This book has not been
evaluated by the FDA
intended to
any disease.
doctor before injesting this or
any book.

Learn To Fly

By Heidi R Hutchinson

Aaron,

[something clever],

Learn To Fly
Copyright © 2013 Heidi R Hutchinson

Cover Design: Penny Reid
Book Design: Heidi R Hutchinson
Cover Photos purchased from Shutterstock

Editors: Hillary Hanson and J. Dan Barnes

Table of Contents

To Laura
they call them betas but
I will always think of you as the alpha
since you were the first believer

Prologue

Cologne, Germany
Two years ago

Luke rubbed his eyes, trying to clear the aggravation and exhaustion from his head simultaneously. His mind raced with flashes and images of the previous six months, compiling a staggering montage of lights, music, chicks, booze, fights, landmarks, more booze, plane flights, brawls, interviews, parties and even more booze.

"This isn't how it's supposed to happen." He realized his words were probably a waste in the quiet hospital room. It didn't matter. He had some things he needed to get off his chest and Mike was the only one he told things to. Ever.

"We were gonna become mega rock stars and see the world, remember that? We had a deal. We promised we wouldn't do all the stereotypical bull crap that so many who'd gone before us did. We were smarter than that."

He sighed heavily and ground his teeth together at the lack of argument that came from the still figure in the bed. Luke would prefer a straight out brawl to the steady sound of the ventilator and gentle beeping of the bedside monitor.

He wished Mike would defend himself. Shout and yell, give him an excuse or explanation. But the soft hum of the machines keeping him alive was the only response.

The past twenty-fours had been the worst kind of wake-up call Luke had ever received. He'd been at a bar with Blake, ignoring Carl's incessant cellphone harassment. All while his best friend and drummer had been rushed to a local hospital for a drug overdose. By the time Carl got through to them, Mike was already in a coma.

No one knew what Mike had taken, but Luke suspected it was heroin. The toxicologist would know soon enough. The real question, the one that had Luke's stomach tied into a thousand and one knots, was whether or not Mike had done it on purpose.

"You can't die." Luke said sternly, his hands raking back his dirty blonde hair. "I need you to wake up so I can kick your ass."

He should have seen this coming. He knew Mike was upset. He had been for most of the tour but Luke was too busy having...a good time. He didn't want to get weighed down by Mike's sour disposition. So he had started avoiding him. Ignoring him.

"I'm sorry," his voice cracked as emotion filled his throat. "I should have been there. I would've stopped you."

But that was a lie. Luke had spent the majority of the tour completely wasted, he wouldn't have known what to do at all. It was a miracle that Carl, their ever-loyal tour manager, had checked on Mike on a hunch. And it still might not have been in time.

"Seriously, wake up." Luke said again, swallowing hard. "I don't know what happened with Ilsa and I don't know where we go after all of this but I promise...I promise you won't go through it alone. And I promise I'll be the brother to you that you always were for me."

Hot tears dripped down Luke's face. "But you can't die...You just can't."

Chapter 1

Keep Your Eyes Open

Lenny glanced down at the silver and pearl face of her watch again. *Ten more minutes, plenty of time.* She pulled open the large glass door to the downtown Los Angeles business building. Her blonde hair reflected briefly in the mirrors behind the front desk as she strode purposefully past security to the elevators around the corner. Going to an interview in a building where her father owned half the floors gave her a twinge of guilt, but nothing more.

The lobby was a smattering of suits, briefcases and clacking high heels. Lenny pressed the button to the lift, shifted on her feet considering her options, and then started up the stairs without waiting.

She took the stairs two at a time at a full sprint, taking advantage of the need to expel some of her nervous energy. She didn't bother removing her high heels and smirked to herself at how stubborn she was about even the smallest things. She couldn't squelch the anticipation that built in her with every stride; as if she was finally headed in a direction that was taking her somewhere better than where she had been. Her long legs quickly carried her to the third floor where she exited, barely winded. She straightened her pressed white blouse and strode to the receptionist's desk coolly.

The woman behind the desk looked up at Lenny's approach with a practiced smile. "May I help you?" Her deep red hair was pulled back into a tight bun and her wide green eyes were framed by thick, trendy glasses.

"I have an appointment with Jerry Douglas," Lenny responded professionally, "My name is Lenny Evans." She almost hesitated saying her full name, but decided that it was highly doubtful the receptionist would recognize it. The woman gave her a split-second double-take; Lenny kept her face impassive. The woman narrowed her eyes slightly but waved her to a seat with a perfectly manicured hand and picked up the phone to announce her arrival.

Lenny sat in the chair stiffly. She hated the scratchy fabric of her dress pants against her legs and the pinch that accompanied wearing heels. Hopefully it would be worth it. She could suffer a few minutes of physical discomfort if it meant changing the direction her life had been going. Nearly any new direction would be welcome at this point.

She adjusted her small purse on her lap, more practical than eye catching, and thought again about the conversation she'd had with Simone

9

the night before.

Simone, the long-suffering girlfriend of her brother Scott, was a well-established photographer from the east coast. At a shoot the day before, she had overheard a conversation involving an immediate job opening and called Lenny that evening.

"I didn't get a lot of details but apparently the job is for a personal assistant and there's a lot of travel involved." Simone's voice was hushed, as if she didn't want anyone to overhear her. That made sense, she was probably with Scott. And if Scott knew Lenny was looking for a way out he'd pitch a fit. Older brothers tended to assume they could run the lives of their siblings.

"Thanks, Simone." Lenny scribbled down the phone number. "I owe you one."

Lenny had called the number and set up an interview immediately. The required travel was the most appealing part. She needed to get away. Now. She really didn't care, apart from prostitution or porn, what she had to do to make that happen.

Double doors opened to her right, and a short, bald man in a suit came out to greet Lenny. When she entered the posh office, she was surprised to see another man already sitting in one of the chairs in front of the desk. Baldy shook her hand and introduced himself as Jerry Douglas.

"This is Carl Darrow," he motioned to the second man who had already stood up and was reaching his hand to Lenny's.

His attire was very different from Mr. Douglas, wearing plain blue jeans, a faded green t-shirt and scuffed cowboy boots. She noted his hand was calloused when she shook it and his posture indicated he was just as uncomfortable in his surroundings as she was. His brown eyes narrowed at her and he ran a hand roughly through his hair as he looked her up and down and failed to hide his grimace.

"Lenny, is it?" He asked, his voice edged with annoyance.

Lenny nodded and smiled, "Or Lenna. It was my grandmother's name."

"We sorta thought you were a guy from your resume." He waived at the paper on Jerry's desk that she had faxed over that morning. He didn't even try to hide his disappointment as he seated himself again and Lenny heard Jerry sigh in exasperation.

"Happens all the time," Lenny tried to reassure him, taking a seat in the chair Jerry offered her. She avoided crossing her legs completely and just crossed her ankles, turning her knees out to the side in the most ladylike posture she could manage.

The men exchanged glances and both sat down. Lenny got the impression they had already made their decision but were going to go ahead with the interview anyway. She swallowed hard and squared her shoulders.

"This job might be a little…unconventional for you," Jerry began, searching for the right words, trying to be delicate. "It's long days, long nights, hard physical labor and you'd be on the road constantly." His eyes skittered around his desk and his hands straightened his pen, then his name plate, then his pen again.

"Is it because I'm a chick?" She asked, seeing the slight break in his serious demeanor and his eyes flicked to Carl.

Carl slouched back in his chair and rubbed his chin with his fingertips. "No, it's 'cause you're pretty."

Lenny felt her mouth tug up slightly on one side. She could see him measuring her, gauging her reaction, testing her. So she remained silent.

Carl studied her placid silence for a long while. But it was Jerry who asked the next question. "What makes you think that being an assistant is where you'd…fit?"

"I'm organized, I work hard and I have nothing keeping me in town," she answered honestly. "I'm not afraid of dirt and sweat and I know I can do the job well."

***

Carl watched closely as Lenny and Jerry discussed the ins and outs of the job. She was focused on Jerry but her expansive eyes would flit around the room occasionally, as if taking inventory.

Her resume said she was twenty-five with little to no employment history but she projected a calm self-assurance that hinted at a wisdom that was gained only by experience.

Jerry seemed flustered at her confidence and Carl could see the interview was getting away from him. The worse he tried to make the job sound, the more interested she became.

Carl was impressed with her quick thinking and directness. He had been hesitant when she had first entered the room, her obvious beauty could be more of a hindrance to the job than a help. However, she didn't seem to be trying to use any womanly wiles to make the interview go more in her favor.

Carl sat back in his chair and laced his hands together behind his head. "You realize this isn't a glamorous job?" He interrupted, drawing her gaze to him. "You'll basically be a glorified babysitter. You'll haul their shit, keep track of their schedules and have eyes on them at all times."

"Easy as pie." She didn't break eye contact and he found himself reassured by her self-possession instead of intimidated by it like Jerry had been.

Carl had actually wanted to avoid hiring a woman if at all possible. Jerry had given him the scripted speech on sexism in the workplace and Carl had finally agreed to hiring an *ugly* woman...if it came to that. But the young lady sitting before them was the antithesis of ugly.

He turned his tone severe and his frown deepened, "Make no mistake, I'm not paying you to be their girlfriend. You cannot, under any circumstance, sleep with them. Do you understand?"

"Loud and clear." Lenny matched his expression and Carl had to hold back a smile. She was definitely not what he had expected.

He sighed and ran both hands through his hair while looking up at the ceiling. He chuckled sardonically, "I have no idea why I'm even entertaining the *thought* of hiring you. You are exactly the kind of girl that can bring this tour crashing down."

"Listen, I know I'm a chick and I know I'm not what you expected," she started, refusing to be deterred, "But I'm stronger than I look and I'm a fast learner. I can do the job and I'll do it well." She repeated, her jaw flexing lightly under her skin and Carl heard the desperation that she tried to hide in her voice. Why did she need *this* job so badly?

He knew Jerry was watching him, waiting for an indication of some kind but he couldn't look away from the determined stare of her midnight blue irises. She was serious, she meant business, and he believed her. Somewhere in her life she had learned to fight for what she wanted.

When he spoke again his attitude had changed from skeptical to decided. "I've been with these guys for nearly twenty years. They tend to be pretty self-destructive and I need someone on the inside. Not just an assistant. I need someone who can be their best friend but stay loyal to me. They have to trust you, need you and like you. I can't have another tour riddled with scandal and the guys have promised they've changed but..." He rolled his eyes and rubbed his chin dejectedly.

"They're so stubborn," he growled, "they keep insisting they don't need an assistant." He shook his head in frustration. "They have argued with me about it every step of the way. They hate the idea of having someone they haven't picked themselves basically be in charge of their lives for the next six months. They have more trust issues than *I* do."

He sucked air in through his teeth as a fresh thought crossed his mind. His eyes flashed at Lenny and a slow smile spread across his face.

"What?" Lenny asked apprehensively, her eyes lighting up as she realized that the job was in her reach.

"I'm gonna stick you on the plane with them tomorrow. Let them think you're another passenger. If you use as much charm on them as you have on us, they'll hire you themselves."

"That's pretty sneaky, Carl," she pointed out, arching one eyebrow at him.

"I'm out of options, kid. These guys have been the collective pain in my ass ever since I walked into their garage and told them to keep it down. They have so many hoops to jump through, you have no idea."

He shook his head and looked over her again. "I like you, Lenny. I almost feel bad asking you if you want the job. It might ruin your life."

Carl watched Lenny as she considered all of the information. At first glance, with her blonde up-do and flawless skin, he thought she was just another pretty face. But she had a spark in her she couldn't hide. A spunky cockiness that appealed to him.

She was undoubtedly perfect for this job.

"You're making a good choice, Carl." She gave him a half-smile and Carl was surprised at his own sense of relief that flooded his veins.

For the next twenty minutes the three of them went over the confidentiality agreement and the touring schedule. She signed some paperwork and asked hardly any questions. They all shook hands and she left.

Carl stared after her, lost in his own musings. He had complete confidence that they had found the ideal person.

"That was easier than I expected," Jerry broke into his thoughts. "I wasn't sure you'd find what you were looking for. Considering...everything."

"She's perfect," Carl agreed.

"I sure hope this works out for you. Better than the last tour anyway."

"It will," Carl said matter of fact as he started to gather his things. He couldn't wait to get out of this office and have a cigarette. He hated coming to this building but Jerry insisted they do the interview in his office. Saying something about how Carl's smelled like cigarette butts and coffee.

"What makes you so sure she won't run off with one of them and end up in the tabloids?" Jerry attempted to joke.

"She's got a brain," Carl responded. "Besides, she didn't even ask what band she's working for. Not once," He took a breath and picked up his bag, "Whatever she's looking for, it isn't fame and drama."

***

Lenny sat patiently in the plane next to the window. It had been a long time since she had flown anywhere alone and she was kind of excited. She tried to suppress the giddiness in her belly, knowing the plane would take off soon and her new adventure would start. The text message she had sent before boarding had been the final goodbye to be said.

The ticket was waiting for her at the counter like Carl had promised and that was what made Lenny realize this was really happening. She was really doing it.

Always early, she was first to board the plane and assumed the band members would be along shortly.

"Hey, beautiful." An attractive man with sculpted shoulders and long, dirty blonde hair pulled back into a low ponytail greeted Lenny. She smiled politely as he sat down next to her. He must have been in his late twenties. His ratty blue jeans and worn, Chuck Taylor's seemed out of place in the first class seating but Lenny didn't mind.

"How did I get a seat next to you?" He asked her flirtatiously, his pale blue eyes sparkling with mischief.

Lenny shrugged and played it cool, remembering her instructions from Carl. "Probably luck," she replied coyly.

"Story of his life, the bastard." Another voice joined their conversation from across the aisle.

Lenny leaned over to see what she assumed to be two more band members seating themselves adjacent to them. Another two men plopped into the seats in front of her as well. They were all in their late twenties to early thirties, had rumpled clothes on, and dark circles under their eyes. As she looked more closely, she began to recognize them.

"Going on vacation?" The friendly young man next to her kept the dialogue going.

"Looking for a change of pace and a new job," Lenny replied, not exactly lying. She was pleased that she wouldn't have to work too hard to get their attention. When Carl had said she was supposed to befriend them, she wasn't exactly sure how that would happen. But it seemed they were impressed with a pretty smile and a hair flip. At least this one was.

He grinned at her and asked, "Unemployed and sitting in first-class? How is this possible?"

"I have wealthy parents." She explained strategically, realizing her slip. She tilted her head and smiled sweetly, hoping they could skip the details about her life.

14

"I'm Sway," he introduced himself and stuck out his hand, not truly interested in Lenny's back story.

She grasped it strongly and replied, "I'm Lenna."

"Beautiful name for a beautiful girl," he winked at her and Lenny suppressed an eye roll. It wasn't exactly the most original line she'd ever heard. She let her hair fall over her face as she dipped her eyes, thankful that she could hide behind it, pretending to be flattered. Her physiology didn't normally respond to a guy flirting with her, she had always told herself she was far too practical for things like butterflies and blushing. And she couldn't respond as she really wanted to because her new job required her to be friendly- whatever that meant.

Her hair was not in its usual tight braid. The elastic restraint had broken in the airport and she was forced to let it hang loose, something she had grown to hate over the past couple of years, but was now finding it a very useful curtain.

Sway, if that was indeed his name, though Lenny doubted it, wasn't traditionally handsome. His face was wide and angular with high cheekbones and soft, full lips. His skin was smooth, freshly shaved, not even a hint of stubble. His fine, blonde hair was probably shoulder length, though it was hard to tell since he had it casually pulled back. Lenny looked at his unbroken elastic with envy; Sway caught her gaze and gave her a suggestive eyebrow waggle. Lenny fought back a chuckle and looked away with feigned shyness.

Out the window, the plane was rising off of the runway and into the air while the flight attendants were going through their perfectly practiced speeches. She swallowed hard to compensate for the pressure change and tried not to think about home.

She had left a note for her parents with very little explanation. Her mom would be unreasonably worried, which is why she avoided the conversation altogether. They would never understand. They had always struggled with comprehending the majority of her life decisions, but even more so in the last couple of years.

As her thoughts kept following their path, her chest started to burn with an irritatingly familiar heartache. She closed her eyes and leaned back in her seat, deliberately pushing those old thoughts and feelings away. The past was the past and she couldn't change anything, so there was no reason to think about it.

Her hand clutched her phone and she checked to make sure she had turned it off at the attendant's reminding. She knew she had though, she had powered it down before boarding, not looking forward to the inevitable string of irate replies when she had to turn it on again.

15

***

Luke Casey tried to catch a glimpse of the gorgeous girl tucked between his bass player and the window across the aisle from him without being too obvious. It was a rare occurrence when a woman didn't start giggling nervously at Sway's obvious flirtation. But he could tell right away that this girl wasn't like others.

He and his band mates had seen her at the airport waiting to board the flight. The entire airport couldn't help but notice her, or maybe that was just how Luke saw it. She was dressed plainly in cut-off jeans and a white t-shirt, her long, naturally blonde hair hung past her shoulders. It wasn't bottle-blonde like so many of the other girls in SoCal and Luke wondered if maybe she wasn't a local.

She had an energy that was captivating. Even sitting still in the airport, Luke could sense an underlying passion just below her smooth surface, like rushing water beneath a frozen river. She had the kind of beauty that reminded Luke of sunsets and mountain vistas. Natural, wild and dangerous.

And she had no idea. Maybe that's why Luke couldn't get her out of his head.

She had fidgeted slightly while she waited for the call to board their flight. Luke noticed her chewing the inside of her cheek as she quickly tapped out a text and then pocketed her phone. Her build said she was probably an athlete, her toned legs hinted she was a runner. Luke wondered vaguely what she was running from.

Now, as he finally got an unobstructed view of her face in the early morning light, he could see her brow furrowed in deep thought, as if trying to will a memory away. On her lap she clutched a notebook with a pen in the spiral.

"Are you a journalist?" Sway asked. Luke knew full well she was not, journalists tended to give off a certain aura that repelled him. However, he was actually thankful that his pushy friend was keeping her talking.

Lenny's eyes fluttered open and she looked at the notebook in her lap, "No, just a poet," she said absentmindedly. Luke strained, trying to listen in on their conversation without being obvious. Damn Sway for getting the seat next to her.

"Oh, so it's a book of secrets, is it?" Sway's tone staying light. He could never resist a pretty girl.

Lenny winked, "Everyone has secrets." She smiled easily and changed the subject, "Why are you going to Chicago?"

Luke could tell Sway was enjoying her spunky back and forth. "We're heading there to kick off our tour," he answered with a hint of pride

16

and Luke rolled his eyes.

Lenny frowned, "Tour? Are you in a band?"

Laughter and snickers erupted from the other members as they overheard. Sway smiled, pretending to be embarrassed that she didn't know who he was. "I guess you could say that," he took a bottle of water from the drink cart as it passed. "I'm sorry, I thought I introduced myself. I'm Ryan 'Sway' Schaeffer, bass player for a band called Double Blind Study."

Lenny's brows drew together, "Okay..."

Sway wasn't disappointed. Instead, he grinned from ear to ear, showing her his dazzling, perfect teeth. "We're kind of a big deal," he bragged.

"Is that why you thought I would be impressed with your flattery? I imagine most girls are," Lenny raised an eyebrow pointedly and Luke smirked. Girls didn't tend to call Sway out on his obvious self-important air. Luke was even more compelled to get to know this one better.

Sway continued to grin. "Of course," he admitted.

"Why are you smiling then?" Lenny narrowed her eyes at Sway.

"You're obviously not like most girls. I'll have to change my tactics."

Lenny was rolling her eyes when Luke had heard enough and crossed the aisle, grabbed Sway by the arm and pulled him to his feet. "You talk too much, Sway," he said, almost scolding. He took Sway's vacant seat and turned to Lenny, "Sorry, he can be pushy with pretty girls."

"With girls in general," Blake, who was sitting ahead of Lenny, snorted.

"I resent that!" Sway defended as he sank into Luke's empty chair, "I have never hit on an ugly girl."

"Good job, dude. I'm sure that little statement will convince her that you are, in no way, a pig," Mike said sarcastically from next to him.

Sway turned to him, "Thanks for backing a bro up."

***

Lenny was amused at their interaction, they reminded her of her brothers. But she couldn't get distracted, she had a job to do. *Time to become their new best friend.*

Lenny had been blessed with a photographic memory. It came in handy more often than not, allowing her to learn tasks quickly and become proficient in them. She noticed and stored details as precisely as a computer. It was her best kept secret, and she had always used it to her advantage.

The guy who had switched seats and was now sitting next to her was the lead singer of the group. Double Blind Study had been her favorite band for some time now. Hard rock with a bit of metal influence. They hadn't toured in two years because of the drummer doing hard drugs when they were overseas and landing in the hospital. The tabloids ripped them apart, sensationalizing the truth of the matter. They printed gossip and pointed blame on drinking, girls and the band's inability to get along with one another. The band members refused to do interviews and took a hiatus. Their fame skyrocketed. Fans demanded new music and a follow up tour.

She covertly studied Luke Casey sitting next to her. He was casually browsing through a guitar magazine, not as interested in her as Sway had been. His short blonde hair was covered by a Celtics ball cap, not a surprise since most of them were natives of Boston. His gray t-shirt was snug against his lean but muscular chest and shoulders. Tattoos leaked out from his short sleeves and down to his elbows. Despite his rumpled appearance and worn jeans, he smelled clean and his face was shaved smooth. His reputation was one of smoldering sex appeal and refusal to get tied down. Typical lead singer qualities.

Lenny put on her most amicable smile, tucked her hair behind one ear and asked, "Are you guys always this nice to each other?" She still hadn't gotten a clear view of Luke's face, and she was wondering if he was as good looking in person as in the magazines. Not that it should matter, she was now on the payroll and Carl had been pretty specific about how he felt with her 'fraternizing' with the band members. However, those facts did nothing to extinguish her curiosity. She was still a woman, after all.

"Pretty much." He thought for a minute, seemingly engrossed in the periodical, then added, "We look out for each other. Some of us don't know our weaknesses as well our friends do. You need someone to watch your six." He turned his stunning blue eyes on Lenny, "You know what I mean?"

Lenny nodded her head even as an electric current ripped through her body. She knew exactly what he meant but she couldn't speak for a moment as her voice had gotten stuck in her throat while she had been busy trying to figure out exactly what shade of blue Luke Casey's eyes were.

He was everything she was afraid he would be. The pictures didn't do him justice. He was even more gorgeous while in motion, as if his raw masculinity had to be *felt* and no camera would ever be able to capture it. And his voice, that voice that could go from soothing and melodic to a fury filled growl in a span of micro seconds, was washing over her like a warm rain shower. She tried not to stare at his perfectly chiseled jaw line as he spoke more words to her. Words she was going to need to respond to any minute.

"I totally agree," she suddenly blurted out. She didn't know what she had just agreed to, but Luke seemed satisfied so it must have made sense on some level. She inwardly cursed herself for turning into an instant jellyfish and resolved to not let her hormones ruin this. She just wouldn't look at his eyes. Or his smile. Or his arms. *Oh, geez, his arms.*

This was unexpected, and in no way normal for her. Her body was betraying her logical practicality. She took a breath and resolved to shake it off. She was nothing if not a professional. Lenny had been ignoring attractive men her whole life, Luke Casey would be no different. Right?

***

"You have a lead on a job in Chicago?" Luke was trying to be polite but he couldn't help feeling uneasy. He had purposed to rescue her from Sway before Sway could start humping her leg. Now Luke found himself trying not to talk to her too eagerly. He kept trying to meet her eyes, they were the deepest blue he had ever seen, almost sapphire. But she continuously looked around the cabin.

"Nothing definite, just an impulse," Lenny smiled, and Luke couldn't help but wonder what it would be like to kiss those perfect lips.

"You look familiar," Harrison was up on his knees in his seat and had turned around to join their conversation. Luke was both thankful and annoyed at the distraction.

"Maybe you saw me at the airport." Lenny raised her eyebrows in an obvious gesture.

Harrison chuckled at himself, "Yeah, that was probably it." He stuck out his hand, "I'm Harrison O'Neil, I play lead guitar in the band you've never heard of."

Lenny grasped his hand and Luke was surprised at the sudden surge of jealously that filled his gut when they touched. He pushed it aside quickly. He was not going to lose his head over a girl he didn't know.

"You have gorgeous eyes, Lenna," Harrison blurted out what Luke and Sway hadn't gotten to yet. Luke glared at Harrison discreetly but Harrison either didn't notice or didn't care.

"Thanks," Lenny accepted the compliment and then added her own, "You have gorgeous hair."

Harrison blushed and immediately ran his fingers through his luscious locks. He worked really hard at making his hair look effortless and Luke knew he enjoyed people complimenting it.

Lenny seemed amused at his reaction and gave him a small, lopsided smile and added, "You can call me Lenny, everyone else does."

"Lenny? That's rather unique, and kind of manly," Harrison waggled his eyebrows and Luke had to suppress his laugh. Harrison flirting was the exact opposite of Sway. No matter how hard the guy tried, he couldn't help but come across as adorable and was immediately 'friend zoned.'

Lenny laughed lightly at Harrison's remark and her eyes darted to Luke's. "I guess I've always been more comfortable just being one of the guys," she explained. Luke felt disappointment drift across him when he realized they had *all* just been 'friend zoned.'

Harrison didn't seem to mind though, and he kept the conversation going. The rest of the band members began to join in the discussion, and Luke was impressed with how well Lenny held her own. She stayed active in the dialogue, adding jokes and quips. Luke had known these guys a long time and it could be difficult getting a word in edgewise, but Lenny fit in like a missing piece that they didn't know had been missing. That was a weird thought. *Don't go down that road, Casey.*

Luke did, however, notice that Lenny continuously steered the conversation back to the band. She spoke very little about herself and the guys preferred it that way. They were entertainers for a reason.

The attendant with the drink cart made another pass and he paused at their row. Luke looked up to see the young man looking at Lenny like he was trying to place her. Luke frowned and turned to her as well. She was still talking to Harrison, having not yet noticed the attendant. Was he just checking her out? That was kind of unprofessional, Luke criticized internally.

"Can I help you, man?" He finally asked the gawker.

"I'm sorry, I just, uh, I..." the young man swallowed and tried again having gotten Lenny's attention now. "You look really familiar."

Wow, this guy was serving drinks to rock stars and yet he'd decided to hit on a passenger with one of the worst lines available. Luke was the opposite of impressed.

"I get that a lot." Lenny smiled apologetically. "I guess I have one of those generic faces."

"Oh, sorry." Th attendant turned red and shuffled on his way.

Luke wanted to disagree loudly with Lenny's assessment of herself. Generic? Was she joking?

***

Lenny eased back into the conversation, letting it flow and grow around her. She'd almost panicked when the flight attendant had nearly identified her. That would end her new career before it really got underway. She couldn't risk the shadow of what she was running from decide where she was going.

That brought her back to the band and her goal to win them over. She was finding herself really liking these guys. They were friendly and good-humored and made her feel equally witty and important. That didn't surprise her; Lenny had always gotten along with guys better than girls. It came from having three older brothers…and of course the male dominated sport she had just abandoned.

The drummer, Mike Osborn was sitting beside Sway. He was tall and lanky, tattoos spiraled up and down his arms and his hair was a shaggy, caramel color. He hadn't shaved in a few days, as evidenced by the dark shadow cast across his jaw. He seemed to be the most subdued of the group, even though he was constantly smacking his legs to a beat in his head.

"How did you guys come up with your band name?" Lenny kept the conversation moving with the intent of learning as much as she could about them and preventing them from asking about her. And the band name had always seemed a little ambiguous.

"It's kind of a long story," Luke shifted uncomfortably in his seat.

Lenny pushed his knee flirtatiously, "C'mon, you can tell me." The longer she spoke with them, the more comfortable she got and the more Luke Casey's effect on her dulled. Lenny was pleased to know she still had a handle on her own brain, rock star or not.

Luke looked over at Sway who shrugged, "I don't care, man. You already ruined any chance of seduction on my part. It's still a better name than what Blake thought up."

"Trophy Wives would have been an amazing name, you jag," Blake Diedrich said from the seat directly in front of Lenny.

Blake was also a guitarist, but played the grungier side of their songs. He was older than the rest of them and had come from a different band years ago. He was more punk rock than metal rock, but his sound blended nicely with the rest of the group. Blake had turned around a few times during the conversation and Lenny hadn't missed the appraising gaze that came from his green eyes. He was tall and lean with jet black, short, spiky hair and just like all the other band members, he had tattoos and muscles.

They could easily fit in with the guys Lenny worked out with at her local gym. Or a random biker gang.

"I always liked Taco Night," Sway smiled impishly.

"Anything is better than Taco Night," Mike interjected, receiving a scowl from Sway.

"So, you guys just picked a name out of a hat or what?" Lenny was trying to follow along.

Harrison turned around to face her and Luke again, "Here's the deal, we grew up in Boston, right?" He waited for Lenny to nod so he knew she was paying attention. "Okay, Sway has always had a…penchant for the ladies." Lenny looked over at Sway who winked and she resisted another eye roll. "When he was only seventeen he started to sneak onto the campus at Boston University to scam on college chicks."

"Why college chicks?" Lenny asked, her mouth ticking up on one side.

"Because college chicks are experienced and usually pretty easy," Sway said matter of fact.

"Dude," Mike grimaced with disapproval.

"Anyway," Harrison continued, "BU does a lot of research, and some girls picked up on the fact that Sway wasn't a student. They developed an experiment in order to study attraction and how strong a teenage boy's libido could be. They did a *double blind study* in which Sway didn't know he was part of an experiment and neither did the girls he was scamming on. It was going great for them until Sway got caught by campus police. They threw him out and threatened to turn him in on charges of seduction."

"Is that real?" Lenny asked, incredulous.

"Yeah, Frank Sinatra was charged for it too, you know," Sway said, making a sexy face and blowing Lenny a kiss.

Lenny shook her head and waited for Harrison to finish.

"My sister was the one who organized the study, that's how I found out about it," Harrison folded his hands together and rested his chin on his knuckles. "We decided that our band was basically that, a double blind study to the public where they didn't know they were part of it and neither did we. 'Course we're more sober now than when we started. So I suppose we're more aware of our actions."

"Yeah, and you really don't want to have to go to all the trouble of changing your album covers and t-shirts," Lenny teased.

"And Blake would have to get that tattoo removed," Harrison added.

"You tattooed the name of your own band on yourself?!" Lenny pulled herself up to look at Blake, "Lemme see it."

Blake tried to feign annoyance but he clearly liked the attention. He stood up on the plane and yanked his shirt up to expose his impressive six-pack and the large tattoo scrawled in black ink across the width of his chest:

DOUBLE BLIND STUDY

"That's nice and subtle," Lenny said sarcastically with a grin.

"I was excited..." Blake tried to defend, putting his shirt back down.

"Dude, you were drunk," Harrison corrected. Blake shrugged in confession.

"Blake came back with the tattoo and we didn't have much of a choice after that," Harrison finished his story.

They spent the entire flight laughing and entertaining Lenny. They talked easily, having no reservations about her seemingly innocent presence. She had built the perfect platform for her next statement. It was time to cast the net.

"You guys make it sound fun but hard. I wish I could come along to help you out," her voice light and sweet. This was it.

They all exchanged glances, momentarily silent. Harrison spoke first, "Actually, we do need an assistant-"

"Dude!" Blake smacked him.

"Ow!" Harrison protested, rubbing his arm. "What?! Maybe it'll get Carl off our back!"

They all seemed to consider this for a minute. Luke turned to Lenny and asked, "What do you say Lenny? You wanna join a bunch of ugly, smelly guys for a few months?"

Lenny smiled. Her plan had worked. She nodded at all of them and kept her tone even as she replied, "What do you mean? Like, work for you?" She tried to look confused.

"Yeah," Harrison's face lit up, "Then you can hang out with us every day."

"That would be amazing," Lenny smiled but she noticed Luke's eyes shift down and away from hers. The other members were already discussing how they could sell the idea to Carl but Luke remained silent. He'd already given his verbal approval and Lenny got the distinct impression that Luke was the leader in more areas than just lead singer. If he had disagreed with this than the deal would have been off.

Luke suddenly came back to the conversation and his easy smile returned. Whatever he had been thinking about had been settled and Lenny tried to push his obvious discomfort with her to the back of her mind. She would just have to prove to him that she could do the job.

Chapter 2

Times Like These

Shane: *Lenny won't answer her phone or any of my texts*
Cody: *so it's over then*
I'd think you'd be happy about this
Shane: *she didn't tell you where she was going?*
Cody: *Nope.*
But you know her, she's not big on confrontation
Shane: *do you think she remembers?*
Cody: *it's been 2 years*
pretty sure it would've come up by now
relax, you're finally off the hook
we both are

***

Luke was uneasy. Again. Hiring Lenny excited him and he knew it shouldn't. She was gorgeous, and that would present a whole set of issues. But, she was also smart and seemed to genuinely fit into the dynamic of the group. It had been a long time since Luke had gotten this flustered over the presence of the opposite sex. It was like being a teenager all over again, hence the unease.

Luke wasn't the oldest, but he felt the most responsibility for the rest of the guys. The band had always looked to him to be the leader, in more ways than simply musically. Luke took it all in stride. He had no problem being the one everyone else expected to make the hard decisions, the one to lead by example. After what had happened in Germany two years ago to Mike…well, he couldn't let anything like that happen again.

Luke was aware of Carl's apprehension in regards to the tour and what obstacles could potentially arise. He couldn't see that they had grown up and things were different now. At least, they all hoped they were different.

Their opening show in Chicago went smoothly. They had gone directly from the airport to the venue, meeting Carl backstage and presenting Lenny to him. Carl had been annoyed, not unexpectedly. They were always coming up with new ways to make his job harder than it needed to be. Most of the time Carl's veto held solid, but he had caved under Harrison's pleas and Blake's outright promise of defiance. The band did need an assistant, and Lenny had been the most decent candidate to come along in a while.

"Decent candidate," Luke rolled his eyes as he recalled Sway's description of the newest member of their entourage. They had each driven away a number of women in the past, be it from heartbreak, exhaustion or restraining order. Luke felt his gut clench at the thought that Lenny would eventually be another casualty of their fame.

But maybe not. She didn't seem nearly as naive as most women he'd known over the years. She was audacious and self-aware. If she had any insecurities or illusions about what her job would be, it wasn't obvious. And with the guys new commitment to being straight laced and sober for the first time in their lives, she just might have a chance of leaving this tour emotionally intact.

Luke raked his fingers through his hair and let out a sigh. He shouldn't be having so many thoughts about the new girl. It was a dangerous path to start down. Luke found it unusual that the rest of the group was so taken with her, they barely knew her. However, he couldn't judge, as he was the one standing on his hotel balcony devoting every stray thought to her. He sighed again and tried to shake some new thoughts into his distracted brain.

He truly felt like the only one who was apprehensive about adding a female into the mix this early in the tour. It had turned out so badly last time. But then again, that wasn't the fault of the women around them; that had been their own poor choices.

His hotel room was on the top floor; and just below he could see the buses getting loaded. They would travel by bus for the tour through the States, and then fly overseas for a few shows in Europe. Departure was to be early in the morning, about twelve hours from now. This was probably the only night they would get a hotel, at least for a while. He and Mike would share a bus while Sway, Harrison and Blake would share another. They had five sleeper buses to accommodate the large crew that their show required which is where Lenny would ride.

Things were sure different than when they started out ten years ago.

Luke returned to the interior of the room and closed the sliding glass door.

Mike came in from the hallway and crashed face first onto one of the beds, "Holy shit, I'm tired."

Luke chuckled, "Maybe you should've slept last night instead of practicing your bluff so late."

"Practice makes perfect...or something like that." Mike closed his eyes, "I'm gonna sleep now. Go away or be quiet."

Luke left the room quietly, thinking that a walk might do him some good. Maybe he could help with something. He hated sitting around anyway.

His nerves were more than likely in direct correlation to the huge tour they were embarking on at dawn and had nothing to do with the chick who seemed to be at the forefront of his thoughts. He had to keep his head clear. He had to stay alert. If he wanted this band to not only survive the industry but their own past mistakes, he needed to focus on the music. Not on Lenny's thousand watt smile.

Easier said than done.

"Carl put you to work already?" He asked as he came up beside her. The wind was tossing loose strands from her tied back hair around her face. She turned to smile at him and his stomach tightened. She was crazy beautiful.

"I like to stay busy." Lenny noticed Luke's frown as he chastised himself internally and she misunderstood its meaning. "I can't justify being your assistant if I'm not actually *assisting*.

"Carl gave me the low down on what's allowed on the buses and what's not," she gestured to the checklist in her hand and motioned for him to follow her inside the bus. She pointed out the items as she listed them, "You have all your gear and favorite foods on board. A fully stocked fridge with soda and *water*," she emphasized, "and not the cheap kinds, mind you, but the good stuff." Luke followed her through the interior of the bus as she showed him where the sheets and and towels were located. "And I went ahead and programmed my number in your phone."

Luke looked down at her hand and saw her extending his iPhone towards him. He took it and his thumb slid across the face as he tried to figure out what to say. Why did her presence muddle his thoughts?

"So you can call me when you need anything," she smiled at his blank face and bit her bottom lip. Probably to keep from laughing at his total lack of cool.

"You didn't have to do all this for me." This was the first time they had really been alone and Luke was aware of the close proximity they were in, standing in the main lounge of the bus. It was unnerving. And intoxicating.

Lenny laughed, "Not just you, all the guys," she shook her head slightly at his expression, "I already gave the others their phones. You're the last one to finally wander down here."

Luke stared at her, realizing she was only doing her job. Taking care of him, of them, was her job. He looked down at the phone in his hand. They had a working relationship. She wasn't a groupie. She wasn't flirting with him. She wasn't treating him like a rock star.

27

"And I already gave the big speech to everyone else so I might as well give it to you too," Lenny continued, her blue eyes taking on a serious glint, "Carl told me that there is to be no booze or babes allowed on board."

Luke felt a smirk beginning on his face and he tried to repress it. He wanted to make a joke about how that meant she was already breaking the rules, but he figured she probably didn't place herself in the 'babes' category.

"Don't make that face," Lenny took on a scolding tone. "I'll be around to inspect regularly and I have no problem being the bad guy."

"You're really taking this job seriously, aren't you?" Luke tried to keep his statement from sounding condescending.

Lenny arched an eyebrow at him as if she was expecting a challenge.

"You have my full support," Luke tipped his head towards her and he thought he detected the hint of a blush starting low on her neck. But maybe he was wrong about that too.

She gave a small, sideways smile that nearly melted Luke on the spot. When she turned to leave the bus, he automatically followed her.

As they stepped down into the humid July evening, Lenny turned and pursed her lips. She narrowed her eyes and Luke braced himself for what he thought was going to be an admonishment for him looking at her butt as they had exited the vehicle. He thought he'd diverted his eyes before she'd noticed, but now he wasn't so sure.

"What?" Luke asked innocently.

Lenny sucked in a breath and hesitated before taking a step closer to him. Luke reflexively inhaled her scent and hoped she didn't notice. If she did, she didn't say. She held his eyes for a beat.

"I know I don't know the whole story about what happened with Mike..." she spoke slowly and Luke could tell she was trying to find the right words, "but I really admire how you all are supporting his sobriety by keeping alcohol off the buses."

"We're a family, and family's support each other," he explained simply. It really was that simple and he was thankful that she had reminded him of that. Of the real reason they were embarking on this possibly disaster-filled adventure once again.

"I don't have parents or siblings or anything like that," Luke had no idea why he felt the compulsory need to spill his life secrets to her, he didn't even know her. He could say it was something in her eyes that he trusted. Or the way she turned her head slightly when she was listening to him that signaled his words were safe in the space that existed between them. "These guys are more than friends to me. They *are* my family."

She reached up to touch her lips, like she wanted to ask a question but had to stop herself. He was curious what she would ask; what direction her questions would take them in this impromptu albeit personal conversation.

Lenny's eyes drifted to something over his shoulder and Luke knew she was suddenly very far away.

"Yeah," she agreed, her voice rough. And then, as if realizing where she was, her eyes snapped back to his and she pulled the clipboard to her chest protectively. "Well, I'm pretty much done here for the day," she began to back away from him and forced a smile. "You better get some rest tonight, you have to be amazing tomorrow."

Luke gave her a nod as she departed quickly, heading for the hotel. He wondered what had spooked her. Maybe that was in his head, but it seemed like something was on her mind, and damn if he didn't want to follow her and ask her what it was. He didn't understand the impulsive need he felt to keep talking to her. Figure her out, let her figure him out.

"Ah, hell," he muttered to himself. Sticking his phone in his back pocket, he watched Lenny's blonde hair disappear through the entrance. He thought about trying to catch up to her but he waited a few extra minutes to let her get ahead. He didn't need to know where she was going. Probably to her room. He didn't need to know which room was hers. He didn't need to think about her at all. In fact, he should probably try to stay as far away from her as possible. She worked for them now, and sleeping with her, while that would probably get her out of his head, wasn't a good idea. Not to mention the fact that he'd be starting out the tour with the same bad decisions that had plagued him all during the last one.

Besides, she didn't seem like the kind of girl to crawl into bed with a rock star. She was better than that.

And that's exactly why he wanted to explore that gorgeous chaos he could see behind her blue eyes.

Luke made it up back to the top floor without seeing Lenny again. He quietly changed his clothes and headed to the hotel weight room. Maybe an hour of intense sweating would help sort out his confused desires.

An hour accidentally turned into two. Even though he kept repeating to himself to stop thinking about her, Lenny was all that filled his thoughts. Where had she come from? What was her story? As he burned out his bodies reserves on another dropset, he realized he knew very little about this woman they had so readily invited into their lives. That was going to have to change.

***

Lenny showered and dressed quickly, opting to skip pajamas and wear her jeans and grey V-neck tee to bed. It would save time in the morning. Sleeping fully clothed wasn't anything new for her anyway; it was practically a way of life living at higher elevations. She combed her long, wet hair and twisted it into her standard braid. Just as she was finishing brushing her teeth, she heard a knock at her hotel room door.

She crossed the room and looked through the peep hole. It was Carl, pacing in the hallway. She grimaced and unlocked the door to let him in. As he entered, she could smell cigarette smoke mixed with his aftershave.

"Hey," she greeted casually, "What's up?"

Carl strode across the room without saying anything. It was obvious from his behavior that he was looking for something. He scowled at Lenny, surveying her appearance and that of the yet to be used bed. The persistent frown on his face relaxed somewhat.

"What's going on, Carl?" Lenny tried again, but she already knew the answer.

"I wanted to check to see if you were alright," he lied.

"No, you wanted to see if I was *alone*." Lenny corrected and the corner of her mouth pulled up into a half-smile as she shook her head. She crossed her arms and leaned against the closed door.

Carl gave up the act, "Well, yeah."

"I understand this whole scenario is new for you, but you're just gonna have to trust me."

"I trust you," he took a breath; "it's those other hooligans I have a hard time with."

"Carl, I appreciate the over protective father routine, but I can really take care of myself." She gently tugged on his arm and led him to the door. "Get some sleep, big day tomorrow." She opened the door and he walked into the hallway. He turned to say something else and she interrupted, "Goodnight, Carl." Then closed the door.

***

Carl stood in the dimly lit, empty hallway for a moment and then started to the elevators. He trusted Lenny, even more so now that she had basically thrown him out. She was a strong, young woman, no nonsense, focused. And she wasn't going to let anyone push her around. He pressed the button and waited. With a "ding!" the door opened. Exhaling a relieved sigh, Carl entered the lift and leaned against the wall. This tour might be successful yet. The boys appeared to be more centered than ever, and with Lenny on the inside, Carl felt like he could relax a little.

When they had come to him months ago, asking for him to return as

30

their tour manager, he had flat out refused. However, he'd known most of them since they were tots and their persistence wore him down. They made a lot of promises. No drinking, no girls, no drugs. And they refused to do the tour without him, so the label had offered him an obscene amount of money.

It had seemed that their hiatus had given the band the time and space they needed to figure out how to be musicians again. They were dedicated to the creative process and claimed to have no interest in their previous...temptations. Carl only halfway believed them. He wasn't a complete idiot, they were terrific liars, that's why he needed an inside man, so to speak.

Carl had agreed to their request and then he started his own search. He needed someone who the band would trust. Someone seemingly innocent and innocuous. Someone they would invite along if they were getting ready to trash the entire eighth floor of a swanky hotel. But this someone would have to have loyalties to Carl, at least enough so he could try to stop whatever destruction the band had in its sights. Because when it came down to it, Carl loved these guys like brothers. Okay, maybe more like cousins. He wanted to see them succeed, not crash and burn.

He was about to give up hope when Lenny had breezed into Jerry's office. She was perfect. Carl couldn't describe it; he had a feeling deep in his gut that this girl was the answer to his prayers. Of course, that didn't mean he thought the next six months were going to be a prance in the park. Carl had gone to Lenny's room to make sure she was keeping up her end of the bargain. He was wonderfully relieved to find out that she was alone. Extra point in her column.

The door opened to his floor and he strode more leisurely to his room. As he got into bed and closed his eyes, he acknowledged the ridiculous feeling of excitement he was getting. He hadn't felt this much anticipation for a tour since Double Blind Study was still a garage band. It felt good. Right.

Last night's show had gone perfect. Playing poker until early morning with his oldest friends had been a welcome change from the infamously crazy after-parties of the last tour. And no one had mentioned Lenny's looks, or even her gender for that matter. Maybe they didn't notice. This might work after all.

***

Lenny was the first one awake. She tucked her small travel duffel into the compartment on the crew bus and hurried across the street to the tiny coffee shop. The wonderful aroma filled her nose and woke her up a little bit more. She ordered enough coffees for the bus drivers, herself and Carl. Shifting the large order into a more manageable hold, she headed back to the waiting buses.

She passed out the coffees to the thankful drivers and sidled up to Carl. He glanced over at her, a bit surprised as she handed him his coffee.

"Thanks," he muttered.

They stood side by side without looking at each other for a few moments. Then Carl spoke again, "Sorry about barging in last night."

"Not a problem," she answered quietly. "But try to keep in mind, I'm on your side." She looked at him with a wry smile.

He chuckled softly and took a sip of his coffee, "It's new, I'll have to get used to it."

The Chicago morning was beautiful. Lenny admired the tall skyscrapers against the periwinkle sky. She had missed traveling and the excitement of waking up in a new place with the city just waiting to be explored. Her heart beat faster in anticipation of the upcoming touring schedule. She had no idea how much free time for her would even be possible. It didn't matter. She'd find a way to make the most of it.

"I was gonna have you ride with the crew for a couple of days but I changed my mind." Carl gave her a sideways glance, "I want you on the Red Bus with Sway, Harrison and Blake."

"Any particular reason why?" Lenny saw this as a good sign. It meant Carl wasn't afraid of her being alone with the band members during the long hours on the road. When he had laid out the rules yesterday, one of them was: "No girls on the buses during travel." Family and committed girlfriends could be the exception, but none of the guys were in a relationship. Lenny had been concerned about the logistics of keeping an eye on them if she wasn't going to be around them without supervision anyway. Carl's directive just changed that.

"You're my eyes and ears," Carl shrugged. "We'll try to switch it up periodically, keep them on their toes."

"You got it, boss." Lenny nodded towards the hotel where the musicians were making a slow and bleary-eyed exit, "Time to get to work." She slammed back the rest of her scalding hot coffee, ignoring Carl's startled look. Tossing her empty cup into a nearby trashcan, she headed for the approaching band members.

Lenny grabbed the suitcases from out of their hands and pushed them onto their respective buses.

"C'mon, ladies! We have a long way to go!" She directed with authority while she loaded their few bags.

"Damn, new girl! Calm down!" Blake protested sleepily. Lenny only laughed and shoved him up the steps of his bus.

"Your adoring public awaits." Lenny dramatically ushered Mike and Luke onto their bus. Even in the the early morning, Luke looked completely rested and relaxed. Lenny held in a contented sigh as he gave her a heart-stopping grin at the foot of his bus. He held her eyes for a second, like he wanted to say something, but he just shook his head and climbed up the stairs.

Lenny gave Carl an exaggerated salute before following Sway up the steps of the Red Bus. He looked amused and impressed with her efforts and Lenny couldn't help but smile. As far as new lives go, this one was shaping up quite nicely.

***

Lenny settled into her seat on the Red Bus. She was a hard worker and she knew it. Her effort and quick success had already won her the respect of the road crew within a day. Even Carl seemed a bit less tense. She was excited and relieved to be on the road. This was new and different and she knew she'd be good at it. Just like everything else she'd put her mind to. And there was more than enough for her to do to keep her from thinking about all the things she was running from. A short seven hour drive, stage set up, show, stage tear down, back on the bus, drive all night. She could totally do this.

"Carl actually trusted you with us?" Blake teased from his reclining position on the couch.

"Yeah, what about the 'No Babes' rule?" Sway added from somewhere in the kitchenette area.

"I don't count." Lenny answered, not even looking up from her notebook.

"What? Why don't you count?" Blake pushed himself up on one elbow to look at her. "Are you a lesbian?"

Lenny smirked and shook her head, "No, I just don't sleep with rock stars. It's a rule I have."

"Screw that!" Sway dropped on the sofa opening a can of soda, shoving Blake out of the way. "We're not rock stars, we're *musicians.*" He shook his head, obviously offended by her word choice.

"Fine, I don't sleep with *musicians* then." Lenny corrected, rolling her eyes.

"So Carl thinks nothing will happen because you have this special rule?" Sway asked, belligerence all over his face.

"Is that all you think of me as, Sway?" Lenny narrowed her eyes at him. "Just another conquest?"

"N-no," Sway stammered.

33

"Then why is it every conversation I have with you ends up being about sex?"

"It's the only thing he thinks about." Blake grinned at his friend who elbowed him hard in the ribs.

"That's not true!" Sway protested. "I have layers, I ain't all about sex."

Lenny tapped her pencil against her knee, contemplating his defensiveness.

"Sway's having a hard time adjusting to the No Bob Tour." Harrison had settled onto the floor and was already rummaging through the video game consoles. He found the setup he was looking for and started plugging it all in. "He has to talk about it a lot before he can let it go. It's his way."

Sway 'humphed' and settled deeper into the cushions of the couch. Blake took a controller from Harrison and joined him on the floor and they began an epic battle involving robots and zombies.

"I'm sorry... No Bob tour?" Lenny questioned.

"Yeah. No Booze or Babes. Bob." Harrison explained as his avatar decapitated a zombie.

"Right," Lenny hid a smile and reopened her notebook.

The cabin was quiet save for the gory zombie deaths that were coming from the plasma TV. Lenny went over her lists for what to do when they arrived at the next venue. She knew she had it down, but she always double checked. Being wrong was not her favorite thing.

"I still don't get why you're the exception to the babes rule." Sway broke into Lenny's thoughts.

Lenny looked up to see him staring at her intently. His blue eyes were hooded and soft. The blonde hair he usually kept pulled back hung forward and touched the stubble on his well-defined jaw. Lenny understood a little more how the girls were so easily taken with him. Five seconds of his direct eye contact and she felt caught, examined. The seduction thing made a lot more sense suddenly.

Sway wet his full, perfect, bottom lip with his tongue as he waited for Lenny to give him an explanation. She swallowed and he must've noticed her unease because his mouth crooked up slightly on one side.

"For shit's sake, Sway!" Blake interrupted by punching Sway in the thigh.

"What?" Sway exclaimed innocently. He rubbed the place where Blake had hit him and winked at Lenny.

Lenny let out the breath she hadn't realized she was holding and looked back to her notebook. She felt the heat creep up her neck in embarrassment. Even as she tried to fight it off, she felt her ears go white-hot and she vaguely wondered if she was going to spontaneously combust on the spot. That would only further Sway's ego she was sure. She could see the headlines now: *Girl explodes from seduction overload after extended eye contact with rock star.*

"Lenny is off limits!" Blake was actually yelling. He hadn't even paused in his grizzly zombie killing spree. He glanced over his shoulder to look between Lenny and Sway.

"I know that," Sway defended himself, "She was turning me down left and right, I had to make sure I still had it." He leaned back on the couch and put his hands behind his head. "And I do." He smiled wickedly at Lenny.

"Just ignore him." Blake directed at Lenny. "He really can't help himself."

"I really can't." Sway shrugged, agreeing with the guitarist. "And I also can't let you believe that you don't fall into the babes category, because you totally do."

Lenny still hadn't spoken. She was certain her face was a lovely shade of maroon. She was having an internal argument on how she would handle this. Acknowledging it seemed to be the best option.

"Yep. You caught me," she gave an embarrassed smile, "I'm a just a dumb girl after all."

Sway's face fell and he leaned forward bracing his arms on his knees, "That's not what I was saying at all."

Harrison and Blake had paused their game and turned around, concern evident on both their faces.

"I was just having some fun, I didn't..."

"He's an idiot, Lenny," Blake threw a glare at Sway. "No one thinks you're a dumb girl. We're really glad to have you here."

"Seriously," Harrison's dark eyes were round and pleading, "You have to ignore him. He just likes a challenge. He hits on me at least once a day."

Lenny smiled at Harrison. He really was the most adorable guitar player she had ever met.

"That's true, actually." Sway added and Lenny laughed out loud then. They seemed to relax a little.

"Guys, it's fine." Lenny was touched by their concern for her feelings but it wasn't necessary. "It's not like I've never been flirted with before. It's just been...a long time is all. I forgot what to do in that kind of a situation," she attempted to laugh it off even as the truth in her words burned her throat.

All three guys exchanged frowns.

"What do you mean, 'it's been awhile?'" Harrison seemed confused.

35

Lenny bit the inside of her cheek, unsure how much she felt comfortable revealing. She liked these guys and all, but that didn't make them best friends by any means. And this subject in particular made her feel more exposed than she had anticipated.

"Yeah..." Blake showed disbelief. "You weren't in prison or something, were you?"

"No," Lenny said, forcing a wide smile. "No, nothing like that. I've been busy for a couple years. Haven't gotten out much." She grit her teeth at the twinge of hurt in her voice.

They eyed her momentarily and decided not to push it. She was relieved when Harrison and Blake went back to their violent game.

She stared out the window, enjoying the peacefulness of the prairie as it passed outside. What a weird first day.

***

During stage setup, the band was sleeping and Lenny decided to learn as much as she could about the equipment. She had never handled musical instruments before; she came from a family of devoted athletes. She understood gym equipment and sports gear; weight plates, dumbbells, sparring helmets and gloves, various forms of physical protection and how to utilize all of those items to the maximum benefit of the user. Guitars, drum kits, amplifiers, mic stands and the like were completely foreign to her. But she was a fast learner and applied herself full force.

She made sure the band got to sound check and then she took her first official break of the day. She changed into athletic shorts, a sports bra, and running shoes. She texted Carl, telling him she would be back in two hours, and went for a run.

The fresh air helped clear her head. The time went fast and she arrived back at the venue. After a couple minutes of snooping around, she found a shower in the stadium and took advantage of it. She dressed quickly in jeans and a blue tank top and went backstage to make sure everything was still on track.

Sam, head of security, greeted her first and pointed her towards Carl, in the sound booth with the technician. Carl looked up and smiled when he saw her. She raised her eyebrows in silent question; his smiles had been few and far between for the most part.

"It's all good," he said happily, "all according to plan."

"Good." Lenny shifted her gaze to the band warming up on stage. "They sound tight." She looked at the sound tech, "Would you mind if I sat in here with you during the show? I won't get in the way."

"Fine with me," he replied.

Carl dismissed himself leaving Lenny and Greg, the sound engineer, alone. Lenny paid attention to all the little switches and knobs, memorizing as much as she could without asking questions. She didn't want to be a distraction.

***

Mike could see everything from his position behind the drums. He watched Lenny walk back to the sound booth but, more importantly, he saw Luke staring at her. His posture and playing changed noticeably. It was like he was trying to show off a little. Mike chuckled to himself, realizing Luke's crush. He made a mental note to ask him about it later.

When sound check wrapped up, Mike took a long pull from his water bottle and followed the rest of the band back to the Blue Bus to chill before the show.

"So, I noticed that someone has eyes for the new hottie," Mike casually remarked as they relaxed in the main lounge.

"Who doesn't?" Sway mumbled, rummaging through the fridge.

"No shit, that chick is smokin'." Blake took a drink from his water.

Mike kept his focus on Luke who shifted uneasily on his feet, looking anywhere except at Mike.

"I wasn't talking about you horn dogs," Mike replied.

They turned to Luke who still hadn't said anything.

"You like Lenny, Luke?" Leave it to Harrison to just be out with it.

Luke looked up, pretending to be confused, "What? No, of course not."

"So you hate her?" Harrison was deliberately trapping him into a confession of some kind.

"No, I don't hate her, don't be ridiculous. She's nice," Luke stammered, looking uncomfortable.

"So you *do* like her." Harrison wanted an absolution, his face the picture of innocence.

"What do you want me to say?" Luke was growing more agitated. "You want me to say I think she's good looking? She is. You all think so, too. Why does it matter if I say it?"

"Whoa, dude, relax," Blake dramatically widened his eyes and motioned with his hands for Luke to calm down, "We're not the ones in love with her."

Luke rolled his eyes and stormed towards the door. "You're a bunch of dicks, you know that?" He left in a huff as the others burst into laughter.

"What's wrong with him?" Sway asked Mike.

"Ah, he thinks his crush is a big secret." Mike shrugged

37

nonchalantly.

"Well, if I'm not allowed to bag her, then I don't think Luke should be allowed to either." Sway sat down on the floor.

"You know you're a pig, right?" Mike asked him in disgust.

"A pig that gets more action than you." Sway pointed out, not even offended.

"I don't think we should be talking about who does or does not get to bag Lenny." Blake interjected from the kitchenette. "I have a feeling she could kick all our asses."

"How was it having Lenny on your bus today?" Mike asked. He had wondered what had possessed Carl to throw her into the dog pile like that on her first day.

"She was cool. Helped me kill some zombies." Harrison responded, exchanging a look with Blake.

"What was that?" Mike asked pointing back and forth between them. "Did something happen?"

"Not exactly." Harrison said slowly.

Blake sighed and ran his fingers through his short dark hair, "Sway put the seduction on her."

"Dammit, Sway!" Mike chastised.

"I handled it," Blake reproved. "I don't think it's going to be an issue."

"Can't you ever let one go by?" Mike asked in frustration. He was so sick of Sway never growing up. The endless parade of girls over the years was making it really hard for Mike to respect his band mate.

And then Mike said what he had said many times before, "You have no self-control."

The remorse that washed over Sway's face was sincere and Mike flinched inwardly. They both had things they struggled to master that had hurt those closest to them.

"I know," Sway said softly. "I'm still sorry about-"

"I know. I shouldn't have said that." The tension in the cabin was thick and Mike regretted having such a strong reaction to Blake's revelation. "We're both trying to be better."

***

Luke decided to take a walk to clear his head. He knew the guys were just giving him a hard time. What he was really upset about was how much he had let it get to him. Lenny was already a sensitive topic for him and he knew that could get him into trouble.

Girls had always been a weakness of his. He liked women and they liked him. He never spent enough time with one to really know what they were all about. The longest relationship he had ever had, he was loaded for the entirety of it. That's probably why it had lasted as long as it did.

Why did Carl stick her on the bus with Sway today? It had pissed Luke off more than it should have. Jealousy was a new feeling and he didn't like it. It's not like she was *his* girl. She worked for the band. She was off limits. Off. Limits.

He shook his head, trying to focus his thoughts. He couldn't have a relationship with Lenny. That would be unprofessional. And a disaster. Carl would be pissed. Luke smirked at that. But, she was going to be around them a lot and she was really fun.

Friends. They could be friends. That would work, he had lots of friends, he knew what a friendship looked like. He would just have to treat her like one of the guys. And ignore the fact that she was his perfect height for kissing. Shit. This was going nowhere fast.

It suddenly occurred to Luke that he had no idea if Lenny even noticed him in that way. She had remained cool and aloof towards him, and all the guys for that matter. Maybe she wasn't attracted to him. That was new. Luke had never had to work for a girl to notice him. Chicks constantly threw their bras and panties to him on stage, and once, Carl had had to chase out two girls who'd tried to stow away on the bus. Maybe Lenny was exactly what she seemed: a hard worker who wasn't interested in getting tied down in a relationship. Why did that make him want her more? Luke was starting to get mad at himself.

The real kicker for him wasn't his physical attraction towards her, though it didn't help matters. Nope, that's not what had him confused and upside down. It was the unpredicted avidity to crack open his chest cavity and show her everything. Invite her to climb inside his mess of a life and add some beauty to it.

He turned back towards the bus; he knew the guys were going to continue giving him a hard time until they got bored with it. He would just have to ride it out until then. And hope he didn't screw everything up in the process. They were depending on him.

"Were you with your girlfriend?" Blake lilted.

"Go to hell." Luke tried to play it casual.

Carl stuck his head in the bus, "Ten minutes."

They started to the stage area, all of them feeling the energy of the crowd beating in their chests. It reminded them all of why they were really there, the exhilaration of playing a live show. They loved the fans and the excitement. They'd been playing together for so long it was nearly effortless.

When they took the stage, the arena went wild. The time always seemed to pass too quickly. From the first note to the last, they continuously gave it everything they had, knowing that they wouldn't be able to live their dreams without the fans making it possible.

They constantly left it all on the stage, returning to the buses completely exhausted. All worry and speculation about any subject matter disappeared; they focused on rocking their fans' faces off. And they never disappointed.

Chapter 3

Best of You

meet me in the mountains
under a star filled sky
build me a fire out of ashes
teach me how to fly
-excerpt from Lenny's journal

Lenny hadn't slept in almost two years. Not really. She could lay down and stare at the dark and hope and pray to slip into peaceful oblivion, but it wouldn't happen.

She would have little bouts of sleep, but nothing solid to cling to, nothing that *felt* like the sleep she remembered from days long ago. It would usually start with the muscle aches, followed by the vivid nightmare replay. Some images never seemed to fade, especially with a photographic memory, and they were in perfect, crystal clear reception when she was alone in her bunk. The traumatic betrayal that left her empty, the physical pain that ripped through her body as her dreams fell apart around her, the gruesome incompetence to stop or change any of the events as she watched them replay again and again. The end always resulted with the perfunctory long-standing headache.

She was a pro at hiding the dark circles under her eyes with special concealer and acting like being a morning person was just who she was. She knew that Carl believed that she took coffee intravenously, and she couldn't deny that it would make the consumption of required caffeine that much easier.

Her inability to sleep came in quite handy for her new job. Everyone thought she was the first one awake. Nope, she was just up. All the time.

Lenny sighed as she paid for the hot, black beverage at the counter in the roadside diner. Yep, another exhausting day. At least Carl loved coffee as much as she did. She smirked as as she grabbed his to-go cup. If only he knew what a pusher she felt like every time she handed him his cup.

***

Trust. Trust was a big deal to Carl. It usually took years of knowing him to earn it. Two weeks into the tour and Carl knew he trusted Lenny beyond the reasonable.

She didn't just do what was expected, she rose above expectation. She inexplicably knew everything about everyone's station. She could fill in at a moment's notice. She was everywhere at once, solving problems before Carl knew they ever existed. And she did all of it with a smile.

Professional barely covered it. The entire tour ran on her timetable, which happened to be more efficient than Carl's. He got more than an assistant out of hiring Lenny. If Carl was the ruthless sea captain, then Lenny was his devoted first officer. And the crew was loyal to her. Probably to the death.

He was starting to wonder how he had done this for nearly twenty years without her. Gone were the days of wild parties, coked out musicians, and random girls filing on and off the buses. She kept the buses clean of any contraband and shooed groupies away. Carl finally slept easily at night and as a pleasant result, his acid reflux was under control.

He knew he should give credit to the band for the lifestyle overhaul they'd promised from the beginning, but Carl chose to believe that none of this would be possible without Lenny. She was his right hand. If Carl was the Emperor, then Lenny was Darth Vader.

It was possible that the power was going to Carl's head.

He still didn't know what she had so readily left behind the day he hired her. He kind of didn't care. Whoever, or whatever, had chased her away was a fool, and he was reaping the benefits of that mistake. All he had to do was keep her happy and his life was smooth sailing.

He rotated which bus she rode on daily, sometimes hourly. However, he still preferred to have her ride the Crew bus overnights. No reason to play with fire.

No complaints had been uttered. The guys enjoyed having Lenny around, and Carl knew they didn't want to screw it up. Having a woman of Lenny's character on the tour had softened things considerably, to the point where even the hardest of roadies watched their behavior around her.

Carl couldn't blame them, she had a charm and exuberance that was contagious. He looked forward to her bringing coffee to him every morning. He never made that part of her duties, but he believed she did it out of the kindness of her heart.

That's where he was waiting when she came to him with a frown.

"What's up?" Carl asked, trying not to sound concerned.

Lenny handed him his coffee and shook her head. "The new opening act is a bunch of dicks," she growled.

Carl laughed out loud; Lenny never talked negatively about anyone.

Even so, he knew what she meant. A new band had opened up for them last night and would be traveling with them for a short leg of the tour, six shows altogether. They were young, immature, and hard-headed. They had their own set of rules that they lived by. They *thought* they were punk rockers, but they seemed to care an awful lot about making sure they *looked* like punk rockers.

"Just a week and they'll be outta your hair." Carl said, taking a sip of his coffee.

"I hope I can make it a week." Lenny grunted. "If that skinny asshat hits on me one more time, I'm gonna punch him in the neck...accidentally. "

Carl choked on his coffee. Lenny smirked at his sputtering. When he recovered he cautioned, "Just stay away from them. The label wants them to get some exposure. They'll burn out soon enough."

"What kind of a name is Juniper Highlights anyway? They think they're *so* tough. I bet I could make 'em cry in under five minutes." Lenny huffed under her breath and then shook off her bad mood. "We still gonna make good time with all the extra stops?"

Carl pursed his lips, "Yeah, for the most part." He grimaced as he thought about the time being wasted on friggin' bathroom breaks. "That's the last time Sway buys tacos out of some guy's trunk."

Lenny tried to hide her smirk behind her cup but Carl caught it anyway.

"I know, you think it's funny."

"It *is* funny!" Lenny grinned at him. "And it's really not Sway's fault. I mean, that Hibachi looked clean to me."

Carl rolled his eyes. "Well then, no more Mexican food on the road. We can't keep stopping every time he's gotta take a dump."

"Gross, Carl," Lenny pretended to look disgusted. "He's just following the rules." She raised her eyebrows at him and he said the rule out loud with her:

"No number two on the bus."

"That should've been the name of the tour." Carl muttered under his breath.

Lenny chuckled at his orneriness. "Hey, day off tomorrow, what's the plan?"

Carl considered before replying, "I was thinking about giving you the day off, too." He raised an eyebrow and gave her a knowing look.

"You mean, tell everyone I have the day off and then sneak around to see if they try to get into any trouble?" Lenny translated for him.

"Yeah, pretty much." Carl nodded.

"Sounds like a good idea. I think the guys are getting sick of me playing Mother Hen. It might be better for me to lay low for a day."

"They're not sick of you, they love you. Everyone does." Carl told her seriously.

Lenny avoided his stern look and gave him her now famous half-smirk, did her trademark move of slamming her coffee and got ready to get back to work. Carl knew it was her exit strategy for when things started to get too personal for her. She was really good at protecting herself, but he was getting to know her despite it. She didn't really allow compliments for herself. She'd get a flicker in her eye and immediately end the conversation. Just like now.

"Time to get back to work, Boss Man." She strode to the end bus to start her rounds, her golden hair reflecting the rising sun and bouncing the color off the shiny chrome. Carl took another sip of his coffee as he watched her depart. Damn, but that girl knew how to find good coffee.

"Hey!" Carl called after her, "Blue Bus today!" She waved her hand at him over her shoulder in acknowledgment.

***

Lenny knocked on the Red Bus's door and waited for a few seconds before boarding the bus. She liked to give a small warning before entering because a couple of days ago she discovered how much Sway liked to walk around in the nude. Growing up with three brothers it wasn't anything shocking for Lenny. But Sway had actually been kind of embarrassed. Which had been pretty adorable.

The guys were sitting in the main living space with guitars and papers spread all around them. They looked up in unison as Lenny entered the room.

"How you feeling, Sway?" Lenny asked the bassist.

He rubbed his belly and made a sad face, "Now that I've shit out half my intestines I feel a little better."

"Nice." Lenny shook her head. "Well, Carl says no more Mexican food on the road."

"Agreed," Blake and Harrison replied as one.

"You ready to hit the road?" She asked as she inspected their refrigerator and bathroom supplies.

"Who are you riding with today?" Blake asked curiously.

"Blue Bus today. Hopefully it'll be less stinky." She teased, waving her hand in front of her face. Sway looked apologetic and Lenny grinned at him. "Don't feel bad, we've all been there."

"Hey, what's the plan for the day off tomorrow?" Harrison seemed hesitant to ask. His large brown eyes looking anywhere but directly at

44

Lenny.

"Um, let's see," Lenny said, pretending to think about it. "A whole day off in Virginia Beach…I think I might actually go to the beach." She laughed at their silent faces. "What? Carl said I could have the day off, too."

"Cool. We were just talking about…how you needed a day off." Harrison quickly covered as Blake gave him a stern look.

"Sure ya were." Lenny smirked, "I know, I've been in your hair a lot. You need a break, I get it." She smiled at their protesting faces but didn't leave room for discussion. "It's cool, I totally understand. I'll see you later," she waved as she left the bus.

Lenny's next stop was the Blue Bus with Mike and Luke. It was her favorite stop of the day, that's why she usually saved it for last. And today was even better because she would be getting to stay.

Lenny tried to stifle the spark of excitement that was bouncing around in her belly. She knocked and paused. She hadn't had any indecent accidents on this bus like the other one but she decided that she really couldn't be too careful. Besides, Luke Casey naked was *not* an image she really needed to have in her head forever. Unfortunately. That would make working for him that much harder.

Making her way into the living space she could see Mike sleeping on the sofa, looked like he'd been there all night. Empty water bottles and candy wrappers littered the floor. Automatically, she started to pick up the garbage and throw it away. Luke came out of the bathroom, having just showered, with a towel slung low on his hips.

"Why is Mike sleeping on the couch? You guys have a fight?" She quipped, refusing to look up, knowing she wouldn't be able to keep herself from staring at Luke's perfectly sculpted chest and abs. *Freaking Adonis.*

Luke retreated to the back room to put clothes on. When he reemerged he was wearing faded jeans and a black t-shirt, his hair still wet and messy from the shower. He had started to grow some scruff on his face a few days ago and hadn't shaved it. But it looked good on him. Made him look older. He stepped towards Lenny and took the now full trash bag from her hands to tie it closed.

"He was watching a movie last night and decided to sleep out here," he explained in a hushed voice. He was standing close to Lenny so that she could hear him and she could smell the fresh shampoo from his shower and his minty breath. Suddenly, she was very aware of her coffee breath and took a step back. She smiled casually, ignoring the flush she felt creeping up her neck, and opened the refrigerator to give it a quick scan.

"What movie was it?" She asked, surprised at the steadiness of her voice despite the pounding of her pulse. The intensity with which her body consistently responded to Luke's presence was alarming, to say the least.

"*Rear Window* with Jimmy Stewart." His voice was close again, just over her shoulder, and she swallowed hard before turning around.

His crystal blue eyes scanned her face slowly. He had successfully backed her into the corner of the kitchenette. She licked her bottom lip nervously and saw his gaze drop to her mouth and stay there.

"I love that movie, too." Lenny reached for the trash bag, grazing his hand with her own as she slipped it from Luke's grasp. He inhaled sharply and she stepped around him, quickly backing towards the door.

"I'll make sure you guys get a refill of water before we take off." She paused, trying to get her heart rate under control, "I'm riding on this bus today so...I'll be right back."

Luke took a step toward her, "What are you going to do tomorrow?"

"Maybe go to the beach with Tanya and the other merch girls," she lied, looking away from his penetrating gaze.

"That sounds like fun..." Luke acted like there was more he wanted to say but couldn't think of it.

"Yeah...so I'll be right back." She repeated, but this time she turned around, finally breaking the tension between them and walked down the steps.

***

Mike watched their interaction through slits in his eyes and held back the deep chuckle that wanted to escape.

"That sounds like fun," Mike mocked softly from the couch.

Luke turned to him, clearly surprised that he was awake. "You're an ass," he muttered to his friend on his way to the back of the bus.

Mike let the chuckle out now; he enjoyed giving his best friend a hard time. Luke didn't really have crushes, so there was so much more material to be worked. Luke had never had a hard time getting women. He'd usually just give them a lip curl and a wink and they were suddenly topless. To Mike, it was very interesting to see Luke struggle so much with basic conversation around a girl.

"Maybe you can help put lotion on her back," he continued to tease.

Luke huffed and closed the door to the back lounge, leaving Mike on the couch laughing.

***

"What's in the notebook?" Mike asked with curiosity, nodding towards Lenny. She looked up and Mike thought he detected a bit of panic on her face, but she quickly smoothed it out.

46

"Just my journal, sort of," she muttered, closing it and tucking it back into her bag.

"You don't have to put it away, I was just wondering," Mike reassured.

"I was finished anyway," Lenny's dark blue eyes connected briefly with his and he gave her a small smile.

"You writing the next Great American Novel?" He kept it light, still trying to get a good bead on her.

"Hardly." She tucked a stay hair that had come out of her braid behind her ear.

She stood up and stretched her arms over her head. "These long hours on the bus sure do get my muscles all bunched up."

"Yeah, you seem like you're pretty active. The drive must about make you crazy." Mike gauged her reaction to a personal assumption about herself. If it bothered her, she didn't show it.

Getting to know the 'real' Lenny was Mike's new hobby. She was an expert at deflection and ambiguity. It didn't upset Mike or bring him any cause for worry. To him, it was a new way to pass the time on the long drives.

"It's not so bad." Lenny answered with a sigh. "Besides, it's not every day I get the opportunity to travel with one of the world's greatest bands."

And there it was, deflecting his personal inquiry into a compliment about the band. It was her MO. If a question required a personal answer, she would stroke the ego of the inquisitor. It was like a weird game of chess, with words and presumptions being the moving pieces. Mike loved it.

"Carl said you go running during sound check everyday," Luke joined them from the back lounge. He'd been noticeably absent, Mike thought. Usually wherever Lenny was, Luke was hanging around nearby. But he'd kept his distance most of the day, which Mike didn't understand. He clearly liked the girl.

"Yeah, it's a habit I picked up a few years ago." Lenny averted her eyes and sat back down.

"I usually run in the mornings when we park. You should join me sometime." Luke's lead singer confidence was back to oozy goodness.

Lenny's eyes flashed to Luke's for a second and Mike was certain she almost blushed. These two were so attracted to one another, and continued to fail at pretending as if they weren't, that it was almost comical to witness.

"Unless you think you wouldn't be able to keep up." Luke playfully provoked when Lenny didn't answer right away.

"That's the least of my worries." Lenny gave him a sideways smile.

47

"I like to run alone, helps me think."

"I promise not to talk," Luke pressed, "You won't even notice I'm there." Mike was beginning to wonder if they noticed *he* was even there.

If Mike's attempts at divulging Lenny's carefully concealed inner-self was like chess, then whatever it was that Lenny and Luke did was like fencing. Fluid. Graceful. *Advance. Passata-soto.*

"Then why do you want me there? Do you need a bodyguard?" Lenny's tone turned playful. *Opposition Parry.*

Luke guffawed, "Maybe. Sometimes I get scared." He winked at Mike. "There could be bears out there." *Forward Recovery.*

"Oh yeah," Mike verified, "Luke picks up wild animals like nobody's business." He wasn't sure if he was helping or even what he was helping with; Luke still hadn't made any declarations to him about his intentions with Lenny.

Lenny let out a small laugh and she pulled her legs up under herself in the chair, slipping off her shoes.

"I guess it wouldn't hurt." She gave Luke a serious scowl. "But I run with a purpose, it's not a fashion show for me. I plan on looking ugly and unkempt."

"Good, better to scare away the bears." *Flick.*

***

Lenny wasn't sure when she had drifted off. She remembered talking with Mike and Luke about the new song they had been trying out the past couple of shows. Then they had lunch. Sandwiches.

Mike decided to get Lenny involved in his favorite soap opera. He had waved her over to the couch so she could have a better view of the show and she settled in between the two men.

The next thing she knew, she was laying in the middle of a field under a perfect bluebird sky. She hadn't seen a sky this crystal clear in so long. The wildflowers surrounding her smelled clean and masculine. Masculine? Wait a minute, that's not right. But it felt sooo right. Lenny rolled onto her side and inhaled deeply. *Mmmmm, you smell like snowflakes.* She heard thunder in the distance, a storm must be coming. She felt the ground rumble beneath her and her eyes flew open when she realized it wasn't thunder but a very deep, hearty chuckle.

A man's chuckle.

Lenny sat up so quickly her vision darkened. She tried to focus on something, anything. Mike was gone. The TV was playing but on mute and the cabin was the golden colors of early evening.

"Whoa, calm down, Len." Luke's voice was gentle as he placed his warm hand on the center of her back to steady her. His blonde, messy hair swung across his forehead, covering his eyes.

"I'm sorry, I didn't know I fell asleep." Lenny's neck was heating up and she used one hand to wipe the side of her face. It was as bad as she feared. Drool.

"It's fine, you were obviously tired. You work your freaking ass off; I think you've earned yourself a nap." Luke's fingers had started to make small circles on her back, soothing her. They worked their way up to her braid and tugged on the elastic, pulling it free.

"I didn't mean to...um...drool." Lenny was humiliated. She moved to try to stand up but Luke put his other hand on her knee, stopping her. The warmth from his touch seemed to melt her to the seat.

"Really, Lenny," he said sincerely, making sure to have eye contact, "You didn't do anything wrong. You need to learn to take a break sometime." His fingers were still working into her hair and untangling the tight twists of her braid.

Lenny gave him a tight smile, wishing she could believe what he was saying. But what if Carl had walked in at that moment? How could she explain why her head had been in the lap of a rock star? She'd have been fired for sure. No, she would have to be more careful.

And she really needed to stop whatever black magic Luke was doing to her hair.

"Besides, who doesn't like being told they smell like snowflakes?" Luke was trying not to smile but he was failing.

Lenny's eyes widened as she realized she had said that *out loud*! How else could she embarrass herself today?

"I was dreaming," Lenny muttered, coolly moving Luke's hand off her knee and tensing to stand up again. Luke's hand in her hair held her still.

"Give me minute," his deep voice commanded. His fingers found the knot in her muscles at the back of her neck and started a gentle, but firm, massage. Lenny let out a small sigh as he worked the tension free.

"Dreaming about me or snowflakes?" Luke whispered low in her ear, causing goosebumps to raise on Lenny's arms.

"Neither," Lenny muttered and she finally broke out of his spell and got up and crossed to the other side of the cabin, settling back in her chair.

"Can I have my hair tie back?" She asked, holding out her hand and disliking the breathless way her words had come out.

Luke's face was unreadable as he watched her. "No," he finally said, "I've noticed you've been getting headaches and I'm worried that braid is adding undo pressure."

Lenny sat back at his statement. It made sense. Her headaches usually blossomed right at the base of her skull where the top of her braid

49

began. But she had no idea that he had been noticing those things about her. Her goal had been to be as invisible and as unassuming as possible. The last thing she wanted was attention.

"And since I can't get you to take any regular kind of break, the least I can do is require you to let your hair down," he grinned at her, "so to speak."

Luke's smile caused warmth to fill her appendages and she bit the inside of her cheek to keep from smiling back.

"Besides, you wear that damn thing every day; it's time for a change." He wrapped the hair tie around his wrist and gave her a serious look. "And anytime you need me to work on the tension you have building in your neck, you let me know." He arched an eyebrow flirtatiously.

"Sure thing, boss." Lenny replied, seeing the slight tick in Luke's jaw when she said the word 'boss.' He didn't like being reminded that they had a working relationship but one of them had to right the rocking ship. He was getting too familiar and she had to keep him at a safer distance.

Lenny flipped her head over and shook out her hair, pulling the strands through her fingers and releasing any tangles. She couldn't deny that it felt good to have it free. Every follicle was rejoicing in triumph. Silly follicles.

When she righted herself, she saw Luke staring at her with hazy eyes. She knew what that look meant, she'd seen it before, on other men looking at other women. She didn't understand why Luke was directing that kind of a look at her. She knew she wasn't ugly but she wasn't anything beyond...ordinary. She chose to ignore it and pulled out her cellphone to check for any messages.

A couple texts from Harrison in regards to Blake eating the last of his Crunch Berries, a dirty joke from Sway and an ETA from Carl.

"We should be in Virginia Beach soon." Lenny informed Luke, hoping the subject change would snap him back to reality.

"You really going to the beach tomorrow?" Luke asked, shifting into a casual slouch on the sofa. The setting sun cast shadows in the cabin and darkened his face so she couldn't read his expression.

"Yep," Lenny lied. She hated that she had to lie.

"You could come fishing with me and Mike," he offered slowly.

Lenny cleared her throat. Honestly? She would much rather go fishing with Luke and Mike then have to play party to Carl's paranoia. But that wasn't an option. "No, I think I better work on my tan."

"I've just never seen you really talk to the merch girls; I didn't know you guys hung out." Luke suspected something. Probably not the truth, but he definitely thought she was up to something else. Lenny could feel him studying her and her pulse quickened.

"Just say what you want to say, Luke," Lenny replied in a low voice, "Ask me the question that's really on your mind." This was a dangerous game, even for Lenny. If Luke guessed outright what she was doing...she would admit it. And Carl would flip shit.

The cabin was quiet save for the hum of the wheels on the road. Lenny thought about turning on the overhead light so she could read Luke's face.

"Are you seeing someone on the road crew?" His voice was dark and rough, as if the question was painful to ask.

Lenny felt a small smile play on her lips. "No, " she let let out a relieved sigh. "Nope, I'm as single as they come."

She connected his suspicions and had to admit that it did indeed look like she was sneaking off to meet a secret lover. She almost laughed at the idea but Luke turned on the lights in the cabin and the serious look on his face sobered her instantly.

He returned to his seat but continued to study her. She met his gaze without flinching.

"Are you seeing Carl?" He asked, his mouth flat.

Lenny's eyes widened and her eyebrows raised at Luke. "Seriously?"

He didn't respond, watching her with that penetrating stare of his. As if he could extract the truth from her by willing it from the depth of her soul.

"No," Lenny shook her head, incredulous, "I am *not* seeing Carl. That would be..." She couldn't think of the correct word to finish with. Absurd, creepy, wrong, insane, all came to mind.

"That would be what?" Luke demanded an end to her sentence.

"Weird." Lenny finally vocalized. "And very, very wrong." She lifted her hair off of her now hot neck and pulled it over one shoulder. "Why would you even think that?"

"You seem really comfortable with him," Luke stated plainly.

Apparently Carl wasn't the only one Lenny was comfortable around. She still couldn't wrap her head around the fact that she had been *asleep* in Luke's lap. Her, the girl who can't sleep. Drooling in Luke Casey's lap. It was ludicrous.

"I guess he reminds me of my brother, Scott." Lenny said slowly.

The tense lines around Luke's mouth seemed to relax and the playfulness came back into his voice. "Then what's the real reason you won't come fishing tomorrow?"

Oh, boy. Lenny was about to spill. She swallowed hard, lying to Luke left a bad taste in her mouth.

"I can't tell you," she finally mustered out. She wanted to smack

51

her forehead with her palm. Why was she so weak when it came to him?

The silence that followed was oppressive and Lenny thought she was actually going to choke. And then Luke let her off the hook.

"I can accept that," he dipped his head in truce. "You don't have to tell me everything, Lenny...just don't lie to me."

"Can I ask you a question?" Lenny took advantage of the familiarity that seemed to erupt between them without her permission. It may have been her imagination, or possibly her ego, but she had the distinct impression that Luke was more open with her than he realized.

"Always." He answered without pause and she felt a tiny shiver race down her spine.

"What changed in between this tour and the last one?" She licked her bottom lip and tried to clarify quickly, "I mean, I know that Mike was in rehab but it seems like this is really important to you. To all of you," she looked at him with soft eyes, "But especially you."

Luke let out a careful breath, "That obvious, huh?" He chuckled nervously and rubbed his hand down the side of his face.

Lenny was a little fearful she'd asked too personal of a question. But she couldn't stop herself this time. She wanted to know. Her need to know more about Luke was sometimes overpowering, like now. It overshadowed her sensible reasoning to keep a safe distance. She wanted to see past the image that was projected to the public and know who he was at his core.

Why did he give her want to make exceptions to all the rules that she believed would keep her safe from defeat? Was it the way his mouth curved up slightly on one side, how his voice deepened when he talked about his friends, the way he seemed to have one more thing to say but never said it? All of the above.

"It's hard to explain." His eyebrows raised slightly and he focused on the center of the floor. "My parents died in a car accident when I was in fourth grade and my great aunt took me in. I met Mike in sixth grade and we were pretty much inseparable after that. My aunt died a week after I turned eighteen, leaving me a ton of money and no relatives."

His eyes returned to hers and she saw something deeper, more vivid, than Luke had ever revealed.

"The band became my family. I'd do anything for them. But we got too big too fast and none of us were super responsible about what to do with that kind of popularity. I was drinking," his eyes widened and he looked into his lap, "a lot. I didn't pay attention to what was happening to us. The night we almost lost Mike, I realized how much I needed him. They're my family, maybe not by blood, but that doesn't really matter. They're my brothers."

"You love them." Lenny said it as a definitive statement, squeezed from her by the emotion she heard in his voice as he relayed his simple story.

"Yes," he nodded. "More than anything." He looked into her face and she couldn't help but see the burden he carried for his loved ones. The inner conviction and loyalty that drove him.

"The music is more than a hobby or something we happen to be good at. It's who we are. It's or heart-breath, our creed, our passion." His blue eyes blazed around the edges. "That's why this tour is so important to me. Because they're important to me."

Lenny's heart pounded at his words. His intensity, his truth...it was exquisite.

She didn't get a chance to respond because Mike rejoined them at that moment. He staggered from the back of the bus, his messy brown hair even more mussed. He rubbed his sleepy eyes and looked back and forth between Luke and Lenny.

"That's not where I left you." He winked at Lenny and she felt her face flush as she remembered where she had awoken only a short time ago.

Mike chuckled at her discomfort and got a bottle of water out of the fridge.

"Hey, throw me one of those," Luke called to him and Mike tossed a bottle his direction.

"You joining us for movie's and popcorn tonight?" Mike directed at Lenny.

"I, uh," Lenny stammered. She had no idea what she was going to be doing that night. She hadn't discussed it with Carl. But more than that, she was still reeling from the complex emotions that Luke had stirred in her.

"When we park we're going over to the Red Bus, you're coming with us." Mike held up his hand to stop her weak protest. "We're the ones who asked you to come on this crazy adventure, it would rude to ditch you."

Lenny sighed in mock disgust but she gave him a smile. "If you say so."

She locked eyes with Luke momentarily. It was enough to cause her heart to stall. He was beautiful. And not only on the outside.

***

They arrived in Virginia Beach around eight that night, the buses parked and everyone disembarked. It had been a long two weeks. Crew and personnel scattered almost immediately.

They weren't staying in hotels for a lot of the tour because they were trying to cut costs. The band had to prove themselves as a big draw

53

again. They had decided to buy their own tour buses which helped keep the crew comfortable during their crazy, sometimes back-to-back performances. The schedule they were on was hairy, but they were more than prepared for it. The investment of the transportation and skipping hotel accommodations for the majority of the trip, had been an easy and efficient way of getting the label's backing for such a date-heavy tour.

The band would all go separate ways tomorrow for the day. But for the night before, they all gathered in the Red Bus to go over music Sway was working on and watch movies. Having Lenny tag along was a natural addition to their close knit family.

Mike could see her apprehension and decided to give her free rein of the remote control. He understood the complex idea of an outsider trying to fit into a dynamic that was already tight and bonded. It couldn't be easy.

Lenny smiled gratefully as Sway placed the popcorn bowl in her lap. That was something concrete Mike had picked up on, Lenny liked to eat.

Blake was already popping more for everyone else. Lenny started to flip through channels, pausing on ESPN sports network for a moment. She casually glanced around, not noticing Mike lounging in the back, watching though half lidded eyes. She turned her attention back to the sports update.

He watched as her body noticeably shifted closer to the screen. Her eyes lit up while the channel showed images of snowboarders practicing in anticipation of the Winter X games coming up in a couple months. Mike caught Luke's eye and raised his chin in Lenny's direction.

"Find anything good yet?" Blake asked abruptly and she quickly changed the channel.

"Not yet." Lenny replied, scrolling through the list again. She eventually settled on an old classic movie. *An American in Paris* with Gene Kelly. Mike was a sucker for old movies and it distracted him from asking Lenny about the snowboarding.

"You don't really like this, do you?" Blake made a face at Lenny.

"Well, it's no *Brigadoon*..." Lenny smiled.

"*Brigadoon*!" Mike heard himself shout. He knew he had just gotten more excited than his usual. Everyone turned to stare at him. "You like *Brigadoon* too?" He asked Lenny, getting up and moving onto the couch so he could be closer to her.

"Holy crap, yes." Lenny giggled.

"You've got to be kidding me!" Blake grumbled. "There's *two* of them?"

"I always wanted to be Cyd Charisse when I grew up," Lenny confessed.

54

Mike didn't know the last time he had been this happy. He was the only one who ever got into the old movies, especially the musicals. He saw Blake roll his eyes but ignored him.

"I made my mom sign me up for ballroom dancing because I wanted to be the next Gene Kelly."

"How did you end up becoming a drummer?" She asked, her smile wide.

"Turns out I have a great sense of rhythm but two left feet." Mike grinned and took some of the popcorn she offered.

Mike and Lenny talked through the whole movie. They raved over the actors and the characters and the plot line. They exchanged quotes from their favorite classic movies, trying to best each other in a guessing game. Mike knew they were driving the others crazy but he didn't care. His chess game with Lenny had shifted into ping pong and she was volleying with equal give and take.

"When did you get into the classics?" Lenny asked.

"I'm not sure, they were always a part of my life. But I got reattached while I was in rehab. " Mike stated matter of fact. He sensed the mood of the room shift. He hated that. Anytime his past drug use came up, everyone started using kid gloves.

"I'm sorry," Lenny's eyes were apologetic.

"It's not your fault," Mike stayed casual. "I have a problem; it's something I have to be able to acknowledge. It's what keeps me on track."

The room was quiet, Lenny looked into her lap.

"Hey, don't feel bad." He said smiling at her, trying to break the tension. "I'm the one who screwed up. I'm thankful I didn't die and I'm thankful I have these idiots to help hold me accountable." He playfully shoved her shoulder. "When did *you* get into classic movies?" He turned the question on her.

Lenny swallowed and tried to push past the awkwardness she clearly felt. "I saw *My Fair Lady* when I was eight. I decided right then and there that no one would ever be as beautiful as Audrey Hepburn."

The air in the bus seemed to relax a little more and Mike asked her questions about her her childhood. Now all the guys were paying close attention, this was the most Lenny had ever shared about herself. She talked about growing up in Wyoming and having three older brothers.

"Dang, three older brothers, that explains your competitive side." Mike acknowledged.

"Yeah," Lenny's face was open as she talked about her siblings. "They definitely taught me a lot. I was sort of an accident. Scott, David and Nathan were all really close together. Scott was twelve when I was born. David was eleven and Nathan was ten."

"So you were the baby, essentially."

"I guess you could say that, though they would never let me feel like it. I wanted to keep up with them so bad and they were more than happy to let me tag along. I think I was afforded a lot more opportunity than others would have been in a similar situation." Lenny got a faraway look in her eyes and Mike could tell she was feeling a little home sick.

"Do you get to talk to them very often?" Mike asked gently.

"Not as much as they would like," Lenny admitted. "Scott calls every day but mostly to lecture me on my priorities."

"Do they know what you're doing now?"

"Yeah, but they just like to worry." Lenny tried to wave it off but she obviously really missed her brothers.

"What about your folks?" Mike wanted to find out all he could before her walls went back up.

"My folks are awesome, honestly. They're really great people. They're just having a hard time with me growing up."

Mike noticed Lenny space off a little in their conversation but instead of drawing her back in, he changed the channel. The movie had ended a few minutes ago and he wanted to try an experiment. He turned the station back to ESPN and the sports broadcasters were still talking about the Winter X games preparation. Lenny zeroed right in on the screen. Mike kept one eye on Lenny and one on the TV.

Her face was pinched and tight, like she was trying to not feel whatever it was she was feeling right now. It morphed into obvious distress as they started to show a profile of a female snowboarder, Cody Carmichael. She was talking excitedly about the upcoming games and the interviewer asked her about her Olympic gold medal from two years ago. Lenny stood abruptly, yanking the remote away from Mike and switching off the TV. Everyone looked up at her sudden movement and she stared directly into Mike's eyes. He'd gone too far.

Checkmate.

"I have to go." She darted out of the bus.

"What the hell?" Sway asked, confused.

Mike exchanged glances with Luke who had been watching from across the room. He put down his notebook and grabbed his hoodie.

"I'll check on her." He waved them off and bounded out of the bus.

***

She was lacing up her running shoes when Luke walked onto the bus.

"Kinda late for a run, isn't it?" He asked, trying to appear casual

56

but his concern was showing through.

"Nope," Lenny answered stoically. Her demeanor was drastically different than it had been most of the day. She was cold towards Luke, closed off.

Luke was glad he was wearing his sweatpants and tennis shoes; he followed her out the door and matched her pace.

"You don't have to come," she snapped.

"I know," Luke answered, not even breathing hard.

Lenny picked up her pace, pushing Luke to keep up. She kept increasing speed until she was at a flat out run, turning corners and crossing streets with unbelievable fluidity. They rounded a corner and came to a large city pond with a bike path that ran alongside of it. Luke matched her step for step, breath for breath. She was running on pure emotion now.

As they crested a small incline she ran out of breath and collapsed flat out in the grass staring up at the star filled sky. Luke looked down at her for a beat and then he took a seat next to her. He let her rest for a few minutes before speaking.

"You can really run."

She snickered a little and sat up, still panting. "I told you that you didn't have to come," she reminded. She pushed her sweaty hair off her face and readjusted her hasty ponytail.

Luke looked up into the sky and then turned his eyes on her. His kept his voice soft as he asked, "What happened?"

He saw a thousand emotions debating across her face but she wouldn't give voice to any of them.

"You know, I had to chase Mike once." Luke began; he brought his knees up and rested his forearms across them. "Of course, he hopped a plane and went to L.A. You were much easier to catch." He leaned his shoulder into hers for a moment and looked into her face again. "What happened, Len?"

"It's nothing." Lenny was building those walls again and Luke could feel her shutting him out. He sighed and put his arm around her shoulders pulling her tight to his side. Trying to keep her from shutting him out completely.

"Okay. I won't push."

At first Lenny stiffened at his sudden embrace but then relaxed and turned her face into his chest.

"I shouldn't have taken off. They're gonna want to know what's wrong with me." Lenny's voice was muffled by Luke's sweatshirt.

"They'll get over it." Luke rubbed her back reassuringly.

Luke had never just held a woman before and he had been able to seize that opportunity twice today. It felt really good to feel her softness

57

against his side. She smelled amazing, the heat from the run mixing with her subtle perfume. He used both arms to pull her a little closer. When she didn't resist he felt a strange satisfaction in that.

"Why did Mike run?" Lenny asked into the silence.

"That's not fair." Luke tenderly corrected. "I can't divulge my best friend's secrets without anything in return."

Lenny's hand fisted against his sweatshirt and he pressed his lips to the top of her head.

"Luke?" Lenny's voice came out small and slow.

"Yeah?"

"How long did I sleep this afternoon?"

Luke thought back to this afternoon when Lenny had snuggled into his side and eventually rested her head in his lap. She had fallen asleep almost the instant he had touched her.

"Four hours." Luke answered honestly and he felt her tense beneath him. "Why do you ask?"

"Why didn't you wake me up?" She asked, ignoring his question.

"Because..." Luke didn't know how to answer that. Not without sounding like a psycho. Oh well. "...I wanted you to feel safe." He tightened his grip around her, trying to drive that point home.

Lenny wrapped her arms around his middle and Luke closed his eyes in relief.

They sat together quietly for a long time before Lenny stood. She had put the pieces back together of her crumbling wall and she was her regular, centered self again.

Luke realized that no matter how comfortable someone may seem being alone, they all needed someone every now and again.

"You wanna go back?" She asked.

Luke nodded and they began a slow jog back to the buses. His head was spinning at having spent so much focused time with Lenny. He had a peek into her world. Even though she had shut him out again, Luke knew that he had been the one to lend her the strength to repair whatever had broken her tonight.

As they rounded the corner and the buses came into view, Lenny slowed her pace to walk to cool down.

"Thanks for letting me hang out with you guys tonight." She said quietly into the humid night air.

"You can always hang with us, Len. You're a part of us now." His sincerity made Lenny smile. He would do anything to see that smile more often.

"And thanks for," she gestured to the way they had come, "all that."

"Anytime." He wanted to pull her into his arms. He didn't want the night to be over. He didn't want her to be alone anymore.

He walked her to the foot of the steps of the crew bus and he had an idea. She might not go for it but then again...

"Hey, we have the extra space for a third person on the Blue Bus if you would like to move over there with me and Mike...permanently."

Lenny raised her eyes at his suggestion, "Don't you think that would be a little inappropriate?"

"Why?" Luke didn't understand.

Lenny let out a small laugh, "Because I'm a girl and you are, well, notorious rock stars."

Luke grimaced when he finally understood what she was implying. "But it's not like that with you; you're like a sister to us."

Lenny took a deep breath, "I'll ask Carl what he thinks."

Luke nodded his head, "Fair enough." He started to back away, "Good night, Lenny."

"Good night, Luke."

Luke turned around and scowled to himself. *You're like a sister to us? Why would I say something so stupid?* He most definitely did not view her as a sister.

He shook his head and climbed the stairs to the Red Bus to say good night to the fellas before turning in himself. They had questions of course, but he deflected them the best he could, protecting Lenny's vulnerability.

It felt good to protect her. Normal. Maybe he was too hellbent on rescuing people he cared about. Maybe it was because there was nothing he could do to save his parents and so he was trying to make up for that by rescuing everyone else, whether they wanted it or not. That was a depressing thought.

Or maybe he was falling in love with her.

***

Lenny's mind refused to let her fall asleep. Again. Long after the crew had come back to the bus and had filled the bunks, she was still lying in the darkness. Waiting for exhaustion to win out over her thoughts. The lines were blurring between her job and her desire to be their friend. Especially Luke.

She couldn't explain the irresistible pull she felt towards him. She got along with the other guys really well, but Luke...he was special. Every time they had eye contact it felt like she was getting electrocuted. In a good way.

She sighed and rolled over to face the wall. Why did he have to be so damn perfect? Tonight he hadn't even made a move; he had simply held her, without expectations. That was new, especially considering his reputation. Then that conversation earlier that exposed so much of his complicated loveliness... and now he was asking her to move to his bus. No way would Carl be okay with that. It had to stop; she couldn't let it go any further.

It was protection for him just as much as it was for her.

An unexplainable tear made it's way out of the corner of her eye and traveled down to the pillow.

Chapter 4

Creatures (For A While)

"I am the king of this castle!" Blake shouted from the top of the bar. He lifted his beer pitcher high in the air and the crowd cheered as he started to pour it down his throat, spilling frothy overflow onto the front of his shirt.

"CHUG! CHUG! CHUG!" The spectators shouted at his feet, pumping their fists in the air.

"How the hell did this happen?!" Carl snarled as he and Lenny tried to push through the mass of people to get to the inebriated guitarist.

"I don't know, Carl! They lied to me!" Lenny yelled back angrily.

The day had started very differently from where it was ending up. Lenny had told the guys she was going to the beach with some of the merch booth girls. But she didn't.

Carl had wanted her to follow the guys and make sure they didn't cause trouble and negative headlines. Lenny thought he was being a touch too controlling but he was her boss, she didn't want to tell him *that* two weeks into her employment.

Besides, she really didn't think the guys would get into any trouble. They'd been on the road for a little while now and they had shown no interest in the former things that had tainted the atmosphere of their previous tour. Lenny had to wonder if Carl was just being overly pessimistic or if there was some truth to his anxiety.

Luke and Mike went offshore fishing. Easy enough. All Carl had to do was follow them to the pier and wait in a small café till they returned.

Sway, Harrison and Blake said they were going to a local water park. Lenny suspected Carl had her follow those three because she was younger and would blend in easier with the youthful crowd. She was thankful that she could wear her bathing suit and still get a tan, adding to her alibi of going to the beach.

The guys rented a private cabana but that didn't limit their social capacity. It did, however, make it easier for Lenny to track them.

Sway had women all over him, constantly bringing him lemonade and reapplying sunscreen to him every ten minutes. Harrison and Blake were much more active, they enjoyed the rides and were very affable with the fans that recognized them, signing autographs and posing for photos. Lenny was impressed with their graciousness and humility.

Sometime in the late afternoon, Lenny lost them. They left the water park early and Lenny got stuck in traffic. This is exactly what Carl didn't want to happen.

Desperate, she called Harrison on his cell, thinking he was the most likely to tell her the truth.

"Hey Lenny, how's the beach?" He sounded nervous, that wasn't good.

"We came back early, Tanya got a sunburn." That would be an easy cover, Tanya was always sunburned. "Where are you guys?" She tried to sound curious but not overly so.

"Um, we're headed to a movie downtown." He didn't sound like himself and Lenny could hear Sway whispering something to him in the background. "I have to go, it's about to start." And he hung up.

Lenny had no choice but to believe them so she pointed the rental car in that direction. But they weren't downtown. They went to the far west side. To a biker bar.

About the same time Lenny figured out they weren't at the theater, she saw a picture sent to her on Twitter of Blake having a drinking contest with the lead guitarist from their opening act, Juniper Highlights.

Cursing herself for being so naïve and cursing them for lying, Lenny called Carl. They each raced to the bar to attempt to stop what they both feared. But by the time they got there, it was too late. Blake had already crawled up on top of the bar. And now he was waving his shirt over his head.

Lenny got to him first and shoved other patrons out of the way. She grabbed him by his pant legs and shouted up at him, "Blake! Please come down!"

"Pretty Lenny!" He smiled at her happily, "C'mere, Pretty Lenny." He wriggled his hips to the beat and attempted what Lenny could only guess to be his best *Coyote Ugly* moves. His words were slurred and he was weaving a little on the bar. Out of the corner of her eye Lenny saw dozens of camera phones taking pictures. The place was packed.

This was a nightmare.

She climbed up on the bar with him much to the pleasure of the crowd. The air was now filled with cat calls and whistles. Ignoring all the requests for her to take off her *own* shirt, Lenny grabbed Blake tightly by the shoulders and began to help him down off the bar into Carl's waiting arms. His skin had a fine sheen of sweat mixed with beer and Lenny's fingers had difficulty getting a decent grip on him. She was forced to hold him close to her to keep from dropping him. The stench turned her stomach and added to her already pissed off state.

As they helped him through the crowd, he stumbled, and Lenny and Carl had to hold him up on each side. Sway and Harrison emerged from the mass of bodies and were met with angry glares from both Lenny and Carl.

"Can we help?" Harrison asked.

"Pay your friends tab!" Lenny bit out. She ignored Harrison's wide eyes. She felt her anger burning low in her belly and knew she was on the verge of losing her temper.

Blake, oblivious to Lenny's ire, started singing along with the music and tried to dance again but fell instead. He sat down hard on the floor with his legs splayed out in front of him like a toddler. He reached his arms up towards Lenny and gave her a sloppy grin.

"Kiss me!" He declared. "Kiss me now!" And then he dissolved into uncontrolled giggles.

Lenny ground her teeth together, her heart beginning to hammer with barely controlled rage. She and Carl helped him back into a standing position and maneuvered him through the door and into the parking lot. Blake's arm was haphazardly pulling her hair as he tried to keep his own balance and Lenny grimaced.

Waiting outside were the punkers from Juniper Highlights, doubled over in laughter. Lenny used all the self-control she had left to move past them and get Blake in the van before any media showed up. But then, they started heckling.

"Your mama had to come get ya, huh?" The tall skinny one laughed. Lenny's face was already flushed with exertion but she felt a new surge of heat bloom across her cheeks.

For some reason, Blake felt it necessary to defend himself; he pushed Lenny and Carl away and held up his fists, charging towards the mockers. "I'll kick your ass!" He was threatening when he stumbled and fell backwards. Lenny and Carl helped him up again. The punkers were laughing even harder now.

Lenny shot a death glare in their direction but kept moving. *We just need to get out of here.* Lenny tried to focus on the task at hand.

"Guess you can't hold you drink as well as you thought, huh, old man!" More laughter. Lenny literally bit her tongue and tasted blood. She exchanged glances with Carl from behind Blake's shoulders and he shook his head at her. He must've been reading her mind.

"There's nothing worse than a talent-less, washed up rock star who doesn't know when to quit!"

That was the last straw. Lenny'd had a long day. She was beyond angry at this point. Of all the mistakes she had made that day, letting some dick-less moron talk trash about someone she considered a friend would not be another one.

"HEY!" Lenny whirled on them, dropping Blake into Carl's arms. "Blake Diedrich has more talent in one earlobe that you have in your entire piss poor excuse of a band!"

Then she charged. She was lunging, her vision completely red, when she felt two strong arms grab her by her waist and pull her back. She pushed the arms away, clawing to get to the punkers. She broke free and tore towards them once more.

"Who do you think you are? Huh? You're no one!" She screamed as she rushed them. She shoved the guy and he fell to the ground with a thud, her eyes blazed with fury as she cocked her left leg up to kick him in the chest. Suddenly Sway's arms grabbed a tight hold of her again and lifted her up and backwards, retreating to the waiting van.

The frightened hecklers had fallen silent. Sway handed Lenny over to Harrison who pulled her into the van and closed the door. He got in the front passenger seat and Carl squealed the tires on the van as he whipped out of the parking lot.

Lenny was in the backseat breathing hard, blood boiling. Her body trembling with the adrenaline surge. Harrison tentatively touched her arm to calm her down but she jerked away.

"Are you kidding me?!" She yelled. "What the hell?" She threw her head against the back of the seat and closed her eyes, angry tears pushing out from under her eyelids.

"I'm sorry, Lenny-" Harrison began, his expression pale.

"Don't!" She snapped, pointing her finger at him. She rubbed the wetness off her face and smelled the beer on her hands from carrying Blake. She let out another growl and wiped her hands on her jeans.

"Lenny," Sway leaned around the seat but Carl reached over and put his hand on his chest, signaling him to stop.

No one dared to speak the rest of the trip. By the time they made it back to the buses, Blake was ready to throw up. Lenny helped him to a patch of grass a few yards away and rubbed his back as he heaved.

Carl took Harrison and Sway inside the bus and proceeded to lecture them for their recklessness and irresponsibility. Lenny would have laughed if she wouldn't have been so mad; he was treating them like teenagers.

She rubbed Blake's back as he clutched the earth, holding on for dear life. As his body expelled the alcohol again and again, he began to cry. Lenny didn't feel it appropriate or beneficial for her to say anything.

"I'm so sorry." Blake sobbed over and over again. "I'm sorry, Lenny... p-pretty, pretty Lenny..." More heaving.

Luke and Mike came around the corner of the bus. Lenny's heart caught slightly as she and Luke held eye contact. She knew she was mirroring the frown on his face but she didn't know what to say. He glanced up at the bus where she could still hear Carl yelling.

Suddenly, Carl came stomping down the stairs and huffed out into the darkness. His lighter ignited his cigarette and then he paced around the parking lot like a caged animal, kicking rocks and randomly yelling.

Luke went up inside the bus and took his turn yelling at Sway and Harrison. Lenny wasn't even surprised. She knew how deeply Luke cared for his mates.

Mike slowly shuffled over and sat down near Blake with his back against a tree.

"You never did know when to stop," Mike remarked pensively. He let his head drop between his knees and rubbed the back of his neck with one hand.

Lenny could tell Mike was thinking about more than just tonight's incident. Her anger slowly dissipated and turned into compassion. They had seen their share of success and failure. They knew each other's ugly sides better than anyone. How hard it must be to see someone you care about slip into old habits, long conquered.

She looked at Carl, still having a fit in the distance, and she understood his worries better. She was wrong. He wasn't being controlling, he was being realistic.

"At least we got there before he went full college coed on us." Lenny joked lightly.

"Yeah? Where's his shirt?" Mike raised his eyebrows pointedly.

Lenny shrugged in mock confusion, making Mike laugh.

"I think I'm dying." Blake moaned from the grass.

"You're not dying, don't be so dramatic." Lenny rubbed his back as he hurled some more. "You're gonna be hella sick tomorrow, though." She added with a touch of sympathy in her voice. Blake groaned in response.

"How was the fishing?" Lenny looked at Mike.

"Good." Mike's expression softened with the subject change. "Peaceful."

"You do anything this exciting?" She gestured to Blake.

Mike chuckled, "Not in a long time."

Lenny motioned to Mike to help her get Blake, who had finally stopped vomiting, into a standing position. They helped him up the steps and into the bus, pushing past the lecture in the front room. Luke stopped yelling and assisted in getting Blake into his bunk.

Lenny set a garbage can next to him and propped pillows behind his back so he was lying on his side. She took a seat on the floor and leaned against the opposite bunk.

"I'll stay with him tonight in case we need to go to the hospital." She was worried and annoyed at the same time. She should have taken Carl more seriously. How was she going to repair this?

Harrison and Sway felt badly, it was obvious. They *should* feel bad. They had broken their promise to Carl, they lied to Lenny and now Blake had to be watched to make sure he didn't die in his own vomit.

Mike nodded and headed for the door. He grabbed Luke's arm, pulling him with, on the way out.

Luke stopped momentarily and touched Lenny's shoulder. "You sure?"

She nodded but couldn't look up at him. She felt too responsible for all of this.

Luke paused just above her then he leaned down and kissed the top of her head. "You're amazing," he whispered in her ear before he followed Mike out of the bus.

Lenny expelled the air in her lungs slowly. Luke's sweet gesture had sent shivers through her. She leaned her head back and stared at the ceiling. The lines between professionalism and friendship were tangling. But she was too tired to care at the moment.

She watched Blake's sleeping form, his mouth hanging open. She was more upset that they had lied to her than she was about the drinking in general. *I'm the worst kind of hypocrite,* she thought bitterly. What kind of right did she have to be angry with them for lying when that's basically all she had done since she'd met them?

She should have kept a closer visual on them. She hoped Carl wasn't going to fire her. It would probably depend on what the media reported tomorrow.

Sway and Harrison hung their heads like ashamed puppies and went to bed without saying a word. Lenny knew she had scared them with her outburst and part of her was satisfied. She chuckled inwardly. If Sway hadn't stopped her she would have given that little douche bag a good thrashing. She hadn't let her anger get the better of her in a long time. It felt kinda good to unleash the back country girl, she had missed her.

***

Mike sat on the couch across from Luke and contemplated how to address the growing concern he had for his band mate's feelings in regards to their new assistant. He had thought it was a brief crush, but now he wasn't so sure. Mike could see the attachment to her gaining strength and he didn't want to see his friend get hurt. Either one of them.

"What's going on with you and Lenny?"

Luke's eyebrows drew together and his mouth ticked up on one side. "I'm not sure what you mean. Can you be more specific?"

Mike rolled his eyes. Was he really trying to play coy about this? It was definitely not his usual.

"C'mon, man." Mike scratched the back of his head in frustration. "It's me."

Luke took a deep breathe and looked down at the floor. He leaned forward, bracing his forearms on his knees and looked back up at Mike. His face was serious and almost inquisitive.

He dropped his voice to just above a hush, like he was afraid someone would hear him. "You know all those things we sing about? Love, passion, truth, beauty, life...?"

Mike nodded, feeling his frown deepen.

Luke shook his head slightly, as if he didn't believe what he was about to say. He rubbed his face aggressively with one hand and chuckled sardonically at himself. "When I look at Lenny...I feel like I finally know what those songs are talking about." He pushed back in his chair and closed his eyes, "Do I sound completely crazy?"

Mike held back a smile and answered quietly, "No, you don't sound crazy."

***

Lenny left the bus early while everyone was still sleeping. She had a lot of time to think throughout the night as she watched over Blake. She was still disappointed that they had lied to her, but this wasn't her first experience with a bunch of guys hell bent on getting messed up. She had three older brothers, after all. And that didn't even cover half the things she'd seen grown men do when testosterone got involved.

She went across the street to a local fast food restaurant and ordered copious amounts of greasy hash browns, breakfast sandwiches and coffee. She had one of the employees help her transport her large order, promising him a free CD in return.

Carl was waiting in his usual spot for coffee. It was a relief to Lenny because she wasn't sure how mad he was at her from the night before. She handed him his coffee and waved him into the Red Bus where she deposited the rest of her bundle. She thanked the employee for his help and gave him the CD.

"Aren't you the girl who tried to knock out Travis Cline last night?" The kid asked, referring to the lead singer of Juniper Highlights that Lenny had attacked outside the bar. The kid had stars in his eyes; he was acting like he had just met a celebrity.

"Were you there?" Lenny asked, eying him suspiciously. He looked too young to have been at the bar.

"Nah, my buddy sent me the video in my email." He held up his phone and showed Lenny a grainy replay of her outburst and Sway throwing her into the back of the van.

She tried to feign indifference. "It's not what it looks like."

"C'mon, that was *awesome!*" The kid argued. Carl gently grabbed the young man's elbow, unsuccessfully trying to hide his smirk.

"Take your CD, kid. Thanks for the help." He turned him over to security at the bottom of the stairs to continue his exit.

"I thought we should have a family meeting," she started to explain, ignoring what had just happened with the internet video as she unpacked her purchases on the table top.

"I'm not mad at you, Lenny." Carl got her to look at him.

"You have every right to be, Carl. I let you down."

Carl gave a lopsided grin, "No, actually, you didn't." Lenny frowned at him and he continued. "I watched all the media coverage of last night's incident and no one has video of Blake's 'King of the Castle' speech. But there is video everywhere of a blonde bad-ass attempting to take out Travis Cline."

Lenny's face fell, "Oh, no."

Carl laughed, "It's alright, Len. You saved the day." He laughed again at her horrified expression. "I'm just glad Sway got to you before you could do any real damage and I had to bail you out of jail."

Lenny finally saw the humor in it and let out a small laugh herself. "Yeah, I woulda hurt him pretty bad." What she didn't say, was that her reason for panic was two-fold. If she was identified in that video it could cause even more trouble. *I'm sure the sponsors would love that kind of publicity.*

They heard a groan from Blake's bunk, interrupting Lenny's thoughts and she went to help him up.

"What the f-." Blake was holding his head and trying to sit upright.

"C'mon, your Majesty," Lenny helped him up and to bathroom.

When she heard the toilet flush she reminded, "Make sure you wash your hands." She was talking too loudly on purpose and Carl chuckled.

Blake staggered out of the small bathroom and Lenny led him to the booth of waiting food. His face turned up at the smell and he tried to pull away.

"No, no, no." Lenny prodded, "You have a show tonight and you need a healthy breakfast." She unwrapped the hash browns for him and raised an expectant eyebrow.

Blake grimaced but surrendered and took a bite. After a few more small tastes he started eating normally and even asked for some coffee. Lenny sat next to him in the booth and put her hand on his back. She ignored Carl's watchful eye. If she expected these guys to be upfront with her from now on, she was going to have to let some of her own walls come down.

Carl texted Luke and Mike to join them and he pulled Sway and Harrison from their bunks, literally. He was obviously still mad at them. They all gathered around the food silently. Carl let them eat for awhile before he spoke.

"Last night was stupid." His voice was calm but serious. "The only thing that saved your asses from a full blown media evisceration was this girl, right here, going all Chuck Norris on that idiot." He pointed at Lenny and the guys snickered quietly. "We've got a few more months before we can call it a day, you know what I mean?" They all nodded.

The air was quiet and Lenny was again struck with compassion for the guys. While she was mad that they lied to her and Blake had come dangerously close to alcohol poisoning, she understood how badly they needed to expel some energy. They were rock stars after all.

"Thanks, Len." Blake gestured with his food and then looked down at the table.

"Don't think you're off the hook with me," Lenny was stern, "I'm still angry with you." She sighed, "but I get it, more than you know."

Mike's brow furrowed at her slight confession and he exchanged a look with Luke who shrugged. Lenny didn't feel the need to explain herself. The time for that would come later.

"Next time you feel the need to prove your manhood, come and see me first. I have some alternatives that might interest you." She slid out of the booth and started for the door.

"Where you goin?" Sway asked.

"I smell like a bar floor, I have to shower. You guys need to get your act together. Just because last night was rough doesn't mean you can slack off at your show." She almost cringed at how much she sounded like her father.

***

Lenny left the bus while Blake swallowed another sandwich nearly whole and wiped his lips. "That chick is a genius; this food is a miracle cure." He belched loudly.

"She's a lot stronger than she looks." Sway said, tearing into a sandwich himself.

"I've never seen anyone so pissed," Harrison agreed.

"I wonder what she did before joining us," Sway mused.

"Probably UFC," Harrison said, half-serious.

"Regardless, this should be a good lesson for all of you," Carl interrupted gruffly. "Don't cross her. She will mess you up." They all nodded solemnly and he added, "She was mad when we got there but she didn't 'Hulk-Out' till she heard that asshat talking shit to Blake. You all know Lenny to be level-headed and focused. Turns out, her line is you." Carl let his words settle over them before he excused himself.

The guys chewed quietly for a few minutes, thinking about what Carl had just said.

Blake cleared his throat, "Um, Luke?" He said hesitantly.

"Yeah, buddy?"

"I don't remember a lot from last night...but I'm pretty sure I told your girlfriend to kiss me."

Light laughter erupted around the table. Luke rolled his eyes. "She's not my girl."

"Not yet." Mike replied quickly, causing more laughter.

"Let's just drop that whole train of thought right now, okay?" Luke was trying to look as serious as possible but the side of his mouth kept turning up. "Lenny is off limits to all of us, remember?"

"Why ya smiling?" Harrison ribbed.

"Go to hell." Luke picked up his coffee and left his band mates laughing behind him. He went outside and stood in the warm sunshine, trying to push their comments out of his mind. He knew they were right; he couldn't stay away from Lenny. He just didn't want them to talk about it so much.

He saw Lenny exit the crew bus, her bag slung over her shoulder. She looked around, taking inventory of her surroundings, having negligible eye contact with Luke, and headed to the backstage area. Luke barely hesitated, jogging to catch up with her.

"Hey," he said falling in step beside her. She flashed a quick smile but kept moving, clearly on business.

"Scouting for a shower?" He anticipated her destination.

"I can usually sneak into one." She grinned at him and he fought back the urge to hug her.

"You can use our shower." He volunteered, already knowing what she would say.

"That would be a bad idea," she replied. "Besides, I like the adventure of finding one. I feel like I earned my shower that way."

"I just wanted to say thanks for all you did last night for Blake. I

70

know it couldn't have been fun watching over him all night." Luke's words came out hurried and nervous.

"It's not like I was going to sleep anyway." She held up her coffee, "Thank God for caffeine, am I right?"

Luke shoved his hands in his pocket, trying to figure out how to ask why she had blamed herself for Blake's actions last night. And why she had gone to such great lengths to protect him.

"I know it wasn't my fault that Blake acted like a colossal moron last night," Lenny said as if reading Luke's thoughts. "I just know that if I woulda been there, it wouldn't have happened."

They rounded a corner and Lenny stopped to face Luke. They had just enough privacy so that no one could hear them but not enough for anyone to think something else was going on between them.

"What about the Street Fighter routine, where'd that come from?" Luke was genuinely curious. He saw the video on the news this morning and couldn't help but wonder at this mysterious woman who had worked her way into their daily lives.

"I told you I have three older brothers, right?" Luke nodded. "Nathan is a MMA instructor and he thought I should have a basic knowledge for self-defense. I just let my temper get the better of me last night." Lenny shook her head with embarrassment. "I guess you were right, I'm part of the family now. I couldn't stand to hear someone ridicule one of my brothers. I wanted to take him out."

Luke chuckled, wishing he could have been there to see it in person.

"Now, I have to go find a shower and get this...ick off of me." Lenny made a face as she glanced down at her messy clothes. She pointed her coffee at him, "Don't follow me, we can't have people talking."

Luke nodded and she gave him a half smile and turned down a darkened hallway. He watched her until she was completely out of sight. He knew she was right, but that didn't stop him from wanting to be around her all the time. She was completely amazing. And a little dangerous. And he couldn't get enough.

Chapter 5

Falling

Lenny took up her usual post in the sound booth with Greg, the sound engineer. Her inability to do any laundry the last couple of weeks had left her with a ratty pair of jeans and a vintage Lynyrd Skynyrd t-shirt she had stolen from her brother, Scott, years ago. Her long blonde hair was in a loose mess around her shoulders due to Luke's 'request' that she not wear the braid anymore. She hated to admit it, but her headaches had gotten substantially better.

She found herself on her feet, swaying her hips to the music and singing along with every song. This band, their music, had always pulled deeply at her soul. She found it difficult to keep up the depiction of stoic observation, like a good employee should, when they took the stage. She could get lost in the words, the beat, the melody... Something about Luke Casey's velvety voice had an energizing yet calming effect on her. It filled her senses like the fresh pine blowing through the trees back home...

After the accident, she had found little to no comfort in those around her. But Double Blind Study on her play-list made her feel like she wasn't alone. Someone out there understood what she was going through. Her friends only added to the pain she was going through and DBS became her safe place. Now, here she was, on tour with them, eating with them, watching over them, taking care of them. They would never know how much they had taken care of her over the past two years. When she went into that interview weeks ago she never dreamed that she would end up here.

The crowd was insane. Bodies jumping up and down and slam dancing without stop. Crowd surfers kept popping up and making their way from one side of the pit to the other. The band played three encore songs and the fans went wild. Lenny smiled with satisfaction, knowing that last night's incident had just drawn a larger crowd.

The band had a small meet and greet after the show before they could get on the road. They had limited the amount of after-show events because of time restrictions so this was a rare occurrence. Less than ten people, a few radio winners and some friends of Carl's that had driven nearly ten hours from Hartford.

Lenny's eyes kept being drawn back to the threesome that had arrived with Carl's backstage passes. The tall, dark-haired girl was lively and friendly, dragging the shorter brunette girl with her in happy exuberance. The short girl seemed...detached. She looked uncomfortable and politely irritated by her surroundings. Like she had something far more important on her mind. The lone guy in the trio chain smoked almost as much as Carl.

Lenny saw Sway zero in on Tall Girl and she made her way that direction to intercept. Sway had barely said a word and the girl's happy face changed to annoyed in a second. Lenny quickened her pace. Sway was going to get slapped one of these days. Why did he think he could hit on anyone?

"You're feisty, I like it." Sway's lip curled up and Lenny saw Tall Girl take on a more combative stance.

"Hi, I'm Lenny." Lenny stepped in between them and stuck out her hand. "You must be Carl's friends from Hartford." Tall Girl shook her hand and turned her glare into a more pleasant expression again.

"I'm E," she introduced herself. "I only met Carl today." She pointed with her thumb over her shoulder at the guy looking too cool for school, "David got the tickets."

"Lenny, I was having a conversation." Sway leaned over her shoulder and gave her a scolding look. E's glare returned and Lenny's smile widened to an uncomfortable degree of fakery that hurt her cheeks.

"Let's get you guys a drink." She turned E and her friends towards the refreshments table. When they had taken a few steps, she turned and grabbed Sway with two fistfuls of his shirt.

"She's going to kill you, Sway," Lenny warned in all seriousness, "You have to back off."

"Take it easy," Sway's grin was adorably naïve. He really thought he could get anyone. He brushed off Lenny's grip and headed after E again. Lenny wanted to stop him but she also kind of wanted to see what was going to happen.

As the evening progressed and things began to wrap up, Lenny was amazed at E's restraint. She would have clocked him by now.

Lenny found out that E was a personal trainer and they exchanged different tips and techniques. Sway's jealousy was apparent. E spoke to Lenny more than him and he started to get huffy. When they were getting ready to leave, E gave her number to Lenny to keep in contact. Lenny was excited; she didn't have many friends who she could talk with about fitness anymore.

"Gimme her number, Lenny." Sway begged like a toddler after they had returned to the bus.

"No, Sway. If she wanted you to have it, she would have given it to you." Lenny staunchly refused.

"Please, Lenny!" Sway dropped to the floor of the bus in a pleading posture, "I have to talk to her again."

"Why this girl, Sway?" Lenny raised an eyebrow at him. "You didn't even talk to the two slutties drooling all over you. I almost had to hose them down. What made this girl so important to you?"

Sway pulled himself up off the floor and threw his body into a chair. "You wouldn't get it," he grumbled.

Lenny crossed her arms and waited. He ran his hands through his long hair a few times and sighed heavily.

"I met her in Spain awhile back. She turned me down then too."

"She didn't mention that," Lenny said thoughtfully.

"She's the only girl to turn me down," he looked over at Lenny and rolled his eyes, "Besides you."

"So, you just want what you can't have?" Lenny was disgusted.

"No, she's...aww forget it." Sway waived his hand at her dismissively, "I'm going to get some sleep." He trudged towards the back of the bus.

"What was that about?" Harrison asked as he handed Lenny a water bottle and sat down on the floor.

"I'm not totally sure," Lenny frowned down at her water.

"You wanna kill some zombies with me?" Harrison asked hopefully. It didn't matter how late a show went or long they'd all been awake, Harrison loved to play video games.

"Might as well." Lenny smiled and tousled his hair as she sank to the floor beside him.

***

The label heard that Travis Cline had tried to pick a fight with a girl at a bar in Virginia Beach and pulled Juniper Highlights off the tour the next morning. They didn't have enough clout for the company to take that kind of a risk. Lenny was pleased, it served them right. But that meant Double Blind Study didn't have an opener. Harrison suggested they use local bands at every venue, giving new talent a platform. It was an instant hit, increasing the band's reputation for staying true to their humble beginnings.

Additional things had changed since that night. The dynamic had shifted between Lenny and Carl. She was going to have to get a lot closer to the guys to prevent what had happened in Virginia. That meant distancing herself from Carl a little more and staying nights on the band's respective buses.

He appeared to understand her point of view and respected it. He

75

had asked her to walk a fine line and he seemed satisfied with how the situation was evolving. He gave the guys a little more space, and only really saw Lenny when she brought him coffee in the mornings.

They were coming up on another day off and the anticipation was palpable. The crew was looking forward to blowing off some steam, but the band wasn't sure what they were going to do yet. Blake's foray into bar-top stripper had made them a little more wary of letting loose.

"Maybe we should just practice," Mike suggested from his seat in the corner.

They were all riding in the Red Bus as the convoy traveled to their next venue. Lenny had been surprised at how much time they actually spent together. It was a lot. She had assumed that bands got on each other's nerves and needed their space. Or maybe that was just girls in high school.

"That's a pretty good idea, actually," Luke concurred with his friend.

Sway and Blake groaned in unison. Harrison had no response except the occasional grunt as he decapitated a zombie.

"I hate this game," Lenny said under her breath from beside him.

"Lenny, you said you had ideas for how we could demonstrate our manhood," Blake stated flatly. The guys chuckled and Lenny turned a wary eye over her shoulder.

"Yeah…" she said noncommittally.

"What can we do tomorrow to be men?" Blake folded his hands in his lap.

Lenny smiled at his phrasing and bit her lip. "I'm glad you asked, actually. I already set something up for us tomorrow." She turned around as her avatar died and Harrison let out a whimper.

"All of us?" Blake asked, one black eyebrow raised.

"Yep. Should be fun. And dangerous enough to keep you out of trouble." Lenny stood up and stretched her cramped legs. Harrison needed a new hobby, this was going to wreck her knees.

The guys tried to persuade her to reveal her idea but she remained tight lipped.

"I've already cleared it with Carl-"

"You clear everything with Carl," Sway grumbled. "That guy is sooo boring."

"He's not that bad," Lenny defended, "He has a job to do and I respect that, you should too." She chuckled as Sway rolled his eyes at her. "You know, you guys aren't always puppy dogs and ice cream either."

"I'm actually hurt that you would say that," Mike remarked as she plopped down on the sofa next to him and he threw an arm across her shoulders. "I strive to always act as puppy-like as possible."

76

She laughed and shoved his leg. "Ha ha ha," she said sarcastically but her smile was genuine.

"C'mon, just tell us what the big plan is." Harrison's eyes were round and dark with pretend innocence. His mother must've had a hard time trying to keep him honest, Lenny thought with amusement.

"Nope, you'll just have to trust me." She crossed her arms over her chest and leaned back against the couch, signaling the argument was over.

The guys grumbled a little while more, a common occurrence as they started to wind down from their performance. It wasn't too much longer and they crawled into their bunks one by one until only Luke and Lenny were still awake. They continued to visit quietly but Lenny was very aware of the shift in mood after everyone had gone to bed. It had predictably become more...intimate.

He could make her palms sweat with a look. Not to mention the fact that whenever they were alone her body suddenly wanted to fall asleep. It was like it knew that Luke had dark powers that could cause her body to relax and finally rest for unspecified amounts of time. It wanted to curl up against him and lose all connection to reality.

She hated her body. Traitor.

"You should probably get some sleep, too," she reminded Luke. His face fell slightly at her sudden subject change and she wished things didn't have to be so complex between them.

"What about you?" He asked with uncertainty.

"What do you mean?" Lenny felt her heart rate quicken. *Stop it! Calm down!* She scolded it internally.

"You don't sleep much...do you?" Luke's gentle confrontation left her without an explanation. She could lie to anyone. Her parents, her brothers, her friends. But not him. It was way too hard and required too much cognitive function, which she was somehow lacking in his presence.

"Not quite," she finally muttered.

"Why not?"

It was a simple question. Lenny wished she had a simple answer. What could she really say? Sure, they had gotten closer during their morning runs every day and Lenny considered him a friend. He told her anything and everything about himself, becoming transparent and real. But there was still so much he didn't know about her. She could change that. She could answer his question honestly and open up to him. It was only fair.

Oh, boy.

"I was in an...accident, a few years ago." Lenny started slow, her hands beginning to tremble. She hadn't talked about this with anyone in a very long time. She clasped her hands in her lap and squeezed them together.

77

"What kind of an accident?" Luke's quiet voice prompted.

Lenny took a deep breath. This sucked. Where the hell was she supposed to start? If she told Luke everything then...then what? Then he'd *know*.

"I used to snowboard," she said flatly, the words falling onto the floor of the bus with a thud. There it was, in the open, her secret. She raised her eyes to meet his confused expression.

"Like, professionally?" Luke sat up straighter in his chair and leaned forward.

Lenny blew air out of her mouth. Why did he have to be so interested in her crappy past? How was she supposed to explain all of this without coming across like a dick? "Yeah...I was an Olympic contender." Shit. Now she sounded arrogant.

Luke's eyebrows rose, "That sounds like a big deal."

Lenny closed her eyes and pinched the bridge of her nose. *Here comes the headache.* When did things stop being black and white? Where did all this gray shit come from?

"Yeah," she declared more forcefully than she intended. She dropped her hand back to her lap and tried again. "Yeah, it *was* a big deal." Luke waited patiently for her to proceed and Lenny fought back the urge to jump out of the moving bus.

"I come from a family of athletes. We're all awesome." Her sarcastic tone made Luke chuckle and she relaxed a little. "I started snowboarding when I was a little kid and decided that's what I wanted to do for..." she shrugged, "Well, forever."

Lenny paused as the memories rushed in. The purity of the excitement. The adrenaline spike of a good run. "My best friend's uncle, Duke, was pro at the time and he took me under his wing. Taught me everything he knew. He was wild. He encouraged us to be risky and find our own lines off the normal, protected ski routes." She shook her head, reminiscing. "My parents were totally freaked out. They wanted me to have regular lessons and train in a more controlled environment. But that's the appeal of snowboarding, there are very few rules. It has a freedom of expression that other sports are lacking. I got better and started winning competitions. My parents were upset at first that I wasn't pursuing a more 'traditional' sport but..." she smiled wistfully, "They eventually got on board.

"My first Olympics, two years ago...almost three now, I thought I was ready," her voice cracked and she tried to swallow the ache away, "I wasn't. I lost control and wrecked."

"How bad?" Luke finally asked after a few minutes of silence had passed.

"Oh, you know, the usual head trauma, broken bones. Stuff like that." Lenny saw the distress on Luke's face and she felt stripped. Raw. When he looked at her, he saw her. Crushed spirit and all. And it terrified her.

"I'm fine now. I made a full recovery, completed all my therapy and I'm clear for launch," she laughed, trying to brush off the severity of her injuries, but it was obviously forced.

Luke frowned at her and cleared his throat, "But you don't sleep."

"Ah," Lenny waved carelessly "It's just leftover side-effects from having your body crushed. I sleep a little. But then the muscle spasms and the anxiety take over and...you know what?" Lenny cut herself off and shook her head with embarrassment, "It's not a big deal. It's totally fine."

"It's not fine," Luke confronted. He suddenly crossed to sit next to her on the couch. He reached up, brushing the hair over her shoulder and touched the tense spot behind her neck, "This. This isn't fine." His fingers began their magical movements, releasing the negative energy that seemed to pool in that area. "And you slept just fine in my arms," his voice, warm and rough, reminded very near her ear.

"I guess..." Lenny sought an explanation, one she hadn't figured out yet. "I guess, you make me feel safe." She thought she heard Luke sigh but she couldn't be sure. She shouldn't have said that. She shouldn't have said any of the things she had said to him tonight. She was losing control of her faculties. This only happened around him.

"You *are* safe with me," Luke gently pulled her into his arms as he reclined on the sofa. He tucked her body between his and the couch, keeping her head on his chest. His fingers stayed on the back of her neck, slowly removing the ache, while his other hand pulled her arm across him, completing the embrace.

Lenny's body was flush against his and her heart hammered in her chest. If one of the guys came back to the main lounge or if Carl caught them-

"I don't want you to worry anymore," Luke broke into her thoughts.

"I didn't say anything," Lenny defended.

"I can feel you tensing up again," he tapped her neck with his fingertips, "Just relax. This isn't anything more than a friend helping out another friend."

Lenny fought the heaviness in her eyelids. Friends. Is this what it was like to have friends? She slowly traced the black swirl of ink that started on his forearm and disappeared under his shirt sleeve. She inhaled his scent, a mixture of soap and spearmint, and sighed.

She couldn't let feelings develop for him. It wouldn't be fair to him or her, for that matter. After the tour was over they would go different ways. She focused on the reason she got this job in the first place, to get away and start new. He was a rock star, she was the assistant. At best, they were friends, but it couldn't be more than that. Besides, Luke Casey deserved someone better than a broken girl from nowhere. It was her last thought before she slipped into peaceful unconsciousness.

***

When Luke woke up the next morning, Lenny was already gone. The buses had stopped sometime around dawn but he wasn't sure when she had left. He wasn't too surprised. He knew he was pushing every boundary she had set up between them since the beginning. But he couldn't help it, from the moment he had first met her, he couldn't resist her. When he found out he could offer her the peace she had been lacking, he jumped at it.

He had tried to stay awake as long as possible, just enjoying the feel of her in his arms. Her softness and warmth, it was a closeness he'd never experienced with anyone. It was terrifying. And perfect.

Luke tried to push the burning apprehension in his gut further downward. He hoped she wouldn't feel weird around him today. He wanted this to be a step forward, not back.

He joined the guys after his shower and they began to speculate what plans Lenny might have for them. They discussed skydiving, water skiing or maybe even makeovers.

"I'd be down for a makeover." Harrison looked at his hair in the reflection of the chrome on the side of the bus and primped a little, "As long as I get to keep my hair."

Lenny pulled up in a rented van and they all piled in. They chattered the whole time, trying to get Lenny to tell them where they were going. She remained secretive for the whole forty minute drive out of town. Then the van pulled onto a gravel road that wound up into the gorgeous Smokey Mountains. She stopped at a ramshackle cabin with a saggy roof.

As the guys quietly piled out of the van, an older gentleman came out of the cabin and approached Lenny. His hair was gray and thinning at the temples but he moved with the energy of a much younger man. He was obviously fit and carried himself with a dignity that had been earned.

"Lenny Evans, it really is you!" He grabbed her in a hug. "I haven't seen you since…oh, it's got to have been four or five years now."

The band looked on, silent. They knew each other?

"Last time you were here you had that friend of yours with you, what's her name? Cody? Did she come along this time?" The old-timer looked around.

Lenny laughed and shook her head, "Not this time, Dale."

Luke frowned as a stray memory tried to connect in his brain.

80

Cody? He knew that name from somewhere…

"Guys," Lenny addressed her group, "This is Dale Larson, he owns this shop and he's agreed to set us up for the day."

"For what?" Harrison asked, surveying the surrounding mountains.

"Mountain biking. All day." She said it like she had expected them to have it figured out already.

The guys were definitely surprised. Maybe a little nervous but Lenny seemed confident that they were going to do just fine. Dale set them up with bikes and helmets and various supplies like water and snacks. He gave all of them different degrees of instruction but nothing really specific, then he turned them over to Lenny.

"Whatever happens, keep your eyes on the lead dog," he rested his hand on Lenny's shoulder, "That's this girl, right here. She's the best I've ever seen on a trail and she'll show you how it's done." With that, he bid them farewell and retreated back into his cabin.

***

Lenny wasted no time; she climbed onto her bike and headed down the road. The guys had no choice but to follow. She tried not to push them too hard at first. She had extra energy she was trying to burn off and she didn't need to take it out on them.

Waking up in Luke's arms that morning had left her feeling a combination of unparalleled rejuvenation and bewilderment. She had slowly peeled herself out of his embrace and promptly begun avoiding him and any conversation having to do with him. She had no idea what was going to come of this new development in their friendship. But she was pretty sure that they were dancing on the edge of the traditional definition of *just friends*.

Blake caught up to her first, "Hate to bust your balls, but I think I know how to ride a bike."

Lenny grinned and ducked off the main road and onto a narrow trail heading uphill. She kept glancing behind her to make sure she hadn't lost anyone. She laughed to herself every time she heard one of them holler in surprise. She pushed them to what she knew was their limit, but nothing too risky or dangerous. As they continued their climb she heard grumblings in the back for a water break. She knew there was a place that leveled off up ahead and she would let them rest when they reached it.

As the last member entered the clearing, Lenny took her helmet off and released her sweaty hair from its tight ponytail. She smoothed it back and replaced the elastic. Then she passed out sandwiches and water, making sure the guys stayed hydrated.

81

"How much further?" Harrison puffed.

"You wanna head back?" Lenny offered.

"No, we'll keep going." Luke answered; he was barely winded and grinning from ear to ear. He patted Harrison on the back, "The fresh air is good for you."

"It's a good thing none of us are smokers," Sway joked.

"Yeah, Carl would be dead by now," Blake laughed.

Lenny smiled at her band of tattooed misfits. They had quickly become her favorite people in the whole world.

She finished her sandwich and walked over to a ledge overlooking the forest below. Mike walked up next to her and whistled.

"That's an amazing view."

Lenny agreed. Mike studied her expression quizzically and asked, "What other extreme sports do you take part in?"

Lenny took a deep breath of the mountain air and smiled. She turned toward the group and answered, "I hang out with rock stars."

***

Luke pulled his bike up next to Lenny's and handed her her helmet. "Ready, Captain?" He asked her, testing the waters of their friendship. Not knowing if she regretted trusting him the night before with her secrets.

"Ready." She buckled the chin strap and smiled up at Luke. If she was ashamed, she wasn't showing it.

"You're gorgeous," he blurted out, not really thinking.

"You too," she teased back. "You seem to be doing pretty good on the trail," she complimented.

"I like a challenge," Luke winked.

Lenny raised her eyebrows and mounted her bike, "Well then, I'll race you to the top." And she was off.

Luke shook his head and sped after her. He had never met anyone with so much passion for everything they did. He loved the way she never stopped going after something and how she managed to completely master something new. He wanted to see how fast he could teach her guitar. Besides, that would offer more opportunity for them to be alone together. He tried to shake off the excited feeling he got when he thought about sitting with her, alone, just talking.

He thought about kissing her all the time. Constantly. But he wasn't about to make her uncomfortable. It would be alright, he would be patient until she trusted him. He was enjoying every minute they spent together anyway. That included hanging with a bunch of people or talking late into the night on the bus.

Lenny beat him to the top and took off her helmet with a big smile. "Was that challenging enough for you?"

Luke nodded, trying to catch his breath, "Well done."

They had a few minutes alone as they waited for the rest of the group to catch up and Luke plunged ahead with his just-born idea.

"You should ride on the Blue Bus with us after tomorrow night's show. I want to try to teach you how to play."

"Play what?" Lenny's brows frowned.

"The guitar." Luke answered like it was obvious.

"Why do you want to teach me the guitar?" Lenny's frown deepened.

"You're good at everything you do. Not just good, you're the best. I wanna see how fast you learn it."

Lenny shrugged, "I suppose it's worth a shot."

"And then maybe you can teach me something I don't know how to do." He was trying to be subtle but he still wanted her to pick up on the undertone of his suggestion.

If she did, he would never know because the guys came huffing and puffing their way up the trail.

"So it's settled, you'll ride with me and Mike after tomorrow's show?" He wanted her confirmation, knowing she wouldn't go back on her word.

"You got it." She smiled openly at him and then greeted the stragglers, "Hello, Lovelies. How do you feel?"

"I'm not gonna lie, Len, I feel like a man." Blake confessed and they all laughed out loud. "Good job, mama," he complimented her as he patted her back.

Lenny let them rest and enjoy the scenery for a while before turning them back down the hill. The ride to the starting point was quiet and Lenny took it easy on them. When they got back to the cabin, they thanked Dale for the loaned equipment and collapsed into the van. They were all too exhausted to even think about going out later. Which, Luke suspected, had been Lenny's plan all along.

Lenny took a longer drive through the mountains instead of driving straight back to the venue. Most of the guys fell asleep right away and the radio played soft country music as she wound her way along the tight mountain highway. Luke sat in the front seat with her and watched her face as she drove along carefully.

"I miss the mountains." She said it so quietly Luke would have missed it if he hadn't been looking at her.

Luke reached over and took her hand gently in his. He didn't say anything and she didn't look at him. He kept her hand in his, resting on the middle seat between them. His thumb softly stroked the tops of her fingers. When they pulled into the parking lot, she tugged her hand free of his grasp.

As she parked, she smiled apologetically at him. He nodded at her in understanding. He had no problem being the guy who brought her comfort on her own terms.

The guys all piled out groggily and onto their buses, thanking Lenny along the way.

"Thanks, mama," Blake hugged her shoulders, "You made me feel like a man and kicked my ass at the same time."

***

The sun was beginning to set, and there was some discussion of getting a pizza and turning in early. Harrison placed a delivery order and gave Lenny the cash. She walked to the gate of the parking lot to wait for the driver. Famous rock stars couldn't just get their own pizza; she smiled to herself at the thought. They were crazy famous to the whole world, to her they were her family.

She sat down on the curb and enjoyed the peaceful calm of the evening. The sky was turning from blue to purple to red with highlights of gold and pink mixed in. She breathed in the clean mountain air and felt the tension in her shoulders ease. She marveled at the strange turn her life had taken in the last month. She had planned on getting as far away from her previous life as possible and now she was feeling the weirdest tingle of homesickness.

She missed her family and the open skies of Wyoming. Tomorrow was David's birthday. She knew they would probably have a big family dinner. Scott and Nathan would be there, as well as David's wife, Felicity, and their four little boys. Lenny would be the only one absent. She should call to wish him a happy birthday. She pulled out her phone and looked at it. She decided to send a text instead; if they were busy she didn't want to interrupt.

Sliding her phone back into her pocket, she was startled when Mike sat down next to her.

"You shouldn't be out here," she jested, "Someone might recognize you."

Mike made a "humph" noise.

They sat quietly together for a few minutes, listening to the sounds of the city below them. Lenny leaned back on her arms and kicked her feet out in front of her.

"I have a confession." Mike looked down at his feet and stirred some loose gravel around with his shoe.

Lenny frowned and looked over at him but didn't say anything.

"I overheard your conversation with Luke last night."

Lenny wrinkled her nose in response.

"And I know that you and Luke," he cleared his throat, "slept together on the couch."

"We didn't-" Lenny sat up and started to protest.

"No, I know," Mike stopped her. "You actually *slept,* not the other thing."

Lenny swallowed and waited for him to continue.

"I just wanted you to know that I haven't told anyone. I know how weird Carl gets about our personal relationships and he doesn't need to know about this."

"Well, it won't happen again so..." Lenny wasn't sure what to say. Embarrassment was beginning to color her cheeks.

"That's crazy, Lenny." Mike finally looked up from the ground and she was surprised at his serious continence. "You work too frickin' hard to have to go without frickin' sleep. If Luke makes you feel like you can relax then I think you should take advantage of it."

"Mike, that's not exactly...professional." Lenny felt a burning begin in the back of her eyes.

Mike rolled his eyes. "Would you let it go for a minute? I'm serious about this." His voice held an edge that she had never heard him use before. "I know what it's like to run away from something you love because of...mistakes." He licked his bottom lip, looked back at the ground and then back to Lenny. "Luke's more than a friend to me. He's a brother. He aided in my recovery like no one else. If he can help you get through this last little bit of disrepair, then let him do it."

"I just don't..." Lenny's throat was dry and her head spun.

"I know, you're embarrassed. You don't want to need help. You think you can figure this out on your own."

Lenny's stomach twisted at Mike's words. When he said out loud what she was thinking internally, it sounded selfish. And weak.

"I enjoy the whole 'Girl Power' thing as much as any dude but you have to be able to admit when you've taken it too far."

A large tear splashed onto Lenny's cheek as Mike continued.

"Sleep is so important. I can't stress that enough. If Luke can help you regain that part of your physiology then let him. I have a pretty solid theory that once you get back in the habit of sleeping regularly, you'll be able to face the rest of your recovery."

"But, I've recovered completely," Lenny argued meekly.

"Sure, physically," Mike nodded and reached towards her, touching her temple softly. "What about all the stuff still happening up here?"

85

Lenny's vision blurred with tears. Her heart thudded in her ribcage as her head spun, trying to figure out where all of Mike's insight had come from and how she had become so transparent. Did she really appear to be this weepy, broken girl, lost and needing help from strangers?

"Hey." Mike's voice had lost its confrontation and his hand gently pulled her face up so he could look her in the eye. "No one knows. And no one has to know unless you tell them." He studied her face for a moment. "The only reason I overheard the whole thing is because figuring you out has become...an obsession for me." He chuckled at his own words. "But after hearing the truth, it felt wrong for me to know without you giving me the permission to hold that knowledge...you know?"

Lenny nodded but didn't reply. Mike's hand dropped from her chin back to his lap. His eyes tugged down on the sides, making him look older than usual.

"You're a part of the band now, Lenny. Whatever happens from here on out, you need to know that we consider you the sixth member. And you're safe with us. All of us."

Tears began to collect in Lenny's eyelashes and she reached up to rub them off her face. Mike had brought out a tangle of emotions in her and she was ashamed at her reaction. She had no words for a reply. Just more tears. She wiped at them angrily.

Mike put his arm around her shoulders and she leaned into him. "Listen, kid. I get it, I really do." He paused and rubbed her arm tenderly. "But you have to go back someday. You can't give up your passions just because of a bad decision. Believe me, what do you think this tour is all about?"

"But I'm not like you, Mike," she softly reminded. "You're awesome and I'm...not."

Mike chuckled at her reasoning. "We're a lot more alike than you would think. You're basically the chick version of me."

Lenny sniffed away her tears and laughed. She sat up straight as the pizza delivery guy pulled up at that moment and Lenny paid for the food. As she and Mike walked back to the buses Lenny asked, "What happens now?"

"Now? Whatever you want, mama. We'll follow your lead, just like always." He winked and Lenny felt relieved.

Now Mike *and* Luke knew. And it didn't seem so terrible anymore.

Luke. Every feeling she had in regards to him caused conflict inside. She wanted to be next to him all the time and yet she wanted to run away as fast as possible. He could make her feel completely safe and completely exposed simultaneously.

As if Mike were reading her thoughts he said, "Luke just wants to help you, you mean a lot to all of us. Try not to freak out about it." She looked over at Mike with a stunned expression and he chuckled at her.

Lenny considered his words for a moment, "You guys really are best friends, aren't you?"

Mike nodded, "I'd do anything for him. He saved my life. He's the only reason I'm back on the road again." Mike sucked air in through his nose and frowned, adding weight to his final words. "He doesn't give up on the people he loves. I owe him more than I can ever repay."

Chapter 6

Short Skirt/Long Jacket

Luke's breathing was labored. His body hummed with adrenaline and he bent down hard against the guitar strings. Sweat poured off his face and his longish bangs stuck to his forehead. He stilled his mouth behind the microphone and looked out over the throbbing mass of people; his arm hovered over the overworked instrument. He felt a mischievous grin spread across his face as the audience screamed for him to continue. He heard the pulse of Mike on the kick drum behind him. Sway had his back turned to the crowd and he waited for Luke's signal. Harrison stood at rapt attention, a smile beaming across his expressive face as he surveyed the arena. Blake stood solemnly in his zone, guitar half-cocked, a statue of rock and roll.

Luke laughed into the microphone and the crowd screamed louder.

"What?" He asked them, knowing the reply. "Oh, you want us to keep going?"

The reaction was physical, and the energy coming off the crowd pushed against him. He loved this moment. Holding the crowd on the precipice of complete rock and roll ecstasy.

Luke nodded once to Sway and the band exploded in a flourish of lights, smoke, and sound. The crowd erupted with them, filling the stadium with even more madness than a few minutes before.

Luke rode the high all way till the end of the show. He was still buzzing as he bounded up the steps of the bus. He flopped on the sofa as Mike threw him a bottle of water.

"There's never enough." He said to no one in particular.

"Never enough what?" Lenny settled next to him, handing him a towel to wipe off his sweaty face. Luke smiled up at the ceiling. How did she do that? Make him relax in an instant?

"Never enough time. Or music. Or voice." He took a long drink of the water and sighed. "I want to do this everyday for the rest of my life."

"You and me both," Mike agreed and Luke reached his hand in the air to fist-bump his drummer.

Luke rolled his head to the side and took in Lenny's fresh appearance. She was in some old jeans and a too big t-shirt, her bare feet tucked up underneath her in the corner of the couch. He squinted to get a better look, yep, she was wearing eyeliner tonight. That was new. Made her eyes look even bluer, if that were possible. Her cheeks were flushed a healthy pink and Luke couldn't resist grinning openly at her. She gave a half-smile and looked away. He knew he was staring but he didn't care. She was too damn pretty to not look at.

Lenny had let him hold her again last night while she slept. On the couch again, but he didn't mind. He'd take what he could get.

Two consecutive nights of decent sleep and her complexion had brightened noticeably. Not only that, but her smiles came easier. And Luke loved to see that smile.

"Is that my shirt?" He gestured to the blue tee that was clearly too big for her.

Lenny scrunched up her nose. "Ha, probably. I used to jack my brother's clothes all the time. I haven't had time to wash anything and I didn't feel like being a dirty girl today." She picked at the hem. "I just grabbed one from the back. I hope that's okay."

"It's fine." It was more than fine, he loved that she was feeling comfortable around them enough to borrow their clothes. And the fact that she had chosen his shirt, whether on purpose or not, gave him a small thrill.

He tore his gaze from her and righted himself. If he didn't purpose to move on to the next task he'd stare at her all night.

He retrieved his old acoustic guitar from his bunk, the one he'd had since he was in middle school, and took a seat in a chair facing Lenny. He began to explain the construction and shape of it, trying to be more conversational that clinical. He told her about the history of the instrument and what had first inspired him to play.

"But I read in *Rolling Stone* that you learned how to play guitar to pick up chicks." Lenny raised an eyebrow. What a tease.

Mike let out a large burst of laughter, "That's right! I remember when you said that!"

Luke frowned at the two of them. "Of course that's what I told *Rolling Stone*...they're freaking *Rolling Stone Magazine*." He shook his head as if to disapprove of their misunderstanding.

Lenny's sudden giggle was unexpected and she tried to cover her mouth with her hand when they both looked at her with lifted eyebrows. Luke couldn't help but notice the flush on her cheeks and the nervous way she bit her bottom lip when she looked at him.

Luke gave her a wink and continued on with his lesson. He explained chords, notes and calluses while the overhead lights bounced tiny reflections off the guitar and the mirrored ceiling.

Mike, for his part, taught Lenny the basics of keeping a beat. He gave her a set of drumsticks and demonstrated how to use her legs to smack

90

out a rhythm. She picked it up quickly and soon they were having an impromptu jam session.

As Luke watched Mike and Lenny try to trip each other up he was filled with more appreciation for his drummer than before. Lenny was laughing easily and openly at this point and Luke knew it was due to the cozy atmosphere in the bus. And Mike was responsible for a lot of that.

Mike caught Luke's eye and gave a slight nod. He got up and kissed the top of Lenny's head, "I have to go to bed or I'll be grumpy tomorrow."

Lenny let out a small groan of disappointment but it was halfhearted. Her eyes flicked to Luke's briefly as she said goodnight to the drummer and Luke felt his stomach do a somersault. He wondered when, if ever, she would stop affecting him with a single look.

Mike retired to his bunk and Luke crossed over to the sofa and placed the guitar across Lenny's knees. She didn't resist as he guided her fingers to the correct positions, letting his hands linger too long on her soft skin.

"Yikes, I can see why you have such thick calluses." Lenny winced as she squeezed her fingers around the neck.

"You're tough; you'll develop some of your own soon enough." Luke could smell her shampoo and it took a fair amount of restraint for him to not lean over and bury his face in her hair. He watched the delicate features of her face as she concentrated on her finger placement. She was learning quickly, just like he had anticipated.

"I like you in my shirt," he softly murmured in her ear. Lenny stilled her motions. She didn't look at him; instead, she readjusted the guitar on her lap and continued to focus.

"It really brings out your eyes," he spoke slow, leaning closer to her. He lightly brushed the hair off of her shoulder, exposing her neck. He wondered if her skin tasted as sweet as it smelled.

Lenny sighed heavily and her shoulders fell. She pushed the guitar back towards Luke and stood up.

"Goodnight, Luke."

Luke quickly put the guitar down, stood up and grabbed her hand. "I don't understand. Where are you going?" His eyes searched her pained expression.

"I'm going to bed. You should too. We're both tired and I really don't think you're processing things rationally." She tried to tug her hand out of his grasp but he held on.

"Len, I'm sorry, please don't go yet. I got carried away; I just like being near you."

Lenny's face was guarded. "When the sexy lead singer of the hottest band in the world starts talking about your eyes, it gets pretty weird."

"You think I'm sexy?" Luke tried to joke with her, hoping to get her to stay. Nope.

Lenny made a face and yanked her hand away. "We're friends, Luke. Don't wreck it just cause you're horny," she snapped.

She was hurt. And offended. Luke was desperate to make it right. He wanted to kick himself for being too damn pushy. He thought she was feeling what he had been feeling; he had read the whole situation wrong. And now she was slipping away from him again.

He gently grabbed her by her shoulders and waited till she looked him in the eye. "You're right, we are friends. The last thing I want to do is make you uncomfortable." He brushed a piece of hair off her face. "I realize our situation is...complicated. It's just..." he stumbled on his words. "You're...this unstoppable force of nature and sometimes...I let myself get carried away when I'm around you."

"It's fine," Lenny replied coolly. "Sway explained the rules to me: What happens on the bus, stays on the bus." She pulled back and tried to give a small smile but she looked entirely too sad. "Old habits are hard to break...I get it."

Luke frowned down at her. "Sometimes I don't think you listen to a word I say."

"I will give you credit, though," she continued, "You rock stars sure have a way with words." She started to back towards the bunk area. "We'll just pretend that this didn't happen and then no one has to feel awkward." She tugged at the hem of the shirt she was wearing. "I'll wash this and get it back to you."

"You can keep it," he waived her words off and tried again. "What about you getting some sleep? Can't we still...?" He gestured to the couch where he had automatically planned on spending every night holding her until the tour ended.

"I don't think that's a good idea anymore." Lenny's eyes pulled down on the sides with a deeper sadness than Luke had seen before and he felt like he'd gotten kicked in the stomach. "I'll see you in the morning." She turned and disappeared into the center of the bus.

Luke slumped back on the sofa, giving up. Not having the strength or mental clarity to convince her she was wrong. He hadn't been trying to take advantage of her, he'd simply gotten caught up in her presence. Caught up in her smile, her laugh, her very *being*. It had been a long time since a girl had made him feel this crazy. And she had no idea. Not even a clue.

He sat in the quiet of the cabin, listening to the hum of the wheels. He picked softly on the guitar, and jotted notes on a sheet of paper he'd been carrying in his back pocket. If nothing else, this girl had inspired some of his best writing.

92

He rubbed the scruff on his face. No one, ever, in his life had started a fire like this inside of him. He thought about what might happen when the tour was over and his heart ached at the idea of her disappearing from his life.

***

Lenny lay in the bunk facing the wall with her arms crossed over her middle. She felt like she was tearing apart her insides. She wanted to go to Luke and crash into him. Wrap her arms around him and not let go. But it would ruin everything. It would ruin him. *She* would ruin him.

Every moment she spent with him was intense. It was all she could do to keep her wits about her. Walking away from him had required more mental fortitude than she could have foreseen. If he would have kissed her... She closed her eyes at the idea; that would have been the end of her. She would have came apart completely and she doubted very heavily that she'd be able to survive that kind of a wreck. *Different worlds. Different people. Different futures.*

She would stay away for a few days; they needed to clear their heads. A little time apart and they would be feeling...differently.

***

Three days. That's how long it had been since Lenny had left Luke standing in the cabin on the bus with a broken look on his perfect face.

For three days she had successfully avoided seeing him and talking to him. Except for those ninety minutes where DBS took the stage. Then she couldn't take her eyes off him. Couldn't stop imagining what that kiss would have felt like had she let the moment continue. Couldn't stop wanting him to make another attempt.

She rubbed her tired face with her fingertips and tried to suppress a yawn. Three days since she'd slept. Yep, it was back to that. She looked at her empty coffee cup and wondered if a fifth refill would be a bad idea. She looked around the small coffee shop, planning on waving down the attendant.

She froze when she saw Luke standing in the doorway. Looking directly at her. At first, she thought maybe she had been daydreaming about him so intensely that she had imagined him. But no, he was as real as he'd ever been. Tall, lean, and perfectly created like a work of art. A sculpture come to life. Her fantasy with living breath.

She was trapped. She couldn't exit without causing a scene. *Of course he's going to come over here,* she thought with barely controlled

93

panic as he made his way towards her. He settled into the vacant seat across from her, never breaking eye contact.

"Hey," she said with a small, sideways smile.

"I've missed you," Luke responded and then winced at his own words.

"I've been busy. This leg of the tour is pretty…intense." His eyes were bluer than normal today. She felt her traitor of a heart speed up at his close proximity.

Luke visibly swallowed. He was obviously trying to keep from spooking her again and she felt a stab of guilt.

"What's that?" He nodded at her notebook.

"Just some poems…stupid stuff, really." Lenny closed the weathered book and laid her arms on top.

"Can I see?" Luke reached across the table, his fingers touching the edge of her hand and setting her on fire. Lenny hesitated but released it to him stiffly. How much was she supposed to deny him? She was already withholding the friendship she had promised wouldn't get awkward. It wouldn't hurt to let him read some old ramblings of a shattered girl in recovery.

Lenny held her breath as he leafed through the pages. She thought a few days apart would cool things off between them. Logically, it should have. She was wrong. Whatever they felt for each other had gained strength.

"These are really excellent, Lenny." Luke was absorbed in the written words and Lenny was rethinking letting him read her most personal thoughts. Sure, not every single one of them was about her in particular. But she had never really shared them with anyone besides Scott. And that was just because Scott was so damn bossy.

"No, it's just pointless…girl stuff…" she trailed off, finding it difficult to have this conversation.

Luke looked up at her swiftly, "Nothing about you is pointless."

Lenny licked her lips nervously. Why did he make her feel like this? She wanted to run away. She glanced at the door, planning her escape.

"Please don't go." Luke pleaded, reading her thoughts. Her chest burned at his request.

"I should get back, Carl wants me to…" She was trying to come up with a plausible lie.

Just then, her cell phone rang and she jumped. She hurriedly pulled it out of her pocket and glanced at the call screen. Speak of the devil, it was Carl. She answered it, ignoring Luke's heavy sigh.

"Hello?"

"Hey, have you seen Luke? He won't pick up my call." Carl sounded irritated.

"Yeah, he's right here" She handed him the phone, thankful for the interruption.

"Hello?...What?...Right now?..." Luke closed his eyes in frustration and brought a hand up to rub his forehead. "Yeah, okay. I'll be right there." He hung up the phone and handed it back to Lenny, "You shouldn't have answered that." Luke's demeanor had shifted dramatically.

"What was it about?" Lenny wasn't sure she wanted to know based on the clench in his jaw and the narrowing of his eyes at the center of the table.

Luke stood up and grabbed her hand pulling her to the door, not worrying about her reaction. "Just some garbage I have to deal with," he growled.

He tucked her notebook under his arm and pulled her down the street possessively. Gone was the Luke who was trying too hard to not cross any lines. Lenny was thrown off by the sudden alpha-male, take-charge Luke that was striding purposefully down the sidewalk. She half-expected him to toss her over his shoulder if she didn't comply. He didn't release the firm clasp on her hand until they were climbing up into his bus, more agitated than Lenny had ever seen him.

As Lenny's eyes adjusted to the darkened inside of the lounge she made out the figure of someone sitting on the couch. A tall, leggy, buxom brunette was filing her nails. She had on a severely short skirt and a cleavage baring top. Alarm bells started to go off in Lenny's head when she saw Carl standing a little ways away with his arms crossed.

"Hey, baby," the boobilicious girl lilted when she saw Luke. She smiled and showed too many teeth, reminding Lenny of the shark from *Jaws*. Her stunning blue eyes were half-lidded, as if in a sleepy, sexy daze.

"What are you doing here, Ashton?" Luke got right to the point.

"She's our opener for the next month." Carl said, not hiding his displeasure. "The label told me a few hours ago."

"That doesn't answer why you're *here.*" Luke emphasized "*On my freaking bus!*"

Lenny was too stunned to say anything. Luke never lost his temper. Ever. And he was beyond livid. She felt like she shouldn't be here except that Luke had brought her. She knew her eyes were wide but she was pretty sure no one was paying attention to her.

"Aww, baby, I thought you'd be happier to see me." Ashton wasn't fazed by Luke's shouting or the angry glares focused on her. Her full, pouty lips made it impossible to look away from her mouth while she spoke. She went on to explain nonchalantly, "My band is riding with Sway and them. I'm gonna bunk with you." She winked.

Lenny almost threw up. She had finally placed who the bimbo was.

95

Ashton James was a recording artist, which was the simple explanation. The more detailed version included her being Luke's ex-girlfriend. Their relationship had been very public and fans blamed her for a lot of the problems between the band members two years ago. Including Mike's overdose and following hospitalization. Modern day Yoko.

"No," Luke said, deadly quiet, "You can ride with the crew."

"Ew." Ashton rolled her eyes and pushed her flawless, chocolate hair back over her bare shoulder on one side. "Carl already said it was okay." She didn't even pause her filing and looked at Luke. "It'll be just like old times."

"I never said it was okay," Carl was trying not to rage. "You backed me into a corner, you *she-devil*." He turned to explain to Luke who hadn't stopped glowering at Ashton. "Her *entourage* filled the empty spaces of the crew buses and the Red Bus. Your bus is the only one with room until we get to Denver, then the label will have one for her."

"Who's the groupie?" Ashton suddenly narrowed her eyes at Lenny and Lenny immediately felt her body shift into a defensive stance.

"She's their assistant." Carl answered automatically, still caught up in his own frustrations.

Lenny felt her face start to redden as Ashton looked her up and down with a knowing smirk. She didn't even know this girl and she already hated her.

"So you guys finally hired a professional to keep you happy? The groupies too inexperienced for you now?" Ashton ran her tongue over her teeth and arched an eyebrow.

"Are you implying that I'm a whore?" Lenny bristled, causing Luke to take a step in between the two women.

"No, I was calling you one outright." Ashton's eyes flared slightly, daring Lenny to react. "You're not?"

"Lenny is our personal assistant." Everyone looked up to see Mike standing calmly in the doorway to the back lounge.

Ashton rolled her eyes and looked back to her nails.

"Lenny," Mike addressed without taking his glare off Ashton, "You don't do anything she says." He took a few steps across the room and stood in front of Lenny with his back to Ashton. "I moved your things for you from the crew bus when I heard Lucifer was joining the tour, you're staying with us. Permanently."

"I knew it, you're all addicted to blondes. I hope she's at least clean. You had her tested, right?" Ashton's voice dripped with disdain.

Mike grabbed Lenny's shoulders to stop her from charging forward. His jaw clenched visibly and he pushed Lenny towards the door. He looked over his shoulder at Luke who was visibly shaking with anger. "Sound

96

check, man." Luke nodded but didn't respond.

When they got out into the parking lot, Lenny yelled to expel her frustration, "What...The...Hell?!" She had never hated anyone instantly before.

A few seconds later Carl stormed off the bus grumbling, "Never hit a woman! Never hit a woman!" Guess Lenny wasn't the only one with self-control issues at the moment.

Mike kept walking; he motioned for Lenny to join him. She got close enough and he hooked an arm around her neck, pulling her towards the stage area.

"Don't let her get under your skin." His jaw was working furiously but his voice stayed even. "She's gonna say and do all she can to make you want to...well, kill yourself." He snorted and shook his head. "No one knows better than me how effectively she can get into your head. Just don't listen to anything she says, okay?"

Lenny was mad. She was mad because Ashton James shouldn't be anyone to fear. She was mad because this person had hurt Mike in the past. And she was mad that Luke was alone with her.

"What about the rule? She can't stay on the bus." Lenny was grasping and she knew it.

"I agree. If I can't have heroin on the bus than *the devil* sure as hell shouldn't be allowed either."

***

Luke took a deep breath and tried to calm the adrenaline coursing through his body. He paced back and forth across the floor and rubbed the back of his head with his palm.

"What's wrong with you?" Ashton asked, focused again on her nails.

Luke stared at her for a minute, not really believing she was back in his life. Just when things with Lenny were...*Were what? I mean really, what's going on with Lenny anyway? Every time I try to make a move of any kind she runs away.* Luke shook his head, trying to focus on the present problem sitting in his view.

"You look good." Ashton eyed him seductively, attempting to change the subject.

He heaved out his breath and sat down in a chair across from her.

"Ashton, look," he began calmly; they'd had this conversation many times. "Please try to listen to what I'm saying." She raised her eyebrow and gave him a bored expression.

"This tour is different; there will be no 'like old times.' At all." He

97

tried to decipher her blank look. "No drugs, no sex, no wild parties. You understand?"

Ashton squinted her eyes as she tried to decide which part to argue with and made a face. "Ugh, you're boring." She flipped her nail file onto the table and crossed her legs. "Any other 'rules', Headmaster?"

That was the thing with Ashton, when they were alone together she could almost be reasoned with. If he approached it right.

"Lenny is our personal assistant, you can't talk to her like that. She deserves respect and she's going to get it."

Ashton leaned forward, her eyes glinting with mischief, "Why, is she your girlfriend?"

"No." Luke knew that Ashton's jealousy could take a nasty turn if she found out he had actual feelings for Lenny. It would be so much worse than if Ashton believed they were only sleeping together.

"Then why do you care how I talk to her?" Ashton's lip curled in a disbelieving smirk.

"She'll kick your ass, Ashton." Luke answered honestly. "And if you don't tone down the attitude, I'm pretty sure no one will stop her."

"Aww, you're worried about me?" Ashton sat back and pouted like a child. Luke's stomach churned. He couldn't believe he had been with her for so long. He had definitely underestimated how wasted he had kept himself two years ago.

"Not exactly," Luke grumbled.

***

Luke was late to sound check and completely distracted. But he promised the guys he would be on for the show. Lenny fidgeted nervously in the sound booth, waiting for Ashton to grace the audience with her presence. She hadn't talked to Luke since leaving him on the bus with her. What could she say? *Hey, your ex is a piece of work, mind if I smother her in her sleep?* Yeah, that's all she could come up with.

The lights dimmed and the band started playing a slow ballad. Ashton appeared in the spotlight. Her body seemed to be completely proportionate and Lenny had to wonder how much of that was credit to an experienced surgeon on the west coast. She worked the crowd over and brought them to their feet. By the time her set was done, even Lenny was clapping. That tramp could really sing. It was completely unfair.

When it was Double Blind Study's turn to take the stage, they were delayed. Lenny started to chew on her fingernails, wondering what was going on backstage. Greg muttered something into his radio, someone muttered back. He cued the lights and Mike struck the first beat of a very shaky performance. They got stronger as they continued but it wasn't great. Lenny was nervous for them. The guys seemed disconnected from each other. This had never happened before. At least, not on this tour.

During the encore, Lenny decided to make her way back to the bus. Her footsteps were heavy as she climbed inside. Ashton, not unexpectedly, was sitting in the lounge reading a *Cosmo* magazine. Her dark hair hung perfectly down her back, not a strand out of place. Her long, fabulous legs stretched out on the couch in front of her. She was wearing a mens t-shirt and lacy panties. That was all.

Lenny rolled her eyes and walked past her.

"You're not special." Ashton's dig was unexpected and Lenny halted in her tracks.

She knew from Mike's warning that she should keep walking but she wanted to see what all the fuss was about. She faced Ashton, taking in her full lips and high cheekbones. Not one thing about this woman was even remotely flawed; and again, Lenny wondered how much of it had been paid for. Her eyelashes were even thick enough that Lenny guessed she probably didn't have to wear much makeup at all.

"You think they care about you and they'll fight for you." Ashton turned her wicked blue eyes to Lenny. "But they won't."

"I don't need anyone to fight for me." Lenny declared, knowing she was letting Ashton do exactly what Mike had warned her she would do.

Ashton laughed mockingly, "You're so clueless. You really think you matter to them, it's actually kind of sweet." She closed her magazine and set it aside. "But you don't have anything to offer they can't get somewhere else. You're a simple novelty, a shiny new toy. You're replaceable."

Lenny took a step towards her but Luke and Mike came inside at that moment. Ashton jumped up and wrapped her arms around Luke's neck, giving Lenny a great view of her perfect ass. Luke had eye contact with Lenny over Ashton's shoulder. Lenny rolled her eyes in disgust and went to the back lounge. Mike followed close behind.

"I didn't have any clean pajamas so I borrowed one of your shirts, I hope that's okay." Ashton's sing-song voice could be heard throughout the cabin. It made Lenny want to rip her ears off and throw them out the window. "I mean, I always used to wear your shirts to bed before…" Lenny gave Mike a look and pretended to stab herself and bleed out. Mike stifled his laughter.

Luke stuck his head the doorway, "What are you guys doing?"

"Probably watch a movie. Out there seemed a little, I don't know," Mike acted like he was searching for the right word, "*whorish* for my taste."

"I heard that!" Ashton yelled.

"Good! Put some pants on!" Mike hollered back.

"Just a couple of days guys and she'll be on her own bus." Luke was trying to keep the peace but Lenny couldn't figure out why. Why was he being nice to her?

"Yep, and I plan on treating her exactly as she deserves until then." Mike stated plainly.

Luke let out a heavy sigh through his tired smile. He looked at Lenny apologetically, "I'm going to bed." He climbed into his bunk and closed the curtain.

Ashton whined for a while before she, too, finally went to bed. Lenny half expected her to try to crawl into the same bunk as Luke but she didn't. *Thank God for small miracles,* Lenny thought.

She and Mike stayed up watching classic movies, not speaking. After Humphrey Bogart put Ingrid Bergman on the plane bound for Lisbon, Mike coaxed her into trying to get some sleep.

She climbed into her bunk and tried to block out what Ashton had said to her. *You think they care for you and they'll fight for you. But they won't.* Lenny took that as a threat, Ashton was planning on getting rid of her. Well Ashton James might have gotten her way in the past, but Lenny didn't lose. Ever. It was so on.

Chapter 7

Breakout

Lenny got up the next morning feeling invigorated despite her lack of sleep. She hadn't had a challenge in a long time, and Ashton James just bit off more than she could chew. Lenny was determined to make her choke on it.

Ashton's presence on the tour was already oppressive. Lenny could sense it in the mood of the crew. It was like a black cloud hanging over each of them individually, waiting for the inevitable lightning strike. It pissed Lenny off to see that Bitch Face could have that kind of power over the people in her life. *Not if I have anything to do with it.*

She showered and dressed quickly, pulling her hair into a messy bun with a few wisps of hair escaping around her face. She threw on her standard jeans, a snug, canary yellow tee and her trusty Chucks and quickly made her coffee rounds. She greeted Carl in their usual spot with a beaming smile.

"You look like sunshine this morning," Carl eyed her suspiciously. "You didn't kill Ashton by any chance, did you?"

"Not yet." She said with a lopsided grin.

"That woman makes my skin crawl." Carl took a sip of coffee. "Are we sure she's even human? I mean, isn't there a separate classification for pure evil?"

Carl gave Lenny an amused warning glare. "You better steer clear of that little nightmare, Lenny." He said in his worried dad voice.

"You have no idea how capable I am of handling her." Lenny reassured him. *No idea at all.*

Carl flashed her a look that said he was still unsure but proceeded to change the subject.

"The good news is that I've arranged to get hotel rooms for us when we reach Denver. I booked you a nice suite since you'll have spent the week in a viper's nest."

"Thanks, Carl," Lenny smiled sweetly at him. Carl didn't do favors for anyone. Lenny recognized the huge deal that it was and she impulsively

101

threw her arms around him. He stiffened at her sudden embrace and she held back a laugh.

"That's enough," he growled but Lenny heard the affection in his voice.

Her status in this band was solid, Ashton was an idiot.

***

The guys were tense. Mike watched them eat quietly as he sipped his orange juice. Lenny had gathered them up and taken them to breakfast but no one could find Luke...or Ashton. Mike knew the guys were already running through their worst case scenarios in their heads. Ashton had successfully thrown them back into a place of angst and distrust.

Everyone except for Lenny. She was irritated but still peppy. Mike watched as she tried to pull the guys out of their glum moods and he again thanked God for her existence.

Mike was pissed too. He was doing his best to not entertain his own dark temperament, but it was still there, lingering in the back of his mind. He really hoped Luke wasn't being stupid. He'd been Ashton's lapdog once before. It didn't work out.

"We need to do something fun." Lenny announced to the table causing the solemn eaters to stare at her.

"What do you have in mind, mama?" Blake finally asked tiredly.

"I heard there is a bungee jumping area near here," her face lit up with rebellion.

"I don't know if Carl would go for that." Harrison eyed her suspiciously and Mike sniggered. Lenny was definitely in a wild mood this morning.

"Who says he has to know?" She dared them, eyebrows raised.

The looks that went around the table ranged from terrified to excited. Lenny didn't bend the rules. Lenny would never go against Carl. Lenny was predictable. Lenny was safe. This wasn't Lenny...was it?

"Hell, I'm in." Mike was the first to commit; he knew why Lenny was feeling so unruly. Ashton's presence was suffocating and Luke wasn't being himself. He had pretty much gone off alone since Ashton had shown up. And he was also avoiding the rest of the band. Lenny was feeling a need to express her frustration and bungee jumping was a way better alternative than what Mike had come up with...binge drinking and smack.

The others turned to Mike, clearly surprised at his easy agreement.

"Dude, we could die." Harrison felt it necessary to point out the dangers, in case it wasn't obvious.

"Yeah, but we won't." Mike winked at Lenny and stood up from the

102

table. She joined him at the door where they turned to look at the others who were still gaping.

Mike chuckled and grabbed Lenny's hand, tugging her into the sunshine that matched the color of her shirt.

***

Mike looked down at the raging water below him from nearly two hundred feet. *This is a very bad idea.* He was having second thoughts at Lenny's choice of activity for the day.

He looked at her getting her harness attached and was amazed at her calm focus. She seemed more relaxed than he had seen her all tour. It shouldn't have made sense, they were easily in the most dangerous scenario he could come up with, and she was acting like it was a trip to the mall, or whatever girls do for relaxation. He had obviously underestimated her drive for extreme adventure.

Harrison, Blake and Sway had agreed to try it if Mike and Lenny went first. But Mike could see the apprehension on their faces. Harrison was visibly sweating. He chuckled nervously to himself, what had they gotten themselves into?

Lenny approached the edge of the platform and listened to the instructions from the operator. She nodded and took a deep breath.

"You're afraid to get on a snowboard again, but this doesn't scare you?" Mike tried to reason with her. Lenny flashed him a grin and then dove off the platform.

Mike's stomach dropped to his feet as he watched her body fly into the open air. She got to the end of the line and her body rebounded and plunged again, continuing to oscillate up and down until all the energy was dissipated. The operators lowered a rope to her, she attached it to her harness and they hauled her back to the platform.

"That was awesome!" Sway gave her a high-five.

"Are you okay?" Harrison asked, his eyes wide, trying to search for any visible injuries.

"I'm great!" Lenny responded, "I'm gonna do it again!" Her face was...serene, her cheeks pink from giddiness.

Mike shook his head; he knew it was his turn. He would have to follow through since he had given the others such a hard time for being scared.

"You're gonna love it," she whispered in his ear as she gave him a quick hug. She stood back, biting her bottom lip and grinning at the same time in anticipation of his jump.

Mike approached the edge and took a deep breath. In a moment of courage he took a flying leap and was airborne. The sensations that raced through him were indescribable. He felt completely out of control but totally centered at the same time. Then he experienced a brand new rush in the recoil. His heart was stuck in his throat, but he knew his face had a silly grin plastered across it. As soon as it had started, it was over, and they were pulling him back up.

His mighty leap impressed the guys and they got geared up to make their own jumps. Lenny let loose more than all of them, jumping three more times herself before they had to call it a day and head back for sound check. It was weird to not have Luke with them but they still had fun despite his absence.

"Can't tell Carl, okay guys?" Lenny leveled a serious look at all of them.

"Why does it matter if Carl knows? We're the ones who hired you." Sway said, and Mike noticed Lenny's lip twitch at his words.

"Let's just keep it between us, okay?" Lenny said again earnestly and they all nodded in agreement.

***

Luke was late to sound check again, looking like he hadn't slept in days. It was amazing, Ashton had only been a part of the tour for twenty-four hours and Luke had aged ten years. His hair was more matted than stylishly messy and his eyes were unfocused and empty.

Lenny was helping the guitar techs, Dustin and Ben, get set up when Ashton pranced across the stage

"Oh good, Ashton," Blake sounded relieved, "It's just you, I thought I heard someone backing over a goat." The guitar techs laughed and Ashton shot daggers at him.

Lenny stopped laughing when she saw Luke watching them. He had never looked so lost. Lenny took a step his direction but he minutely shook his head, signaling her to stop. She frowned at his pinched expression, silently asking her question from across the stage. He held eye contact with her for far too long, as if attempting to dump every thought and feeling he had into that one, simple communique. Lenny nodded, understanding as much as she dared.

She left the stage in search of Carl. No way Ashton was going to force the alienation of Luke from his friends. *Home-wrecking sociopath.*

***

The show that night was better than the previous, but only

104

marginally. The rest of the band was tight but Luke struggled with playing and remembering all the lyrics. He would look up from the mic and back to the sound booth but Lenny wasn't there. He didn't know where she was and it bothered him. He knew he was the only one at fault for why she had to stay away. Punishment for past sins.

Luke trudged to his bus, no autographs or photos with fans. His shoulders pulled down and he felt like shit. He dreaded seeing Ashton. She would be half naked again and obnoxious as hell. He paused outside the door and took a deep breath, bracing himself for the inevitable chatter that she would start hurling at him.

He heard a stirring to his left and he frowned into the darkness. He made out a shadowy figure waving him over. Taking a few steps in that direction, he recognized Sway.

"What's goin' on?" He asked his shifty friend.

"Come with me." Sway waved him to be quiet and just follow. Luke shrugged and crept along the back of the venue in the dark with his bass player. As they made their way along, Luke could hear more whispers and they came around a corner to an ugly brown van and the rest of his band.

The van was half hidden behind a dumpster but it looked like a throwback to their days when they were just starting out. Complete with the rust over the wheel wells and graffiti decorating the outside. The rest of the band members stood waiting for him in a semi-circle. Luke was surprised at how relieved he was to see Lenny amongst his friends.

"We're ditching the buses tonight. Lenny hooked us up with a private ride." Harrison smiled eagerly, "You're coming with us."

Luke looked around at the faces of his oldest friends and the girl he was falling for even more. How did he ever deserve to find not just one good friend in this world but five? He nodded and they all piled into the decrepit van.

Luke noticed that Slim, their regular driver, was behind the wheel. He slid into the seat next to Lenny and whispered a question in her ear, "If Slim is here, who's driving the Blue Bus?"

Lenny tried to hide her smile, "Slim's brother, Mo." Her eyes met Luke's and he squinted, trying to figure out if she was serious.

"Slim's brother is named...Mo?" He asked slowly.

Lenny bit her bottom lip to keep from laughing and nodded.

Mike slid the door closed and settled into one of the captain's chairs. Harrison occupied the other captain's chair and Blake was sitting cozy next to Luke and Lenny. Sway took his position in shotgun and started calling out options for music to be played.

Luke patted Lenny's thigh affectionately and asked, "This was what you were doing during the show, wasn't it?" She nodded with a smile and he squeezed her leg. If she only knew the significance of what she had done, of what she did everyday...

"Don't worry, though," she whispered to him, "Carl knows, this is completely sanctioned."

Slim made his way out of the parking lot and onto the road before he turned on the headlights.

"I feel like super spies!" Harrison whispered excitedly.

Sway pushed an old tape into the ancient radio and cranked up the volume. As Tom Petty's 'American Girl' started to play, the whole band joined in, singing at the top of their lungs.

***

As the van sped down the interstate, the band sang song after song together. Lenny felt the icky stench of Ashton evaporate and she smiled in satisfaction. This was the most liberated she'd seen the guys all tour. That included when they were jumping off that bridge earlier in the day.

"This is exactly what it was like when we were young." Harrison reminisced happily.

"You guys traveled by van?" Lenny asked, she loved to hear their old stories from before they made it big. Especially when Harrison told them.

"Yeah, in a crappy van just like this one," Harrison swiveled haphazardly towards Lenny. She laughed as he almost spilled onto the floor. He regained his balance on the loose bolts holding the seat down and continued. "Our van was brown, too. We called it the Brown Streaker. We were very creative musicians back then."

Lenny started with a small giggle but it grew into out of control belly laughter as Harrison kept going. "I was getting puked on nightly, and we couldn't always afford showers at the truck stops so..."

"Gross!" Lenny cried. "Who was puking on you?"

Harrison pointed his thumb over his shoulder, "Usually Sway's current shag."

"Hey! It wasn't my fault that they always seemed to have a lot to drink." Sway defended from the front.

"Sure," Harrison nodded in sarcastic agreement. "But all we had was this one van, with all of our stuff and us in it. And Sway was always using it for...extracurricular activities."

"Eww." Lenny scrunched up her nose.

"Tell me about it." Harrison shuddered at the memory, causing Lenny to laugh harder.

"Who drove?" Lenny asked curiously.

106

"Not Blake!" Mike said with force and Lenny waited for the explanation as Harrison put on his professor face.

"Blake does not drive."

"I drive just fine!" Blake defended from the other side of Luke.

"Blake...how do I put this...hit a building." Harrison stated flatly.

"One time!" Blake interjected. He leaned over so Lenny could see the sincerity on his face. "One time, Lenny! It wasn't my fault."

"Right, it was the building's fault, how dare it be built where you wanted to drive." Harrison continued, just as flat. He raised his eyebrows at Lenny and she laughed even more. "Oh, I forgot, not just any building...the courthouse."

"What?!" Lenny exclaimed, "How did you accidentally hit a courthouse, Blake Diedrich?!" Her disappointed mother tone came out and all the guys laughed.

"I don't know! It was dark...I have night blindness...I thought I saw a dog..." His voice trailed off as he gave up defending himself.

"But at least he didn't set the van on fire." Harrison gestured to Luke. Lenny turned to him in shock.

"Why do you think I gave up smoking?" Luke grinned.

"Wow, you guys. How did you ever get anywhere?" Lenny was genuinely surprised.

"Oh, you know...hard work, good looks," Harrison ran his fingers through his hair, "and of course we're freaking talented out the ass."

"Of course," Lenny agreed but she was still laughing. She adored these guys, no one could replace them. She was past the point of no return; she couldn't see herself leaving them. Ever.

The guys started to get tired after a few hours and eventually began nodding off. Lenny stayed awake, watching her fellas sleep. Ashton wasn't getting her claws into them. She leaned her head against the window and looked out at the stars.

Luke shifted in his seat next to her and she glanced over to see him and Blake snuggled up together. She smiled, *big, tough rock stars*.

Whatever power Ashton used to have over Luke was in no way stronger than the bond that this band shared. Lenny had to remind them of that. Ashton was simply a distraction, she didn't matter. That's why Lenny had talked to Carl about renting the van and going ahead of the convoy. The guys needed to harken back to the days of their youth, where this whole crazy thing started.

Two more shows before Denver, twelve total before Ashton left the tour. Then a four week break over Christmas.

Lenny tried to focus on her job, but in the dark cabin with just the sound of the wheels on the road, her thoughts drifted to home. She wondered what she would do during break. She couldn't go home. She hadn't called her parents in over a week. The last phone call had been tense, they wanted her to come back. She missed them, but she needed to be out here more. She wasn't ready to face...all of that.

Maybe Carl would give her some sort of assignment over break to keep her occupied. She could ask him later.

Scott was pissed; she'd stopped answering his calls two weeks ago. Her voice mail kept filling up. She wouldn't even check it if she wasn't afraid it would be Carl. Scott had been the most persistent of her family members. She wished he would just back off and let her figure this thing out.

He didn't understand, none of them did. How could they? She wasn't exactly being the most forthcoming with any of them. Most of all, she was disappointed in herself.

Lenny pinched the bridge of her nose and squinted against the headache revving itself into full blown migraine. Suddenly, Luke's arms were around her, pulling her against his chest and pressing his lips to her temple. The headache fled as she instinctively buried her face in his shirt.

"Sshh. It's okay, I got you." Luke whispered against her ear.

Lenny ignored her previous logic of avoiding more situations like this. She needed him right now, it was that simple. And somehow...he just knew.

***

Slim pulled over for breakfast at a little roadside diner. He opted to eat alone at the counter but the other six squeezed into a booth. They pushed each other playfully, taking up more space than they needed to. The waitress was not amused at their antics and she grumpily took their order and walked away.

"This was a great idea," Sway spoke for them all, "We should get rid of the buses altogether and just travel like this again." He leaned his elbows on the table and started to play with the sugar packets.

"You feeling better, dude?" Blake asked Luke who was sitting directly across from him.

"Yeah," Luke smiled, feeling like himself again. "Sorry, I was acting so-"

"Menstrual?" Blake finished for him.

Luke chuckled and nodded. "Yeah, I guess that's how I was acting, huh?"

"You guess? Dude, middle school girls are less moody than you," Blake grimaced.

108

"I don't know why you let your tampon get all twisted just because Ashton James, walking bitch-fest that she is, happens to be around. What? Does she have your balls in a jar somewhere?" Blake's dark eyebrows rose accusingly.

They were giving him a hard time and Luke knew he deserved it. "It's hard to think clearly around her, I guess I just shut everyone out. Sorry about that. Again."

They took their time eating breakfast, enjoying the time together without any distractions. They were in such a good mood they even got their grumpy waitress to smile before they left.

"We have enough bunks in the Blue Bus for all of us," Luke looked around at the band, "why don't we all just ride together?"

"I like it," Mike looked to Lenny for approval.

"Hey, I'm just the assistant. You don't need my permission." She held up her hands to show she wasn't protesting.

"I don't know man," Sway began, "I really hate that girl. I don't want to sleep in the same vehicle as her. What if she tries to molest me?"

"Gross, Sway. Gross." Lenny frowned in disgust and Luke smiled at how cute she looked when she was correcting Sway. Like she was still shocked by some of the things he said.

"But it might be fun to make her miserable," Blake pointed out.

"We could go on a shower strike like last time," Harrison suggested.

"Yes!" Blake snapped his fingers and pointed at Harrison. "That! We're doing it."

Lenny closed her eyes and rubbed her forehead with her fingertips, "Oh, geez."

"Sorry, mama. But we did promise you the full 'Rock Star' experience, smelly guys and all," Sway grinned at her.

"We should definitely be as authentic as possible," Mike was nodding his head.

"You have to participate too, Lenny," Blake said, "You're one of us now." He arched an eyebrow, daring her.

Luke was surprised when she took the bait and replied cheekily, "I can hack it if you can."

***

They pulled into the parking lot of their next venue and their spirits were high. As they made their way to the buses, Ashton came running out and grabbed Luke by the arms.

"Baby! Where have you been? I was so worried!" She glared at Lenny over Luke's shoulder and Lenny rolled her eyes. It was weird, when

109

Ashton called Luke, 'baby', Lenny didn't hear it as a term of endearment. It sounded more like piglets squealing at their mother's teat.

Luke stepped around her, "I was with my friends, I don't have to check in with you." She backed up at his curt reply.

Ashton shook it off and ran to catch up to Luke, snaking her arm around his. Lenny had to give it to her; the girl was either very persistent or thick as a brick. Luke pulled his arm away and entered the bus, Ashton close on his heels.

"My coffee angel," Carl greeted Lenny as she handed him a cup of steaming coffee she had brought with her from the diner. "I thought you might forget since the plans were a little different."

"I could never forget you, old man," she flashed a smiled. "How did it go?" Lenny asked, she'd been slightly concerned for Carl's safety once Ashton found out they had ditched her.

"I think she put a hex on me," Carl said honestly.

"That girl has issues, that's for sure," Lenny agreed. "The guys have decided to all ride in the same bus until Ashton gets her own." Carl nodded his approval. "And, they've started a shower strike," she added slowly.

"Not that shit again," Carl sounded annoyed but his eyes held a hint of amusement, "This is gonna get gross, you know."

"They made me agree to it, too." Lenny winced at her own confession and watched for his reaction.

Carl burst out laughing, "Ashton is gonna be so pissed."

***

Sound check was amazing. The guys were presenting a united front and it greatly improved the mood of the crew. They weren't going to let Ashton get her way anymore. In fact, they were doing a pretty good job of humiliating her. She was constantly lurking about and it only provided more fuel to rip on her. It's like she couldn't take a hint.

"Why don't you go hang out with your minions? They like you...at least that's what you pay them to do," Blake remarked as Ashton stood in the way of everyone.

"Shut up, Blake," she bit. "No one likes you, you're just a washed up has-been from the gutter."

Blake's jaw worked under his skin and he growled back, "That's better than being a vapid whore with daddy issues."

"Who says you don't have daddy issues, orphan?" Ashton's sneer was heard more than seen.

"I like your spray tan. What shade is that? Overcooked yam?"

The exchange of insults continued throughout the afternoon until Ashton threatened to call the Orphan Bus to reclaim Blake and he, in turn, threatened to set all of her undergarments on fire during her set.

Harrison intervened at that point, and convinced everyone to separate for the remainder of the evening so they could concentrate on why they were really all there...for the fans.

When Double Blind Study played their opening song, the crowd went nuts. The place erupted with the standard crowd surfers and slam dancers but they were fueled by a more intense energy than ever before. Lenny thought the roof was going to blow off, the fans yelled so loud. She was tempted to jump into the crowd and let them carry her away.

"They're *on* tonight." Greg shook his head as he tried to keep up with all the changes to the set list. The band pulled out some classics they hadn't played in a while. Fan favorites and B-sides. It felt more like a jam session then a regular set. Lenny knew it was due to their impromptu road trip so they could reconnect to one another.

Ashton's witchcraft be damned.

***

It was day three of the shower embargo and Lenny felt her greasy hair with her fingertips. She made a face and brushed it into a tight bun on top of her head. She was really looking forward to that suite that Carl had promised her at the end of the week.

The plan was working very well. Ashton was so mad she couldn't spit straight. She complained about the smell constantly and she stopped trying to get close to Luke. She kept making digs at Lenny about her trucker appearance, but Lenny always had a quick comeback that shut her up. For the most part.

Lenny was alone in the bus, restocking and refilling the supplies. She was making a list on the counter when she felt the hair on the back of her neck stick up. She raised her eyes to see Ashton staring at her. She was wearing a little pink dress that could be mistaken for a negligee, her voluptuous breasts proudly on display.

"Don't forget to put *soap* on your list," she snarked.

"Good one," Lenny said flatly.

"Aren't you embarrassed of yourself?" Ashton looked her up and down, "I mean, the grunge look is a little outdated."

Lenny glanced down at her dirty jeans and stained t-shirt. She wasn't feeling great about how she looked but she wouldn't give Ashton the satisfaction of knowing that. She shrugged and responded, "At least no one has mistaken me for a hooker."

111

Ashton's nose flared and her lips pursed together tightly.

Sway skipped up the steps of the bus and into the room. "Uh-oh, do I smell tension?" He waggled his eyebrows.

"No, that's Lenny's ass," Ashton said haughtily. She started to wave her hand across her face and scrunched up her nose. "Sway! You stink, too!"

Sway only laughed and got a water bottle out of the fridge.

"How was sound check?" Lenny asked, blocking out Ashton's presence.

"Good. Solid." Sway thought for a minute and then asked Lenny, "You wanna make-out?"

"Sway, you really would screw anything, wouldn't you? You have no standards." Ashton said with disgust.

"That's not true." Sway said sweetly, pushing his long, stringy hair out of his face. "I can honestly say that I have never wanted to bag you."

Ashton sputtered something unintelligible and stomped outside.

Sway laughed as she left then hugged Lenny to his side, "I don't really wanna make out."

"I know."

"I mean, unless, you want to," he arched an eyebrow at her.

Lenny pushed him away and rolled her eyes.

"Okay, okay. But let me know if you change your mind," he winked and left again.

Lenny changed the sheets in the bunks and picked up the garbage that littered the floors. She considered not changing the sheets in Ashton's bunk but thought better of it. As she was pulling out the dirty, used blankets her notebook fell out onto the floor.

Lenny slowly picked it up, remembering that Luke had been the last one to have it. Why was it in Ashton's bunk? Lenny paged through it and noticed some marks and notes had been made. She recognized Luke's handwriting but that still didn't explain why she found it where she did. She wasn't that upset about it. She wasn't *thrilled* but she figured Ashton was planning something devious and Lenny had caught her before she could pull it off.

She tucked the notebook into a small cupboard behind the TV in the back lounge and checked the time. A half hour till Ashton's set. Lenny opted to leave her jacket despite the chilly fall air. She knew the arena would be hot with all the bodies jumping up and down. She jogged over to the stage area and took her seat next to Greg.

The lights came down and the band started up. Ashton appeared on stage and began wooing the crowd with her haunting voice and complicated, nonsensical lyrics. Her set was the usual, nothing extraordinary, until her

112

closing song.

"I wrote this when I was going through a tough time in my life. I finally feel comfortable sharing it with you tonight." Lenny gagged at Greg and he laughed. But as Ashton's delicate vocals drifted slowly and seductively over the air, Lenny got a sinking feeling in her stomach and goose bumps stood up on her arms.

"That bitch!" Lenny said out loud. Greg frowned at her, confused. "She stole my song! I wrote that!"

Chapter 8

Lines In Sand

As soon as the encore finished, Luke threw his guitar to one of the nearby techs and hurried to the bus. He had to get to Lenny before she got to Ashton. During the entire set he struggled with focus as different scenarios flashed through his mind. Most of them ended with Ashton slapping Lenny with a restraining order and Lenny having to leave the tour.

Luke couldn't let that happen. He had no idea what was in the future for them but he couldn't lose her. Not yet.

The bus was empty. His heart started to beat with something akin to panic. He checked the other buses. Empty. The stage was getting broken down when he checked the sound booth.

"Where did Lenny go?" Luke asked Greg who was closing down his equipment.

"I don't know, man, but she was pissed. Are you sure you want to find her?" He called after Luke's retreating back.

Luke was in a full out run, he hadn't seen Ashton or Lenny since the end of the show and he wasn't liking the disappearing act. He knew that Ashton had crossed the mother of all lines and she deserved whatever she was getting but Luke didn't want Lenny to have to deal with all that alone. Ashton would ruin everything if given the opportunity. She knew exactly what she was doing and it made him sick to his stomach.

He ran back inside the venue and almost knocked over Carl.

"Have you seen Lenny?" Luke panted.

"Yeah, she's in the office," he pointed to the door he had come from, "I was just coming to find you. Have you seen Ashton?"

Luke shook his head dumbly and entered the small, dimly lit room. She was sitting in a chair at a desk talking on her cell phone and jotting down a few notes. She looked up at Luke and gave him a quick smile and went back to her conversation.

"Yep, we'll be in Denver tomorrow....great, see you then." She hung up the phone and turned her attention to Luke's worried expression.

"That was my lawyer," she explained, looking almost annoyed.

"Your lawyer?" Luke was trying to follow along. His head swirled with confusion from adjusting to the drastic change in what he had expected to find and the reality sitting before him.

Lenny frowned at him, "Are you okay?"

"Are you?" Luke didn't understand why he had hadn't found Lenny with her fingers wrapped around Ashton's throat.

"Yeah, why?" She smiled, "Oh, because of Bitchy McThievery stealing my song?"

Luke nodded, watching her warily. His heartbeat thudding in his ears as he tried to calm down from the last few minutes of anxiety that he had experienced.

"Scott, always trying to protect me," she rolled her eyes, "came across my journal awhile back and made me get a copyright...So, I'm suing her." She ended with a wink.

Luke closed his eyes and a low chuckle started that grew into full on belly laughter as he released the tension that had been building during the whole show. He reached over and grabbed Lenny's hand and pulled her into a hug, still laughing.

"What's so funny?" Her voice was muffled against his shirt.

"You're the best." He pulled her back and looked into her face. "I was afraid you were going to kill her and I was going to have come and visit you in jail."

It was Lenny's turn to laugh, "Believe me, I thought about it, but I decided this option would be way more satisfying. I'm not an idiot, I know what she's trying to do. I just won't play her game." He grinned and squeezed her against his chest again.

Lenny pushed him away playfully, "You stink!"

"You should talk!" Luke gave a hurt look but Lenny wasn't falling for it.

"C'mon," she moved to the doorway and looked at him over her shoulder, "let's go hang out with other awesome people."

Luke shook his head to himself in wonder. How did a woman like this come to be in his life? She was such a stark change from every other girl he'd ever dated or been around.

When they entered the bus, Ashton was sitting in her usual perch on the couch with a smug smile on her face. The rest of the guys were clustered around the kitchenette, avoiding her entirely. Luke nodded to Harrison to pass him a couple of waters for him and Lenny.

"Um," Harrison questioned openly, "shouldn't there be some sort of, I don't know, discussion? About what happened tonight?"

"What do you mean?" Luke decided to play dumb, wanting to know what Ashton had told the guys.

"Well, you took off after the set and Ashton told us just now that you guys wrote that last song together..." Harrison trailed off, confusion all

116

over his face.

"Are you writing songs with Ashton?" Blake asked, more agitated and confrontational than Harrison.

So that was how Ashton was playing it. She wasn't only trying to get rid of Lenny, she was trying to pull the guys away from him too. She really needed to revamp her diabolical planning skills.

"Actually," Lenny interrupted as she flopped herself onto the sofa right next to Ashton. "*I* wrote that. She stole it from me."

Luke held back a smile as he saw Ashton shift awkwardly. She obviously didn't expect Lenny's blasé reaction.

"But, thank you, Ashton," Lenny's tone danced on the edge of sarcasm. "You made it sound beautiful." She took a long drink from her water bottle as Ashton scowled at her.

Just then, Ashton's cell phone rang.

"You might wanna get that," Lenny gestured. Ashton frowned at her and took her phone to the back of the bus. Lenny held up her hand, signaling the others to wait for it.

"WHAT?!" Ashton shrieked.

"There it is," Lenny said, satisfied. "I imagine that was her lawyer telling her the happy news that I'm suing the crap out of her." She held her bottle of water up in toast, "Here's to a successful shower strike and copyright infringement!"

***

Shane: *Scott texted me, he said that she's going to be in Denver tomorrow*

  Cody: *no shit? Are you going to see her?*
  Shane: *I don't think that would be a good idea*
  Cody: *I'll do it*
  Shane: *let me know how it goes*

***

Lenny sank deep into the bubbles in the over-sized tub. She relaxed into the hot smell of jasmine and closed her eyes.

The suite Carl had gotten for her was by far the greatest perk of her job that she had experienced yet. It was three separate rooms, a living room with a fireplace, an office area and a spacious bedroom with a King-sized bed. The bathroom had an elevated round tub and a separate shower area.

The first thing Lenny did when she got her room key was take a shower. While the shower strike had been highly successful in irritating

117

Ashton and bringing the band closer together, Lenny silently vowed to never do that again.

When she felt thoroughly cleansed of the 'on-the-road-ick,' she filled the tub with bubbles and proceeded to soak her tired muscles.

She planned on enjoying her last day of freedom as much as she could. She knew that calling her lawyer was going to open up a whole new sack of cats but teaching Ashton a lesson was totally worth it.

Lenny heard a knock at her door and sighed. *That was fast.* She grabbed a towel and dried herself off and then wrapped the hotel provided robe around herself. She crossed her spacious living quarters as another knock sounded.

She opened the door to find Carl, pacing, per his usual.

"Carl, what a surprise," Lenny said dryly.

Carl smiled reluctantly and entered the suite as Lenny extended her arm signaling him to do so. He looked around, admiring her accommodations.

"How do you like your room?" He asked too casually.

"I like it a lot. What's up, Carl?" She didn't want the small talk. She wanted to return to the bathtub and pretend she wasn't getting ready to have a crappy night.

Before Carl could answer, someone else knocked on the door. Lenny opened it and found Harrison and Blake. They entered without being invited in.

"Nice digs," Blake whistled. He dropped into an over-stuffed navy blue chair and swung his legs up over the arm rest.

"Hey, Carl." Harrison opened the in-room fridge and started rummaging for snacks.

Before the door to the hallway closed completely, Sway slipped inside. He kissed Lenny's cheek on the way by, "You smell nice, is that jasmine?" He joined Harrison on the couch and turned on the giant plasma screen.

"What are you guys doing here?" Lenny asked, trying to stay patient.

"Waiting for Mike and Luke." Sway answered like Lenny should've known.

"What? Why?" She frowned and crossed her arms over her chest.

"'Cause we're going out tonight." Harrison said matter of fact and then looked at Blake, "Aren't we?"

Blake rubbed the scruff on his face and nodded, "Yeah, karaoke, right Carl?"

Lenny turned her attention to Carl who smiled sheepishly.

"You told me I could have the night off, Carl," her tone was more cross than she intended and Carl winced.

Sway looked up and his eyes narrowed, "What do you mean, 'night off'? We're just hanging out. Geez, Lenny, is being our friend really work to you?" His tone was lighthearted but Lenny could tell he was fishing.

Lenny pursed her lips and swallowed, sidestepping that relational landmine and replied, "I just meant that I have a meeting with my lawyer tonight. And I thought we could all use a rest." Sway seemed satisfied with her answer and went back to the TV.

Lenny motioned for Carl to step aside so they could talk privately.

"I'm meeting my lawyer in a couple of hours, I can't go to karaoke."

Carl nodded his understanding, "Okay. But I just wanted to let you know, Sway was right, this isn't part of the job. I thought you might wanna blow off some steam with us tonight."

"You're going, too?" Lenny frowned.

Carl laughed quietly, "Well, yeah. I get a day off too every once in a while, you know."

Lenny conceded to that point but it still surprised her that Carl could so easily cross those lines of real friendship and professionalism so quickly when he'd been on target the whole tour.

"Where you meeting the lawyer?" Blake spoke up from his lounged position in the chair.

"Um, there's a fancy restaurant up the street," Lenny's stomach started to dive to the floor.

"Can we all eat together and then go out after you're finished talking to your rep?"

Lenny shifted uncomfortably. She didn't really want the guys around when her attorney brought down the hammer. The stuff with Ashton was simple, Lenny just had to sign some papers, but she knew there was going to be a more serious conversation after that. Her mind raced as she tried to think of an excuse to not have them there without having to tell them the whole story anyway. And she really didn't want to relive that nightmare.

She resigned herself to Blake's suggestion, "Yeah, that'll work. But it's gonna take me a little while to get ready."

"That's fine, we'll chill here." *So much for my relaxing bath,* Lenny thought.

"Carl, how come Lenny has a bigger room than us?" Harrison asked.

"'Cause she's better than us, dummy." Blake answered, Harrison nodded like he agreed.

Lenny shook her head and closed herself in her room to finish getting ready. As she was applying her mascara she heard Mike and Luke show up and Blake fill them in on the plan.

Lenny shimmied into the little black dress she had purchased at the boutique across the street from the hotel. She hadn't packed anything to wear to a formal restaurant and needed something fast. The dress was modest in the front, it was snug but the hem reached her knee and the neckline draped gracefully across her collarbone. It was sleeveless with a beaded embellishment at the shoulders.

She finished blow drying her hair and slipped into a pair of black platform stilettos. She applied a light coat of champagne colored lip gloss and took a deep breath. She hadn't been part of this world in a while and she wasn't sure how the guys would react, or if they would even recognize her.

She glanced at the clock on the nightstand, time to find out.

She opened the door and stepped into the living area, moving quickly to the door and pulling a knee-length black coat out of the closet. She turned around to face the guys as she slipped her arms in the sleeves. The reaction was what she had dreaded. They gaped at her with open mouths and she felt heat move up her neck.

"C'mon, we have to go," she motioned for them to get up, not caring if she sounded impatient.

"Damn!" Blake finally said something, "You look..." he trailed off.

"Let's not make a thing out of this, okay?" Lenny was cross, she clenched her jaw and led them out of the hotel room.

Sway whistled, "We are severely under dressed."

"You guys will be fine," Lenny sighed in exasperation, refusing to have eye contact with any of them on the elevator or their quick trip through the lobby. She couldn't handle seeing herself through their expressions. She had always hated this part of her life and she had tried her best to keep them out of it. As unrealistic as that might be.

"It's just a block north of here," Lenny was already walking down the sidewalk, as Luke tried to hail a cab, "We can walk."

"In those shoes?" Mike exclaimed. But she was already striding purposefully forward. The guys followed, she wasn't giving them the choice.

Fueled by her frustration and irritation in the impending events, she barely noticed the disdainful looks given by the wait staff when they entered the restaurant.

"Miss Evans, we've been expecting you." The host greeted her, eying her group suspiciously.

"They're with me, Louise," she knew she sounded bitchy. She hated herself for it. He nodded reluctantly and motioned to a girl standing nearby. The girl proceeded to lead them to a table in a private room towards the back of the crowded restaurant.

The room was empty except for a flurry of waiters rearranging the table and settings to accommodate the group they hadn't expected. The girl who had seated them took their drink orders and disappeared.

The guys began to relax somewhat and the table buzzed with hushed conversation. Lenny sipped her water and sat perfectly still, staring at the center of the table in deep thought. This was never part of the plan.

She hadn't *just* come from a family of athletes like she had told Luke. Both her father and mother were Olympic gold medalists, so was her brother Nathan. They were also incredibly wealthy, owning several high-end restaurants and resorts all around the world. Including the one they were in. Brushing shoulders with the upper class of America had been part of her upbringing. It's one of the reasons snowboarding had appealed to her, it was the opposite of everything that surrounded her. But she could do it. She could put on the clothes and walk in the shoes and say all the words, but it literally felt like every cell in her body was screaming to run away.

She focused on her breathing while she stared at the flickering candle in front of her. She felt eyes on her but didn't look up to see who they belonged to. Probably Luke. She could sense his concern from across the table. She hated that he was worried. She hated that it had to do with her. She had wanted to do this meeting privately but it wasn't feasible. Hopefully it would be over soon.

As three men approached the table wearing very expensive suits, Lenny sighed. She should have known that Patrick would call her father.

She stood up as he leaned in to kiss her cheek.

"Lenna," he addressed with a smile.

"Dad," Lenny acknowledged wearily, "I didn't know you would be here."

"Who are your friends?" Lenny's father asked politely.

The guys stood up to shake the man's hand as Lenny introduced them all by name.

"This is my father, Bruce Evans." She saw the realization dawn in each of their eyes as they greeted him and knew another piece of her anonymity was slipping away.

"*The* Bruce Evans?" Harrison asked excitedly. "Three gold medals and world record holder for the Men's 200m backstroke?"

"That's right," Bruce humbly smiled.

"It's an honor to meet you, sir." Harrison continued to gush, "I had no idea you were Lenny's father."

"Well, she looks more like her mother," Bruce's eyes crinkled on the sides as he smiled warmly at his daughter. Lenny's heart was stabbed with guilt at how wonderful he was treating her friends.

121

Lenny introduced the second man, who was easily a younger version of the first, "This is my brother, Scott."

Scott Evans stood a great deal taller than most of the men around the table. His athletic build fit nicely into his tailored suit. His dark brown hair was a contrast from Lenny's blonde, which he kept shaved nearly bald. He shook hands with everyone at the table and seated himself at the end. Lenny's lawyer, Patrick, sat on the corner next to Scott with Lenny to his left.

The rest of them took their seats with Lenny's father sitting at the head, so he could best converse with all present. Lenny avoided speaking with her father and her brother. Instead, she focused on the papers her lawyer had already presented to her. Bruce entertained her friends by regaling them with tales from his youth. They were completely star struck. Food and drink flowed easily and Lenny was surprised at how effortlessly they got along with her father. They didn't exactly move in the same circles.

"Wait a second!" Harrison looked at Lenny, shocked, "You're Lenny 'Freebird' Evans?"

At Harrison's words, Lenny's mouth went dry. She took a drink of water and slowly put the glass back on the table, not really acknowledging Harrison's question.

"No way," Sway looked at Lenny as if meeting her for the first time.

"I remember you!" Blake couldn't hide the awe in his voice, "You could really fly."

"I don't do that stuff anymore." It was all she could think to say, her ears turning red with heat. Her father allowed a lengthy pause before speaking again.

"So, you are the group of ruffians my one and only daughter decided to run off with?" Bruce's tone was serious but his eyes sparkled with mischief.

"Maybe you can convince her to come home," Scott spoke up from his end of the table.

"We're in the middle of a tour, Scott. I have responsibilities," Lenny spoke to him sharply.

"Yes, you do," he leveled at her. She grimaced; she had walked right into that one. "Speaking of," he gestured to Patrick, her lawyer, sitting next to her.

The well-dressed attorney picked up on his cue and explained to Lenny flatly, "You're in breach of contract with your sponsors. They are threatening to begin litigation."

Lenny's shoulders stiffened, "Can't you just settle and give them some money?"

"If they proceed, they'll try to clean you out."

"I don't care about the money," Lenny stated forcefully.

"Honey," her father addressed, and Lenny turned to him for the first time since they'd sat down. His face was filled with compassion for her and her heart stalled in her chest, "They'll take the Lodge."

"They can't do that!" She was combative. "That's my home!" Her voice cracked slightly. "That's Duke's home..."

Her hands started to shake and she gripped her napkin under the table. She looked to Scott for an explanation.

Scott softened his expression, "Why do you think I've been trying to get a hold of you?"

Lenny stared hard into Scott's eyes, looking for some sign that this wasn't as bad as her gut was telling her it was. Honesty looked back. Her attempts to avoid having to deal with her mistakes had created a much bigger problem than she had anticipated.

She let her shoulders drop, defeated. That was her one weak spot. The Lodge wasn't just her home. It was Duke's home too. She could always move on and buy a new house, but Duke had nowhere to go.

Always the renegade, Duke refused to live in the public eye. Rumors swirled of him being too mentally deficient to understand what it meant to be paid for snowboarding. He denied sponsorship and remained relatively untamed, a mountain boy to the core. As such, he couldn't make a decent enough living to buy his own place and continue doing what he loved most. Big mountain riding.

Lenny had purchased the Lodge years ago when the money had started rolling in. It was a massive estate-like cabin in the mountains of Wyoming with five bedrooms, six bathrooms, multiple living areas and lounges. She had bought it with the intent of her and her friends being able to live there and snowboard the mountains right out the back door. Duke had been such an influential mentor to her, she made a deal with him. He could live there for free, forever, as long as he maintained the property. If she lost the Lodge, Duke would be homeless. And it would be her fault. She couldn't do that, Duke had done too much for her. He meant too much to her.

"What do I have to do?" She asked, quietly submissive.

"Just make a few appearances until your contract runs out. You know, smile, wave and take pictures." Patrick explained it all so simply. He had no idea how hard those things were actually going to be for her. "The Winter X-Games is the next one, it's in January. Can I confirm to your sponsors that you'll be there?"

"That's during break, Lenny, it's completely fine," Carl tried to comfort her, misunderstanding the duress on face.

"Yes, I'll be there," she said, refusing to meet anyone's eyes. She was humiliated that this had to happen so publicly for her. But this is how she had set herself up so she really shouldn't be surprised.

"We'll all be there," Luke interjected earnestly.

Lenny's head jerked up at his words. She tried to read his expression but was too distracted by her own messy thoughts to make sense of anything.

"Yeah, we'll be your assistants for a change," Mike said with a sly smile, backing up Luke like always.

"Just let me know how many will be in your party and I'll get rooms reserved at The Inn," Patrick said, diligently on duty.

Lenny realized everyone was staring at her and she needed to snap out of her funk or there would be more questions. Questions she didn't have answers for yet. She couldn't start thinking about Aspen and who else would be there. She would have to deal with that later. Alone.

She forced a smile and set about trying to make the meal more pleasant. She discussed business with Scott, told some stories of what life had been like so far on the road and reminisced with her father. As the evening progressed, more of Lenny's life came into detail and was suddenly up for discussion.

"So, let me get this straight," Carl was really having a hard time believing that the Lenny, who had worked for him ardently for the past couple of months, had ditched on her own manager and brother, Scott. "You just left town? You were supposed to be in a meeting and you just...got on a plane?"

"Pretty much," Lenny laughed a little at Carl's incredulous look.

"What's the big deal, Carl? So she got on a plane," Harrison was attempting to defend Lenny by making it seem like her actions were insignificant, "It's not like she took the talent bungee jumping or something."

Carl blinked and did a double-take at Harrison, "Why...why would you say that?"

Harrison shrugged, "I've had a lot of wine."

Carl started to ask Harrison more but Blake interrupted, "I think what Harrison is saying is that, Lenny's still a responsible person. She just needed a change of scenery." Blake looked to Lenny for approval, "And it worked out great for us; we ended up with the best assistant in the world."

"You guys went bungee jumping without me?" Luke was catching on quicker than Carl but not as fast as he should have.

Lenny covered her mouth with her hand to block her smile. She wondered how many secrets were going to all spill out tonight. Subtly wasn't really in the rock star repertoire.

As they all stood on the sidewalk outside of the restaurant saying goodnight, Lenny's father held her in a tight embrace.

He kissed her forehead and looked at her lovingly, "You have always made me proud."

Lenny fought the lump rising in her throat at his affectionate display. Bruce Evans had never had a problem showing his daughter how much he cared about her, not even in public.

"Be good and call your mother," he hugged her a final time before getting into his waiting town car.

Scott wrapped his strong arms around his sister and gave her a tight hug, "You need to give Duke a call, too. He worries."

"No, he doesn't," Lenny scoffed.

"Yes, he does…and try to come home for Christmas. We miss you, too." Scott hugged her again before getting in the car with their father.

Mike put his arm around Lenny and pulled her towards the hotel, "Feel better, darlin'?"

Lenny only nodded. She really did. She wasn't exactly looking forward to bringing them to the X-Games, she still had a lot of thoughts and issues to work through before they got there. But as she looked at her unconventional surrogate family she felt better knowing she wasn't going alone.

Hopefully she'd find the strength to face her demons before then.

Chapter 9

Beautiful Disaster

Luke stood outside Lenny's room, his hand poised to knock. He just wanted to see her. She had looked great at dinner. Beautiful, but...sad. He felt the pull to her from the lobby and didn't resist it. He knew she would be alone. He knew she needed him.

He knew this could all blow up in his face.

He looked down at the guitar case in his hand and blew all the air out of his lungs as he knocked on the door. They finally had a break from the long, dragging hours on the bus and all he wanted was to be in the same room with her. Since Ashton had shown up, he'd felt like he'd hardly seen Lenny. He missed her.

"Hey," Luke didn't have more than that for a greeting. Lenny leaned against the door frame before smiling and standing aside to signal his entrance. She had changed out of her dress and her face was washed clean of makeup. Hair piled loosely on top of her head, she was in sweatpants and a white tank with a band hoodie half-zipped over the top. She was breathtaking.

"Didn't you go with the guys?" She asked as she closed the door behind him and then crossed the room and folded herself into an overstuffed navy chair.

"No, I wanted to see you." He sat opposite her on the couch and tried to look as relaxed as possible, placing the guitar case down on the floor next to him.

Lenny was more subdued that usual. She sat quietly, not responding to his statement. Her pensive gaze was fixed on the sleeves of her jacket and her vulnerability was conspicuous.

"Big night." Luke hated how his voice sounded harsh in the quiet of the suite.

"Yeah," Lenny gave him a small smile and he saw that her attention had left her shirt sleeves and she was now watching him quietly. Her countenance hinting at the softness he knew lay inside her, buried deep for safekeeping.

"So, what happens with Ashton now?" He asked, not wanting to talk about his ex but needing somewhere to start.

"She'll have to pay me some money and she'll probably stay away

127

for a while." Lenny answered with a half-smile on her face. Luke adored her half-smile.

"What about this thing with your sponsors? How you feeling about that?" Luke didn't miss the flicker of fear flash across her face; it was very uncharacteristic of her.

"Um," she looked back to her lap, "it'll be weird, but I can't lose the Lodge. So..." Her voice trailed off and Luke didn't miss the fact that she wouldn't look at him when she answered.

"Your brother is a beast." Luke tried to bring the conversation somewhere lighter. He needed her to be comfortable if he was going to go through with his original intention of seeing her.

"Yeah, he has that effect on people," Lenny laughed a little then and eased back in her chair.

"And your dad seems pretty cool, too," Luke added, trying to get a decent conversation flowing. He'd never been good with small talk.

"I probably give my family a harder time than they deserve." Her demeanor was shifting, ever so slightly back to confidence. The strange awkwardness that had been present a moment ago was dissipating and Luke internally high-fived himself.

"I'm sorry I'm so weird about the snowboarding thing," Lenny suddenly blurted out. "I haven't dealt with it very well, or at all, actually." She looked up at him sheepishly, "I don't handle failure gracefully, if you hadn't noticed."

Luke chuckled and leaned forward resting his elbows on his knees, "You think *we* deal well with failure? I'm pretty sure that's just part of being human."

He began to point to his fingers one at a time, "Let me give you some of my favorite examples of how well we dealt with the failure of our last tour. Mike: started his own carpet laying business after he was clean and then refused to speak to me. Sway: got married to a stripper in Vegas and divorced within the week, *twice.* Harrison: tried to become a carpenter with disastrous, and might I add expensive, results. Blake: tried his hand at the culinary arts but mostly he gained twenty-five pounds. It wasn't pretty."

Lenny snickered at his examples, "What about you?" she asked, "What did you do?"

"You've met my ex, right? Tall, brown hair, answers to Satan?" Luke rolled his eyes at himself, "Yeah, I bought her a house."

"Whoa! I didn't know that! No wonder she had a hard time moving on, you were her sugar daddy." Lenny teased, trying to stifle her laughter.

"As you can see, you don't have anything to be embarrassed about," Luke reassured her.

"Did you love her?" Lenny asked, unexpectedly serious.

128

Luke was taken aback, he had never thought about it. He shook his head, "No, I just hated being alone and she was hot. Not my proudest moment." He paused as he thought about it, "I didn't even like her back then. I think I bought her the house because I was hoping she would stay there, and away from me.

"What about you?" He turned the question around, "Have you ever dated someone you couldn't stand?"

A mixture of confusion and hurt swept across her face and Luke knew he'd touched a nerve. Her brows drew together and she licked her lips before answering.

"I really only ever had one boyfriend. I liked him a lot." Her voice grew quiet, "I never got to know him enough to find out if I could love him."

"What happened?" Luke tried to sound mellow. But he wasn't. The idea of another man in Lenny's life had him feeling on edge instantaneously.

"We broke up after the accident." Lenny was being dodgy and he could tell there was more she wasn't saying.

"That was kind of a dick move." Luke defended her. How could someone let a girl like this get away? Whoever it was, was an idiot.

"It wasn't...I'm the one who ended it. I broke up with him," her voice was strained and she was avoiding his eyes again.

"He should've fought for you," Luke argued. Her words weren't matching her demeanor and Luke was suddenly very angry at the guy who had obviously put a fracture in her heart.

"That's not really..." Lenny shook her head and closed her eyes, "It wasn't meant to be, that's all."

After an uncomfortable pause Luke spoke again, needing to drive his point home. "I would've fought for you."

When Lenny looked at him, his heart about stopped in his chest. Her eyes were watery and her lips were parted, as if to say something into the silence. But nothing came. Her eyes sought an explanation, one she couldn't outright ask and Luke knew this was the moment.

Very few times in Luke's life did he know exactly what step he was supposed to take. He usually guessed wrong and had to go back and try again. His past was filled with apologies, misunderstandings and broken fences that no one could mend. Not this time. Not with this moment.

He unpacked his guitar and set it on his lap, his hands beginning to tremble. He grit his teeth. He needed to do this. It would be worse not to. He ached to hold her, to kiss her, to make her feel what he felt. He needed to have some sort of absolution to the dance they were in. He couldn't possibly be the only one feeling overpowered by his own heartbeat.

"Lenny, I haven't done the best job at showing you or telling you what you mean to me," he cleared his throat, "But I communicate better through music so..." He took a cleansing breath before he brought the pick to meet the strings in his chosen method of confession.

"You're not pushing but I'm falling
you're soaring and I'm stalling
and it's not a secret
that my strength is your weakness

the beauty you have inside
shines out through your eyes
you wear your heart on your sleeve
your wings flutter and you leave

and when you fly
can I be your blue sky
when your heart beats alone
let my arms be your home
if I say it first
will you say it second
if I give you this verse
will you feel protected

I need you
could you need me too..."

He waited for what felt like too many breaths before he sought her eyes. Did she understand the enormity of what his soul had admitted? Did she know that this wasn't some elaborate attempt to get in her pants but that he meant every freaking word?

"I do need you." Her voice came out rough and Luke stared at her mouth, wanting her to say it again. She licked her bottom lip and took a shaky breath.

For the all the daydreaming that Luke had done about her and exactly how he would kiss her for the first time, he was suddenly very nervous. The first kiss with her could very well be the most important of his life.

Luke put the guitar down and crossed the small space between them. He pulled Lenny to her feet and grabbed her around her waist with one arm, pressing her against him. With his other hand he cupped her neck and angled her face upwards. He looked from her eyes to her lips, hesitating for a fraction of a second. She didn't pull away. She didn't protest. His mouth came down against hers, feeling the firm softness of her lips as they returned his kiss. He thought that the taste of her would finally quench his desire, but it only fed his hunger for more.

He had planned on kissing her slowly, taking his time, making it last. But when the moment came, he lost control. He lost himself in her.

He felt her hands fist into his t-shirt, pulling him closer. His heart raced as he realized his eagerness was being reciprocated. The intensity of their kiss grew as their weeks of self-restraint were suddenly released in that one moment. Her hands worked their way into his hair and Luke let out a groan.

They were yanked back into reality by the sudden knock at the door. They jumped apart as if they'd been shocked.

Luke took a deep breath to steady himself. Lenny straightened her clothes and made her way to the door, checking the peep hole. She took one more calming breath before opening it.

"There you are," Carl smiled at Luke, "The guys wanna know if you want to join us for a game of poker in Blake's room?" He looked back and forth between Lenny and Luke, frowning. "You guys weren't fighting, were you?" He asked, misreading the tension.

Lenny smiled, "No, just talking. I'm actually pretty tired so I'm going to get some sleep. But you should go, Luke, win some money back from Blake."

Luke tried to read her face but she was as unreadable as ever. He nodded as he thought about it, "Yeah, I'll be right down."

"Great!" Carl turned to leave, "See you in a bit. Goodnight, Lenny."

"Goodnight, Carl."

The door closed and Lenny and Luke stared at each other in silence. Everything between them had changed in the span a few breaths.

"I don't want to go." Luke finally said, his soul screaming at him to say more.

"I know, but you have to," she whispered.

Her cheeks were still pink from their momentary passionate embrace. She looked at him with clear eyes and Luke knew she wasn't asking him to leave because she didn't want this. It was because she wanted it as badly as he did.

Luke charged across the room and crushed her to him. His hands started on her hips, making their way up to her hair as he kissed her desperately. She responded strongly, wanting him just as badly.

He stepped back, breathless, her kiss making him dizzy. He held her face in his palm and touched her lips with his thumb. "This is far from over," he whispered roughly.

He left reluctantly, looking at Lenny one last time before closing the door. As he walked down the hall and to the elevators he tried to calm down. He had kissed lots of girls, more than he could count. But no one had knocked the wind out of him. No one made him feel like the earth had been slightly knocked off it's axis.

He smiled to himself as the lift opened and he stepped inside.

She had kissed him back.

***

Luke stared at the ceiling. He had lost every hand in the poker game. He didn't care. He kept thinking about Lenny, alone in her room. He wanted to go to her, keep her company. Hold her. Kiss her. Explain the things that remained unexplainable without her around.

"I kissed Lenny." He said out loud to the ceiling.

Mike was lying in the next bed and he propped himself up on his elbow and looked at Luke in the dark. "Whaaat?" He sounded like he was laughing but Luke couldn't see his face.

"When?" Mike asked.

"Tonight. Before the game."

Mike was definitely laughing. "Where?"

"On the mouth."

Mike really laughed then, "No, dude, where were you when you kissed her?"

"Oh, in her room."

Mike waited for more information then asked, "Was it awesome?"

"Yeah."

Mike laid back down and chuckled again. "It's about freakin' time, that's all I have to say."

Luke smiled broadly.

"It also explains that stupid grin you had on your face the whole night."

"I lost a lot of money to Blake."

Mike guffawed.

"Is it wrong? Am I screwing up all our lives?"

"Don't be ridiculous," Mike chided. "You two make the most sense of anything ever."

"You really think so?" Luke felt his nerves settle into a bundle in the pit of his stomach.

"Oh yeah." Mike said confidently. "She's your song."

"What do you mean?"

"Every good lyric, melody or riff is Lenny in a package. Anyone can see it. You look at her and you just know...she's the one you've been singing about all this time. You just didn't know it."

132

Luke felt his mouth tug up on the side in a smile. That's exactly why he told Mike stuff like this. For answers like that.

"Mike, don't tell the others yet."

"You know me; I always got your six, brother."

Luke sighed contentedly. He knew they were moving in the right direction finally but he didn't want to go too fast and scare her away. This was a whole new ballgame.

***

Lenny was all smiles when she woke the next morning. She had slept better last night than she had in years. She took a shower and dressed in jeans and a white t-shirt with the black band hoodie. She literally skipped to Carl with his coffee.

"You're awfully spunky today," he eyed her suspiciously.

"The healing power of sleeping in a real bed," Lenny joked. "Well, that and finally having all those secrets come out last night lifted a weight off me."

Carl nodded, "That's why honesty is always the best policy."

A wave of guilt washed over Lenny and she changed the subject quickly.

"I better get the buses put back in order before we leave tomorrow." She was already hurrying off before Carl could ask any more questions. She had promised him that nothing would happen with any of the band members and something had definitely happened.

She had a lot to do, moving Blake, Sway and Harrison's things back to the Red Bus, changing the sheets in the Blue Bus and restocking food.

She was just finishing up in the Blue Bus when Luke appeared. They had eye contact and Lenny couldn't hide her excitement to see him. He grinned and rushed to her, kissing her face and lips passionately.

He looked over his shoulder to see if anyone was coming. Satisfied they were alone for the time being, he let his fingers linger in her hair as he kissed her again and again.

"I missed these lips," he whispered between kisses.

"We have to keep this quiet, Luke." Lenny pulled away from his kisses and gave him a serious look. "If Carl finds out, he'll fire me so fast."

He gave her a lopsided grin, "Hey, I totally got this."

She rolled her eyes and he planted one more kiss on her lips before he really had to go. Someone would get suspicious if they weren't careful.

He walked to the door, turned and let his eyes rove over her face, unapologetic. He tapped the door frame with his fingertips like he had something important to say.

133

Instead, he gave her a wink, "I'll see you later." And he ducked out the door.

Lenny grinned, she felt like a teenager. She knew she was behaving ridiculously but it was hard to stop. For the first time in a long time, she felt like she could breathe again.

***

Cody bullied her way into the arena using a combination of flirting and threats. It always seemed a touch harder to get what she wanted than she thought it should be. *You catch more flies with honey.* Her grandfather's words echoed in her head and she rolled her eyes at the memory. Foolish old man.

She spotted Lenny immediately despite the security giants trying to block her way. Her hair was longer and not in that god-awful braid she had insisted on wearing since...well, since then.

"Lenny Effing Freebird Evans!" Cody shouted at the top of her lungs, ignoring security as they tried to muscle her back out the door. Her voice echoed through the open space and she smirked with satisfaction when she saw that brilliant head of golden hair whip around in her direction.

Lenny nodded to security and they let Cody through. She sauntered to the stage, taking careful note of Lenny's posture and body language. Cody wasn't sure if Lenny was happy to see her or not. She'd been pretty guarded since the wreck and even more reserved in the months leading up to her unexpected departure with a rock band.

"What the hell? You're in town and you weren't gonna call me?" Cody smiled widely and ignored the fact that Lenny didn't smile in return.

"Scott called you?" Lenny asked instead, slipping her hands into her back pockets and walking to the edge of the stage.

This would be easier than Cody thought. The only reason she was here was to keep up appearances anyway. What kind of a best friend would she be if she didn't at least feign interest in Lenny's life? Besides, if she thought Scott was her source then maybe that meant she was thinking about coming back.

"Damn, girl. When you want to disappear, you do it in style." Cody didn't answer her question, the same as Lenny had done to her. She would play every game Lenny wanted to. She would just do it better.

Cody hopped on the stage and hugged her oldest friend. Their relationship had always been complicated, but Cody had never found anyone who could truly replace Lenny. She was one of a kind. Perfect Lenny, with her perfect hair and her perfect teeth and her perfect life. She was so...perfect.

Mike watched Lenny talking to her friend from his usual place behind the drums. Was it just him or did Lenny look a little stiff? He shifted on his stool and saw Sway texting out of the corner of his eye.

"Who you talking to?" He asked. It wasn't any of his business and normally he could care less who Sway was talking to, but Mike was feeling curious today.

"A girl," Sway mumbled. "You don't know her."

Mike frowned. Sway didn't give his number out to girls. Weird.

"She a friend?" Mike was actually pushing. He seriously didn't even want to know, he didn't know why he was asking.

"Yeah, dude, she's a friend. Why do you care?" Sway looked up in exasperation.

"I don't," Mike rubbed his hand down his face and turned away.

"Whatever, man. I really wish you'd get over it."

Mike glared at Sway whose head was bent back to his phone. He wanted to yell at him, curse him, tell him to shut up but he couldn't. Sway was right, Mike was acting paranoid. Again. Private conversations always set him on edge.

He knew being on the road would make him jumpy after a while. The stress and the travel and all the crap that somehow goes along with it. Having Luke around helped. A lot. But being alone still sucked. And now that Luke and Lenny had finally kissed...kind of solidified his forsaken nature once again.

Why *did* he care who Sway was talking to? Because he knew who he was hoping it was... But it wasn't. And it never would be again.

Mike looked up to see Lenny approaching with her friend. He really didn't feel like meeting new people today but Lenny meant a lot to him so he'd attempt his best behavior. *Fake it till you make it, right?*

"This is my friend, Cody." Lenny introduced with a tight smile.

Mike shook the girl's hand and ignored the once over he received. He wasn't interested. She seemed nice enough and being Lenny's friend, she probably was. Mike just wasn't that guy.

Sway was overt in his praise of the new girl and Mike found himself backing away from the group ever so subtly. Lenny caught his eye and they exchanged what he could only describe as a painful look. She didn't want Cody there either. And she needed an ally. Mike sighed inwardly; he could be that for Lenny. It might give him something to focus on besides the turmoil.

"I'll stick around." Cody was nodding her head. "Someone's got to fill you in on this chick," she elbowed Lenny in the ribs. "I bet she hasn't told you any of the good stuff."

Mike wondered where the hell Lenny had connected up with this girl. She was like the night to Lenny's day. And Lenny looked like she was going to lose her lunch. He looked around at the rest of the guys, why didn't they see whatever it was he was picking up on? Why did stuff like this always fall on him to fix?

***

"So what's the deal with you and the guys? Have you hooked up with any of them?" Cody was trying to get Lenny to open up a bit more. She was being particularly cagey. Even for Lenny. They had covered the Ashton mess, Lenny coming to Aspen and life on the road. All that was left was Lenny's love life.

"Cody!" Lenny exclaimed, looking around the sound booth nervously. "No! I work for them and they're my friends."

"C'mon, Luke Casey has a bangin' bod. Totally doable." She saw Greg look over his shoulder at her and she winked.

"Please stop." Lenny was blushing uncontrollably at this point and Cody realized that nothing in that department had changed. Good to know.

"Frickin' virgin," Cody smirked. "You have got to loosen up, babe." She took out her phone and tapped out a short text to Shane. For a guy who claimed he didn't care if Lenny had moved on, he definitely needed a lot of reassurance.

"Can we not talk about that?" Lenny pinched the bridge of her nose and Cody wondered if maybe she *was* taking it too far. The headaches hadn't been an issue until after the accident but Cody always seemed to be trigger. Or maybe it was talk about sex in general that made Lenny's head hurt.

"Sure." Cody sighed. "When are you coming home?" It was the question of the year. When would Lenny return to the mountain and claim it as her own again? Cody found it hard to believe that Lenny could give it up altogether, not when she had so easily dominated.

"Maybe for Christmas." Lenny replied, relaxing again at the subject change.

"I saw Duke last week, he misses you." Cody swallowed the gag that wanted to surface. Those two had always had a much closer relationship than she cared for. She still didn't know why Duke had decided to mentor Lenny over his own niece but whatever. Cody didn't need anyone's help anyway. She'd proved that by winning the gold medal, hadn't she?

The lights dropped and the show started and Cody felt relieved that the 'catching-up' was over for the most part. Being with Lenny was exhausting. Trying to anticipate what may or may not upset her got old quick. Cody wished they could go back to being kids, when things weren't so complex.

She would stick around after the show for a bit and fish for information. If Lenny had remembered anything surrounding the circumstances of the accident, it was sure to be obvious during a session of sentimental reminiscing. And she really wanted to know if Lenny was considering a comeback anytime soon.

***

Lenny was doubled over in laughter. She couldn't breathe at all and sat down on the floor to try to catch her breath. But Cody wasn't going to let her off that easy. She kept going with her story, even as Lenny tried to wave a 'time-out' at her with her hands.

"So, Lenny, brilliant as she is, decides we need something edgy to do for the talent show. I went along with it because, well, let's face it, she's amazing and I trusted her."

Lenny was wiping away her tears as Cody brought back some of her best memories. Pre-accident memories.

"She convinces me that we should sing and dance to Salt N Pepa's 'Shoop.'" She paused as the room exploded in laughter, then continued. "No, seriously. We practiced for weeks, learning all the words and the dance routine. We were so proud of ourselves." She smiled at Lenny. "Keep in mind, this was a private school that our parents paid thousands of dollars a year for us to attend."

"What happened?" Harrison asked, wide-eyed.

"We got kicked out." Cody said flatly. "We didn't even make it through the first chorus and Mrs. K shut off the power."

Lenny was finally catching her breath when Cody dove right in to another story from her past that she hadn't thought about in a long time. Maybe she shouldn't have dreaded seeing her friend after all. This could work.

***

The guys had a lot of questions and Cody was more than happy to give detailed answers. She wasn't even a tiny bit surprised that there were five dudes drooling all over Lenny. It was typical. Lenny always had to have all the boys to herself.

137

"What about the nickname 'Freebird'?" Blake nodded a question at Cody. "Where did that come from?"

"You haven't told them anything, have you?" Cody accused Lenny playfully.

Lenny shook her head but kept smiling. Another thing that hadn't changed from the accident, Lenny didn't talk about snowboarding. And the fake humility was a nice touch.

"Um, let me think, when did that start?" She looked up at the ceiling as if trying to remember. "We were in high school, Lenny was starting to gain some attention for her talent on the mountain." She sat next to her friend on the floor and leaned her back against the wall. "Lenny was always taking off to go test the powder in remote areas of the world. The boys at school loved her and were always trying to get with her." Lenny shook her head to disagree, embarrassment starting to color her neck. "Yes, Sweetie, you've always been hot." Cody dismissed her silent argument and sighed, "But Lenny couldn't be tamed, just like the song. I think the first time it was used publicly though it was Shane Brookings, was it not?" She looked to Lenny for verification. Lenny bit the inside of her cheek and shrugged. Cody chose her next words carefully.

"Yeah, it was. Shane was doing an interview with ESPN and they asked who he thought had the most potential in the young crowd that was staring to blaze their trail on the mountain. And he said, 'Lenny Freebird Evans, that girl can fly.'"

"That's a pretty hefty endorsement. Isn't that guy like, the best?" Mike asked. Cody narrowed her eyes at him. He had been paying way to close attention and she didn't trust him.

She forced a laugh in response, "Yeah, he basically rules the effing sport."

Lenny was quiet; she was still smiling but had calmed down considerably. Cody watched heedfully, looking for any telltale signs of grief, heartache, regret, etc. But Lenny was an oak.

"And it stuck; announcers and commentators started talking about this amazing new talent and they hardly used her first name anymore."

"Why did you say publicly? Was it used before that?" Luke asked.

Cody calculated his question. She knew men and she knew them well. And it was more than obvious to her that Luke not only wanted Lenny but he also wanted to protect her. *How in the hell does she always make that happen? Hottest guy in the room and he's her frickin' lap dog.*

"I started calling her that in high school every time she turned down another poor boy that had fallen desperately in love with her. I had mentioned it to Shane the first time we met him. Remember that?" She elbowed Lenny. "He kept trying to flirt with Lenny but she wasn't having it.

So I explained that she was a free bird and she wasn't gonna be caged." She smiled at Lenny with mischief. "Shane liked it so much he got a tattoo of it on his bicep."

Luke might as well know the truth. If he's going to be her whipping boy he should know he's not the only one.

"Whoa! Some dude got your name tattooed on his arm for you?" Sway gaped.

"No, it wasn't my name, it was a nickname and also a famous song. It really had nothing to do with me." Lenny's expression was nonchalant and she waved it off. Cody pursed her lips before changing the subject.

The seeds had been planted, the rest was their fault.

"Remember that time Duke got stuck in the tree?" Cody asked Lenny whose eyes widened at the memory.

"Yes! I still can't believe he did that." She said, shaking her head.

"What happened?" Harrison egged on.

"Okay, Duke, my crazy uncle who taught Lenny everything she knows, he prefers to find his own line."

"What's a line?" Sway was confused.

"The line is the track you take down the snow to get to the bottom." Lenny explained.

"Anyway," Cody continued. "We had gotten way up in to the backwoods area that is seldom run and decided to be a little more risky with our chutes." Cody's eyes sparkled with humor at the memory. "The rule has always been: if you can see the bottom, follow Duke's line; if you can't see the bottom, do not follow Duke."

Lenny started to giggle again but tried to keep it quiet so that Cody could finish telling the best part.

"Duke took this wild line down the hill and instead of following the open area where he could clearly see what was coming; he veered to the left and went over this small ridge. Well, he thought it was small." Cody paused to let Lenny laugh heartily, everyone's eyes were wide in anticipation. "Turns out, it was this huge cliff that dropped into nothingness and he ended up in a tree."

"It was really fortunate that tree was there," Lenny pointed out. "He could've gotten really hurt, otherwise."

"Who? Duke?" Cody rolled her eyes, "That guy is invincible; he'll out live us all." She turned to Lenny, "You should really call him. Seriously, Lenny," Cody let out her aggravation. "No one loves you more, not even your own parents. The least you could do is give him a call and tell him you're okay."

"Fine, I'll call him." Lenny conceded with frustration in her voice. "You're right, he deserves better."

Cody put her arm around Lenny's neck and hugged her close. "Thank you. It'll be good for you, too, ya know." And now they all knew that Lenny abandoned those closest to her. *Zing.*

They continued to visit for another hour and then Cody leaned over and kissed the top of Lenny's head. "I have to go, Bird. I have an early morning appointment." She stood up and Lenny joined her.

"Hey, call me if you need anything." Cody looked into Lenny's face with a serious expression. "I'll see you in Aspen." Cody paused. "Or maybe at the Lodge if you decide to go home for Christmas."

Lenny nodded but didn't speak. Cody left feeling satisfied with her visit. They were obviously still friends which meant that the memory lapse around the accident was still intact. Shane always worried for no reason. Now if Cody could just convince Lenny to come back to competing, maybe she could find out once and for all who was actually the best.

***

The next few days all sort of blurred together for Luke. They had a show every night so they were pretty much on the bus nonstop. Anytime he and Lenny had a free moment they would make out like high schoolers. In the back of the bus, behind the bleachers, in the dark behind the venue. And every night, he would sing his song to her, hoping she would fall for him just a little bit more.

The weirdness from Cody's visit had passed but it had taken a few days. Luke had noticed Lenny's distance but didn't confront it. He wouldn't even have known where to start. He and Mike had had a conversation that left Luke feeling leery of Cody and unsure of how to address it. How do you tell someone that their best friend is a poison in their life? Besides, he was having too much fun with Lenny to want to spoil it.

The excitement of sneaking around was new for Luke. His past relationships had all been very public and nearly completely physical. Not this time. They talked about everything, all the time. The only one he had ever shared so much with was Mike. But Luke was still very aware of how gun-shy Lenny had been even recently. He wasn't going to push for anything more than what they had right now. He liked her and she liked him.

And the kissing was fantastic.

Luke was making his way to sound check, his standard grin plastered on his face from having just spent the most amazing three minutes with Lenny in the back lounge of the bus. He jumped when Ashton stepped out in front of him.

"Shit!" He said, startled, his smile gone. He stepped past her and

140

continued on.

Ashton looked annoyed at being blown off and ran to catch up to him.

"I need to talk to you, Luke." She tried to get his attention.

"No you don't, Ashton." Luke frowned straight ahead.

"I'm sorry for what I did to Lenny and I want to make it up to you." Luke kept marching forward without pause.

Ashton's voice was getting desperate as they neared the stage.

"I know that she's your friend and you're really mad at me but I want to make things better so we can go back to what we had." They had made it to the stage area and everyone was watching as Ashton nervously spit her words out. Her voice was getting shriller and she was starting to cause a scene. "We need to fix this, baby! You're just not your best self without me!"

Luke stopped in his tracks and turned his scowl on her. "I'm going to be as clear with you as possible, Ashton." His voice was low and gravelly. "We," he pointed to her and himself. "No longer exist. That ended a long time ago and never should've happened in the first place."

"We had a fight, Luke! That's what couples do, but we can still make it work."

"No, Ashton! We are not a couple." Luke's voice was growing in volume.

"But, baby-!"

"You have to listen to me! I don't *like* you!" Luke's voice was sharp.

The arena went dead quiet and Luke felt all eyes on the commotion at center stage.

Ashton wasn't giving up that easy. She tried to reach for Luke's hand but he stepped back, away from her.

"I know you still have feelings for me!" Ashton shouted, she was forcing the issue. In the past, when Ashton wanted her way she threatened to make a public spectacle, knowing it made Luke uncomfortable and he would give in to get her to shut up. "That song you sing for encore every night, I know that you're singing it to me!"

"Ashton, you wanna know the truth? Okay, here it is. I *never* had feelings for you. Never. I was lonely and you were *convenient*. I feel bad about that, I really do, but I'm a different person now. You're the *same* person. You're shallow, vapid and cruel. You're mean to me and my friends and your own employees. The song I sing every night is for someone who is the exact opposite of you. She's amazing and sweet and I'm crazy in love with her."

Ashton's mouth fell open. The guitar techs nodded their approval.

141

Ashton reached for Luke again and again he pulled away and shook his head at her. She turned in a huff and left the stage. The onlookers broke in to applause.

***

Lenny's stomach felt like she had gone over a hill. Her head was a little foggy, maybe she misheard. Maybe Luke hadn't actually just announced that he loved her to the entire band and crew. She took a breath and focused on trying to stop her hands from shaking. *Okay,* she thought reasonably, *he didn't actually say my name. No one else knows he's talking about me.* That only offered a few seconds of comfort because the next thought was *Luke just said he was in love with me.*

She decided to not overreact. She could handle this. Obviously, there was going to be a rational explanation and Luke would tell her later. She went about the rest of her night trying to behave as normally as possible.

Ashton's set was a blur, Double Blind Study was outstanding. Luke took his seat during the encore and sang his song to Lenny, the one he had written for her. He sounded almost desperate, urgent. She couldn't tell because she wasn't looking at him. She wanted to, it was just that the lights seemed particularly bright from her seat.

After the set finished, she headed back to the bus and turned on the TV, looking for anything to distract her and get her brain working properly again.

Mike and Luke entered the bus, joking and laughing, acting like everything was normal. Lenny did her best to participate in the conversation. She knew they were talking to her but she wasn't paying attention to what they were saying. She was answering mechanically. After an hour or so, Mike excused himself to bed and Lenny and Luke were alone.

He moved over to sit next to her on the couch and she stiffened. He gave her a gentle smile and reached over to hold her hand. She didn't pull away but she did flinch a little.

"Hey," Luke's voice was a soothing balm on Lenny's frayed nerves. "I only said that to get Ashton off my back."

Lenny let out her breath like a deflated balloon.

"I know." She lied, still trying to appear fine.

Luke chuckled, "No you didn't, you were totally freaked out."

She smiled then, "Was it that obvious?"

"Yes." Luke confirmed. "But don't worry, I'm not saying that yet."

"I don't know how I feel and-"

"Neither do I." Luke cut her off. "Really, it was just to make a point to Ashton." His eyes were pleading with Lenny to believe him.

142

She folded into his arms and he held her close. Weirdly, she felt better believing that he wasn't actually in love with her. She loved the feel of his strong embrace and smell of his aftershave as she leaned against him. The anxiety she had been feeling all night had completely disappeared in his arms. She didn't know what that meant, and she refused to try to define it or examine it.

***

Luke and Lenny spent every spare moment together. They joked around with the familiarity of old friends and when no one else was around, they were kissing. Lenny started to go through Chap Stick a lot faster and it made her smile to know she had a secret reason for that. What she wasn't thinking about was all the things she was putting off. She used her secret 'fling' with Luke as an excuse to not fulfill her promise to Cody to call Duke. She didn't want to have that conversation.

They had wrapped up the last show on this leg of the tour and the bus got stuck in a snowstorm on its way back to Chicago. They had made it to a truck stop but the drivers announced that it would be too dangerous to continue, they would have to wait for the roads to clear. It was fortunate that it happened that way and they didn't have to cancel or postpone any shows.

The band members gathered in the Blue Bus and were playing various games and having a few laughs. They toasted to a successful tour, they toasted to no one killing Ashton and they toasted to the promise of a successful overseas tour after the break.

"Are you coming with us?" Blake asked Lenny in regards to the overseas tour starting at the end of January.

"I don't see why not." Lenny raised her eyebrows, "Unless you don't want me around anymore?"

"No, we voted last night. It was unanimous, you have to come with us." Harrison said from the back of the bus, joining them.

Lenny nodded, knowingly. She smiled at the rag tag group of dudes who had become her family over the past couple of months. She couldn't picture *not* being with them.

"Are you going home for Christmas?" Sway asked.

"I think I should, yeah." Lenny admitted. It was strange how things had changed so much for her and how different she felt. When this tour had started she had expected to end up in a different town with a different life. But now she was thinking that maybe she should salvage the life she already had. If she still could.

"What about you guys, where do you go for the holidays?" Lenny asked.

"We'll all head home to Boston." Mike explained, "It's where our families live." He nodded fractionally at Luke who looked down and rubbed his brow line casually.

Lenny knew so much more was said between them in that moment than she would ever understand. What must it be like to not have a family to go home to? But to have a friend so close that you know you belong in their family events without the verbal invitation? Lenny's heart hurt at the thought of Luke being alone for the holidays. And she suddenly felt very selfish for having avoided her own for so long.

"Except Blake," Sway interrupted her thoughts, pulling her back to the conversation. "He goes home with Harrison."

Lenny frowned, waiting for the explanation.

"I'm not from Boston." Blake glared at Sway.

"Can we still come with you to the X-Games?" Harrison asked suddenly, changing the subject.

"Of course," Lenny said, a little confused by the question. "Wasn't that the plan?"

Harrison breathed a sigh of relief, "I was afraid you were going to change your mind. You can get pretty elusive when it comes to you *other* life."

Lenny chuckled, "That's true, I suppose."

She thought about it for a minute and realized that the guys would be totally out of their element in Aspen. They were used to being the rock stars, she wondered how they would fair being regular civilians. It was true, they would be recognized and some people would probably ask for autographs but she knew that there was a whole other reason for the crowds.

"It could get weird for you guys, you know." She thought she might try to prepare them.

"Oh, we know." Mike grinned. "The roles will have flipped: we'll be *your* assistants."

Lenny felt a tinge of apprehension. It must have showed on her face because Luke rested his hand reassuringly on her thigh. She looked at him and his expression quieted her mind instantaneously. She loved how just looking at him had such a powerful effect on her.

"You guys gonna be okay during break, being separated and all?" Sway addressed Lenny and Luke. The room laughed at their startled expressions.

"What do you mean?" Luke tried to play it off and be cool.

"Seriously?" Sway raised his eyebrows at where Luke's hand was resting familiarly on Lenny's thigh.

"Yeah, it's the worst kept secret around, guys." Blake prodded.

Lenny blushed and looked down.

"I don't know what you're talking about." Luke obviously knew he was caught but kept trying to signal the guys to drop it. "We're friends, what?"

"Yeah, okay." Sway said sarcastically, deliberately ignoring Luke's attempt to deflect the truth.

Luke looked to Mike for help but he shrugged.

"It's really okay, guys." Blake said. "We've known for a while."

"Known what for a while?" Luke continued to play dumb. Lenny smiled at how he was trying and she knew it was only to make her comfortable.

"Yes," Lenny finally said. "We are a little bit closer than just friends but we're not labeling it right now."

"Frickin' hipsters," Blake snorted. "Fine, I'll label it for you. Perfect for each other, there! Was that so frickin' hard?"

Lenny didn't know what to say after that. Luke smiled at his friends. Leave it to them to take something to a whole new level. He squeezed Lenny's leg and chuckled low in his chest.

"How long have you guys known?" Lenny asked them.

"Since Denver." Blake answered, surprising both Luke and Lenny.

"How?" Lenny was perplexed; she thought they had been careful.

"Well, it was kind of obvious. I mean, Lenny had needed a good kiss for a while. Why do you think I was always asking to make out?" Sway joked.

"Yeah, you were both suddenly *very* happy." Blake winked at Lenny.

Lenny shook her head and smiled. She was afraid they wouldn't approve but that wasn't the case at all. Carl might be a different story.

"So, you guys gonna see each other before Aspen?" Sway asked again. "The reason I'm asking is because it is gonna be weird not having you around for like, two weeks."

Lenny shrugged, "I guess we hadn't really talked about it." She looked at Luke who was beaming at her. "I talked to Scott the other day and I decided to stay at the Lodge with Duke and see if I can talk him into joining us for dinner on Christmas Day."

"Have you even talked to him yet?" Mike asked.

Lenny clenched her jaw slightly. "No. I was gonna surprise him." She tried to clear the emotion from her throat.

"What's the deal with you guys anyway?" Harrison asked. "I mean, I get he's like your Miyagi and all but why the avoidance?"

It was a legitimate question. One that Lenny didn't really have a legitimate answer for. Duke had been more than just a mentor. He was the only one who had truly supported her in ...everything. They had a similar spirit and drive, hating the social norm and rebelling against the standard. She never had to explain things to him, he already knew. Even when she decided to be more 'conventional' and pursued qualification in the Olympics, he supported her. But she knew he didn't agree. He thought her best lines were made in the back country, amidst the unpredictable elements.

She felt like she had let him down more than anyone. She became too cocky, ignored her instincts and that's what really caused her to lose control out of the chute. How was she supposed to talk to him now? What could she say?

"I guess I just wouldn't know what to say." Lenny's words sounded lame even to her. She looked at her hands in her lap and picked at a stray thread on her jeans.

"You want me to come with you?" Luke's voice was so sincere and full of concern that it made Lenny feel even worse about her actions.

"No, I think it would better if I see Duke alone at first. Besides, if he's mad, I don't really want to get yelled at in front of you guys." She smiled, indicating she was half-joking.

"You think he'll yell at you?" Blake questioned.

"Trust me, I deserve it." Lenny rolled her eyes, "So much you don't know." An idea came to her then, "Hey, you guys wanna come out for New Year's? We can chill at the Lodge for a couple days and then all fly to Aspen together."

***

They all exchanged glances, thinking similar thoughts. Lenny was so elusive about her past; she would never really talk about herself openly. Now suddenly, she's inviting them to her home in the backwoods of Wyoming for a major holiday. This was such a big step that they agreed without much thought.

Lenny relaxed against Luke's side then, leaning her head onto his shoulder. Luke squeezed her leg again and smiled faintly. The guys resumed their video game session and Luke let his thoughts wander. He was concerned about Lenny but couldn't explain it. He knew there were issues she still wasn't dealing with and he wasn't sure if she trusted him enough to let him help her through it. Being on the road had its advantages of keeping them separated from 'real life' and he knew how jarring a return to the norm could be. Especially for someone who was running away from their reality. He tried not to let his concern cloud his mind, but a fear was lurking he couldn't seem to shake completely.

***

146

Cody: *she's coming to Aspen*
Shane: *are you sure?*
Cody: *yes, don't be a baby about it*
Shane: *don't be a jealous bitch, Cody*
Cody: *you're such a dick*
 Shane: *at least I'm not fake*

Chapter 10

The Outsiders

Snow had started to fall as Lenny approached the Lodge. She was always amazed by its massive beauty, no matter how many times she had seen it. It was enormous, with a wooden and stone structure, perfectly nestled into the mountainside with an expansive view of the range from the back.

She hadn't planned on coming up until tomorrow, but after dinner with her parents and a disconcerting conversation with her father about Duke's whereabouts, she had felt a rush to check on him sooner rather than later. She knew she was worrying unreasonably. He was a grown man and had no trouble taking care of himself. But, then again, most of their relationship had been fairly irrational.

Lenny parked her old Bronco in the drive, not bothering with the garage door. She grabbed her duffel and started up the walkway. When she opened the front door, all the interior lights were off.

"Hello?" She called into the darkness. She reached for the switch on the wall by the door, flicking it on.

"Hello?" She called again, stomping the snow off her shoes and slipping them off before leaving the foyer.

"Duke?" She called into the living room, but received no answer. She traveled through the empty area and into a smaller den off to the side. She flicked the light switch, but the room was empty. She backtracked and went through an adjacent door leading to the kitchen. The floor to ceiling windows faced the west, and the sun was beginning to set, giving the illusion that the stainless steel appliances were made of pure gold. But it was also void of human presence.

Lenny touched his cellphone on the counter and picked up her pace across the granite floor and sprinted up the stairs leading to the bedroom area. She saw a light on in Duke's room at the end of the hall and she breathed a sigh of relief. *He's here.* She slowed to a walk, her socked feet silent on the wood floors as she came to the open doorway.

Duke was sitting with his back against the headboard, reading a book. His thick, dark hair matched his full beard, making him look older than he really was. Lenny smiled at his red flannel pajamas, a mountain man to a fault. He was wearing reading glasses and his lips moved just noticeably with the words as he read. Lenny leaned her body against the door frame, watching quietly.

A million different emotions began to toy with her heart and she felt its pace quicken the longer the silence continued. She hadn't been fair to him. Of all the people she had been trying to escape, Duke should have never been on that list.

"It's kinda early to get ready for bed, isn't it?" She finally asked into the stillness.

Duke didn't even look up. "Nope." He continued reading.

Lenny swallowed; she knew she deserved the cold shoulder. She slowly slid down the door frame and pressed her back against it, bringing her knees up to rest her arms on them.

"I'm sorry I didn't call, Duke." She said trying to keep the tremble out of her voice.

Duke turned the page in his book and kept reading. Lenny sighed and leaned her head back.

"I made up your bed for you." Duke broke the silence but still didn't look up.

Lenny felt a smile start at the corners of her mouth and her heart started to make the long climb from the floor back to its proper place in her chest. "How did you know I would be here?"

"The wind told me."

Lenny chuckled softly, "Scott told you I was coming, didn't he?" She shook her head as realization swept over her. "You weren't *missing*, you guys planned this."

"I have no idea what you are talking about." Duke kept his tone even and conversational.

"I was really worried about you, you know." Lenny tried to make him feel bad even though she knew he wouldn't. She didn't have a right to that anyway.

Duke finally closed the book and put it down on the nightstand, giving Lenny his full attention. She shifted uncomfortably from her seat on the floor. Maybe this is where she'd finally get lectured, she had it coming and she knew it.

***

"Did your mom send any of her chili with you?"

Lenny frowned, confused. "What? How did…no, what?"

Duke stood up and shuffled past her and down the hall. He turned to see if she was coming. She pushed herself to her feet and followed him

150

down the stairs and into the kitchen. Duke opened the fridge and started to pull out ingredients for a sandwich.

"Here, let me do that." Lenny took the packages of lunch meat out of his hands and gently shoved him out of the way. Duke made a satisfied grunting noise and meandered over to one of the stools against the counter facing Lenny.

As she sliced cheese and tomatoes, he watched her movements closely. Her hands were steady, they'd lost the tremble she had the last time he had seen her. She moved deftly around the kitchen, like she hadn't been away at all, remembering where each and every thing was kept. Her hair was loose and more than halfway down her back, very different from the tight braid she had insisted on after the wreck. Her cheeks were a healthy pink and she had put on some muscle, filling out the sunken places the accident had left her with two years ago.

Duke rested his elbow on the counter and put his bearded chin in his palm, rubbing his whiskers above his lips. Six months, that's how long it had been since he had last spoken with Lenny. Six months ago she ran off with rock stars and scared him nearly half to death. And now she was suddenly back, making him a sandwich in the kitchen in the home they had shared for five odd years.

"How long you staying this time?" He asked gruffly. He noticed she winced just a bit but she looked up at him and met his eyes.

"Through the New Year...then I have to go to Aspen...then on to Europe for the end of the tour." She placed the perfectly structured sandwich in front of him.

"What happens after Europe?" Duke sunk his teeth into the thick, wheat bread. It was perfection. He hadn't had a sandwich this good in a long time.

"I'm not really sure..." She came around the counter and sat on the stool next to him. He swiveled slightly so he was angled toward her.

Duke chewed thoughtfully for a few minutes. "When do I get to meet the guy?" He tried not to smile at Lenny's surprised expression.

"What?" Lenny blushed and she tried to fight the dopey grin that wanted to commandeer her face. "What guy? What are you talking about?"

"C'mon, Lenny, don't bullshit with me."

"How did you know there was a guy?" She narrowed her eyes at Duke.

"Don't insult my intelligence. Of course there's a guy. No other reason why you'd have that dumb grin on your face."

"How are you not mad at me?" Lenny frowned at him, perplexed.

"I was mad at first. But I got over it." Duke finished his sandwich and rubbed the crumbs out of his whiskers. "Don't change the subject, which

151

one was it? The drummer? The guitarist?" He studied her coy expression. "Nah…you're too flashy for that, you went for the lead singer, didn't ya?"

Lenny's eyes widened and she smacked his shoulder. "Flashy?"

Duke chuckled, "I knew it."

She shook her head, her hair falling over her face, hiding her expression. "We're still working out the kinks, it's all very new."

"What's his name?"

"Luke Casey." Lenny couldn't hide the grin as she said it and Duke chuckled.

"Geez, you got it bad." Duke shook his head in mock disappointment. "Is he coming for New Year's?"

"How do you already know everything?" Lenny exclaimed. "Seriously, are you spying on me?"

Duke chuckled again, "I told you, I know you better than anyone." He looked out the big windows and watched the sun slip completely behind the mountain line. "Well, I hope he's better than the last guy you brought home."

"Shane was nice." Lenny chastised seriously.

"He was an idiot. All caught up in the technical." Duke let out a tiny belch.

"You just didn't like his style." Lenny quietly defended.

"What style? The guy was afraid to even try fresh pow. Besides, who has more style than me?" Duke raised his eyebrows and pointed to his red flannel pajamas.

Lenny laughed, "You're right, no one compares to you."

"Damn straight." Duke gave a satisfied grunt.

He watched her as she gazed out across the last few flashes of orange sunlight shooting through the clouds. He willed her to soak in the calm climate of the the home they had created together. Could it be the refuge that they had planned so long ago? Could she finally feel safe again?

Her face had lost its pinch, her eyes were soft in the low light and she wasn't nearly as jumpy as she had been a few months prior. Duke felt a combination of elation and heaviness settle over him. She was better, but still not whole.

"Well," Duke stood up and scratched his belly. "I'm going to bed, I have a five am alarm set to get out there."

"You're not coming to the house for Christmas?" Lenny asked.

"Nah, you're the only gift I need." He reached over and messed up her hair. She pushed his hand away and pulled her head back, laughing. A full, hearty laugh, like when she was a kid.

Duke moved toward the stairs but turned around before ascending them.

"I'm glad you're back. Even if it is only for a little while." He said sincerely, wanting to say more but finding the timing all wrong.

Lenny smiled faintly, "I am too."

***

After Duke went to bed, Lenny went into the foyer and grabbed her duffel and headed upstairs to her third floor bedroom.

When she had first purchased the Lodge years ago it had come fully furnished, which had been a major appeal to her since she really didn't have the patience or eye for interior decorating. Her mother, on the other hand, had taken it upon herself to completely gut the furnishings and start fresh. She had said that Lenny's home should be a reflection of Lenny herself. Lenny had agreed mostly because she really didn't care, and also, she wasn't sure she'd be able to talk her mother out of it.

What had transpired that summer still amazed Lenny to this day. She was ever thankful that she had let her mother have free reign over the decorating process. Kelli Evans had simplified everything. Creating the perfect, comforting atmosphere that made Lenny feel at home despite the massive size of the estate. Every room was modest yet elegant, a symbol of Lenny's riding style. But out of all the rooms in the house, her bedroom was her favorite.

The entire third floor was a master suite. Floor to ceiling windows covered the westward facing wall with a majestic view of the Tetons. A King-size bed with heavy, down comforters that had always kept Lenny warm despite the subzero temperatures of a Wyoming winter was centered against the east wall. Her walk-in closet could have been another bedroom in and of itself and it was adjacent to her equal sized bathroom which boasted a shower and full-size bath tub. The walls were adorned with original paintings done by her grandmother when she had been a younger woman.

Lenny slung her duffel into the purple armchair facing the small gas fireplace and sighed. She didn't need to turn on any lights in the main room as she changed for bed due to the brilliance of the full moon coming through her windowed wall. She was looking forward to sleeping in her own bed again, and actually *sleeping*. The stress dreams and muscle aches had stayed largely absent since...well, since that first kiss.

Lenny touched her lips absentmindedly and smiled. Luke Casey's kisses had a powerful effect indeed. She snuggled under the heavy covers and checked her cellphone. One new text. She bit her lower lip as she opened the message.

Luke: *I miss you already. It's crazy since I just saw you a few hours*

153

ago. I hope this week goes fast. Merry Christmas, Lenny.

She tapped out her reply and placed the phone on the nightstand. Pulling the covers up to her chin she smiled into the starlit bedroom. Homecoming had never felt so sweet.

***

Duke slept restlessly. He tossed and turned most of the night before he finally got up way too early and made himself some breakfast. He watched the mountains wake up in the chilled sunshine and contemplated changing his morning plans. He would be thirty-six next month and it *was* Christmas after all. Maybe it was time to do more 'grownup' things.

He washed his breakfast dishes and started a pot of coffee. Now that Bird was home he was going to have to get back in the habit of making extra again. He rubbed his hand down the front of his face and tugged on his beard. Except she wouldn't be staying for long. Maybe he should go with her to Christmas dinner at her folks' house.

He shook his head in silent disagreement. He didn't think he could get along with Scott for that long of a time frame. And she should really be with her family for the holiday. He hadn't ever fit into that mix. No, he would spend the day with his first and only true loves. The mountain and the board. His mistress and his passion.

He jogged up the stairs lightly, being careful not to disturb the other house guest. He needed to get changed and get out of there as soon as possible. If Lenny asked him to change his plans, he would. He struggled with telling her 'no.'

That girl always managed to turn his world upside down.

***

Lenny closed the door to the cold world outside and looked up the open staircase of the home she had grown up in. Mom had the place completely decked out in holiday festooning. Lights, ornaments, wreathes and ribbons hung from every doorway, railing and light fixture. The air was thick with cinnamon and opulence. Lenny took off her scarf and hung it on the hook, she slipped her jacket off and placed it in the closet.

"Auntie!"

Lenny was suddenly accosted by four little boys, all under the age of eight. They surrounded her and hugged her while she struggled to stay upright. She finally gave in and collapsed on the floor, laughing.

"Boys!" Their mother, Felicity, clapped at them from the top of the stairs. "Let your auntie up."

154

Lenny hugged each one individually and they ran off into another part of the house. Felicity had made her way down the steps and embraced her. She started to guide her towards the kitchen,

"Sorry, about that." Felicity chuckled, "They've been pretty excited to see you."

"Not a problem," Lenny smiled widely. She inhaled the delicious aroma of turkey as she entered her mother's state of the art kitchen.

"Lenny, you're early!" Her mother exclaimed from behind a a stack of pies. "Did Duke come with you?"

"Um, no. He said last night that he wanted to get out there early and I heard him take the sled when I woke up."

"I never see that man when there's snow cover." Kelli muttered more to herself than anyone else.

"Geez, ma, you think you got enough pies?" Lenny teased her tiny mother. Kelli Evans was only five feet tall but made up for her lack of height with extra spunk. Lenny had gotten her father's tallness but otherwise could have been a carbon copy of her mother, same blonde hair, same dark blue eyes.

"I hope so." Kelli answered seriously, eyeballing the tower of pies arranged on a tiered pie stand. "We ran out last year, you know. It was awful, your father cried."

Lenny snickered at her mom and made her way to the stove top to get herself some apple cider.

"Len, dinner won't be ready for a while yet, do you think you and Nathan can take those little boys outside and burn off some energy?"

"I would love nothing more." Lenny smiled and drained her cider. She went in search of Nathan to challenge him to a snow fort building competition. They each claimed two of the little boys for their team. In a matter of minutes they were all suited up and out in the cold.

While the four rambunctious boys started to build their piles of snowballs in their finished forts for the eminent fight, Nathan and Lenny had a little heart to heart.

"I'm really glad you could make it home for Christmas." He looked at the house. "I wasn't freaked that you took off, I totally understood. They have always set the bar a little higher for you than the rest of us."

Lenny nodded, "Yeah, I should've done it differently but I am glad I got away for a while. It really helped to put some things in perspective."

"You ever think you'll go back out there?" Nathan nodded to the mountains in the distance.

"I don't know." Lenny answered honestly.

"I heard you have a boyfriend." His eyes twinkled, teasing her.

Lenny rolled her eyes at him. "It's still pretty new. I don't know

155

what I'd call it." She knew she would have to deflect any discussion of Luke all day. She wasn't sure what to say.

"Well, he's coming up for New Year's, right?"

"Yeah, but the whole band is coming. All of them. So it's not like a special thing." Lenny could see that Nathan wasn't buying it.

"I don't know, Nate." She said, exasperated. "I like him and he likes me. That's all I have figured out right now, okay?"

"Okay, but I may have to question the young man on his intentions with my sister."

Lenny hit his coat with her mittened hand. "Stop it! You will not!"

Nathan was laughing, delighted that he'd gotten her so riled up. "Oh, now I *have* to." He was dodging more smacks from her. Pretty soon Lenny picked up a snowball and hurled it square in Nathan's face.

"Snowball fight!" One of the little boys yelled and it was instantly a free-for-all. The air was filled with volleying balls of snow and excited yells. Lenny and Nathan were ducking and trying to ward off the sudden onslaught. It was the adults against the kids, they were completely outnumbered.

***

They clamored into the mud room off the back of the house, Lenny instructing the little boys to take off all their wet clothes before going through grandma's kitchen. They happily obeyed, satisfied that they had won the snowball fight against their aunt and uncle.

"I don't know how you do it, Fe." Lenny said to her sister in-law as she got herself another cup of hot cider off the stove.

Felicity laughed, "Neither do I!"

Lenny leaned her back against the warm stove and breathed in the amazing scents in the kitchen.

"You ladies sure have been cooking up a storm in here. It smells so good!"

"Thanks, Lenna! Would you mind checking the table to see if Scott needs anything?" Her mom asked as she scurried down from a step stool with an enormous turkey baster held like a weapon as she headed for the oven.

Lenny nodded and walked onto the dining room. "Mom, wants to know if you need anything else." She addressed Scott who was pushing the kids table into the corner.

"No, I think I have it all."

"Kay." She sipped her cider, studying her tall, older brother. "Where is Simone?" She asked about Scott's longtime girlfriend who was

156

always at every holiday. The photographer he had met in New York a few years ago was tall and willowy with vibrant red hair and a smattering of freckles. She was noticeably absent this year and no one had mentioned her. In fact, Lenny hadn't spoken to her since the night before her interview with Carl.

"We decided to take a break." Scott didn't look up from his task.

"What does that mean?"

Scott straightened up and put his hands on his hips. "She wants something I'm not ready for yet. We decided to take a break and see how we feel after the holidays."

"That's stupid." Lenny couldn't stop herself from declaring her view point.

"That's your opinion."

"Whatever. She's too good for you anyway, I can't believe you won't just marry her already. It's been what, five years of dating?"

Scott frowned at his sister's reprimand. "That's interesting, coming from you."

"What's that supposed to mean?" Lenny could feel her neck heating up.

"You've had one boyfriend your whole life and now this thing with the rock star that we all know won't last, and you think you should give relationship advice?"

Lenny knew he had a point but it irritated her. "I liked Simone, that's all."

Scott grunted and went upstairs to get more chairs. Lenny took her cup back to the kitchen and checked to see if they needed her help. They were fine and sent her out to the den to see her father and other brother, David.

Lenny curled her legs under her and sat on the big leather sofa in front of the fire while her father and David played chess. What Scott had said about Luke bugged her. He didn't know if it would last. How could he? It was still brand new. Lenny wasn't even sure where it was going. Maybe that was the problem.

She leaned her head against the arm rest and stared into the fire. She thought about the guys and the road and how exciting going to Europe would be. She also thought about Duke and the Lodge and the whole life she had waiting for her here, whenever she decided to rejoin it. Was there even the possibility of a future with Luke? Wouldn't he just move on to the next girl when the tour was over? Yes, more than likely, that's what made the most sense. She could just enjoy what little time they had left. New Year's would be fun. And Europe would be great too. But Lenny decided that after Europe she would come home to the Lodge. She may never snowboard again but she could be close to see her nephews grow and be around if her parents needed her.

It was time to make grownup decisions.

"You okay, kiddo?" Her father broke into her thoughts. "You look like you're thinking about something pretty hard."

Lenny twisted her head so her chin was on the armrest and she was looking at her dad. "Yeah, just thinking about New Year's."

"Your mom and I are leaving for the Caymans tomorrow, you need us to stay?"

"No, I think Nathan and I have it pretty much handled." Lenny gave him a small smile.

"How is Duke?" David asked, making a move on the chess board that caused her father to grunt.

"He's the same." Lenny replied. Duke really was the same. Nothing with him ever changed. She smiled to herself as she thought of him. Christmas Day and he was out on a run. This was the first one in a long time where she wasn't sharing it with him and wishing she was.

***

Duke slowly peeled off his sweater, being careful to not tug on his left shoulder. He rotated that arm a few times, trying to loosen the tightness that had built up.

"You tweak your shoulder again?"

Lenny's voice startled him. He hadn't seen her sitting at the bar when he'd come in the backdoor.

"Aren't you supposed to be in town?" He ignored her question, continuing to strip out of his wet clothes without grimacing from the pain running through his arm.

"Ma sent home some leftovers. And an entire pie." Lenny wasn't being fooled. He saw her watching him closely and irritation shot down his spine. The last thing he needed was for her to be worried about him.

"Can I help you with that?" She jumped off the stool and started towards him.

"I got it." Duke didn't mean to snap but that's what had happened. Lenny wasn't even fazed. She rolled her eyes and smacked his hand out of the way as she grabbed the bottom of his shirt and tugged it over his head. Duke didn't have the coordination to fight back even though he knew what would happen next and he wasn't disappointed. As Lenny dropped his shirt into the pile on the floor, she gasped.

"Oh, stop." Duke growled. He tried to push past her with the intent of going to his room and closing the door. But Lenny wasn't having it.

"Holy crap, Duke." Her eyes were wide as they took in the bruises that adorned his torso. It must have been worse than he had expected by the shocked look on her face. "What the hell happened out there today?"

"I took a spill." His mouth crooked up on the side, "Maybe a few."

"Well," Lenny scrutinized his wounds and he had to fight off the self-conscience feeling washing over him from her careful gaze. "You look terrible. But," she turned him around and gingerly touched some of the marks, feeling for cracked ribs, "I don't think anything is broken." She gently rubbed his sore shoulder and gauged his reaction. "I don't like that you keep messing this up, you might need to see a doctor one of these days." She raised her eyebrows at him and her sweet concern made is heart melt.

"I'll be fine." Duke reassured her. "It's not like I've never wrecked before." He grinned as he hobbled towards the stairs, this time she let him pass. "How about I put some clothes on and you heat me up some of that food you were talking about." He didn't turn around to see if she would comply, he knew she'd do it.

In his room, Duke surveyed his body in the mirror. *Yep, I do look terrible.* He slipped his arms in a loose button up flannel, only bothering with half the buttons. His skin still burned from where her fingers had touched him and he silently scolded his anatomy for letting her affect him like that. He put on some baggy pajama pants and stood before the mirror again.

He gave himself a stern look and let out all the air in his lungs. *Get it together, dumb ass.*

He took a few more minutes to clear his head before he made his way back to the kitchen. Lenny had an impressive spread set out for him on the bar; turkey, sweet potatoes, stuffing, gravy, biscuits and green beans. She was sitting on the counter top across from the bar, her legs dangling.

"I thought you said there would be pie." Duke grumbled as he took his seat.

"You can have pie if you finish all of that." Lenny laughed and Duke relished that sound that had been missing for way too long. And he knew the credit belonged to someone else. Not that he hadn't tried, they'd all tried to snap her out of her funk after the wreck but no one could reach her. Now, she seemed closer than she'd been in ages.

"How was the family?" He asked between forkfuls.

"Good, everyone's happy and healthy."

"Scott?" Duke looked up in time to see her scrunch her nose.

"The usual."

Duke nodded knowingly. Scott was always harder on Lenny than Duke felt she deserved. One of the many reasons he couldn't get along with that guy.

159

"What's the plan for New Year's?"

"Nathan will move up here tomorrow to help me set up. He has mom's gift for decorating." She smiled at him crookedly. "I'd really like it if you were here for it. I really want you to meet all the guys."

"I'll be around." Duke nodded as he took a drink of water. He knew what she was really asking. She wanted his approval of the new guy. He had never approved of Shane and he suspected that was one of the reason's she had stopped talking to him about the important stuff. Now that things with Shane were over, Duke was back in Lenny's confidence...for the most part.

***

Lenny went through her closet and packed what she would need for Aspen and then packed a separate suitcase for Europe. She was glad she would be able to bring some fresh clothes for the second leg of the tour. No hasty packing this time around.

Duke had been out on the mountain daily since she'd come home. Every night before he went to bed he asked Lenny if she wanted to come with him in the morning. She always said no. She wasn't ready for that. She might not ever be.

She busied herself preparing for her guests. The upstairs had several single bedrooms and one large room with six bunks in it. She made sure all the sheets were clean and all the bathrooms were fully stocked. It was weirdly similar to her job on the road.

Every night, she and Duke would sit by the fire and visit. She didn't get personal and neither did he. But it was soothing and Lenny enjoyed the knowledge that no matter how far away she went or how long she was gone, she would be able to come home to Duke's solid presence. His loyalty never wavered.

Chapter 11

Tensioning

Duke stared into the fire, *just a simple conversation,* he thought. *It shouldn't be that hard. You guys used to talk all the time.* He didn't look up as Lenny entered the room and handed him a mug of homemade hot chocolate. One more thing he was going to have to miss in a week.

She'd only been home for a few days and she had easily settled into their old routines; cooking all his favorite winter comfort foods, cleaning up his wet clothes after a day's run, going into town for gas for the sled. She wouldn't go out on any runs with him, but he never stopped asking. He knew there was still so much more to say, to talk about. Too many things were getting ignored and he wasn't even sure where to start.

"When does their plane get in tomorrow?" Duke asked instead. That was another thing that he was trying hard to come to terms with. The guy who had set her world right again was going to be in his, er, *her* home the very next night. He had no idea how far this little relationship had gone, but he wasn't going to be cool with them sharing the same room.

"Around noon I think." A lazy smile played on Lenny's lips. "Nathan is gonna pick them up when he goes to get his brothers."

"It's still weird that Nathan was part of a fraternity." Duke shook his head.

"No, what's weird is that they still show up at *my* house every New Year's Eve."

"But it's really Nathan's party. We both know you wouldn't throw a party...ever." Duke smiled as he sipped his hot chocolate.

"Very true." Lenny agreed.

Duke let the silence become comfortable again. They had talked a lot the past few days. Lenny had shared nearly every detail of being with the band. Duke was positive he'd be able to identify them by name on sight. She had obviously made lasting friendships with these guys. He understood why she was going to at least finish the tour. But he hoped she wasn't using that as an excuse to walk away from snowboarding permanently. That was what he needed to ask her...now, where were the right words?

"Is this our last night alone for a while?" He kept his gaze focused on the flames but he felt her shift a little on the couch.

161

"Just for a little while...I'm coming home after Europe."

Duke didn't reveal his surprise at her answer. He took another slow slip of hot chocolate before asking his next question.

"What about Luke?" He didn't want to know, but he had to just the same.

"I don't know, Duke." She let out a deep breath. "I like him and stuff but he's a rock star. And, I guess, I just don't see a future there." She stretched her legs toward him and reclined against the armrest. "I miss being here, with you. This is nice, right?"

Nice? This is my personal heaven. "Yeah, it's nice." Duke knew she was staring at him so he finally turned to meet her eyes. She gave him a small smile and he deepened his frown. "You ever gonna go back out there?" Her smile faded and she looked away.

"I don't know." Her voice just above a whisper, "I'm scared."

Duke narrowed his eyes, "Of what, Lenny?" He matched her tone, not wanting to make her jumpy. Her eyes lost focus as she stared into the fire and Duke knew the answer lay there, in her perfect memory. But she wasn't telling him tonight.

***

Lenny watched as Nathan hung the giant silver and gold wreath in the main foyer. He really loved decorating way too much for a mixed martial arts professional.

"Does that look centered to you?" He asked, leaning back on the ladder trying to get a better vantage point.

"Yes, it's perfect, stop obsessing." Lenny chuckled and crossed her arms over her chest. "The whole place looks perfect, you've outdone yourself this year."

Nathan grinned at her and she swore he was seventeen again instead of his actual age of thirty-five. His blue eyes shone brightly as he hopped off the ladder and surveyed his latest achievement.

"I am pretty awesome, aren't I?" He stood proudly with his fists on his hips, a happy smile spread on his face. "This party is my favorite every year and this one is probably my best yet."

"Why *did* you decide to pull out all the stops this year?" Lenny picked up a box of extra decorations, handing it to Nathan and then picking up another one for herself. He followed her through the house and towards the garage.

"I don't know, last big hurrah I guess."

Lenny spun suddenly, nearly colliding with Nathan as she stopped short. "What? This is the last one?"

162

Nathan chuckled, "I guess you haven't heard then?"

Lenny shook her head, waiting for his explanation.

"I completed my coaches certification a few months ago and to make a *very* long story short, the USOC has tapped me to be assistant coach for Team USA. I'm going to be busy for a while. Like, years."

"Oh my gosh, Nathan!" Lenny set her box down hastily and threw her arms around her big brother's neck. "I'm so proud of you! Congratulations!"

Nathan shifted the his own box to one arm and hugged her back, his smile stretching from ear to ear. "Thanks, Len. I'm pretty excited about it. I've always loved coaching and the Olympics is the ultimate for me."

Lenny picked up her box again and they resumed their trek through the house to deposit them in the garage. She asked him questions as they popped into her head, truly looking forward to her brother's new future. As they entered the garage and Lenny turned the lights on she froze in her place by the door. She had gotten distracted by her excitement for Nathan that she had momentarily forgotten her earlier trepidation at entering this specific part of the Lodge.

Nathan stood next to her and let out a low whistle, "That is a lot of equipment."

All along the back wall of the the oversized garage was a huge assortment of snowboards. It looked like a display from at an athletic gear store. Every size, shape and color imaginable adorned the entire length of the wall. Duke had expertly hung the shelving and track lighting in order to make it look like an art exhibition. A huge cabinet with a glass front showcased her various helmets, goggles and boots.

Lenny swallowed twice before setting down her box. It was an odd feeling, like walking into a funeral of someone you used to know well but just didn't anymore.

"You okay?"

Lenny snapped her eyes to Nathan, his face was filled with concern. Her throat was dry and she swallowed again before she answered.

"I'm fine." Her voice was clipped and and she knew he didn't believe her but she didn't want to have this conversation.

"Lenny," Nathan had already set his box down and he took a hesitant step towards her, "let's talk about it."

Lenny stiffened. "There's nothing to talk about. I'm fine. We have a party to get ready for." She spun on her heel and left the garage with Nathan hot on her trail.

"There's no way you're okay, you're very clearly *not* okay." He wasn't exactly shouting but his voice was louder than Lenny thought necessary. She ignored him and rounded the corner leading down a long hallway that would take her to the dining room. She had a lot to get done before the caterer arrived.

"Lenny, please!" Nathan grabbed her elbow from behind and she yanked it away. "I'm your brother, please talk to me about it."

Hot tears started to burn the back of Lenny's eyes and she grit her teeth in frustration. She came into the dining room and ran full-on into Duke. He grabbed her by her forearms to keep her from falling but he didn't miss the agitated look on her face. She turned away and tried to move past him.

"What's going on?" Duke asked, not letting go and directing his question more at Nathan than Lenny.

"She won't talk to me." Nathan's frustration was obvious.

"About what?" Duke's deep frown looked down into Lenny's eyes and she silently begged him to not pursue this.

"The same thing she always hides from...snowboarding." Nathan ran his hand through his short hair and let out an exasperated growl. "Just forget it. I have to get to the airport." He paused and took a deep breath. "I'm sorry, I hope this doesn't ruin your night." He exchanged a look with Duke and left them alone.

Duke's frown stayed put and Lenny felt her heart rate returning to normal.

"You okay?" He asked, letting go of her arms finally.

"Yeah." Lenny gave a him a small smile and cleared her throat. "Um, can you put the ladder in the foyer away? I'm going to go take a shower."

Duke nodded but he didn't say anything. Lenny headed to her room, relieved that Duke had been there. Always backing her play.

***

The music had started pulsing long before the party started. Nathan hired a DJ every year and they had moved the furniture in the ginormous living room to make way for a dance floor.

Lenny wondered if Nathan was back yet. If Luke was there.

She had spent considerable extra time getting ready. She hadn't seen Luke in a while and she wanted to look...pretty. She curled her hair in loose waves that hung down her back and lined her eyes with charcoal, giving a slight smoky effect. She considered wearing a party dress but settled on skinny jeans and a dark purple top that showed off her shoulders.

Nathan's New Year's Eve parties were unique in that they were amazing and alcohol free. He wasn't taking any kind of an ethical stand. They were a family of athletes, and winter was the height of training, it just never combined well. When Duke moved in, an alcohol free environment became the rule since he was a recovering alcoholic. It was one of the reason's Lenny had been so impressed with the band's support of Mike's sobriety. It was an obvious indication of loyalty and devotion.

But the lack of alcohol never made the party dull by any means. Nathan's frat brothers usually had a pool tournament, snowmobile races in the back and of course dancing.

Lenny took a deep breath and looked at herself in the mirror one last time.

***

Cody rubbed her temples with her fingertips while Clara prattled on and on about something she had absolutely no interest in whatsoever. Where did she find these people? Oh yeah, they were her friends. The limo bumped along the snowy road and Cody knew they were getting closer to their destination.

She took a slim bottle out of her purse and drained the remaining contents. She knew Lenny's little soiree would be dry and she was going to need to be decently lubricated if she planned on being a good guest.

"What is that?" Erin asked, her wide brown eyes watching Cody swallow the remaining liquid in a flourish.

"Fun in a bottle." Cody winked, "Want some?" She produced a second bottle and uncapped it, handing it to Erin.

Erin took a swallow and sputtered; she passed it to Clara sitting next to her who also took a swallow.

"I thought there was no drinking at this party." Clara downed more than she needed and Cody was delighted. This might be more fun than she had originally anticipated.

"That's why we have to do it now." She answered and took the bottle back, pouring more down her throat and then shoving the bottle back into Erin's hands. She raised her eyebrows in silent expectation and Erin caved. She tipped the bottle back and took several gulps. Cody pursed her lips, this was most definitely going to be fun.

***

Lenny hugged Cody in greeting, shocked that she had shown up at all. They hadn't spoken since Denver and she hadn't intended to invite her. Cody had brought her usual entourage of girls in skimpy party dresses but it was the overwhelming smell of vodka that rolled off of the group that made Lenny recoil.

165

"Have you been drinking?" Lenny asked in Cody's ear. The response was loud laughter followed by Cody heading for the dance floor.

Lenny shook her head disgustedly, going back to the kitchen to check on the caterers. That girl was walking a line that Lenny never understood. She wanted to throw her out but she also didn't want to end the party just as it was starting.

She found Duke who had actually dressed up a little, for Duke anyway. He was wearing his nicest flannel and he'd trimmed his beard. He looked at Lenny with a twinkle in his gray eyes and stole another little sandwich off of a tray that a young lady was feverishly trying to fill.

"I'm glad you decided to come off the mountain and join us." Lenny smiled and got a bottle of water out of the fridge.

"Well, someone has to keep an eye on the food." He winked at the little attendant again as she moved the tray out of his reach.

"You should come mingle, Cody is here. She brought her usual entourage."

"How 'bout Nate the Great?"

"Yeah, his old frat brothers are here, makes for a weird mix." Lenny laughed at the absurdity. Cody's friends were all in their early twenty's whereas Nathan's friends were a good ten years older and had careers.

Just then, someone came up behind Lenny and touched her elbow. She turned to see Luke's smiling face. A thousand different frequencies of joy washed over her. She impulsively put her arms around him, hugging him close.

"Hey, you." She greeted warmly.

***

Luke held her a little tighter and a little longer than would normally be socially acceptable. He breathed in her familiar scent and made a rumbling noise in the back of his throat that could only be described as pure contentment. He had missed her.

The man Lenny had been talking to cleared his throat from behind her and Luke released his embrace. He looked into steel grey eyes and stuck out his hand.

"Hi, I'm Luke Casey."

"Duke." The man replied with a firm handshake.

The way Lenny and Cody had spoken of him, he had expected an old man. Instead, he found himself face to face with someone maybe only five years or so older than himself. His athletic build was evident despite his thick flannel shirt and Luke found himself standing a little straighter. This

166

was the guy Lenny had been living with for the past week?

"Duke, this is the lead singer for Double Blind Study." Lenny introduced and Luke struggled with his sudden desire to put his arm around her possessively.

"Right, the circus you left town with." Duke nodded.

Luke squinted slightly, trying to decipher the undertones in which Duke spoke.

Mike, Sway, Harrison and Blake descended upon Lenny at that moment, crowding the kitchen and making it even harder for the caterers to maneuver.

Blake picked Lenny up and gave her a bear hug. She squealed in surprise and slapped his shoulder so he would put her down. She hugged the rest of the guys, happy to see them, then introduced them to Duke as well. Handshakes happened all around, manly grunting and stiff greetings. Lenny must have noticed the subtle tenseness that lingered and tried to break it up.

"Let's get out of the kitchen so these people can do their jobs." She led them out to the open living room where the dancing was in full combustion. Luke saw Cody at the center of the mess and he wasn't surprised.

Some girls spotted the rockers and pulled most of them onto the dance floor. Luke hung back, wanting a few minutes alone with Lenny if it was available. It had been far too long since he had kissed her perfect lips. He slipped his arm around her waist resting his hand high on her hip, having brief eye contact with Duke but acting as casual as possible.

Maybe Duke picked up on Luke's not so subtle hint, maybe he was just hungry but he suddenly announced he needed more sandwiches and left Luke and Lenny alone together.

Lenny watched the band members dancing with Cody's friends and she scrunched up her nose. "Maybe this was a bad idea."

"You're not on duty, they're gonna be fine." Luke lightly laughed at her reaction.

A thin girl with short, caramel colored hair was laughing too loudly and Luke suspected she had been drinking before her arrival. She staggered off the dance floor and came towards Lenny.

"Do you know where some water is? I'm so thirsty." Then she burst into giggles again.

Lenny pulled the girl towards the kitchen stopping just in the doorway. She ducked inside and came back quickly, handing the girl a bottle of water. As the girl thirstily sucked the water down, Luke saw Lenny's face become unreadable.

***

167

"How do you know Cody?" Lenny asked the girl tightly.

"I'm Erin, I met her through my boyfriend, well, I guess he's not really my boyfriend, I don't know what we are." Erin giggled again and a hiccup escaped.

"Where is he tonight?" Lenny tried to sound casual but she was getting the weirdest sensation in the pit of her stomach.

"He said he shouldn't come because it would be too hard to see his ex and he thought she might be here." Erin rambled nervously and looked around the room like she was expecting the girl to pop out and scare her. "It took him a long time to get over her, I guess she really broke his heart."

"That's too bad." Luke said tenderly and Lenny shot a frown his way but he missed it. "New Year's Eve is always such a special night, I'm sorry he couldn't be here with you."

Erin nodded emphatically, "I don't know who the ex is but I guess she totally obliterated him. We've had to work through a *lot* of issues involving trust and honesty and stuff." Erin noticed Lenny's eyes narrow and she stammered. "I'm sorry, I'm talking too much." She giggled nervously.

"No, it's fine." Lenny forced a smile and put her hand on Erin's arm. "Just keep in mind, there's always two sides to every story."

"Sounds like the ex is a real bitch." Luke interjected and Lenny felt her mouth fall open as she looked at him.

Cody shimmied her way over to them and threw an overly friendly arm around Luke's waist. "Hey, whatcha talkin' bout?" Her face was flushed from the excessive alcohol in her system as well as the dancing.

"Erin was just telling us about the guy she's seeing…" Luke began not moving from away from Cody's side.

"Yeah, Shane." Cody nodded, "Bet you guys could compare notes." She laughed as she winked at Lenny who only returned a slow subtle shake of her head. But it was too late. Even though Erin's faculties had been reduced due to her drinking, she wasn't completely brain dead. She turned towards Lenny, eyes wild.

"Wait, *you're* the ex?" Erin's giggling was replaced by a a more heated expression.

"Shane who?" Luke frowned, not following along.

"Shane Brookings, *my* boyfriend!" Erin pointed at herself and took a step away from Lenny like she was afraid of her suddenly.

"You told me that wasn't serious." Luke's voice was dark and he looked at the floor.

"It…wasn't." Lenny looked from Luke to Cody to Erin. How was this happening? Her eyes settled on Cody who had the slightest of smirks on her face, arm firmly in place around Luke's waist.

"Yeah, for *you*!" Erin exclaimed. "*I'm* the one who had to try and to pick up the pieces after you *left* him six months ago!"

"Six months? You made it sound like you had been broken up for a lot longer than that." Luke's frown was deepening and he started to back away from them, pushing Cody's arm off of him.

"I'll talk to you in a minute." Lenny said to Luke and then she turned to Erin. She needed to get this back under control. Too many things were unraveling at the same time and she wasn't prepared. "Please, try to understand that there is a lot more to the story than what you know. I never meant to hurt Shane."

"I suppose you had this guy just waiting around for you." Erin pointed at Luke. "You were probably seeing both of them at the same time."

Lenny looked at Cody who was watching everything unfold with a look of sadistic glee smeared across her face.

"I need some air." Luke said brusquely and stalked off.

Lenny wanted to follow him but she needed to end this nightmare first. She turned back to Erin who was almost in tears.

"Erin, I'm sorry for whatever hurt I've caused you by breaking up with Shane. I never cheated on him and if he has trust issues that's *not* my fault." Lenny's words were forced and clipped but she was too angry about what was happening to care.

"Whatever, I'm going home." Erin grabbed one of the girls off the dance floor and began to cry until the girl agreed to find her a ride home.

Lenny glared at Cody. "Wow, was that planned or what?"

"I forgot she was seeing Shane-" Cody started to lie but Lenny cut her off.

"Bullshit, Cody! That's how you met, she already told me." Lenny rolled her eyes and crossed her arms over her chest. "I put up with a lot of your shit because of Duke but I've about reached my limit."

"Don't get mad at me because Shane moved on." Cody's face grew venomous.

"This isn't about Shane!" Lenny was starting to shake. "This is about you being a horrible friend!"

"Excuse me?" Cody raised her eyebrows aggressively. "You were the one who skipped town the day of one of the biggest meetings of my life! I needed your backing to land that sponsorship and you didn't even call!"

"I'm sorry, I didn't know it was up to *me* to secure *your* future for you!" Lenny replied sarcastically. "Maybe you should have been a decent human being instead of alienating everyone around you."

"You're such a spoiled little bitch! You have always had every little thing handed to you and what wasn't given to you, you had no problem taking!" Cody's lips twisted savagely and Lenny stepped into a defensive stance. Cody had been drinking and Lenny knew that if she attacked it would be sudden and sloppy.

"Ladies, how about we take a breather." Nathan inserted himself into the confrontation. He nodded at one of his frat bros who came over and took Cody's elbow, leading her away. Lenny didn't break eye contact with her until they had rounded the corner.

"What was that all about?" Nathan asked when they were finally alone.

"Cody brought Shane's new girlfriend to the party. Did you know that he's telling people I cheated on him?" Lenny felt her eyebrows go up when Nathan nodded. "You don't believe it, do you?" *How did I end up the villain in this?*

"No, I don't believe that you cheated on him. But he was really hurt by your leaving and I think he's just handling it badly."

"This is unbelievable." Lenny's face was hot and she wished she could go outside for a break from this...insanity.

Nathan took a breath and continued. "You have to remember the facts. You and Shane dated for over two years. He got your name tattooed on his arm, he moved to Wyoming to be closer to you, and I have it on pretty good authority that he was getting ready to propose to you before you dumped him…in a text message."

"Geez, Nate. You make me sound like a monster." Lenny was really growing tired of how people assumed they knew what had happened between her and Shane.

"I'm not trying to. I just think you need to realize someday that your actions have consequences. Just because you weren't invested in the relationship didn't mean he wasn't. You kind of treated him like crap and he was a really great guy."

A really great guy? What-the-frick-ever. "What are you saying?" Lenny was trying hard to bite her tongue. Nathan had no idea what he was talking about.

Nathan let out a heavy sigh. "If you weren't in love with him I don't understand why you waited two years to end it. And I have to wonder about the new guy." Lenny shot him a glare and Nathan swallowed hard. "If you're not in love, don't lead him on. End it soon and be gentle."

***

Luke found himself on the back patio, without a coat in the cold mountain air. Someone approached him from behind and handed him a heavy jacket. Luke slipped it on and turned to thank the individual. It was

170

Duke. Perfect.

Duke nodded at him and gestured to a set of chairs off to the side of the patio. Luke followed him and sat down, not sure what to expect from this conversation. A lot had happened so far tonight and he hadn't processed any of it. So far, all he had gathered was, Lenny had a much more serious relationship with Shane than she had led him to believe. Oh, and she was living with a very attractive man who stank of testosterone in the backwoods of Wyoming.

"Saw that little display in there," Duke started.

Luke grunted and looked up at the stars.

"If you wanna be with Lenny you're in for one hell of a ride." Duke chuckled to himself. "She probably spent too much time on the mountain, never learned all the 'girl stuff.' Her mom was always after her to hang out with people her age doing regular teenage things like, go to the mall." Duke shook his head, "But Lenny wouldn't have it. Nope. Our Bird had to be free." Duke nodded to the starlit mountain line. "Out there, the only place I've seen her truly happy." His words hung in the silent cold for a while.

"So you're saying that it's probably not gonna last." Luke responded quietly, feeling his gut twist.

"I didn't say that." Duke countered. "I said it would be one hell of a ride." Duke gave a sly smile. "Don't give up. You're already loads better than that tool, Shane."

"I thought Shane was perfect." Luke grumbled despondently.

"Ha! Yeah, he sure was pretty." Duke let out a dark chuckle. "He wasn't all that. He was nice but he wasn't any good for her."

"What makes me different?" Luke couldn't help but ask. Here he was, with someone who probably knew Lenny better than she knew herself. What made Luke the guy?

"After her accident, a little piece of her died. I know that sounds macabre but it's true. She left a chunk of herself out there. Shane tried to bring her back to life, I tried, her folks tried but it was no use. It was like talking to a walking corpse." Duke breathed out through is nose. "But she's suddenly back. I look in her eyes and I see her in there." Duke's voice grew thick with emotion. "You're the one who found her."

Luke looked back up at the stars. He wanted badly for what Duke said to be true. He had never felt for anyone the way he felt for Lenny. But was that enough? She obviously had issues with commitment and an addiction to fight or flight.

"It's worth it." Duke said into the darkness as if reading his thoughts. "Grab that light and don't let go."

171

Chapter 12

Magpies On Fire

After several minutes outside with Duke, Sway came and got Luke, asking him to be his partner in the pool tournament. Luke had reluctantly agreed, wanting more to sulk in the cold.

As the game got underway, Luke regretted even more that he'd agreed to this. For some reason, Cody was the only girl in the room and she was being very...vigilant. She kept finding reasons to stand very close to him. She hardly spoke to him, but he could feel eyes on him wherever he took a shot.

He and Sway won the first round and moved on to the next. All Luke could think about was how he hadn't seen Lenny in over a week and he was playing pool with a bunch of dudes he didn't know with a drunk chick attached to his hip. It was not his ideal situation.

Some of the guys cleared out to race snowmobiles and Luke and Sway went onto the next round.

"You're really good at this game." Cody leaned over and Luke caught a whiff of vodka off her words. She must have some stashed nearby, Luke hadn't seen any being served.

"Thanks." He responded tersely as he lined up his shot.

Cody pressed her body against his side and he felt her hot breath in his ear. "After this game you want to go...somewhere?"

Luke's stomach roiled inside and he clenched his teeth. He made his shot despite Cody's interference and he walked away from her to the other side of the room. Sway gave him a perplexed look and Luke ignored him.

Cody was close behind, not deterred in the slightest. Luke wasn't sure how to deal with this. He was used to women pawing at him, but it had never been the best friend of the girl he was with. Wasn't this against girl code? Did girls have a code?

Just then, Blake walked into the room. Shirtless. Luke could have kissed him.

"Hey," Luke handed him his cue, "Play for me, I have to go do a thing." He pointed with his thumb over his shoulder.

Blake didn't hesitate, he grabbed the cue in one hand and Cody around the waist with the other. "Be my lucky charm?" He grinned down at her and she giggled.

Luke was thankful for his brash and bold band mate as he booked it out of there. He needed to find Lenny. He knew a couple of hours had passed and he had to talk to her. This wasn't right.

***

The snowmobile races wrapped up and Duke put the sleds away. Lenny watched from the patio, her hands shoved deep in her coat pockets. What a crappy New Year's. For her anyway. Everyone else seemed to be having a wonderful time. Did it bother her that she hadn't seen Luke in a while? Yes. Did it bother her that she also had not seen Cody during that time? More than she liked to admit.

***

Luke didn't want to appear frantic. So he casually strolled through the huge Lodge that was packed with people. He smiled and chatted with those who recognized him but he was searching for Lenny.

He glanced in what he assumed was some sort of den. It was fairly dark, lit only by a few candles artistically placed around the room. No one else was in the room and he took a few steps inside to see if there might be another room beyond a door or something. This house was massive and damn if he hadn't already gotten turned around a few times in it.

"There you are."

Luke turned to see Cody closing the door and smiling at him seductively.

"Hey, Cody. Have you seen Lenny?" Luke tried to remain polite but she was testing his patience.

Cody curled a lip up, "Why do you care where Lenny is? She's not here, that's all that matters." She began to step towards him and Luke shook his head in wonder. How were they even friends?

"You can do to me all the things you want to do to her. She's never gonna love you. She only cares about herself." Cody slid her hands up Luke's shoulders and pressed her body against him. Luke grabbed her hands and took a large step backwards.

"You're drunk, Cody." He tried to give her an excuse but he knew in his gut that this is who she really was. And it sickened him.

"Cody, your ride is here." A gruff voice interrupted them and Luke looked up, startled to see Duke standing in the doorway. Cody didn't even seem to notice. She leaned towards Luke again.

Duke entered the room and grabbed Cody by the arm. "Your ride is

174

here." He repeated, his eyes flashing to Luke's. Cody struggled against him as he forced her out the door.

"What's your problem, Duke?" She shrieked, wrestling out of his grasp.

Duke scooped her up and flung her over his shoulder. He nodded at Luke, "Can you help me with the door?"

Luke had no words; he just did as the man asked. The way to the front door was cleared of human presence and Luke wondered how that was even possible. But it would probably benefit Cody some if no one saw the degrading way she was being asked to leave.

The limo driver waiting outside didn't even look surprised as Duke shoved his niece into the car. The rest of her friends were already inside and Luke heard a plethora of questions being hurled in Cody's direction. Duke slammed the car door and the driver made haste getting underway.

Duke placed his hands on his hips and gave Luke a hard stare. "You want to tell me what that was?" His words coming out as white puffs in the cold air.

"I was looking for Lenny." Luke knew what it must have looked like when Duke had opened the door but he had to know the reality. Didn't he?

Duke met him with silence. His frown deeper than Luke had seen it all night and he realized that with one word, Duke could turn Lenny against him. If Duke didn't want him around this was the perfect opportunity to make that happen.

***

Lenny cruised through the Lodge reminding all the remaining guests that the countdown to midnight was happening in fifteen minutes. She had no explanation for why Blake and Sway were both playing pool in only their boxers and she didn't ask. She found Harrison and Mike had taken over the DJ's job and were playing a mix all their own. It seemed that Cody and the rest of her friends had vacated early and Lenny felt a mixture of relief and apprehension. She still hadn't seen Luke and her worst fear was that he had left with Cody. He wouldn't do that? Would he?

"Nathan," Lenny almost ran into her brother as he came in from the backyard. "Have you seen Luke?"

Nathan nodded over his shoulder, "He's out back with Duke. They're having some sort of heavy conversation."

Lenny frowned. What? She had just been back there and hadn't seen either one of them. She grabbed her coat and hat and went back out into the cold.

***

The sound from the party got louder and then quieted again as someone came outside from the patio door. Soft footsteps on the granite came toward them and Luke looked up to see Lenny approaching slowly. She had put on a dark coat and a black stocking cap, making her blonde hair and creamy skin stand out. She shoved her hands in her coat pockets and stood in front of him.

"I think we need to talk." Her eyes flicked over to Duke momentarily and Luke had to wonder again at the extent of their friendship. He knew what Duke had told him but how could he be sure there wasn't more there?

"I think so, too." Luke agreed. He definitely had some questions.

"Duke, could you give us a minute?" Lenny asked.

Duke sighed as he slowly stood up. He grumbled something unintelligible to himself. He patted Luke on the shoulder. "Remember what I told you."

Luke nodded but didn't reply.

Lenny sat down in Duke's vacated chair and frowned at his figure as he let himself into the house. "What did Duke tell you?"

"Guy stuff," Luke hedged. "What do you want to talk about?"

Lenny closed her eyes like she was trying to get her thoughts in line before she spoke. "I'm sorry about what...Erin said in there. I had no idea...*any* of that was going to happen."

"Was it true?" Luke kept his voice flat.

"What do you mean?" Lenny was playing too innocent, she was hiding again.

"Were you and Shane more serious than you led me to believe?" Luke asked evenly, not wanting it to come out like he was threatened.

"I don't see how that matters," she answered darkly.

Really? "C'mon, Lenny." Luke's eyes bored into hers. "Was he in love with you?"

She swallowed several times before answering, "I don't know. I mean, how can you really know what someone else feels? He said he did but that doesn't mean anything. But I...I didn't love him back. And I never told him I loved him."

"How long were you guys together?" Luke was afraid of the answer but he had to know. He had to know where that put them. If there even was a *them* to be worried about.

"A little over two years-" Lenny broke off as Luke cursed under his breath.

176

"And you broke up with him how long before you met me?" He knew he sounded accusatory but he was too agitated to stop.

The corner of Lenny's mouth twitched and she looked cornered, trapped. Luke hated himself for making her feel that way. But she didn't run away, instead, she set her jaw and spoke plainly. "I sent him a text, telling him it wasn't working. From the airport. Right before I boarded the plane and met you." Her voice was devoid of emotion.

"A text? Lenny? A text? To a man who is in love with you?" Luke was losing it. Lenny's lack of emotion seemed to amplify his. He knew he was overreacting, but his train of rational thought had derailed a few minutes ago and he wasn't getting it back anytime soon.

"I don't understand why this so upsetting for you." Lenny spoke coldly. "I'm not with him, I don't have feelings for him, why does this make you crazy?"

Luke shot up from his chair and put both hands on top of his hair as he stepped a few paces across the patio and stood with his back to Lenny. She was the first girl that he had ever revealed so much of himself to. The first one who looked at him and he really felt like she saw *him*. Not the public image of him, the one girls wanted to sleep with so they could feel famous. But who he was at his center. At his most real.

He took a couple of breaths and then turned back to her, his heart racing with both hope and fear. Mind numbing, logic splintering fear.

"Because, Lenny." *Because I'm in love with you and it's turning me into a freaking basket case.* He took a step forward. "Because I'm crazy about you. Because I love just being near you. Because I want to be with you all the time. Because you mean so frickin' much to me. And, from what everyone else has said, I can't help but think that Shane felt the same way and you..." He shook his head and raked his hands through his hair in exasperation.

"I what?" Lenny narrowed her eyes at him.

Luke dropped his hands against his thighs, "You...you don't care. You already said you didn't have feelings for him. For two years." He sighed heavily. "Am I just supposed to wait around until you finally figure out that you don't have feelings for me either? Will it just come in the form of a text?"

Lenny's frown was deep as she responded. "What we have is different than what I had with Shane. You can't compare the two."

Luke sat down again and grabbed her by her hands, looking her in the eye. "Then tell me what we have. What is this?"

He stared into her dark blue eyes, eyes that were the same color as the night sky. Eyes that just a few weeks ago had looked at him in peace and adoration but seemed deep and empty tonight.

177

The noise from the party grew as the countdown began to midnight. Luke kept hold of her, waiting for a response.

"I don't know." She said stiffly, giving him the exact answer that he had been afraid of.

Luke held her hands a moment longer and then slumped into his chair, defeated.

***

The revelers started to go home after an hour or so and the house became quieter. The caterers and DJ had cleaned up and cleared out. Lenny walked through the dark, empty Lodge, picking up trash and leftover drinks. She blew out the candles and turned lights off in vacant rooms.

After she had told Luke she didn't know how to define their relationship, he had gotten up and gone for a walk. Lenny had stayed on the back patio long enough for everyone to leave or go to bed so she wouldn't have to talk to anyone. She could barely feel her fingers and toes when she had slid the back door open.

She stuffed the last of the trash into the bag in her hand. This was not how she was hoping tonight would have gone. She was glad the rest of her guests had had a good time but things with her and Luke were...awkward at best. He wanted some kind of absolution from her and she didn't know what to think, let alone what to feel. She knew she had...affection for him. But there was no way that could sustain a relationship. Especially when one of them was as busy and famous as Luke.

She took the full trash bag out to the garage and put it in the can, pausing to look at the back wall. She sighed heavily as she slowly walked towards what had been her vehicle to freedom since she was a child. She missed it. Desperately. Like the way a person misses air from the bottom of a pool. She hadn't felt free...in a long time.

She turned when someone in the doorway cleared their throat. Duke stood watching her in navy blue pajama pants and a long sleeve white tee shirt. She thought he had gone to bed with everyone else.

"Deep thoughts?" He asked.

She half-smirked, "Are there any other kinds?"

He stepped down into the garage and stood next to Lenny with his hands in his pockets.

"What happened with you and Eddie Vedder?"

Lenny smiled at Duke's nickname for Luke. At least it was better than 'Tool Shed' which is what he had called Shane the entire time they were together.

"Nothing. We argued, sort of. I don't know." Lenny said, regret

178

touching her voice.

"Did he tell you that Cody made a play for him?"

Lenny felt like she'd gotten kicked in the gut. She wasn't surprised but to have it confirmed made it harder to deny Cody's true nature. "No," her mouth was instantly dry. "He didn't mention it." And why should he?

"That didn't shock you." It was a statement.

Lenny didn't reply, she was running out of words to try and explain things away.

"What did you argue about then?" Duke pressed.

"He wants something I can't give him." Lenny rolled her eyes at the absurdity. Imagine, a man stressing over the girl not ready for a commitment. "He wants to know how I *feel*." She scoffed, thinking Duke would laugh with her.

"How do you feel?" He asked her seriously, looking at the garage floor.

"I don't know, Duke." Lenny frowned at him. "Why do you care?" Her stomach tightened as the mood in the room shifted with her words.

"C'mon, Lenny. Don't you think you're kind of being a brat about this?" Duke's tone had an edge he had never directed at Lenny and she was taken off guard.

"What do you mean?" She felt bitterness crawl into her mouth and she grit her teeth together. Duke's sudden coldness was neither helpful nor warranted.

"I'm not gonna lecture you or give a big speech. Just…" He took a few seconds to collect his thoughts and when he started speaking again she felt his agitation towards her in a way that she never had before. He was disappointed in her. "Life is hard, Lenny. And people tend to suck, I mean, no one's perfect. We need someone in our lives to help us through it. We make each other better, stronger."

"Yeah, but who's to say that I need Luke?" Lenny clipped, feeling herself getting defensive.

Fed up, Duke waved his hand at the back wall of snowboards and raised his voice, "That's your passion, right there, hanging on the wall like a dead animal! You really just gonna walk away from your first true love?" He turned and waved at the Lodge, "That man in there, brought you back to life when the rest of us were afraid you were beyond hope. And you don't know how you *feel*? The reasons you won't get back on the board or admit your feelings for Luke are the same. You're afraid of losing the *control*. You think you can't get hurt if you can control it. Well, guess what? Love isn't like that. You're either all in or not." He let out a disgusted breath and paced a short distance across the garage floor.

Lenny's face was hot. She was angry. Duke didn't have the right to tell her her reasons. They were hers and hers alone, she didn't owe him an explanation. And she didn't owe Luke one either.

"I thought you said you weren't going to lecture me," she bit out.

"I lied!" Duke snapped indignantly. "Your family and I have been far too forgiving and coddling to you. You need to grow up one of these days."

"This coming from a guy who hates organized sports and lives *alone* in a house *I* paid for!" Lenny was taking it too far but she wanted to hurt him the way he was hurting her.

"Hey!" Duke stormed towards her, pointing his finger in her face. "I don't need your charity, say the word and I'm gone!"

Lenny stood her ground, she was afraid in that moment that maybe Duke actually would leave but she was too stubborn to take back her words. Instead she jutted out her chin and clenched her jaw.

"You can't keep running away from the things that scare you!" Duke threw his hands out to the sides in exasperation.

"I didn't run away!" Lenny shouted back, angry tears burning the back of her eyes.

"Really?" His sarcasm thick, "Then what would you call it?"

"Escaping!" Lenny's stomach fell to the floor as she shouted her truth across the garage. His eyes grew wide at her response and she felt her hands starting to tremble. The room was quiet and Lenny could hear her pulse roaring through her ears. She looked down at the floor, unable to watch Duke's face as he tried to read her mind. Tried to figure out where she had gone. She was tired of carrying her secret for so long. She knew it had changed her. She had let it change her, propelled that change. She didn't want to be who she had been. She wanted to be someone else. She wanted to be safe.

"Were you a prisoner?" He asked, his voice calm, concerned.

***

"I'm not...I'm not doing this." Lenny's voice sounded tired and scared. Duke knew he was almost there. He didn't want to push her. He had wanted her to come to terms with it on her own. She was more stubborn than he had given her credit for. He knew that there was a huge likelihood that she would hate him after this. He had to take that risk. She needed him to.

"What happened, Lenny?" It was the question everyone kept asking her, the one she had never answered.

"I told you, I don't remember." She crossed her arms over her middle and stared at the floor. Duke thought she looked especially small like that.

"You've never forgotten a detail in your life. Tell me the truth." His voice was hard, unforgiving. A flash of terror went across her face. How he hated himself.

"What happened to the girl who looked fear in the face and laughed as she found her line?" Her eyes unfocused and he knew he was reaching her.

"What happened to the girl who flew past seasoned backwoods riders and raged down the ridge line in Alaska?" She shifted and turned away from him. Duke was close, he could feel it. He was going to have to wreck her before he could save her. He raised his voice again, forcing the issue. "What happened, Lenny? Where'd she go?"

"I can't do this." Lenny started to the door of the garage but Duke got there first.

"No, we do this now. No more running." He blocked the way with his body and Lenny tried to push past him but he was solid. He grabbed her by her shoulders and looked into her face as she stared at the center of his chest.

"Let me by, Duke." Lenny said, a false fire on her tongue.

"No." Duke repeated. He clenched his jaw, having a final debate with his insides on whether or not he should be doing this. "I want to know what happened to you." He swallowed his own fear and took a deep breath. "I wanna know where the girl is that I fell in love with."

Lenny met his eyes at last and he saw pain and betrayal covered by confusion.

"What?" The word was a whisper and he almost didn't hear it due to the ringing in his ears at his own confession.

"Yeah, Lenny." His voice low. "Where is the strong, powerful, confident woman that I am hopelessly in love with?" He'd said it twice now. He hoped he didn't throw up before they got through this.

Lenny looked down at the floor; she reeled like she'd just gotten the wind knocked out of her. She turned to walk away but Duke grabbed her arm and whirled her back to face him. Lenny pushed him away with force, her face twisted in anger.

"Stop saying that!" She yelled. "Stop using that word! What is wrong with you people?"

She backed away from Duke, her eyes wild. "Shane, Luke, now YOU?! You don't know what love is! Stop throwing that word around like it means something!" She screamed at him, her hands clenched into fists at her sides.

Duke felt his tears pool in the corners of his eyes as he watched her fall apart in front of him. He couldn't stop now, he was committed, and they were almost there. He grabbed her by the shoulders again and looked her square in the face.

"Tell me what happened, Lenny! Tell me what *really* happened before the accident! 'Cause I know damn good and well this isn't about a bad wreck!"

Tears started to spill down Lenny's cheeks as they stared at one another. The look of defeat that hung in her eyes broke his heart. A sob caught in her chest as she tried to breathe normally and Duke folded her into his arms. He held her body as it shook with released emotion.

"Shane slept with Cody." She clung to him as the truth escaped her lips.

Duke closed his eyes and held her close. So that was it. That was the big secret.

"When?" He asked gently, pressing his cheek to the top of her head.

"At the Olympics, the day before my event...the day before the crash." Her breathing steadied as she brought her emotions under control again. "I caught them. They said that it was my fault for being," she swallowed and her voice was laced with cynicism, "Such a tease. They said I was incapable of love and Shane needed a *release* before his event. And I was too *selfish* to help him with it." A disgusted shiver swept through her body and Duke resisted the urge to put his fist through a wall.

"I couldn't get my head right, I lost focus." Lenny continued shakily. "That's how I wrecked."

She pulled away from him and tried to wipe the watery mess off her face. She was red and splotchy but her eyes were clear. Finally.

Duke didn't want to let her go. He wanted to hold her until she felt safe again. But that wasn't his place. Instead, he sat down on the garage step and she settled next to him.

The rest of the story spilled out unencumbered and he had to bite his tongue to keep from going off on his own tangent against Shane and Cody.

"After the accident, they both came to see me in the hospital. The doctor said I had enough brain damage that I probably would never remember the previous twenty-four hours. So I went with it. I just couldn't foresee trying to figure out how to walk again while dealing with their shit, you know? I thought they'd get tired of the whole thing and move on if I ignored them. Then Shane moved out here and Cody wouldn't shut up about a rematch and I guess I just decided I wanted to try a different life for a while. One where I didn't have to see those two every day."

"Why didn't you just confront them after you'd recovered?" Duke couldn't help but ask.

"Because then they would have known that I lied about forgetting it.

182

And I was afraid that would make me just like them."

"You could never be like them." Duke put an arm around her shoulder and pulled her against his side.

"I didn't realize how much time had gone by until I found the engagement ring in Shane's truck. I couldn't live a lie, I had to leave." She paused and looked up at Duke, her face sorrowful. "I'm sorry I didn't tell you sooner."

"No, Lenny" Duke cut her off. "They were wrong on so many levels. I understand why you split. You don't have to apologize."

Lenny was quiet for a long time and then she said, "I can't stop thinking that they might be right." Duke looked at her with a frown. "What if I *am* incapable of love?"

Duke sighed heavily and held her tighter. "You're just incapable of their twisted version of love. You have more heart and passion than anyone I have ever met. I see you with your family and your friends and even complete strangers. You're kind and compassionate and you honestly care." He paused, letting his words sink in. "You're capable of great love; greater than those two will ever experience in their lifetime."

He wrapped both of his arms around her and blinked back his own tears. Finally. After so much avoidance and running away, maybe now she could begin to move forward. He knew there had been a connection between her accident and her resistance to fall in love. If he could just get her past her fear, she'd fall headlong in love with the man who deserved her the most. And as much as Duke hated to admit it, it wasn't him.

"We need to get you on a line as soon as possible. You can't let them take that away from you. And not up at Aspen, here, on your home turf." His voice was thick with emotion.

"What if it's been too long? What if I forgot everything you've taught me?" She asked honestly.

"Then I can *re-teach* you." Duke replied. "I'll always have your back, you know that."

She seemed to consider his proposal and he felt a thrill go through him that she didn't outright say no this time.

"How about you get some sleep, and we'll talk about a plan tomorrow over breakfast." He helped her into a standing position.

She gave him a contrite smile, "I think I really screwed things up with Luke tonight."

"One thing at a time. Let's get you on a line first. We can fix everything with Thor after that."

"Thor?" Lenny asked quizzically.

"Well, you know, he has that chiseled jaw and those piercing blue eyes." Lenny laughed as Duke directed her up into the house and shut off the lights to the garage.

***

    They took the sleds as far as they could and then started to hike up the mountain, the terrain getting steeper the further they climbed. Lenny refused to think about what was waiting ahead. Instead she focused on the climb. She tried to drink in the wilderness. Savoring every breath that included the scent of fresh pine. Her steps were solid, she didn't have trouble finding safe footing the whole way up. Duke was ahead of her and she could tell he was making sure to clear a little of the path to make it easier for her. She was, after all, out of practice.

    The band had protested, when then found out what the plan was but Lenny calmly explained that this was something she had to do. She could tell they felt left out by being left at the Lodge, but she had to do this without an audience. Luke, especially, seemed jilted. But like Duke said, one thing at a time.

***

    Duke was proud of Lenny for telling him the whole truth last night; he knew it hadn't been easy. He was determined that she see this through. Nothing had ever seemed so right like when Lenny took to the slopes. His insides were still churning from all the new information. Shane had better stay away or Duke would end him. And Cody, even though she was Duke's niece, was no longer welcome in his home. Lenny was really the only one who had ever mattered to Duke.

    She'd saved his life at a time when he was falling apart. He'd gotten into the Hollywood scene of snowboarding and things went from awesome to terrifying very quickly. You can only drink yourself into a blackout so many times before you decide that enough is enough. He got off the bottle and moved to the mountains where he met his niece's best friend.

    Lenny had been only twelve, but she was bold and daring and full of natural talent. Duke took the little bird under his wing and taught her all he knew. She gave him a reason to get up even when the depression threatened to force him to drink again. She took the information he gave her and turned herself into a legend. He started to only see her in the winter as school and competing took first place. But they stayed in good contact by phone.

    Then, after she had graduated high school at midterm, she wanted to take a trip into the back country of Alaska and ride some fresh powder. Duke hustled up some of his old riding buddies and arranged a two week trip

184

for his protégé.

But when Bird showed up, she wasn't this gangly little middle schooler anymore. She was nineteen and had transformed into a woman with unrivaled beauty. Her time spent on the mountains all over the world had given her an untamed, natural allure that was fiercely captivating. Duke spent most of the trip threatening his friends every time one of them so much as glanced at her.

His buddies did their best to show off but Lenny would match them, challenge for challenge. She had finally come into her own and Duke had nothing left to teach her.

That's where it had happened. That's where Duke began to look at her with brand new eyes. She was wild and unstoppable and fearless. He admired her for her talent and strength and courage. And little by little, he allowed himself to fall in love with her, knowing that nothing could ever come of it. She saw him as an old man, and a friend. And Duke was content with that, feeling blessed to have her friendship, to be that close to a wildfire and not get burned.

Duke had turned thirty during that trip to Alaska. He was in the prime of his physical riding career. But even at the top of his game, he took a little spill. He wrecked pretty majorly, cracking a couple ribs and getting bruised all to hell. Lenny had taken careful diligence to patch him back up, chewing him out the whole time for being reckless. He knew he would never forget the way her hands felt on his skin. Or how her hair fell past her face and tickled his bare chest as she leaned over to pack ice around his shoulder. He knew that was the closest that he'd ever get. And he had savored every second.

His little confession the night before hadn't come back up. He knew she hadn't forgotten it, not with her perfect memory, but he didn't want to talk about it anyway. He knew she needed someone that could offer her more than he could. He had accepted that years ago. He had risked his heart and his heart alone, he could deal with that.

***

They crested the top of Lenny's favorite ridge and she felt her heart beating faster and it wasn't just from the climb. The mountains opened up before her and she could see for miles.

"I never get tired of that." Duke breathed next to her. Lenny could only nod.

He turned and waited for her to make the first move.

"I don't know if I can do this Duke." Lenny was thinking about trying to convince him that it wasn't time, she wasn't ready.

"This is how it's going to work." Duke was all business. "You're gonna strap in, then you're gonna dig your chute, then your whole life is gonna change."

"How do you know?" Lenny was half stalling and half really wanting to know. "How do you know this is the answer?"

"Lenny, you have to try," he said gently. "I'll be right here if anything goes wrong."

Lenny took a deep breath. She leveled off the space where she would start her line and looked down the mountainside. Her legs were trembling and her heart was racing. She looked at Duke, her eyes pleading for another way, but she knew she had to do it. Now that she was up there, she could feel an old persistence creeping up from her toes and making its way to her head.

She had to go.

She had to fly.

She knew she was moving quickly but it felt like slow motion. She could feel the texture of the snow as it bent beneath her, carving a perfect path. She let go of all she had been holding back and images started to flash through her mind. Her fight with Shane, walking in on him and Cody getting dressed, the following argument. The initial crash, the slow process of recovery, fights with her parents, avoiding Shane, running away with Double Blind Study, Luke. Luke and his voice and his lips and his amazingly strong arms.

She veered to the left, following her instincts, taking her line over a ridge and going airborne. The rush was intoxicating. It was better than she had remembered. She landed gracefully, fluidly. Her body a perfectly oiled machine, moving and adjusting with the terrain before her. She controlled her speed, enjoying every twist and edge. Her mind was finally starting to put things in order.

This is where she belonged, out in the open. Free.

Not the condescending "Freebird" that Cody and Shane had constantly called her which was more a ridicule than a nickname. No, more innocent than that. Duke had given her the nickname "Bird" the first time he met her. He compared her to a lark and would always quote lines from his favorite George Meredith poem to her while they hiked up to a new chute. As she went over another lip and caught even more air than before, his voice echoed through her mind:

"He rises and begins to round,
He drops the silver chain of sound
Of many links without a break,
In chirrup, whistle, slur and shake,
All intervolved and spreading wide,

Like water dimples down a tide
Where ripple ripple overcurls
And eddy into eddy whirls;
A press of hurried notes that run
So fleet they scarce are more than one,
Yet changing-ly the trills repeat
And linger ringing while they flee, ..."

In that moment, as she seemed to hover in the air with Duke's voice echoing through her head and the images of what had happened flashed before her, she realized that it wasn't her fault. What Shane and Cody had done was their choice. She didn't *earn* their betrayal. The blame belonged on them. And it had been wrong for them to try to put it on her. But it had been even worse that she had allowed them to blame her.

She allowed them to make her feel like she had no worth, like she was nothing. And she had started running, slowly at first and then gaining momentum with her decision to make that interview with Carl. She thought if she got far enough away, she'd stop feeling so trapped in her own weakness. But only facing the truth of what had happened could truly release her. She finally felt absolved of the guilt that had accompanied their disloyalty and vilification.

Lenny landed safely again, nearly breathless. Her mind having been put right and finally at peace. She guided the board expertly to a stop and pushed her goggles up on her head.

She could see Duke making his descent and she shook her head. He never followed her line. It was like an unspoken rule between them. They each had to find their own way. He came to the edge of a ridge she knew was too steep of a drop, that's why she had avoided it. She held her breath, hoping against her own gut that he wouldn't go for it.

"Sonofabitch..." Lenny muttered as Duke dropped off the ridge and out of view. She waited for a few seconds, her heart starting to thud in her chest. Suddenly, Duke sprang over a slope and raged down the rest of the mountain. Lenny breathed a sigh of relief.

Duke came skidding to a stop right in front of her, huge grin plastered on his face.

"Did you see that? Thought I was a goner for sure!" He yelled excitedly.

"You scared me half to death!" Lenny yelled back, laughing.

Duke disengaged his boots and scooped her up in a huge hug. She laughed freely as he swung her around. She hadn't forgotten how to fly after all.

187

Chapter 13

The Deepest Blues Are Black

Lenny and Duke had been gone all day. It was only mid-afternoon but it might as well have been midnight with the way Luke's head was messing with him. He was trying really hard to be the rational, reasonable guy that his band mates knew and loved but having Lenny out in the wilderness with a man who was undoubtedly in love with her had pushed his rationality over a cliff.

Jealously wasn't something that Luke had ever had to deal with. Not since high school anyway. He felt like an idiot. Even after Duke had all but given his blessing the night before, Luke still felt...tense.

"Here they come." Mike interrupted his brooding and nodded out the large windows facing the back of the house. Sure enough, two snowmobiles were pulling up out back.

Lenny disembarked and said something to Duke before entering the house through the back door. Duke drove his sled towards the garage to put it away.

"Hey guys!" Lenny's face was red from the cold and she had snow stuck in her hair. She took off her hat and gloves and started removing her coat.

"How was it?" Harrison bounded across the room and jumped onto the back of the sofa, eager for the recap.

Lenny laughed at him and Luke noticed that it was louder, more released than before. Her smile was wide and her face radiant. He thought she was beautiful before, but this was a whole new experience.

"It was...perfect." Lenny giggled again and the guys exchanged puzzled smiles.

Mike was the only one who seemed to not be surprised. He grinned broadly and wrapped her into a hug. Her arms encircled him in return and they shared a moment that Luke knew he'd never fully grasp.

"So, what happens now?" Blake frowned and crossed his arms. "Are you leaving the tour or what?" Luke hadn't even considered that Lenny being able to return to snowboarding might mean her leaving their lives.

"Of course not!" Lenny exclaimed as her hug with Mike ended.

"You can't get rid of me that easily." Her eyes swung over to Luke and she said a thousand different things to him with that one look. A recklessness burned on the edge of her irises and he realized that something in her had been awakened in the past few hours. It was a definite turn on.

"But, I have to fill you in on a few...unsavory details of my life." Lenny made a face as she entered the kitchen. "You guys hungry? I'm starving, I need nutrients."

The band gathered in the kitchen and Lenny fixed them up with sandwiches. Duke joined them after he had put the sleds away and Lenny calmly explained the details of her 'reckoning' as Duke had called it. The group absorbed the information and came to the same collective opinion. That Shane was the worst and Cody was the devil.

Luke hoped that he and Lenny would have a second chance at their conversation from the night before. Having been filled in on the details of her relationship with Shane now, Luke could absolutely see how the two didn't compare. He wasn't Shane, and he never would be. He needed to make sure that Lenny understood that.

"This probably changes a lot of things about Aspen." Sway stated the obvious.

"I still have to go." Lenny threw a towel at Duke when he rolled his eyes. "Contractual obligations. But I would still love it if you guys all joined me." She looked around at them hopefully.

"Of course we'll be there, mama." Blake grinned mischievously.

"Absolutely." Sway agreed, linking eyes with Blake and mirroring his smile.

"Are we gonna have a talk with Shane?" Harrison asked, noticing his friends weird behavior.

"You're awesome at subtly, you know that?" Blake closed his eyes in frustration.

"What?" Harrison asked, perplexed.

"Are you coming too?" Luke directed at Duke.

"Nah, you guys got this. I hate it up there, too many people."

Luke inwardly breathed a sigh of relief. While he respected Duke and his position in Lenny's life he couldn't help but feel like Duke's presence would keep he and Lenny from getting any closer.

***

They packed their bags that night and got ready to depart for the weekend in Aspen. Duke would drive them all to the airport early the next morning. Lenny was actually looking forward to the trip now, her conscience clear and her mind focused. Shane and Cody may have held her

190

back in the beginning but she had chosen to stay there. Now she was back.

She stood in her room looking out over the dark mountains being lit by the moon. She stretched her tight muscles and closed her eyes. She started when she heard someone in the doorway. It was Duke, again. He looked a little more friendly than he had the night before in the garage.

"You always did have the best view up here." He nodded out the large, wall sized windows.

Lenny smiled, walking over to her bed and sitting on the edge. She motioned with her head for Duke to join her. She saw him consider it for a moment before relenting and sitting down.

"When you coming back?" Duke asked softly.

"We have to leave for London right after Aspen."

"So, you're still gonna be the assistant?"

"Yeah, for now. It's really fun." Lenny's voice got wistful. "And they're really good guys, I like being there for them."

"You've always been a good friend." Duke looked down at his hands and then back out the window.

"I'll come home after that." Lenny leaned her shoulder against his, sensing his melancholy mood.

"You don't have to promise anything right now. Things can still change between now and then." Duke pointed out.

Lenny let out a heavy sigh, Duke was right. Anything could happen she supposed.

"I'll call you." She decided to promise instead.

Duke chuckled. "Good. That'll be nice."

The silence became comfortable, like it always did between them. She felt him take a deep breath and he put an arm around her. She eased into his embrace and closed her eyes.

"For singing till his heaven fills,
'T is love of earth that he instills,
And ever winging up and up,
Our valley is his golden cup,
And he the wine which overflows
To lift us with him as he goes..."

Duke's deep voice reciting his favorite poem to her, the poem he had given to her when she was still a child, along with all the heavy emotions they had shared with one another over the past few days, it was almost enough to make her heartbeat stop. He did love her. She had no doubts.

"Thank you, Duke." She whispered into his chest.

"For what?" Duke grunted.

"For never giving up on me." Lenny said quietly.

191

Duke didn't know what to say, so he didn't say anything. He was content to hold her until she had fallen asleep. He picked up her resting body and placed it carefully on the bed, pulling a blanket over her bare arms. He stared down at her, wanting to be the one who could...just wanting to be the one.

Duke walked down the steps slowly and made his way to his room. He crawled into his own bed in the dark and listened to the quiet of the house. He enjoyed living alone but he would miss Lenny desperately.

Part of him hoped that she and Luke would run off and get married in Europe and never come home. All he ever wanted was for her to have an unending adventure. He knew that Luke could offer all of that and so much more. Besides, Luke was totally in love with her. She would be safe with him.

***

Spinning around quickly, Lenny shoved the last of her clothes in the dresser in her suite. She knew she only had a few minutes before the band showed up at her room and she really didn't want to be unpacking her underwear in front of them. She slid the empty duffel into the closet just as there was a knock on her door.

Her loud and rowdy group entered the room with more fanfare than was necessary but it still made her smile.

"Check out the view you have!" Sway whistled as he flopped himself onto her bed.

"See? I told you." Harrison said to Blake. "Her room is *always* better than ours."

"And *I* told *you* it's because she's better than us." Blake replied.

"And I told both of you to knock it off." Lenny reprimanded with a smile.

The view was pretty stunning. Buttermilk Mountain had been turned into a phenomenal course for the Winter X Games. Hundreds of people had worked tirelessly on it for weeks now, constructing the perfect place for one of the most exciting competitions in the world. Thousands of pounds of snow had been moved and rearranged to create both ideal and difficult terrain for the athletes.

Lenny and the guys had been some of the first to arrive. She had a room to herself but the guys split three rooms between them. She wasn't sure how that worked out and didn't ask.

Luke had his hands in his pockets and stood regarding her carefully. They still hadn't had a moment alone together since their last very tense conversation. She felt heat creep up her neck as his blue eyes flicked up and down the length of her. She couldn't stand the wall that seemed to be between them and she impulsively threw her arms around his neck.

His arms wrapped around her immediately and he buried his face in her neck letting out a small groan, "I missed you."

"I missed you back," she whispered in his ear.

"Um, do you guys want to be alone?" Blake interrupted from behind her.

Luke let her go and smiled crookedly. Lenny rolled her eyes at Blake and readjusted her hoodie as she turned around.

She walked to the dresser and grabbed their VIP passes she had gotten from Patrick and passed them out. "These will get you into all the events and the VIP tent." She stepped back and put her hands in her back pockets as she further explained. "I have X Fest today and tomorrow. Patrick stacked my schedule to appease as many sponsors as possible. I have two interviews today, an hour in the autograph booth and a demo. You guys can have free reign, just don't embarrass me." She added with a grin, she knew they would be amazing, she had no doubts. Not even about Sway.

Her phone made a 'chirp' noise and she picked it up off the dresser glancing at the screen. It was Cody, wondering if she was here yet. Lenny put the phone in her pocket without bothering to reply.

"Hey, when do we get to meet Shane?" Harrison asked from his corner.

"In a perfect world, never. But chances are he's lurking around here somewhere. He's kind of a media whore." Lenny replied sourly.

"We're famous, too," Sway pointed out.

"Not as famous as he is in this place," Lenny countered. "Why do you want to meet him at all?"

"No reason." Blake elbowed Harrison before he could reply.

Lenny rolled her eyes, "Just don't get into any trouble." She moved toward the door, "C'mon, let's go see who is here before I have get to work."

They hung out in the VIP lounge for a couple hours, rubbing shoulders with sportscasters, celebrities and the best athletes in the world. The band knew a lot of the people there and it was sort of a mini reunion. They visited with other artists who also happened to be fans of the X Games and made fast friends of those they didn't already know.

Nearly everyone was surprised to see Lenny, she had been notably absent in the last two years. She was hugged and high-fived and congratulated on returning to the sport. She downplayed the accolades and didn't really explain the reason for her attendance.

Her first interview only wanted her to talk about how exciting the Games were so far and who she thought would do the best today. She smiled and answered honestly, complimenting all the talent that she had witnessed so far. Fans had started to gather around the media tent, her appearance causing a stir.

When the interviewer announced Lenny was heading to the autograph booth next, the crowd moved in a wave that direction. Lenny always like this part, she enjoyed talking to fans and taking pictures with them. Especially the kids. She signed photos and passed them to fans, deflecting questions about her return to the sport. Some people had her sign their equipment or had even brought posters from home. She was more than happy to accommodate them all, posing for pictures and giving hugs.

Afterward, she headed back to the VIP lounge to see her friends. All of them were busy enjoying themselves and she felt good about that. Lenny had been worried they might not fit it but realized that was a ridiculous assumption. They fit in anywhere.

Luke approached her, looking bothered. She frowned at his worried expression.

"What's up?" She asked him, wondering when they would ever have a quiet moment alone together again.

"I just talked to a guy from…I don't know, some sports thing. And he said that your next interview will have Shane there." He eyed her warily.

Lenny's stomach gurgled uncomfortably. She knew she would have to deal with him eventually so this wasn't that big of a surprise. She just didn't want to do it on national television. Typical Shane, still trying to intimidate her into shutting up. She wouldn't be surprised if he had arranged it like this, he loved attention.

"I'm glad you told me." Lenny smirked. "That would've been a shock."

"Maybe you can get out of it. Fake food poisoning or something." Luke was trying to be helpful but Lenny knew this was something she needed to do. She was angry with Shane for what he'd done. Her fire was back and she was looking forward to giving Shane a good burn.

"No." She shook her head at Luke's suggestion. "Thanks. But I think I got this."

She turned on her heel and strode back to the media tents, prepared to give the interview of a lifetime.

***

It was long ago and far away, but for Lenny, the memory crept back to her most vividly. She had been fourteen when she had first lain on eyes on the smoldering hunk of athleticism that was Shane Brookings. He was four years her senior, but had dominated the half-pipe circuit for the better part of his short career. Tall, with wide, strong shoulders and rippling muscles, he looked too large to be so agile on a snowboard, yet he moved with a seductive fluidity. His strength carrying him to record breaking heights and crossing boundaries of flight. His square jaw and perfectly unshaven stubble gave him a roguish appearance that made girls swoon.

Lenny made it her purpose to show up on his radar. It took a few years, she was just a kid to him in the beginning, but after her trip to the back country of Alaska she gained a little more media attention, and Shane took notice. They flirted off and on for a couple of years, creating speculation in the sports world about them having super beautiful athletic babies. And then one day it happened. Shane decided he had to have her.

Looking back, Lenny realized there were several warning signs. Shane was always way into his own body, constantly working out and taking offers to pose half naked for whatever magazine wanted him. He would flirt shamelessly with every pretty girl who walked by; Lenny wrote it off to him having an outgoing personality. Just a few weeks into them dating and Shane started to get weirdly controlling about who Lenny could and could not talk to. She got an offer from *Sports Illustrated* to be in their swimsuit issue and Shane had pitched a fit. She turned it down to appease him but then Cody had swooped in and taken the gig. Lenny should have caught on right away. But she'd never been in a relationship so she really had nothing to compare it to.

Lenny knew it was unusual by the world's standards to be a twenty-three year old virgin, but she'd been busy having a life and never really thought about having sex. It was there, in the back of her mind, she just assumed that when it was time she would know. Completely confident in every decision she'd made in her life thus far, it was normal for her.

So when Shane had started to pressure her into having sex the night before the biggest run in her career, Lenny balked at the idea.

"No, I'm not ready for that step. And besides, I don't want a big distraction in my head for tomorrow."

They were sitting in her room, a small dorm-sized bedroom with two sets of bunks. She and Cody were roommates with two other girls who had recently left because they had won their medals and wanted to go home. Shane had started to make more frequent visits to her room to make-out.

"C'mon, it'll make you do even better tomorrow." He whispered in her ear as his hand traveled from her knee up her thigh.

Lenny shoved his hand away and stood up. She was not liking this side of Shane at all.

"There's no way for you to know that." She frowned. *"I don't want*

to, it's not a discussion."

Shane put on his best puppy-dog face, trying again.

"Please, baby, you're just so hot I can hardly keep my hands off you." He stood up and pulled her close against his body. *"I want you so bad and I love you so much."* He started kissing her neck.

Lenny shoved him away from her. *"Knock it off. I'm serious, Shane."* She crossed her arms and her frown deepened. *"This isn't happening."*

Shane's face shifted to affronted and he put his hands on his hips, scowling at Lenny. She stood firm, not sure what to expect.

"What the hell, Lenny? What's your problem?" He barked, all sweetness leaving him.

Lenny narrowed her eyes. *"I'm pretty sure I'm not the one with the problem."* She grabbed her jacket and slipped it on.

"Where are you going?" He demanded, grabbing a hold of her arm.

She twisted free as she yanked open the door. *"To get some fresh air, I suggest you do the same."*

She left in a huff, slamming the door behind her. Lenny stalked though the Village, calming down quickly. She ran into a few Olympians she had just met that week and they invited her to join them for their evening activities. She relaxed in the fun atmosphere watching other events and competitors. She was feeling in a much better mood when she went back to her room to get rested before her own run the next day.

She opened the door and stopped in her tracks. Her voice stuck in her chest as her eyes that never missed anything viewed the heart wrenching scene before her.

Cody's toned and tanned body was only in a bra and panties and she was hastily yanking a shirt over her head. Shane was in his boxers and pulling his jeans up. Their faces were flushed and they were still breathing heavy. They must have just...finished... Lenny felt her stomach turn as her brain tried to wrap around this blatant betrayal.

She finally found her voice. It sounded strange and angry in her own ears. She wondered what it sounded like to them.

"You have got to be kidding me." She stood still in the doorway, not wanting to enter the room and have to feel the remnants of their recent passions.

"What did you expect?" Cody glared at her, running her fingers through her caramel colored tresses to smooth out the tousle they'd just been through. *"You're such an effing tease. I'm just glad I could be there to fill in. Didn't come in second this time."* She said smugly.

Lenny's eyes widened at her friend's words. *"You're not seriously*

196

suggesting that this is okay?"

"Calm down, Lenny. Don't make a big deal out of this." Shane spoke to her like she was child as he pulled his shirt over his head.

"Don't make a big deal? Are you serious?" Her voice was starting to get louder and people walking by in the hallway were taking notice. A small crowd started to gather a few feet away, listening in.

"I needed a release, I gave you first dibs, and you declined. I found it somewhere else. You shouldn't be mad about this. This is what you wanted, isn't it?" Shane taunted.

"You're an asshole!" Was all Lenny could get out. She was losing her resolve and starting to crumble. She couldn't believe what they had just done but what was even harder to swallow is that they were defending themselves.

"I told Shane that you guys would probably never have sex." Cody said haughtily. "That you have a hard time showing love. That you're broken." She let her words dig in. "But don't worry friend, *I'm always happy to help out."*

Lenny was going to be sick. She could feel the bile rising in her esophagus and swallowed hard to push it down. It didn't work; she ran to the bathroom a short distance down the hall, locked the door behind her, and wretched into the toilet. Then she sat down on the floor and cried.

It had always been hard for Lenny to make friends. With three older brothers she had gotten along with guys better. Girls tended to not like her. It didn't bother her too much, she had always had Cody. But now...Tears ran down her face, uncontrolled. She had never felt so alone in her life. Her family wasn't allowed in the Village and Duke was on an expedition and couldn't be reached. She had no one.

Their words had done more than stung. Lenny had always feared in the back of her mind that maybe romantic love wasn't something in her future. What if Cody was right? What if she was broken?

That week had been the worst of Lenny's whole life. She crashed the next day, allowing Cody to take gold and propel her into superstardom. The recovery from the accident had been slow. Shane and Cody kept coming around, trying to see if she remembered what they had done. Apparently they weren't feeling as secure in their lusty decisions after the fact. Lenny's confidence was sapped. She couldn't even rely on her own body to take her where she wanted to go. She decided to focus on recovery, hoping Cody and Shane would tire of the daily torture and leave her alone.

As she made progress, Shane used her accident as another way to be in the spotlight. He was constantly giving interviews about her well-being and their future together. It didn't take too many weeks of that before Lenny understood why he was in a relationship with her in the first place. It looked good. It made him look even more attractive, he was using her to stay visible. No appeal remained for her to return to snowboarding.

Two years flew by. Shane moved to Wyoming, he wanted to move into the Lodge but his condition was that Duke move out. Lenny declined that idea. She was getting so tired of him. Getting sick of all the fake 'I love yous' and empty gestures. She could feel herself growing colder and more distant with everyone around her. Her atmosphere was suffocating her and she started to fear she would die if she didn't leave.

Snowboarding was more than a sport for Lenny. It had been an extension of herself. It offered a freedom that other sports lacked. Her brothers said that it was her rebellious nature finding a home. It made her feel limitless and challenged. She hated the rules and propriety of growing up in an upper class family. Snowboarding gave her an outlet, a way to express love, rage, passion and grief. The mountain had been her canvas, the board her brush. Losing her confidence in that had been devastating. She was afraid that she would never feel at peace with herself again.

Not anymore. She was back, and her nonconformity had been stifled for too long. She had some catching up to do.

Lenny smirked to herself as she entered the media tent, instantly drawing attention to herself. She smiled politely at the staff, shaking hands and exchanging greetings. A little gal came over and fitted her with a mic and showed her which chair to sit in.

"Wow, you're even pretty up close." The girl giggled nervously, Lenny just smiled, remembering how graciously the guys dealt with the attention they received wherever they went and aimed to appear as comfortable as they always did.

She sat in the chair she was directed to and Brad, the interviewer, engaged her in small talk while they waited for Shane. She and Brad had been on good terms since she had started to gain attention in her early teens. He was apprised of all her success and failures and knew her family relatively well, too. That was the thing about sportscasters, they stuck around the industry for a long time and made friends. It gave them better interviews.

"There's been quite a bit of pressure on me to ask you some hard questions ever since it was announced you were going to be here." Brad said, testing Lenny's reaction.

"You can ask me anything you want, Brad." Lenny replied with a sincere smile, hoping he'd get the hint.

Brad's eyebrows went up at the open door invitation. Normally, a celebrity such as Lenny would have limits or guidelines set up at the beginning of the interview. He smiled with intrigue at her unflinching response.

198

Lenny's attention was drawn to the flurry of activity coming towards her. Shane Brookings entered the tent and flashed everyone his dazzling smile. The mic girl got so flustered she forgot her job and blushed a deep maroon. Lenny hadn't seen Shane since the day before she'd had her interview with Carl. He looked good. Not great, but good.

He approached Lenny and Brad and coolly took his seat. He had kept his dark hair trimmed short and had grown a nice goatee that showed off his angular jaw. He was tall, well over six feet, his large, muscular frame engulfing the chair he sat in. His eyes were pools of amber that glinted in the sunlight that peeked through the seams of the tent.

"I wasn't sure you'd show." He raised an eyebrow at Lenny, obviously surprised to see her.

Lenny didn't reply, she just smiled politely and faced Brad.

"So let's begin," Brad got the ball rolling, turning to speak into the camera. "Today at the Winter X Games we have snowboarding's elite, the sweethearts of the sport. Lenny Evans, eight time X Games gold medalist, once the darling of big mountain riding and Shane Brookings, reigning World Champion in the Half Pipe and current Olympic gold medalist. Also, snowboarding's most eligible bachelor. The world thought you two were going to get married and ride off into the sunset on Burton's newest design but that hasn't happened. How long since you've seen each other?"

"She left me about six months ago." Shane answered quickly, not looking in Lenny's direction.

"That's true, I did." Lenny nodded, keeping her face flat.

"Have you left the sport entirely?" Brad directed at Lenny.

"I thought I had, but I may be making a comeback." She smiled coyly.

She noticed Shane tense up next to her. So did Brad.

"What do you think about that, Shane?"

"I think...that's a pretty big decision and she should probably take it easy." He chuckled nervously. "I mean, she had a pretty major wreck, it might take a while for her to get back to the level she was at."

"Oh, I'm just as good as I always was." Lenny answered, relaxed and confident, a small smile tugging at the corners of her mouth.

"Is that why you guys decided to call it quits, difference of opinion?" Brad questioned, his eyebrows bobbing up and down.

"Yeah, sort of," Lenny answered before Shane could. "I should've ended it years ago. He had the opinion that it was okay to sleep with my best friend and my opinion was that it was wrong." She was laying the sarcasm on pretty thick and saw Brad swallow his grin.

She looked to Shane to voice his opinion on the matter; he was obviously blindsided. He started stuttering, trying to come up with something to counter Lenny's words. But nothing would come out.

"Is that true?" Brad asked Shane.

Shane couldn't answer; he just stared at the ground.

"There was speculation at the time of your wreck that you were distraught before approaching the chute." Brad, realizing that Shane was worthless at this point, pointed back to Lenny.

"Yeah, I had just caught them a few hours prior. In my room." She heard a collective gasp around the tent.

"When you say 'them' you mean…" Brad prodded, a light sheen of sweat was becoming visible by his hairline and Lenny knew she was standing on the edge of acceptable interview protocol. She could practically hear Patrick-the-lawyer reading her retraction statement to the press now. He'd probably cite exhaustion or something.

"Shane and my best friend at the time, Cody Carmichael."

Lenny heard a screech from somewhere off camera but she didn't let it distract her.

"That must've been pretty awful." Brad prodded Lenny to elaborate.

"You know, it really was. The worst part was how they made me feel less than myself. It took me some time to really come to terms with that." She glanced sideways at Shane but he was still mute and paralyzed.

"Shane has been acting like you were the one who broke *his* heart." Brad was trying to get Shane to react to something, anything.

"Weird, right?" Lenny made a face and Brad couldn't stop himself from laughing. "I feel bad for all the girls he's ever suckered into believing his sob story just so he can get pity sex."

"C'mon, Lenny." Shane had suddenly come back to life. "We don't have to do this here. Let's go talk somewhere in private."

Lenny ignored him and kept her focus on Brad.

"So you think you might be coming back to the sport in a full time capacity?" Brad asked, putting every ounce of professionalism into his voice as he could muster.

"I haven't made any decisions yet. But it's something I am considering." Lenny answered with a smirk. "I'm still damn good."

"Think you could win a medal in two years?" Brad speculated.

"If you're asking if I think I'm better than the gold medal defender, Cody Carmichael, then…" Lenny lifted her chin in defiance as she answered. "Yes. I am better than her, in a lot of ways."

Shane, completely humiliated, yanked off his mic and stormed out of the tent. Lenny smile apologetically at Brad.

"So, all good news here today." Brad turned to look into the camera. "Lenny Evans is considering making a return to snowboarding in time for the Winter Olympics and if today's interview is any indication of her passion, the rest of the world better start paying attention."

The red light on the camera went off and Lenny got up to leave. Brad stopped her and shook her hand.

"It's good to have you back, Lenny," Brad said sincerely. "And if you want to trash any other ex-boyfriends on TV please call me first."

"Okay, will do," Lenny laughed.

Luke greeted her in the VIP tent with a huge hug.

"That was amazing." Luke was positively beaming.

"You don't think it was a little over the top?" Lenny asked with a touch of anxiety. Sure, it felt good at the time but she was aware there could be significant fallout.

"Are you kidding me? I make my living by being over the top. I am the foremost expert on what 'over the top' is." He smiled at her again. "You were completely within reason."

"Thanks." She breathed a little sigh of relief. She had dealt with Shane, now she would have to deal with Cody. Lenny knew there would be trouble after she labeled her as the whorey, second-rate best friend.

"I think Blake and Sway were a little disappointed they didn't get to talk to Shane first." Luke said as he directed her back to the hotel.

"Oh, is that right?" Lenny laughed. "What did they think they were gonna do, rough him up?" She laughed again at the idea. She allowed Luke to lead her back to his room without really thinking about it.

He slid the key card into the door and let her inside. His room was smaller than hers. Just one bed and a bathroom.

"You and Mike sharing the King-size?" Lenny joked.

"No, I got my room to myself for the first time in…a while." He finished slowly.

"I bet that's gotta be nice." Lenny smiled and slipped off her hoodie, revealing a white tank underneath. She sat down on the bed, playfully bouncing a little. She watched Luke take off his outerwear.

She hadn't really looked at him yet since they'd arrived. He was so fit and lean, his muscles flexed and moved under his skin and were clearly visible beneath his shirt. His tattoos peeked out from under his long sleeves as he pushed them up and sat down on the chair. His blonde hair was a little longer than when they had first met, she noted as he raked it back off his face with his fingers. He had grown a short beard that only defined his chiseled features even more. His crystal blue eyes were crinkled at the sides, as if in perpetual smile. Her stomach did a back flip. Luke Casey could still take her breath away.

She wasn't sure what to say so she waited in the silence. Hoping Luke would speak.

After several minutes, Luke turned his terrible blue eyes on Lenny. Those eyes that had the power to make her heart stop.

"I'm here for *you* this week. Not the events, not the celebrities, not the weather. Just you. Whatever you need from me, you have it."

Lenny bit the inside of her cheek. She had been keeping him at a distance and yet here he was, offering more for her to misuse if that's what she chose. Her heart beat fast as she began to grasp his unrestricted devotion to her. It was a lot stronger than she had realized.

"I just got my head back on…" Lenny started slowly, she didn't want to hurt Luke but she wanted to be honest with him. "I'm sort of just starting to feel comfortable in my own skin….I still can't give you an absolution on what that means for us." She watched his expression go from thoughtful to forlorn.

"I really like you, Luke." Lenny wanted to grab him and kiss him. "But, logistically, how do you see this playing out?" He frowned at her and she continued. "You're a rock star and you have this hugely successful job that requires you to be gone for long periods of time. And I'm considering going back to competing which also requires a lot of travel." She took a breath. "We might not see much of each other after the rest of this tour."

"We could make it work." He said moving to sit next to her on the bed.

Lenny nodded, knowing that was a possibility.

"I don't think it would be smart for either of us to promise something that huge before we know if that's something we really want."

Luke took one of her hands in both of his. "Are giving me the 'let's just be friends' talk?" He smiled, only half-kidding.

Lenny's eyes widened. "No, not at all. I just think we should enjoy what we have right now and not put so much pressure on what might be."

Luke looked down at her hand and chuckled. "Maybe Blake's right, maybe we are just a couple of hipsters."

Lenny took her other hand and touched his face, directing his eyes back up to hers. "I'll tell you what this is." She whispered. "I'm your girl, and you're my guy."

When his gaze traveled to her lips she felt her pulse quicken.

"I really enjoyed watching your interview." Luke said slowly, his eyes flicking back and forth from her eyes to her lips.

"Oh, yeah?" Lenny raised an eyebrow in question.

"Yeah," Luke leaned in fractionally. "I've never seen that reckless side of you before, it was kinda hot."

Lenny smiled slowly as Luke leaned closer. "You thought it was hot?"

His lips finally touched hers and an electric current ripped through her body. He delicately and determinedly worked his lips against hers. She grabbed his shirt in both hands and pulled him closer. One of his arms slipped around her back while the other cupped her face, directing their course of action. The kiss heated quickly and her body responded. Her hands found themselves twisting into his hair, pulling him closer. Lenny had only been kissed a handful of times in her life and no one ignited her the way Luke did.

She let an involuntary whimper when Luke slowly ended the kiss and stood up. He took a steadying breath and gave her a knowing smile.

"We have to be careful," he whispered in his gravelly voice. "I haven't kissed you in a long time and I'm afraid I could ask for too much too fast."

Lenny's stomach trembled as she understood what he was implying. And she agreed, she hadn't kissed him like that in weeks and it was like someone had set her lips on fire. She would have a hard time saying no. Unlike with Shane, where her thoughts never progressed past kissing, Luke made her want to throw caution to the wind.

She waited for her heart to return to a normal rhythm before she cleared her throat and stood up. "Maybe we should get some dinner after my demo. My dad is in town and he wanted to see you guys again."

"That's a really good idea," Luke nodded. "Knowing your dad is around will help keep my thoughts where they should be." He grinned and then winked. "Well, for the most part."

***

The table at the lodge-style restaurant was long and wide, comfortably fitting the group of seven. The lights were low, and tiny candles inside glass lamps created small pools of radiance on the table cloth. Lenny looked around at the faces that she had become so fond of over the past few months. Blake and Harrison, Sway and Mike. Luke. Her father.

Her gaze locked on Luke sitting across from her, his affection for her evident. It was less frightening than it was in the beginning, but it still left Lenny lightheaded and confused. Luke was carrying on a conversation with her father easily. Not something many people could do. Bruce Evans was always suspicious of those who had the potential to hurt his family. It was part of the reason Lenny had a hard time fully trusting someone, it's how she was raised.

She looked at her father. He was a good man. He had always encouraged Lenny to follow her dreams but he never made her decisions for her. He liked Luke. Lenny could tell by his laugh and the way he listened to Luke's stories. They had a lot in common, both from Boston, Celtics fans, avid fisherman, hated the same politicians. Lenny found herself picturing future holidays with both of these men, her mother and brothers. Was there a future there? With the rock star? Lenny didn't know how that could work. Maybe the details didn't matter right now.

"You're quiet, Lenna. Does your food taste okay?" Her father interrupted her thoughts. His face was relaxed and not pinched and worried like it had been for the past two years.

"Yeah, it's good...I was just thinking." Lenny answered softly, not wanting to break the quiet ethereal spell that had seemed to settle over the table.

"What were you thinking about, honey?" Her father genuinely wanted to know.

"I got on a board today." She let the words hang in the moment.

Her father sat up a little straighter in his chair and a smile began to stretch across his face. He was proud. It was always obvious when he was proud.

"And she did great," Luke added.

"You got to see it?" Her father asked in an excited whisper.

"It was just a short demo ride." Lenny couldn't hold back her delight, "But it felt really good."

The guys started to bombard her with questions, suddenly sensing that the subject was no longer taboo. They knew Lenny's dad didn't know she had been riding again so they had been trying to be careful. Apparently they had a lot they had been wondering about. Lenny gladly answered their queries and told some stories she hadn't thought about in a while.

***

Luke loved seeing Lenny's face glow with enthusiasm as she finally spoke about her most cherished pastime. He could never imagine giving up music for anything. Her return to snowboarding was obviously liberating.

"It's because of you." Lenny's father leaned over and spoke to Luke without the others overhearing. "Don't think I haven't noticed the remarkable change in my daughter since you entered the picture." He took a drink of his water and replaced his napkin on his lap. "I hope you stick around."

Luke watched Lenny's bright expression and replied, "I intend to." He knew, without knowing how, that the love he felt was so much more than anything he'd felt before.

He also knew that it was Duke, and not himself, that had pushed her to trust herself again. That gnawing feeling was still in the pit of Luke's stomach. Duke and Lenny had a connection that couldn't be explained and

204

Luke didn't know if he would ever be able to fill that role. Duke had boldly encouraged Luke to pursue Lenny; he seemed pleased with the arrangement. But Luke had been able to sense Duke's underlying feelings for Lenny, even if Lenny didn't know about them. And wasn't it ultimately Lenny's decision in the end anyway? Or could two men, both in love with the same woman, just decide between them who would get her?

Lenny wasn't a piece of property that could be passed back and forth, exchanging one master for another. She would have to decide. She was the only one who had that power.

Luke looked at her from across the table and tried to relax. She was his girl right now. He chose to focus on that.

Chapter 14

All Apologies

When dinner had ended, Lenny said farewell to her father and climbed into the shuttle van with the rest of the band. She slid the door closed behind her and took a seat in the middle next Luke, who rolled his eyes at the argument taking place behind him. Lenny looked over his shoulder and saw Mike with his arms crossed over his chest and a glower on his face. Sway was against the window, his focus on his cell phone. And poor Harrison, squashed between them.

The van was quiet as it bumped along the road, returning them to the hotel. Lenny wasn't sure why it seemed so tense and awkward; obviously something had happened when she wasn't looking.

"I didn't say you were hiding anything. I just asked a question. That's all." Mike broke the silence. Lenny felt Luke sigh heavily next to her.

"It's none of your business, so back off!" Sway snapped.

Lenny's head whirled around in surprise but Luke put his hand on her knee and signaled her to not get involved. The van stopped and Luke gestured for Lenny to exit quickly. The rest of the guys bailed out behind them.

"Sway-" Mike tried again.

"Seriously, Mike! Stop being so frickin' insecure!" Sway cut him off. "I have a freaking friend! Can't I have a *one freaking friend* outside of this *stupid* band?!"

Lenny stood stock still. The guys argued sometimes but this was intense, even for them.

"Okay, Sway and I are going to see if we can catch that half-pipe shit." Blake calmly put an arm around the bassist's shoulders and directed him away from the group. Sway threw a final glare in Mike's direction.

"He's overreacting." Mike tried to defend himself but Luke just shook his head at his friend.

"You guys push each other's buttons, you always have." Luke placed a hand on the small of Lenny's back.

Mike's brows pushed together and his mouth formed a hard line. Harrison clapped a hand down on Mike's shoulder, drawing his attention.

"C'mon, man." Harrison's eyes filled with compassion. "Let's take a walk." Mike's jaw clenched momentarily before he relented and followed his friend.

Lenny looked up at Luke, completely confused. "What was that all about?"

Luke directed her back to the hotel and opened the door for her. "They have a rocky history. Some wounds take longer to heal than others. They'll be fine, Blake will talk Sway down and Harrison will figure out what's eating at Mike. They'll all be best friends again in no time."

Lenny frowned, Luke seemed pretty sure of the outcome but she had never seen Sway that pissed off before. They walked to her hotel room and she opened the door, still thinking about the scene she'd just witnessed. Luke sat on the couch and patted the seat next to him so she'd join him.

"Don't let it worry you. They can act like they want to kill each other sometimes, but its short lived."

"I guess I have to take your word for it." Lenny pursed her lips. "I don't know them as well as you do...obviously." That last thought troubled her. She had been under the impression that she'd gotten close to these guys, but there was still so much she didn't know. She rested against Luke's side as he switched on the TV, she would probably never know them as well as Luke did.

"You said..." Lenny bit the inside of her cheek, not sure if she should allow her curiosity to get the better of her. "You said something about old wounds...?"

Luke sighed and raised his eyebrows. "Yeah...a few years ago, Mike had a girlfriend."

Lenny adjusted herself on the sofa and laid down with her head on Luke's thighs. She folded her hands across her stomach and waited patiently for him to continue.

"Her name was Ilsa. She was a model from Berlin." Luke rubbed his stubble with one hand and placed the other hand across Lenny's. "Mike was crazy in love with her but she was...undecided. She had a problem with him using and she went to Sway for...advice."

"Oh." Lenny breathed as she followed that train of thought.

"Yep. Long story short, Sway and Ilsa got closer than friends and she dumped Mike for him. Mike overdosed the next day."

"Damn." Lenny had no idea. No wonder they had issues. That would be hard to move past. She felt guilt cramp in her stomach having the information inside of her now.

"Hey, don't feel bad." Luke ran his finger across her hairline. "They would've told you eventually, you're part of the band."

"It's so personal, I feel like I shouldn't know."

208

"That's because you have a good heart." Luke smiled down at her and Lenny involuntarily blushed.

He stared down at her for few minutes, not speaking, a look a pure contentment on his face.

"I like this." He said quietly. His deep voice vibrating through his chest and into Lenny's shoulder.

"What's that?" Lenny asked.

"Just being here with you."

Lenny closed her eyes and smiled. She liked this too. Finally, after all the drama that had occurred during the past few days, they had time to just...be. Together.

His hand traveled down hers and his fingers worked their way into her own. They had nowhere to go, no one expecting them.

"What?" Luke asked her.

Lenny opened her eyes. "What?"

He grinned at her, "You're smiling. I wanted to know why."

"I guess I'm just happy." Lenny answered honestly.

"You're not gonna jump up and run away from me?" Luke teased.

"Nope." She chuckled lightly. "Not today."

***

Luke was just about to say something when there was a knock on the door, interrupting their cozy moment.

Lenny sat up and went to answer it. Luke watched her move with more self assurance than before. Getting her back to the sport she loved was still multiplying in subtle improvements. Luke had to wonder if he could handle all of Lenny at the top of her game. He sure wanted to try.

Lenny opened the door and Harrison stood before her, eyes wide.

"What's up, Harry?" Lenny asked and Luke smiled at how sweet she was to his friends. He got off the couch and joined her at the door.

"I thought maybe I should come and get you." Harrison's voice was nervous and Luke suppressed a chuckle. "Cody's calling you out."

"What do you mean?" Lenny's eyebrows drew together.

"She finished her event and set a new world record and she's challenging you to come out and beat it." Harrison was positively giddy with excitement. "She's really working up the crowd."

"That's ridiculous, Harrison. I'm not registered for an event." Lenny was shaking her head. Luke rested his hand on her back, letting her know he was there.

"Maybe you should try to talk to her," Harrison shrugged.

"I was gonna have to deal with it eventually." Lenny rolled her eyes as she grabbed her coat and hat.

***

The air outside was electric as Lenny made her way through the crowd. With the sun down it had grown considerably colder than it had been that afternoon. The sky was clear with stars making sharp pin pricks in the night sky.

Lenny made her way up to the small press booth at the top of the X Course. It was a long walk and she had time to get an idea of what she would say to Cody. She would probably have to apologize for slandering her to the media. She again pictured
Patrick, paperwork in hand.

The crowds started out overcharged and exuberant but as Lenny trekked through the terrain to the top of the hill, they quieted considerably. Luke and Harrison were flanking her. It was eerie, Lenny noted, like they were all watching her walk fatefully to her demise. She laughed off the thought internally. Sports always brought out the dramatics in people.

As she approached the booth she recognized Brad from earlier, Cody of course and Shane, not surprisingly. They would have to provide a united front to the public, Lenny supposed. A handful of others stood around and nearby, either with the media or with the X Games organization itself. Sway, Mike and Blake waited with their arms crossed, whatever previous quarrel they may have had was forgotten in this moment and they were once again united.

Lenny met Cody's eye contact and felt a twinge of guilt for having betrayed her friend earlier that day. Cody had betrayed her long ago, but Lenny had always hoped she was just little better than that. Turns out, she wasn't. She couldn't go back now, none of them could. What Shane and Cody had done was irreversible, Lenny could never trust them again. Maybe someday she'd work on the forgiveness aspect of it, but not yet.

"What do you want Cody?" Lenny addressed her former friend.

"You said you were better than me earlier today." Cody answered with a smugness Lenny knew was completely genuine. "I want you to prove it."

"Cody, I'm not registered in any events. I haven't qualified for anything." Lenny tried to speak slowly, like she was explaining the facts to a small child. "I know you're pissed but you can't just expect me to strap in and compete."

"Actually," Cody crossed her arms, "All events are done for the evening and my good friend Grant, here, said we can run the course. Just you and I."

210

Lenny looked at the course manager whose face was bright red. He nodded and looked down sheepishly. Cody could manipulate anyone, Lenny thought, her face twisting in disgust. She glanced up at Shane who had positioned his large frame behind Cody like he was her muscle. Lenny looked around at the band who had taken up positions of support around her. *This is sad, it's like the jocks against the band geeks all over again.*

"Unless all that stuff you said today was just a lie," Cody baited her. So that was her play, Lenny mused. If Lenny didn't take the challenge, than everything Lenny had accused them of earlier that day would look like a lie, tarnishing Lenny's integrity with the press and her fans forever.

Lenny sighed in resignation. Whether or not she was ready for this, it was going to happen.

"You don't have to do anything you don't want to do." Luke was talking to her now. "You don't have to prove anything to anyone. We know the truth."

"Yeah," Harrison added, "We know that you're better than this hussy."

Cody frowned at his word. "Hussy? What, is this the 1800's?" She rolled her eyes. "Idiot."

"Hey!" Blake snapped, "He may be an idiot, but he's *our* idiot!"

This was quickly turning into a television sitcom, Lenny noted. She needed to get a handle on her guys. She turned her back to Cody and grouped them in a huddle.

"I can do this," she whispered with excitement. She was near giddy with anticipation. "I can beat her."

"Lenny, you haven't competed in almost three years. I'm sorry, but a couple of good runs down the hill at home aren't the same thing." Sway patiently pointed out. Lenny appreciated his concern, it was a side of Sway that he didn't show often and it was kind of sweet.

"What would Duke say if he were here?" Mike wanted to know.

Lenny considered that for a minute before a wide smile spread across her face. "He'd tell me to kick her ass."

Luke winked at her and nodded his approval. "Then, kick her ass."

Lenny faced Cody again. "I don't have any of my equipment so I'll have to borrow someone's." Lenny was addressing the crowd more than Cody. She took pleasure in the shocked look that sprang to Cody and Shane's faces. They obviously had expected her to back out. How little they remembered of who she really was.

Fellow athletes started to outfit her with everything she would need; a board, goggles, gloves, boots. Lenny was touched by their words of encouragement and anticipation for the upcoming race.

"What, exactly do you have to do to win?" Luke asked as she put

211

on her borrowed gear. She heard the anxiety that he was trying to hide and it made her smile. Luke had never seen her compete before and she was looking forward to showing off just a little bit.

"The course has variable terrain, with berms and gap jumps, turns, drops and steep and flat sections. Basically, everything. Whoever gets to the bottom first, wins," she grinned at him.

"You sure you're ready for this?" He raised an eyebrow at her.

Lenny looked around at the crowd, a familiar buzzing pressure in the back of her skull. Their faces were full of wonder and excitement and she was feeling it. While back country riding was indeed her forte, performing for an audience was her guilty pleasure. She enjoyed knowing she was the best and knowing she was going to completely dominate her opponent. The fact that it was Cody and that Lenny had finally come to terms with what she and Shane had done, made it that much more exhilarating.

Normally, snowboard cross was run in the daylight with four riders at a time on the course. It was way past dark and spotlights had been turned on in order to light the run. It would still be tricky, blind spots everywhere. Lenny was even more confident in her ability to conquer. She had a connection with the snow and her board that she'd never been able to explain. It was as if she could feel the ground change before it actually happened.

She had the advantage.

"I got this." She winked at Luke. "You're about to see something amazing." She wasn't trying to be cocky, she was being honest.

***

Luke was incredibly turned on by Lenny's attitude. Sometimes girls put on a front to look tough but there was nothing fake about what Lenny was feeling. He'd seen her do things with ease that trained professionals struggled to accomplish. He was proud that she was willing to call herself his girl when she was as wild and untamed as the mountains she came from.

He impulsively grabbed her face with his mittened hands and kissed her lips passionately. A loud roar broke out from the observers and Luke realized that their relationship had just gone public. He had been so careful to protect it, not wanting Lenny to get caught in the tabloid's cross hairs. But it was out now. Camera's flashed and the TV crews scrambled to get a better angle. He pulled away from Lenny and tried to downplay what had just happened.

Lenny smiled at him, her crooked half-smile that said everything would be fine. She turned and waved to the crowd and cameras, blowing them kisses.

The girl he had met months before, the one with the carefully guarded heart and a past full of painful secrets had all but disappeared. Lenny had been a mystery wrapped inside a riddle and somewhere along the way, Luke had cracked the code. He knew that to share his life of crazy travel and hard work he would have to find a partner who was strong and could adapt to changing situations. She stood before him now, a bundle of outerwear and a smile that lit the sky.

He walked with her to the chute, his nerves melting away. They were replaced with a shiver, not from the cold, but from the clarity his heart had just experienced. Lenny had to be in his life for the remainder of it.

Luke kissed her one last time before heading to the finish line. He promised to be there when she came in first. Sway and Blake went with him while Mike and Harrison stayed at the top to send her off.

***

"Aren't you afraid you're gonna choke?" Cody sneered at Lenny, "You know, like last time?" Her grey eyes were flat and cold, and Lenny found it sad that eyes identical to Duke's could be so foreign.

"I'm sorry it has to come down to this Cody," Lenny responded coolly, "But I'm gonna crush you." Lenny lowered her goggles and covered her face with her mask, sealing out the cold.

"Yeah, you're not a nice person." Harrison added his own dig. He wasn't very good at trash talking. It was really best if he stuck to lead guitar, Lenny thought.

"Whatever." Cody mumbled and lowered her goggles.

The pressure in the back of Lenny's head had grown to a full scale roar in her ears. It drowned out the crowd and Mike and Harrison's final words of encouragement.

She had an uncanny ability to separate herself from the rest of the world when she focused really hard. She could create a mental barrier, where only she and the task at hand existed. That's where the pressure, the buzzing, came from. She relaxed her mind and enclosed herself in the moment. This was it. She completely blocked out everything around her and took a deep, steadying breath. She felt a smile spread across her face underneath her mask and waited.

***

The start signal rang through the air and the two riders took off.

213

Mike and Harrison strained their necks with the other screaming audience members, trying to get a good view. The girls dipped and disappeared and then reappeared, twisting and flying down the slope.

"Holy crap." Harrison muttered under his breath and Mike laughed out loud.

***

Lenny could feel the perfect snow bend under her board and she almost laughed at how easy the course was. She could feel the curve beneath her and anticipated the jump ahead. She knew she had reached quite a height as her board made contact with the snow again. She saw Cody in her peripheral vision as she tried to cut across Lenny's path. Lenny just slid to the side and shot past her.

***

Luke couldn't see a lot from his vantage point at the bottom but he could hear the rise and fall of the audience's reaction to what was happening. He caught a glimpse of Lenny, flying high and he was reminded of her nickname 'Bird.' She seemed lighter than air. It was as if coming back to earth was a challenge and she belonged among the stars.

***

Lenny's speed was increasing. She crouched lower, gaining more momentum, knowing it was dangerous and knowing she could handle it. Cody wasn't even close. Lenny hadn't seen her in a few turns. The pressure in Lenny's head compressed and exploded in a brilliant star burst in her mind's eye as she took the last jump. *I love my life.* She had enough height and speed so she threw in an elegant stalefish, grabbing the board behind her back heel with her back hand and stretching out her body in the air. *You know, for fun.*

The crowd erupted, finally registering in her awareness. She landed easily and had to quickly slow herself as she crossed the finish so as not to hit the barriers.

Luke was with her in seconds, hugging her and yelling along with the crowd. Lenny removed her goggles and face mask and kissed him.

Thirty seconds after Lenny had landed, Cody finally crossed the finish line.

Lenny unhooked the bindings on her boots and walked over to Cody.

214

"Good race." Lenny stuck out her hand, she hoped this would end Cody's ridiculous vendetta.

Cody unhooked her bindings and picked up her board.

"C'mon, Cody, we used to be friends." Lenny tried to reach out to her, wondering if there was even anything salvageable left in their relationship.

"We haven't been friends in a long time." Cody clipped angrily. "It should've been *me* that Duke coached, he was *my* uncle. It should have been *me* with all the sponsorships and the popularity. You never would have even *tried* snowboarding if I wouldn't have invited you. And this is how you repay me? Some friend you are."

"Cody, this whole thing was your idea. I have no idea how you can continue blaming me for your shortcomings. It isn't my fault."

"Stay away from me." Cody spun around and stalked away.

"Geez, sore loser." Luke said from beside her. Lenny shrugged. She couldn't change Cody. She had met her challenge and had beaten her at her own game. What more did Cody want?

***

Lenny's time wasn't an official recording because it wasn't an official race. But that didn't matter, it still made headlines the next morning. Well, that and her now public relationship with Luke Casey.

Suddenly, it seemed, the crowds realized that rock stars were among them and the guys were inundated with autograph and picture requests. Lenny was proud of the guys. They never expected special treatment or attention but when it happened, they always handled it with class. Giving each fan eye contact and listening to them gush. Especially Luke, he could make whoever he was talking to feel like that was the most important conversation he was going to have all day.

The entire next day was busy for all of them. Lenny had two interviews to do and a few more stops at X Fest for the sponsors. And the guys were the newest attraction. Cody and Shane kept out of the ruckus as much as possible. Lenny felt a little bit bad for embarrassing Cody the night before but Cody had asked for it. Right?

During both of her interviews, Lenny was asked about her and Luke's relationship and she just smiled as a reply. That wasn't the public's business. Her feelings for Luke were definitely growing but he deserved to hear those words from her firsthand, not from a sound bite.

The sponsors went gaga over her performance the night before and started to throw more deals at her. Lenny deferred them to Patrick, choosing to make those kinds of business decisions when the tour was finished. She didn't want to overbook herself again. She was feeling more in control of her life than she had in a long time. It seemed that the downward spiral she had feared had leveled out into smooth riding.

As more of the X Games events wrapped up that night, Lenny snuggled close to Luke in the Athlete's Lounge at the Inn. The Lounge was nearly vacant, just a few people here and there. It was a nice place to relax since media and civilians weren't allowed.

Lenny was happy. Not ecstatically or anything. Just regular, normal, happy. She liked having Luke with her for her important life stuff. She wanted him to stay forever.

"I don't have any obligations tomorrow." Lenny said quietly, her fingers making a trail across the top of his strong hands.

"Mm-hm." Luke mumbled in her soft hair, his eyes closed.

"We could leave tomorrow if you want." Lenny added.

"Where do you wanna go?" Luke was only half-listening to her.

Lenny didn't know. She didn't have a plan. She just had an impulse, a feeling, and acted on it. All she knew is she wanted to be with Luke, on another adventure.

"Just somewhere with you." Was all she could think of to answer.

"I'll go anywhere with you." Luke said slowly his voice rough with an emotion Lenny couldn't define.

***

Luke didn't have a word for what he felt in her presence. He had known for a while now that Lenny was the one. His one. The one he wanted to be tangled up with forever. She was his exception. And he dared to hope he could be hers.

Chapter 15

Glycerine

It had been a long time since Duke had considered getting drunk. Years, in fact. But as he watched the coverage of Lenny flying high at the X Games, he thought about it.

He sighed and clicked off the TV. It wasn't the fact that she was back, the center of a whirling media frenzy. It wasn't that she had just made his niece look like a chump. It was that kiss she had shared with the rock star. Duke didn't realize how much seeing something like that could hurt.

He checked the clock on the wall, it was too early for bed and too late to go back out. He shoved himself into a standing position and made his way to the front door. Maybe a drive in the mountains would help clear his head.

***

Being back on the tour was different for Lenny than it had been a few months ago. She couldn't run errands anymore because the anonymity was gone. Not only did the press know her name but they kept plastering her face all over everything.

Carl was not pleased. He hadn't said anything to her but she knew by the look he'd given her when they arrived in London that he was pissed.

"At least I'm not cross-eyed in this one." Lenny observed the cover of a paper tabloid they were passing around backstage at the venue. They didn't chill on the buses like before because they were rentals for the overseas tour and Carl was afraid they'd trash them. So during their down time they hung out backstage or in the hotel suite.

"I didn't think the last one was too bad, I mean, besides the face you were making." Mike joked dryly as Lenny passed him the magazine.

"I'm sorry about that." Luke wouldn't stop apologizing. Lenny had told him that she was fine with it, it's not like she'd never been famous before. These were just different circumstances, the same rules applied. The media would hound you and try to find a reason to hate you and then move on when someone prettier or crazier came along.

"Don't worry so much." She waved it off. "Really, it's not that big of a deal. I don't forget important things, like underwear, when I leave the house. I'm pretty boring, they'll move on eventually."

"Ten minutes," Carl stuck his head into the dressing room.

The guys gathered themselves and headed for the stage area. Luke kissed Lenny lightly on the lips before leaving. She planned on waiting until they got situated before making her way through the crowd and joining Greg in the sound booth.

She was getting ready to exit the dressing room when Carl stopped her. She reversed her trajectory as his imposing presence demanded to have a conversation. He shut the door behind him. Crossing his arms over his chest, he let out what Lenny could only assume was a snort.

"So how pissed are you?" Lenny asked, her mouth ticking up on the side.

"I told you that under no circumstances were you allowed to sleep with any of them." His voice was restrained but the veins in his neck were pulsing at his pent up anger. He was more red than Lenny had ever seen him and she had a fleeting thought in regards to his heart health.

"Is that all your mad about?" Lenny asked cautiously.

"That was the deal!" Carl barked.

"Well, then we don't have a problem." Lenny said diplomatically, softening her features in an attempt to calm him down.

"What?" Carl snarled with a glare.

"We haven't slept together." Lenny stated matter of fact and stuck her hands in her pockets.

"What?" Carl asked again with less roar.

"Carl, I'm not like other girls, you should know that by now." Lenny said patiently, the same tone she had used on her father many times. "Luke and I are not having sex. We haven't had sex. And we aren't planning on having sex. I have kept my word."

Carl did a combination squint and grimace. He paced back toward the door and then back to Lenny. "But you guys are…together."

"Yes, Carl. We're dating. I like him and he likes me. I realize it's unusual in this day in age for two people to just enjoy one another without getting naked but that's just how weird we are."

Carl almost smiled. "How long before…?"

"For crying out loud, Carl!" Lenny exclaimed, "I'm not thinking about that and if I were I wouldn't discuss it with my *boss*."

Carl, satisfied with her answer, moved to leave and he looked over his shoulder. "Good to have you back, by the way."

Lenny shook her head. That guy.

She resumed her trek to the sound booth hoping she hadn't missed too much. The crowd was on it's feet as the band played it's opening song. Lenny slid into the sound booth and Greg gave her a cursory nod. She had missed this. The energy that reverberated between the band and the fans was breathtaking.

The guys had warned Lenny that the overseas crowds were different than the ones Stateside. They were right. They were even crazier, if that was possible. Not an angry crazy or a dangerous crazy. It was more like their love for the music was completely uninhibited. In a word, it was beautiful.

They hadn't had time to rehearse before flying into Heathrow and only had a small sound check that afternoon. But they were *on*. Lenny was continuously blown away by how effortless they made it all seem.

Luke was magnetic on stage. The women literally threw themselves at him. Harrison kept kicking panties off the stage. Sway would sometimes grab a pair and hang them off the neck of his bass, but that only encouraged more throwing of undergarments. Lenny used to be amazed at the shamelessness of the women but now it didn't even phase her. It also seemed to not phase Luke. He never acknowledged the suggestive antics of his female fans.

Lenny lost herself for a moment in the haze that was Luke Casey. She had never felt for anyone like how she felt for him. He was strong, dependable, sexy and all those things girls dream about in the perfect guy. But there were many other things that Lenny knew about him now that the rest of the world probably never would. Like, he also had this tiny scar behind his left ear that he'd gotten when he was seventeen while he was windsurfing with Harrison in Malibu. And he got too emotionally invested in the contestants on reality shows. And he sang the wrong words to popular songs to make Lenny laugh. He didn't pretend to have it all figured out, he was constantly striving to make himself a better person.

Somehow, amidst the insanity of being a hugely successful musician, he hadn't let the fame get to him. He was genuine and humble. In a world full of flakes, Luke Casey was the real deal.

And for some reason that Lenny hadn't yet deciphered, he wanted to be with her. He didn't just like spending time with her, he acted like she was a vital part of his every day existence. And she felt the same about him. It was strange, she had never believed that Shane loved her, no matter how many times he said it. But she knew, without question, that Luke loved her. It was in everything he said and did, the way he talked to her, how he touched her, leaving no room for doubt.

Lenny was afraid she had finally done what she said she wouldn't do, she had fallen in love with a rock star. No other explanation made sense for everything that was going on between them. It had become even more apparent to her at Aspen. He so willingly lent his strength to her to help her achieve things she hadn't done in years. Her heart hurt a little because she

219

knew the tour would be over soon and things would change.

She closed her eyes and tried to silence the scream that wanted to erupt from her lungs every time she thought about the coming end. How could she part with him? How could she say goodbye after they had come so far? The logical, realistic side of Lenny told her that this was always temporary, she should have guarded her heart better. But the romantic, idealistic side of Lenny wanted to hope that Luke would chase her home. They could get married and have fat babies. Maybe they could bring the whole family on tour and Lenny could compete in the off season. That could work, right?

Reasonable Lenny said no. The tour would end and so would their affair. They would go home. Lenny to the mountains where she would begin training again for the Olympics. And Luke would go home to Boston and record a new album and forget all about her. *That was always the plan,* Lenny reminded herself. *This was supposed to be about finding your way into a new life and moving on. Falling in love was never part of the plan.*

The set was over before Lenny realized it and they were almost finished with the encore. She chewed on the inside of her cheek, contemplating the inevitable.

"You okay?" Greg interrupted her thoughts.

"What? Yeah." Lenny forced a smile and stood up.

She exited the booth, making her way backstage as the band wrapped up their final song. Luke was descending the stairs and he saw her immediately. He scooped her up in a big hug, lifting her off her feet and making her smile. He brought her back to the earth slowly, being sure to kiss her deeply before letting go.

"You wanna get something to eat before going back to the hotel?" Luke grabbed Lenny's hand and they started for the green room.

"Sure, what do you have in mind?" She asked, enjoying the warmth of his hand against hers.

"Let's go on an adventure." Luke raised his eyebrows at her as he held the door open.

"I like that idea." She agreed and then laughed at his excited grin. No matter how much time they had left, she was going to enjoy every second of it.

***

The thing with touring overseas is that Luke felt more like he was on vacation than on tour. They didn't have to sleep on the buses, they had fancy suites in hotels every night. The travel was all by private plane so they had more time to explore the cities and countryside. Plus, they still got to play sold out arenas every night. Each band member had a tendency to go a little wild and really enjoy themselves.

Luke loved Europe. He'd split off from the guys and do his own thing, the whole time wishing he had someone he could share it with. Now, he had Lenny, he could share those things with her.

He had taken her to a small pub that he had discovered many years ago on one of their first trips overseas. They ate some of the local cuisine and talked and laughed until way too late, finally making their way back to the top floor of the hotel.

"Stay with me tonight." He whispered in her ear after he had walked her to her door. He couldn't stand the thought of her staying in her room all alone. She was meant to be near him always. "I don't mean in the same bed, just stay in our suite." He clarified, cupping her cheek in his hand and resting his forehead against hers.

He could see the debate behind her sapphire eyes and he stepped back, letting his hands trail down her arms and rest at her fingertips. "I'll be a perfect gentleman, you can have my room and I'll take the couch. It would be so much nicer waking up with you there instead of just Sway...I need a buffer with that guy sometimes."

She smiled shyly, "You make it really hard to follow the rules."

Luke grinned, "Then it's a yes?" He raised one eyebrow at her.

She sighed in pretend frustration. "Yes. But I have to get my things and I want take a shower tonight before going to bed."

She retreated to her room and Luke waited in the hallway. He was...giddy. He wasn't sure if he'd ever been giddy before, it was all very new. Everything with Lenny was new. Even after they had returned to his suite and explained to Sway that she'd be staying with them, Sway didn't seem surprised. It's like she just *fit*. Into every part of his life.

When Lenny emerged from the bathroom she was showered, and dressed in shorts with a sponsor's logo and a t-shirt with a faded Double Blind Study band script on it.

Luke eyed the shirt thoughtfully as she took a seat next to him on the couch.

"That's an old shirt," he observed. Lenny didn't respond so he added. "I thought you said you didn't know who we were." Referencing back to the day they met.

Lenny blushed, "I lied. I've always been a fan."

Luke smiled and pulled her into his chest, resting his chin on top of her head. He didn't care how she had come into his life, just that she was there now.

He could sense something was bothering her, it had been just below the surface all night. But he decided to wait for her to bring it up. She was in his arms now, and that meant she was safe.

***

The sun began to peek through the cloudy skyline of the London backdrop and Lenny sipped her coffee from the couch. She had woken early, jet lag was confusing, and ordered room service. Luke woke up when the food came to the door and then headed to the shower right away. Lenny poured herself a cup of coffee and slipped into a melancholy repose.

One more show in London tonight. Two more weeks is all they had left. After last night, the feel of a real date for them, Lenny was falling harder and faster. It wasn't enough. It would never be enough. She would never feel like she'd gotten enough kisses. Or smiles. Or embraces. She could and would try to soak up as much of Luke Casey as possible in the next couple of weeks. But then what?

She blinked back the sudden tears that threatened to overtake her. She couldn't imagine the days ahead without him. She sighed with frustration at herself. She should have never let anyone become such a necessity in her life. Nothing lasts forever. And while Luke Casey was her best friend today, in a month she would just be some girl he used to know. She should end it before the awkward conversation of the logistics came up. That would be horrible. It was bad enough that she knew it wasn't going to last, it would be worse to have him have to explain it to her like she was just another...groupie. She didn't think her heart could take that kind of a conversation.

"Good coffee," Sway startled Lenny out of her thoughts. She hadn't even noticed when he had joined her.

"Yeah, it's good." Lenny agreed, having a brief thought about making sure someone brought coffee to Carl.

"What were you thinking about? It looked deep." Sway asked.

"Just...stuff." Lenny couldn't come up with anything she really wanted to share. Too many thoughts, not enough words.

"You feeling okay?" Sway's eyebrows pushed together in concern.

"Yeah." Lenny forced a smile in his direction but didn't meet his eyes. "Fine, why?"

"Just asking." Sway wasn't buying it but he dropped it anyway.

"How come you're splitting the suite with Luke instead of it being Mike?" Lenny changed the subject. Sway was never one to be insightful but she didn't need him suspecting her of anything and then telling Luke before she could tell him herself.

"Because Europe still turns Mike into a pussy and Harrison and Blake will be better at watching him than Luke." Sway twisted his face in annoyance.

"What do you mean 'better than Luke?'" Lenny bristled.

"'Cause Luke's busy with you." Sway picked around the fruit on the food cart and glanced up to see Lenny's offended expression. "Not that it's a bad thing. We all discussed it, it's the solution we came up with."

"Why does Mike have to be babysat? That's a little condescending, don't you think?" Lenny said, knowing that that was what Carl had hired her for in the first place but still feeling the need to defend the drummer.

"Look," Sway tried again, "Mike gets really emotional when we go overseas. He knows it, we know it. He has a lot of triggers here. London is where he met Ilsa." Sway stopped talking and looked up at Lenny. She nodded, silently confessing that she knew the private details of their quarrel, guilt washing over her again. "He needs us to watch out for him, it's what brothers do." Sway settled on a large pastry and came back over to the couch. He sat down next to Lenny, his face serious and thoughtful. "And Luke needs to be with you right now."

Fresh tears started to form in the back of Lenny's vision and she swallowed hard. "What do you mean?" Her voice coming out raspy and thick.

"You guys are good for each other. And no one wants to get in the way of that. It's that simple."

"How is the sexiest girl in the world?" Luke interrupted Lenny's stunned thoughts as he came into the room and bent low to kiss her on the lips.

"I'm okay, kinda gassy." Sway replied, making Lenny and Luke laugh. "I think it was that salmon I ate last night. That was salmon, right?" He pretended to be embarrassed. "Oh, you meant Lenny. Never mind."

"I'm good, how did you sleep?" Lenny looked into the most beautiful blue eyes in the world and her heartbeat quickened. His hair was still wet from his shower and he hadn't put his shirt on yet. She tried not to stare at the body that she was positive was cut from pure granite by the hand of God. *Now stop that!* She scolded herself internally. *You have got to get a handle on yourself.*

"Fantastic." Luke replied in a low voice as he leaned in for another kiss.

"Hey!" Sway jumped in. "I'm sitting *right here*." He shook his head in mock disgust and got up for another cup of coffee.

"Sorry, man." Luke stared into Lenny's eyes. "I just can't get enough of her."

Uh-oh, here comes the jelly legs. Lenny could feel herself turning into mush, good thing she wasn't standing or walking, or holding something highly valuable.

223

"You guys need to just do it and get it over with. The sexual tension around here is unbearable."

Lenny's eyes widened at Sway's words. "Wow, Sway! Inappropriate much?" Sway rolled his eyes.

Luke slipped his t-shirt over his head and pulled Lenny to her feet. He planted another perfect kiss on her lips. He moved his arms around her waist and started kissing her neck.

"Go get dressed, I want to take you around London today before the show." He murmured in her ear.

Lenny hoped she could walk, she wasn't so confident in her knees ability to not buckle. She flashed him a smile and then hurried to change her clothes. Two weeks left, she wasn't going to waste it.

***

As Lenny closed the door to the bedroom to get dressed Luke helped himself to the fruit on the table.

"Lenny was right, that was inappropriate," Luke rebuked Sway quietly.

"C'mon, you guys are constantly macking on each other and talking all cute and stuff. Just do it and get it over with. I don't know what you're waiting for." Sway grabbed an apple off the platter and examined it. "I mean, I know Lenny's special and blah, blah, blah but it's been...a while now. You've never waited with any other girl before." He took a bite. "I don't get it."

"It's not about that." Luke said, his mouth curving up slightly on the side. "I love her. I'll wait as long as it takes."

"What's that supposed to mean?" Sway tried to ask around his mouthful, losing chunks of apple in the process.

"She's the only one I want to be with ever again. I never want to be without her."

"You're talking code, dude. You're gonna have to explain to me." Sway's eyes went wide in exasperation.

"I don't want to have sex just because it seems like it's time. I've done that, it doesn't mean anything. Not this time. She's the only one I ever want to be with in *that* way, for the rest of my life." Luke poured the hot coffee into an empty cup on the tray.

Sway choked on his apple as he finally understood what Luke was saying. He gasped for air as he tried to ask a question but couldn't get around the chunk of apple lodged in his throat.

Luke laughed at him and looked out the window at the London landscape. "Yep." He confirmed Sway's fears. "I'm gonna marry her." He smiled to himself and brought the coffee cup to his lips, "I just have to figure out when and how to ask her."

Chapter 16

A Drop In The Ocean

It was as it had always been for Duke. Growing up the youngest of five kids, his siblings had left home long before he was born. He had been his parents 'surprise' baby. Raised like an only child on the backside of the Ozarks, Duke had few friends and kept to himself. He enjoyed people and he wasn't shy by any means. He just didn't *need* people. And that's where he found himself again. Alone. His third long drive in as many days.

He passed by the local tavern a couple of times and considered pulling into the parking lot. Maybe just feel the warmth of the neon for a few minutes, it didn't mean he'd have to go inside. He'd shake off the feeling and continue driving.

The drive was always the same. Long. Lonely. Unchanging. He never saw anything he hadn't seen a thousand times before. He passed all the same little cabins and 'no trespassing' signs that had always been there. Now, it was starting to snow. Not regular snow. Big, thick, lazy snow. The kind that would pile into slush on the ground, quickly making driving conditions more treacherous. Duke turned the wipers on and peered into the gray.

Up ahead he could almost make out a car pulled over on the side of the road. It's hazards were on but the falling snow was so think it was almost unnoticeable. Duke pulled in behind the small compact car, this was no place to have car trouble. It was a blind turn and with the weather, it was a tragedy waiting to happen.

The plates on the little Ford said *California. Figures, out of towners always think they can drive in the snow,* Duke thought to himself. He set his brake and turned his own hazards on and got out of the old Bronco.

As he approached the driver's side of the car he saw a woman talking on her cellphone. He tapped on the window, startling her. The windows were foggy and starting to frost on the corners from the cold. The woman held up her finger for Duke to wait and she slowly stepped out of the car.

She was tall, Duke observed, for a woman. She was probably close to six feet because she was nearly eye level with him. She had raven black hair that easily reached her waist but was twisted into a loose braid that came over one shoulder. Her almond shaped eyes were a beautiful chestnut brown. She was stunning, to say the least. But her physical appearance isn't what caught Duke's eye first. It was the .45 pointed at his chest.

Duke raised his hands slightly. He wasn't sure if she was being overly cautious or if she was going to rob him.

"I'm waiting for a tow truck, you would do best to get back into your vehicle and be on your way." She spoke with authority and held the weapon like an experienced professional. Duke didn't want to argue. But it was in his nature.

"Nice Sig," He complimented her. He kept his hands raised. "I just thought I might be able to help." He looked back up the road. "It's a blind turn, someone might not see you."

"I'll be just fine." She spoke assuredly but Duke saw her swallow just a little too hard.

"I'm in no mood to cause you any trouble, ma'am." Duke thought he'd try one more time. He had a soft spot for stubborn women with guns...apparently. "Did you call the Highway Patrol?"

He could see her mind working quickly behind those dark eyes. She nodded but didn't answer.

"You can call and confirm with them who I am. I live just a mile up the road, I help them pull cars out of ditches all the time. I'd be glad to help you now, 'cause who knows when the tow truck will make it up here in this snow."

"Do you have ID?" The woman asked, raising an eyebrow.

Duke fished his license out of his back pocket and handed it to her. She gave him a hard look and then got back in her car and on the phone. She spoke for a few minutes to what Duke assumed was the local dispatch. She gave him a sideways glance out the window and nodded to whoever was on the phone. When she stepped back out of the car she had holstered her weapon somewhere Duke couldn't be sure but at least it wasn't pointed directly at him.

"How far can you tow me?" She asked, handing back his ID.

"As far as you need," Duke replied.

"I'll need to get the car repaired in town, is there a mechanic's shop?"

"Yeah," Duke was headed to the Bronco to get his tow cables. "You staying in town or do you need a lift back up here?"

"I'll rent something and drive back up, thank you." She was definitely not a friendly lady, Duke thought. But his thoughts changed quickly when he saw her getting a bundle of blankets out of the backseat of her car.

It was a child, maybe four years old, all tucked and rolled inside numerous blankets and afghans.

"Can we wait in your truck?" She asked, her lips making a hard line on her face. No wonder she had been so quick to suspicion. She had precious cargo.

"Absolutely." Duke dropped his tow cables and helped her and the child into the warmth of the still running Bronco. He made sure they were buckled safely inside and then he maneuvered the Bronco to the front of her tiny car. Duke jumped out and quickly connected the tow cables, rigging everything securely.

When he got back into the truck he tried to give her a reassuring smile.

"We're all set." He put the Bronco in gear and started slowly back down the mountain, paying extra close attention to his driving. He'd never transported kids before. He wasn't sure what would be an acceptable rate of speed. She still had that .45 somewhere and he really didn't need her pointing it at him while he drove.

"Are we going sledding, Mom?" A little voice from the middle seat asked sweetly.

"Mom's car broke so we'll have to go sledding tomorrow." The woman explained gently. Her tone was so different with her child that Duke had to look over to see if it was the same woman. Her face had softened as she looked at her son and Duke was caught off guard by her sweet smile.

She looked up at him and they had eye contact briefly before Duke turned his gaze back to the road. *What the hell was that?* He reprimanded himself. *Keep your eyes on the road, Duke. She has a gun.*

"Who are you?" The child asked Duke bluntly. He couldn't help but smile at the forthright question.

"His name is Mr. Dukane and he's giving us a ride to the place where we can get our car fixed." She explained to the boy.

Duke had never been called *Mr. Dukane* before. He'd been Duke for as long as he could remember. She had gotten that off his ID.

"Actually, you can call me Duke. It's what everyone else calls me." He said with a grin to the boy. His eye caught hers again and he decided to wink. *She's going to shoot me.*

"What's *your* name?" Duke asked the boy, deciding not to steal anymore glances at the exotic beauty to his right.

"I'm Tyler and I'm four." Tyler said proudly.

"Pleased to meet you, Tyler." Duke said and then asked, "What's your mom's name?"

"Mom." Tyler responded making Duke chuckle.

"My name is Natalie." She replied with her own soft laugh.

"Yeah, Natalie." Tyler confirmed. "Is this your truck?" He inquired next.

"Yep, it sure is." Duke confirmed. He was liking how easy it was to talk to Tyler, way easier than talking to Tyler's mom.

"It sure is big." Tyler said trying to peer over the dash. Then, "Do you go sledding, Duke?"

"Sometimes," Duke said with a small laugh. "But I stand up on my sled."

"That's not allowed." Tyler reported, "You could get hurt."

"That's true." Duke agreed, "Sometimes I do get hurt."

The conversation continued on like this for another thirty minutes as Duke carefully drove through the ever increasing storm. Tyler, obviously tired, snuggled up against his mother and the cab fell quiet again.

"Thank you." Natalie said, breaking the silence.

"Not a problem." Duke responded, "I'm just glad you didn't shoot me up there." He grinned at her impulsively.

She smiled a little. It was a lovely smile.

"I couldn't take any chances." Natalie explained as she stroked her son's hair. "He's all I have."

Duke wondered what she meant. He didn't want to cross the boundaries of the social norm but he'd never been good at following those rules anyway.

"Where's Tyler's father?" Duke blurted. It sounded awful as it spilled out of him but he couldn't take it back now. Maybe she would just shoot him after all.

"He died in Afghanistan three years ago." She answered with a touch of regret in her voice.

"Army?" Duke asked.

"Marine," Natalie corrected. That explained the Sig.

"I'm sorry," was all Duke could think of to say.

"He was a good dad." Natalie continued, "Tyler won't ever remember him, but I've never seen a man love his child the way Mark loved Tyler."

"So, it's just you two against the world then." Duke said it as a statement more than a question.

"We do okay on our own." Natalie quietly defended.

"I have no doubt." Duke agreed. "I've never had a gun pulled on me for offering to help with a tow." He gave her a sideways grin.

"Sorry about that." She attempted to apologize but Duke stopped her.

"Don't you dare." He said sternly. "More women should do exactly what you did."

She turned her head to hide her smile but Duke saw it reflect on the window.

"So, you live around here?" She changed the subject and Duke let her.

"Yeah, I live in this ugly lodge up in the mountains."

She chuckled at his description and he felt warmth creep into his cheeks. He liked making her laugh.

"So…" Duke didn't want to come across as a creeper but he wanted to know if he should be aware of any other men in her life before he proceeded with his train of thought. "Do you have a boyfriend or fiancé or anything?"

"Ha!" Natalie laughed again. "That was real subtle." She was smiling openly now.

"I'm not good with women." Duke muttered, embarrassed at his actions. He knew he had just blown it.

"No." Natalie snickered. "The answer to your question is no, there is no one like that in my life." She looked down at her sleeping child. "I don't have time for any of that. Most guys aren't looking for a package deal anyhow."

Duke considered her words, not totally sure what she meant. Guys didn't like her because she came with a kid? That was shallow. And stupid.

"Why are you in Wyoming?" He decided to ask instead.

"We needed to get away and Tyler had never seen snow before. My dad owns a cabin in the mountains. I haven't been up here since I was a little girl, I don't even know if the cabin is livable." She confessed at the end.

"Well, if you were looking for snow, you came to the right place." Duke said, pulling into the parking lot of the best mechanic in town. "Who's your dad?" He asked thoughtfully, he knew pretty much everyone in the area.

"Colonel Henry Clay."

Duke whistled under his breath. "I know that cabin. That's a sweet piece of property. Has he had anyone taking care of it?"

"I'm not sure," Natalie responded. "Dad passed away last year and left the cabin to me. I thought now would be a good time to check it out." She rolled her eyes at herself. "Smart, in the middle of winter."

Duke had parked the Bronco and now he leaned back in his seat and rubbed his short beard thoughtfully.

"Well, it's still early enough in the day. Let me go in and get Earl started on your car and then I'll drive you up there and take a look over it myself." He saw her hesitate and quickly added. "If you don't mind, that is. I'm a pretty good handy-man."

231

He saw her mind working swiftly. She was as smart as she was beautiful. If she thought he was still a threat she would turn him down, but Duke didn't see it going that way. Besides, if he tried anything, she could just shoot him.

"Thanks, Shawn." She smiled, the warmth of it making Duke blush under his beard again, "I'd really appreciate that."

Duke grinned and jumped out of the truck. He jogged into Earl's, unable to hide his delight. No one had called him by his first name in a long time. He liked the way it sounded. It made his heart beat just a tad bit differently.

***

The rest of the European tour was a blur for Lenny, it went entirely too fast. In every city, Luke had something he wanted to share with her. He was excited and energetic, showing her all the little shops and non-touristy attractions that were his favorite. She giggled at his antics and thrill for the adventure.

They hardly spent any time with the other band members anymore, they were nearly always alone. Lenny couldn't tell if it bothered the guys, they hadn't said anything. She only half-cared. The days were flying by and she wasn't going to miss a single second with Luke.

Her attitude became one of passionate desperation. She absorbed every word, every smile, and every kiss. She tried to memorize the lines in his hands and how the calluses on his fingertips felt against her cheek when he would touch her face.

And before Lenny could be satisfied, the tour was done. They were on a plane bound Stateside, decompressing and relaxing. They talked of the successful shows, the fantastic reviews, the sold out performances. Carl was more at ease than Lenny had ever seen him. He pulled his ball cap down low over his eyes and fell fast asleep.

Ever diligent, Luke was already discussing the next album. Where should they record? Who should they go with for a producer? What kind of vibe should they try to capture? It was all very interesting and Lenny tried to keep up with as much of the lingo as she could. She had a pressing in her heart that she was trying to ignore. Luke still hadn't talked about 'them' and she was afraid it was because he didn't know how.

She could broach the subject. After all, it was on *her* mind. What if he changed? What if he shut down and pulled away and got cold? Lenny didn't think she could bear it if Luke started to treat her differently. She felt foolish for feeling that way. She'd never been in love before, she had no idea what to do with it. Especially in circumstances like this, where her reality and her ideal were complete opposites.

She thought about telling Luke that she loved him. He hadn't said it since his outburst at Ashton. That was okay because Lenny didn't really want to have to say "I love you, *too*." She just wanted to say it. Without requirement or expectation. So he would know there were no stipulations. She simply loved him. But the timing always seemed off, and she didn't want it to come out forced or trite.

Of course, the next fear was that he didn't feel the same. Based on the things he said, how he acted and treated her, Lenny knew in her heart he loved her. She'd known since the first moment they kissed. *But rock stars fall in love all the time,* she reminded herself. *That's how they make such great music.*

***

Sway saw the small interaction between Lenny and Luke. It was subtle but perfect. The guys were thrilled with Lenny's presence in their lives. They didn't care that Luke had taken to spending every waking moment with her. She was good to him and he deserved that.

When Luke had told Sway he was planning on marrying the girl, Sway had been stunned at first. But as he considered their relationship, it fit. Sway had never been in love. Sure, he'd made a lot of what looked like love. But he'd never felt for one person the way Luke obviously felt for Lenny. And they hadn't even slept together. It blew Sway's mind. And yet, as he watched them together, it made perfect sense.

***

Harrison and Blake were arguing not so quietly about what they think should've happened on their favorite daytime soap opera. It kind of distracted Lenny from her fear of flying closer to good-bye. She quietly laughed at their antics and felt a lump rise in her throat. She would miss them. All of them. Not just Luke. She would miss Blake and Harrison's petty arguments and ridiculous capers. She would miss Sway asking her to help him with his flyaways and split ends. She would miss Mike's dry humor and his ability to anticipate the next step. She would miss Carl's crankiness and ranch foreman mentality.

She leaned her head against the back of the seat. She was going to have serious withdrawal after she left these guys. She wondered who would take her place for the next tour. Would they treat them as good she would? Would they follow Carl's guidelines and put the band first? Would they fall in love with the lead singer?

233

Lenny couldn't handle anymore thoughts. She squeezed Luke's hand instinctively and closed her eyes. Maybe she would feel better about her plan after she had gotten some sleep.

***

Luke felt the gentle pressure on his hand and frowned slightly at Lenny's resting posture. Her eyes were closed but her face wasn't relaxed. She appeared to be thinking hard, trying to will sleep to happen. He wondered what was bothering her. Well, it had been a long trip, Luke decided. She was probably just tired.

***

The plane landed in New York and they had a two hour layover before their next flight to Boston. The guys napped in the waiting area, jet lag was a bitch. Lenny was kind of surprised that there was a ticket for her to Boston as well and not somewhere further west. She assumed it was Carl and decided that Boston would be as good as any place to say goodbye.

The flight was fast, only an hour, from LaGuardia to Boston. Lenny barely had time to collect her thoughts. As they were disembarking, she knew what she had to do. She tapped into that special feature in her brain that she reserved for competitions. She shut everything out and took a deep breath. The wall came up, separating her from her surroundings. She had a mission, and it was time to execute.

They were at baggage claim and Lenny waited for the guys to gather in a huddle around her. No one noticed that her bags hadn't arrived. They naturally gravitated toward her and she waited till she had their attention.

"I'm going home." She said plainly, her tone gentle. She didn't want to hurt them but someone needed to rip the Band-Aid off. She'd already gotten a connecting flight that would have several stops before she reached home. All she had to do was catch her next flight.

"What do you mean? I thought you were going to Luke's house." Harrison's eyes were already starting to water. Lenny loved his tender heart, he didn't like change.

"I was not aware of that plan." Lenny looked to Luke but his eyes had lost focus. The reality had hit him.

"This is where you guys live, I don't. My job is ended." She got a confirmation nod from Carl and continued. "But I have had the *best* time of my life with all of you." She looked at Luke again. He was staring at her with the saddest eyes she'd ever seen.

234

"I have a whole other life that needs tending to out west." She paused, her mental barrier starting to strain against the heavy emotion that was threatening to overpower her. "I will miss *all* of you, more than you know."

The guys hugged her one by one, their heads low. They backed off a little to give Luke and Lenny some space.

Lenny's resolve was weakening as she looked into Luke's eyes that were starting to turn red from held back tears.

"I will miss you the most." She offered a small smile. She grabbed both of his hands in hers and whispered, "I have never, in my life, felt for anyone what I feel for you."

"Then why are you going?" Luke's voice was hoarse with emotion.

"Because it's time," Lenny whispered. "I can't hang around like a fangirl the rest of my life. I have to grow up one of these days." She tried to get him to smile but he wouldn't.

Luke suddenly took her in his arms and held her tight. He whispered in her ear, "I don't want you to go."

This was Lenny's moment. She gave him a long embrace and then pulled back, kissed him tenderly on his lips and looked him in the eye. She wanted to make sure he knew she was for real.

"I love you, Luke Casey. I will *always* love you." She stepped back and took a shuddering breath. "Now, go." She smiled as sincerely as her heart would let her. "Be amazing." She allowed herself to behold his masculine perfection one last time, trying to memorize every single striking detail, and then she turned around.

He didn't call out to her or chase her. He was letting her go. A tear escaped and splashed onto her cheek. Her legs carried her onward and her heart quaked in her chest. She would feel better in a few days. This was how it had to be. He couldn't face reality, so she had to do it for the both of them. The longer they tried to make it work, the harder it would be to end it. They would each resent each other, making it an ugly end. And Lenny didn't want that. She wanted to remember her time with Luke as the greatest adventure of her life. Because it truly was.

Chapter 17

Drive All Night

Lenny rubbed the sleep out of her eyes and looked around. She had to reorient herself. Where was she? *Oh yes,* she thought, *layover hell.* She had flown from Boston to Atlanta and what was supposed to be a ninety minute layover turned into three hours. Then she flew from Atlanta to Salt Lake City where a blizzard greeted her and the other passengers. She had been waiting in the terminal for six hours until they were cleared for flight to Jackson Hole.

She sat up in the chair and tried to straighten the kinks in her back. She grimaced as it popped and pulled. *It's tough getting older*, she thought wryly. *Being an adult sucks,* she had concluded during her first layover of the trip. Leaving Luke was the most painful thing she had experienced and she still wasn't in a place where she could properly grieve. Surrounded by strangers and airport personnel, she couldn't very well break down into choking heaving sobs, she would cause a panic. She would have to wait till she got home.

Home. It was still so far away. She hadn't told anyone she was coming home so no would be expecting her. She figured she'd rent a car, drive to the Lodge and crash for a few days until her clock readjusted. Maybe she would just stay in bed for the rest of her life. Yes, that was the new plan.

At long last, the call came over the intercom to board her final flight. She shuffled through the line with the other passengers, feeling more raggedy than she had her whole life. Just an hour more. She focused on the next step.

As she settled into her seat, the flight attendants reminded them to please turn off their cellphones during takeoff. Lenny glanced at hers painfully. She had left it on, hoping Luke would call. But he hadn't. No one had. Not Harrison or Sway or Mike. No one had called or texted to even check on her. The heaviness in Lenny's chest increased substantially as the plane started its taxi down the runway.

***

When they left the airport in Boston it got ugly. Harrison openly wept and Blake was so pissed he threw his luggage at a sign and they had to be escorted from the building. The guys had yelled at Luke. They demanded to know why he had let Lenny walk away. Why didn't he chase her? What was stopping him? Wasn't he supposed to be in love? They were beyond disappointed in their fearless leader. He had no answers for them. Instead he set his jaw and got in a cab and took off.

Sway got incredibly emotional and called a girlfriend to come pick him up. Carl shrugged, muttered something about "rock stars" and got his own cab.

Mike was angry. But he was handling it better than Blake, whose face was now a lovely shade of purple. He rubbed his temples in the back of the taxi that he was sharing with Blake and Harrison.

"Harrison, please stop crying," Mike grit his teeth together.

"I'm sorry," Harrison sniffed pitifully.

"It's alright, man. Just try to calm down." Mike tried to be understanding. But he didn't understand. What was that bullshit Luke had said about wanting to marry her?

"I'm gonna kick his ass!" Blake declared. "I don't care if he is Luke freaking Casey. I'm gonna knock him out."

"Get in line," Mike muttered.

"What the hell are we supposed to do now?" Blake asked pointedly. "I thought Lenny was a permanent member of this band. Sonofabitch!"

"So did I," Mike said.

The cab brought them to their building where they all had their own separate loft in the same massive structure. Luke had bought a large colonial style house in the countryside. Sway's living quarters were a small apartment near the TD Garden where he lived in complete anonymity. But Blake, Harrison and Mike had lived in the same building for years.

The elevator slowly rose to their floor, Harrison leaning heavily against the steel doors.

"Let's go get her." He muttered, his breath making a fog on the metal.

Blake and Mike exchanged glances but didn't respond.

"We can go to Wyoming and get her. Tell her it was a misunderstanding. She'll believe us. We'll bring her back and Luke will be so happy he…" His voice trailed off.

"He'll what? Propose?" Mike reacted with more bark than he intended. "Right. She tells him she loves him in the airport but that's not enough to ask her to stay. But we forcibly bring her back and suddenly he sees the light?"

238

The door to the elevator opened on Blake's floor and they all got out.

Harrison hung his head and shuffled along in front of them, stopping at Blake's entry. "We have to do something." He said quietly.

"Yeah, get over her," Mike said sardonically.

Blake wrestled with his key before opening the door and going straight for the refrigerator.

"God bless you, Claudia," he said out loud, pulling a huge chocolate cheesecake out of the fridge and setting it on the counter. Claudia was his housekeeper and she faithfully left a massive dessert in the refrigerator for Blake on the day he returned from a long tour.

"You guys want to drown your feelings in some serious calories?" Blake produced forks and tossed them down.

"Why not?" Mike answered. It was better than going down to the corner and buying a bindle, which he had thought about for maybe a millisecond.

Harrison took a bite of the cake and started crying again. "We have to get her back," he lamented.

"How?" Blake asked contemptuously, "If Luke doesn't want her around what can we do?"

"We can fire Luke and put Lenny in his place." Harrison's eyes lit up at the prospect and it made Mike chuckle.

"That might work actually." Blake assented with an emphatic nod. "I'm so pissed at him, I don't want see him for a very long time."

"Me either." Harrison shook his head in disgust. He pulled out his phone, "I'm calling her."

"Nah, man. Her phone is probably off. Just wait a couple days, let her get home first." Mike said reasonably.

"Okay." Harrison begrudgingly put his phone down.

***

Luke had been driving for a while, he wasn't sure how long. He had gotten home and unloaded his luggage inside his big empty house. The house he had been planning on bringing Lenny to. Then he got his old pick-up out of the garage and started to drive. He didn't really have a plan; he just didn't want to be in his house. Not without her.

He stopped at a tiny gas station to fill up. It was cold and he pulled his leather jacket tighter around his neck as he waited for the pump to stop. He looked around at his surroundings and decided to buy a map.

He spread the map out on the seat next to him and gave it a good look. Pennsylvania. Why did Wyoming have to be so frickin' far away?

239

He started the truck and pulled back out onto the road. Maybe the drive would give him time to think about what he would say to her when he got there.

The guys were pissed at him. He knew they blamed him for Lenny leaving. *Shouldn't they, though?* He didn't want her to leave, that was the last thing he had been expecting. He'd been completely blindsided. But as she broke down the details, the obvious dawned on him. They lived in separate worlds. Goodbye had been inevitable.

No, that wasn't right either. She had left because he hadn't explained his plan to her. He had left her out of it. Of course, she had been making plans, too, it seemed and had left *him* out of it. Why hadn't they been talking to each other about this? Because they were enjoying the moment. Moments. All of them.

Sure, he could've dropped to his knees in baggage claim and proposed right there. But wouldn't that have seemed forced? Especially since he didn't have a ring yet? And what if she had said no? That thought scared him the most. She said she loved him but then she left. She just...walked away.

He regretted everything that had happened so far that day. He needed to get away and think. He had to fix this somehow. He had to get to her. Show her that he loved her, not just say it.

***

Lenny didn't know how long she'd been sleeping but it still didn't feel like enough. She pulled the covers tighter over her head and cursed the daylight filling her bedroom.

She had taken a cab all the way to the Lodge when she had landed in Jackson Hole. It was not a cheap ride but she hadn't called anyone she knew because she didn't want to talk to them. Anyone.

She had heard Duke coming and going downstairs but he had never come up to check on her. He had to know she was home, she'd left her luggage strewn at the bottom of the stairs. It only added to her self-inflicted misery. No one cared about her.

She checked her phone again. Still nothing.

Lenny angrily pushed the covers off of her and glared at her giant windows letting in all the horrible light. Out of the corner of her eye she saw her luggage stacked neatly in the corner. Obviously Duke had brought them up. That meant he had checked on her after all. Lenny felt worse for thinking harsh thoughts about him.

She got out of bed and dragged herself to the bathroom. She stared at her face in the mirror with loathing. She looked terrible. Black mascara

240

smudges all the way to her chin, her eyes were red and puffy from hours of crying into her pillow. Her hair was matted and greasy, she hadn't showered in days. She was wearing an old ratty pair of shorts and Luke's t-shirt that she had kept after he said she could.

So, this is my life. She thought as she examined her atrocious appearance. *No wonder Luke doesn't want me. I look like death.* She heard her stomach rumble and frowned. She hadn't eaten in a while, maybe there were some cookies or something stashed in the kitchen.

She took the stairs slowly, trying to listen if Duke was home or not. She didn't want to see or talk to anyone right now. She crept into the kitchen and started rummaging through cupboards, finally finding an unopened package of Oreos. She poured herself a glass of milk and shoved a few cookies in her mouth as she headed for the stairs to go back to bed.

"Hey, she lives!" Duke said from behind her. Lenny froze in her tracks. She thought about continuing on upwards without saying anything. But she slowly turned around, swallowing her mouthful of cookies.

She was confused at first by Duke's clean shaven face, it took her a moment to adjust. She'd never seen him without a beard and she almost didn't recognize him.

"You look awful." Duke stated with a serious frown.

"Thanks," Lenny said forlornly, shoving another cookie in her mouth and wiping some milk dribble off her cheek.

"I mean, you look like you need a shower." Duke tried again, frown not flinching.

"You're not helping," Lenny glowered. "What happened to your face?

Duke reached up and stroked where his beard used to be. "I thought it might be time for a change. It was making me look older."

"Whatever." Lenny said with no conviction.

"Sorry." Duke took a step towards her, discomfort all over his face. "You wanna talk about it?"

"No." Lenny said and turned to go back to her room. "The world is a horrible place and I'm going to die alone in my room."

She heard Duke stifle a laugh at her response. "Maybe you should have something better to eat than cookies."

"No," Lenny said belligerently.

"Lenny…" Duke began nervously, "I…there…are some people I'd like you to meet."

Lenny paused and turned on the third step, staring at Duke dumbly.

"They're gonna be here soon-" He tried to speak calmly, looking at her not-ready-for-guests appearance.

"How soon?" Lenny asked.

As if on cue, the front doorbell rang and Lenny's eyes widened at him. "No, Duke. Whoever it is, tell them I'm sick or dead or something."

But there was no time, a young boy came racing into the kitchen and grabbed Duke around his middle.

"Hey!" Duke greeted the boy and hugged him back briefly. Lenny watched with the eyes of a woman who thought she might be losing her mind. Before she could process the child's presence, a tall, black haired beauty entered the room with an apologetic smile.

"Sorry, Tyler figured out the door was unlocked."

"That's okay." Duke answered her with a smile. What was that in his eyes? Adoration? He was beaming at this stranger in Lenny's kitchen as if he had known her for years. And she was looking at him the same way.

What is going on? Is the boy Duke's? How long have I been asleep? Am I even here anymore or did I finally die and I'm a ghost watching my friends and family move on with their lives?

"Hi, you must be Lenny. Duke has told me so much about you." The raven haired woman reached her hand out.

So they can see me, that rules out ghost. Lenny stepped down into the kitchen, adjusted her milk and cookies into one arm and shook the tall woman's hand. She knew she was gaping but she really couldn't stop. She had high cheek bones and the straightest, shiniest, blackest hair Lenny had ever seen. Her scent filled the kitchen, Lenny couldn't place the fragrance but it was warm and intoxicating. Not overpowering, but comforting, like a blanket that Lenny wanted to wrap up in and sleep forever.

"Lenny, this Natalie Rodgers. Her father was Colonel Henry Clay, she and her son, Tyler, are moving up to the Clay cabin." Duke introduced proudly.

"Oh," was all Lenny could get out.

Duke shifted uncomfortably as he waited for Lenny to say more. He grimaced again at her appearance and she knew this was not her best look.

"I'm sorry for my…" Lenny looked down at herself, "Hideousness," she finished.

Natalie gave her a smile as warm as sunshine. "Don't apologize, I've been there." She was so gracious that it caused Lenny to want to fling herself into the woman's arms and start sobbing all over again.

"Are you the girl that can fly?" Tyler inquired with wondering eyes.

Lenny turned her gaze on the young boy and felt tears start to form in the back of her eyes. "I used to be," she choked out.

Duke grabbed Tyler around the shoulders and turned him around. "Let's go see if we can find a snowboard your size, what do ya say?"

242

"Okay!" Tyler agreed amicably with the distraction.

Duke glanced over his shoulder, "Nat, can you try to get her to shower or...something?" He motioned his head in Lenny's direction and Natalie nodded at him.

As the guys disappeared into the other room, Lenny continued staring at the gorgeous woman in her kitchen. She studied her openly and shoved another cookie in her mouth. Maybe she was some sort of angel. Or mystical princess.

"How about we get some real food in you." Natalie said and took away the package of cookies. She removed her coat, hat and gloves, setting them aside. Then she went to the fridge and effortlessly whipped up eggs, sausage and toast presenting it to Lenny who had managed to shuffle to the counter and sit on a stool. She was still staring.

"Where did you come from?" Lenny finally asked as she apathetically shoveled food into her mouth.

"My car broke down and Shawn towed us into town."

"Shawn? You call him *Shawn*?" Lenny was incredulous. And weirdly jealous. Duke was hers, she'd never had to share him with anyone before.

"Well, that's his name," Natalie smiled.

"He's always been Duke to me, I guess." Lenny mumbled. Shawn? That was new. This whole thing was new. So, was this woman Duke's girlfriend? She had a different last name than her dad, she was probably married. Was she going to get Duke killed?

"Are you married?" Lenny asked bluntly.

"Widowed. My husband was a Marine. He died in combat three years ago." Natalie poured Lenny a glass of orange juice.

Lenny swallowed hard. Now she felt like a vile wretch.   "Sorry."

"It's all right." Natalie leaned across the counter on her elbows and looked Lenny in the eye. "Bad break up?" She asked with such compassion that Lenny started to cry again.

Natalie came around the counter and gently hugged Lenny to her side. Lenny sank against her. She didn't know this woman but she suddenly needed her.

Natalie pulled Lenny up and towards the stairs. As they made their way to the top floor, Lenny spilled her heart out.

"I told him I loved him! I mean, how stupid is that? I just said, 'hey, I love you, goodbye.'...He hasn't even called!...I know, I know, *I'm* the one who left but I thought they would call. I thought *someone* would call. Even *Shane* called! I thought I was important. I guess I'm not. I'm just a...loser!" Lenny collapsed on her bed, face down. She twisted her face out of the pillow and continued, "And I know it would have never worked. I

243

mean, how could it? He has this whole other incredible life. *Of course* he didn't want me hanging around forever. I was a...*fling*...an experiment...*convenient.*" Her breath caught on the last word. "Just like Ashton." Fresh tears pooled in her eyes.

Natalie moved to the bathroom and started a hot shower. She came back and helped Lenny into a standing position.

"You're not a loser," Natalie spoke firmly. "But you really need to get cleaned up. Just because he hasn't called doesn't mean you can forgo basic hygiene."

Lenny nodded begrudgingly and began the arduous task of getting showered. She toweled off and Natalie coached Lenny into getting dressed in fresh clothes. Then Natalie sat Lenny down on the bench at the end of her bed and took careful time to comb out Lenny's long tangled hair.

"Why are you being so nice to me?" Lenny whispered.

"You're important to Shawn." Natalie said simply. "And Shawn is important to me. Besides, I've been through my fair share of break ups, it helps to have a friend."

"How long have you guys known each other?" Lenny was touched at this woman's kindness and compassion.

"Oh, about two weeks." Natalie laughed lightly. "I know that seems fast but when you've been through as much as I have, you know what to look for in a person."

"I used to think I knew what to look for." Lenny said, more tears threatening to spill over. What was wrong with her? She'd never acted this emotional before in her whole life. She was stronger than this. She had to be. She'd forgotten or something.

"Just because he let you walk away doesn't mean he didn't have feelings for you." Natalie came around to look Lenny in the eyes. "Sometimes, guys get scared and they act badly."

"He hasn't even called." Lenny whispered, folding her hands helplessly in her lap.

"I know, and he might not." Natalie said honestly. "It's important to grieve. You're not doing anything wrong."

"But I'm acting like a crazy person," Lenny protested. "This isn't me! I'm always focused and in control and level headed...Now I'm...just a mess."

Natalie touched Lenny's chin gently and offered a small smile.

"It's okay to be messy. Love does that to us."

"When will I feel better?" Lenny asked.

"It'll take some time." Natalie admitted. "But from what Shawn has told me about you, you're strong and courageous. You'll get through this."

"I've never been in love before." Lenny mumbled, looking at the floor. "It hurts so bad. Like a piece of me is missing. Not something small like a finger...more like a lung."

Natalie patted her knee. "Yep. I know what that feels like." She swallowed hard. "But it will get better. I promise."

Lenny looked into Natalie's dark eyes and wanted so badly to believe her. She had to hope it would get better. She just wished she didn't have to miss Luke so badly while she was waiting for it to get better. Was that too much to ask?

***

Duke brought Tyler back inside to warm up and found the ladies in the living room sitting by the fire. It brought a special peace over him that he couldn't explain.

"There's hot chocolate on the stove," Natalie directed him.

Duke filled a cup for both he and Tyler and then they joined them in the other room. Tyler lay down on the floor and took off his socks, propping up his feet to face the fire. Duke sat in the chair adjacent to the couch.

"I'm glad you got cleaned up," he lifted his chin to Lenny, taking in her fresh face and clothes. She was wearing a fuzzy gray sweater that he hadn't seen her in since their trip to Alaska a few years back. She had bought it in a little shop of handmade items. It reminded him of a phone call he'd gotten a couple days prior.

"Yeah, I guess I just didn't know what to do with myself...I still kinda don't." Lenny was blue.

Duke frowned. He had really believed that Luke was the one. It had all seemed so clear but he'd just let her walk away. *What a fool,* Duke decided internally.

"Hey, Nick called the other day." Duke changed the subject.

"Nick?" Lenny frowned quizzically, "Nick Federa?"

Duke nodded, "Yup. He and Serge and a few of the guys are heading to Alaska this week. He heard you were back in the game and wanted to know if you'd be up for it." His offer hung in the air. The perfect escape. A two week trip to the back country of Alaska with some of the best riders in the world. No television, no distractions. Nothing but the purity and thrill of riding ancient mountains.

"Are you going?" Lenny questioned, a small spark stirring in her blue eyes.

Duke sighed and glanced at Natalie. "Nah, I'm gonna stick around here. I've been helping Natalie get her cabin in order and I can't very well bail on her now."

245

"You've done enough already," Natalie's eyebrows went up. "I can get the rest finished. I wouldn't mind if you wanted to go on a trip with your friends."

Duke's eyes crinkled at the sides as he smiled at her. "I know *you* wouldn't mind. I think I'd miss you guys too much." He stared adoringly at Natalie, forgetting for a moment that Lenny was sitting right there until she cleared her throat in an obvious manner.

"Anyways, I told Federa I wasn't going but you might be up for it." Duke directed back to Lenny. He knew she didn't have any plans, her future was wide open if she wanted it. All she had set out to do was die in her room under a pile of blankets and cookie crumbs.

"Yeah, I'll go." She sat up straight. "When do I have to get out of here?"

Duke was a little shocked by her abrupt agreement. Maybe he shouldn't have been. She did have a history of running away when things got tough. Was this another example of that? No, she told Luke goodbye, she didn't just disappear. He knew where she was going and he hadn't called or tried to get a hold of her at all. Going to Alaska on a whim is exactly what the old Lenny would have done.

"You'd have to fly out tonight." Duke challenged her.

"Dang, I don't even have time to pack." Lenny showed a small lopsided smile that gave Duke hope. She wasn't gone, she was just hurt.

"You don't have to impress those idiots, you know." Duke lightly scolded.

"I know." Lenny stood up, "I'm gonna call the airline and see if I can even get a ticket."

After Lenny had left the room, Duke moved over to sit next to Natalie on the couch.

"You really think it's a good idea for her to do this?" He asked her softly. Tyler had fallen fast asleep on the floor.

"I do," Natalie nodded. "Sometimes you have to run away to see is someone if going to chase you." Her dark eyes shined in the firelight and Duke found himself leaning in to kiss her.

He paused, considering what this next step would mean. He studied her delicate features and soft lips, savoring the closeness that they were sharing at that moment.

"I'd chase you anywhere." He whispered and then he pressed his lips to hers. This was it, he decided, no more screwing around. This was the ride he'd been waiting on for some time now.

Chapter 18

February Stars

Luke had gotten as far as Ohio before his truck got a flat tire. It wasn't a big deal, he changed it and continued on. Another hundred miles and something under the hood started to smoke. He was basically in the middle of nowhere and it was cold.

He slammed his hand against the steering wheel and yelled. He had left town in such a way that he didn't have a car charger for his phone and the battery had died the day before. He hadn't thought, he simply headed west.

Luke flipped his hazards on and popped the hood. He stepped out into the bitter wind of the Ohio interstate and tried to figure out what was wrong this time. He'd worked on this truck for years. It had been passed down to him from his grandfather and was one of the only possessions he'd inherited when everyone started dying off. Luke had babied it and had kept it running like a top. But like everything else in this world, it could and would fail on occasion.

Maybe it was a sign. Nothing about this trip had been going right. If Lenny wanted to be with him she would've stayed, right? Obviously she had gotten whatever she had needed from her stint as a roadie and was ready to return to her real life. *I was just collateral damage,* he thought cynically.

He slammed the hood down on the truck and cranked the motor. It fired right up and Luke yanked the wheel back onto the road. He saw the next exit fast approaching and he took it. Why should he have to drive clear across hell and gone for her? If she wanted to talk to him, she knew where to find him.

He pointed the truck east and slammed on the gas. Luke was tired. He was tired from the drive, he was tired of the games, he was just too damn tired of everything. The guys would have to get over it. Just like he would have to get over it.

***

Lenny hadn't been able to get a flight that day but she called Federa and said she would only be a couple of days late. He agreed to pick her up at the airport in Anchorage so she wouldn't have to drive to the interior alone.

That gave Lenny an extra day to wash her clothes and pack. It was nice to have something to do keep her mind off of Luke. She tried to stay as busy as possible, even making a few runs with Duke and Tyler.

Natalie and Tyler hung around pretty consistently and Lenny could see the bond between them and Duke growing. Whatever feelings of jealousy she had experienced initially had completely disappeared. Duke was a good man and he deserved a good woman. It warmed Lenny's heart to know that he wasn't going to be alone anymore.

She shoved the last of her socks in the suitcase and paused, Luke's t-shirt was neatly folded on the edge of her bed. She bit the inside of her cheek as she considered taking it with her. No one would know who it belonged to, only her. She grabbed it and shoved it under her socks and zipped the suitcase shut. She couldn't have Luke with her, she should at least be able to take a piece of him. Especially since it felt like he had retained rights to a fairly large chunk of her heart.

She checked her phone again. It was becoming compulsive. Still no calls or texts. She sat down on the edge of the bed and stared at the screen. Her heart started to beat crazy hard as she typed out Harrison as a recipient. What could it hurt to say, "hey"?

Lenny : *Miss you guys, how is everything?*

She pressed send and set the phone down, hands shaking. Was it too much? Should she cut all ties? What if he didn't respond?

Lenny stood up, frustrated with herself for being so weak. *She's* the one who decided to end it. This wasn't their fault. The blame landed entirely on her.

Her stomach clenched when her phone chirped softly. She grabbed at it, eager to read the reply.

Harrison: *Miss you too. Luke is a douche bag. We want to come and see you.*

Lenny smiled. Leave it to Harrison to spill the opinion of the group. She impulsively called him, texting would no longer suffice.

"Hello?" Harrison asked cautiously.

"Hey, it's me," Lenny greeted quietly.

Harrison sighed audibly, "Did you get my reply?"

"Yeah, but I wanted to call." Lenny tapped her knee with her forefinger.

"I'm glad you called. I've missed your voice. Blake and Mike aren't as nice to me as you."

"They love you." Lenny admonished with a smile.

"I know…But seriously, we were thinking about coming to see you."

"Well…" Lenny looked over at her suitcases. "I'm actually leaving in the morning…for Alaska."

The phone was quiet as Harrison processed the information.

"How long will you be in Alaska?"

"Probably two weeks. It's a trip for some pro's and old timers. Just for fun. We live in these cabins with no plumbing and spend all day riding these crazy huge lines. It's pretty awesome."

"That sounds cool…How about when you get back?"

Lenny paused. She missed them. A lot. But wouldn't that be like joint custody in a separation? That wasn't fair to Luke, they were his friends first. What was she even doing calling Harrison? She had no right. She was being completely selfish.

"Maybe." Was all Lenny would commit to. She didn't want to make it harder for her to get over Luke and she didn't want his friends to feel like they had to choose between them.

"Is it okay if we call you and stuff?" Harrison sounded hesitant.

"Of course, you guys can always call me…I might not have great reception in AK but you can leave me messages." She tried to laugh and ease his mind.

"Has Luke called you?" Harrison's voice was guarded.

Lenny swallowed hard, "No."

The line was quiet for a long time, neither of them really knowing what to say.

"It's okay, Harry. It has to be like this," Lenny said gently.

"I disagree." Harrison was more serious than Lenny had ever remembered hearing him.

"You'll see…we'll stay friends and Luke will move on…One of us had to be the grown up…" Lenny tried to pour comfort and belief into her tone even though she didn't feel it.

"We're gonna come and see you when you get back. You're part of us now, Lenny. It's not the same without you around."

"I appreciate that." Lenny smiled into the phone. She meant it. But she knew that given enough time, they would move on too.

They would all move on.

***

Duke and Lenny had ridden to the airport in the Bronco quietly and he helped her get her luggage and equipment checked in. She turned to face him, all she had to do was head through security, so this would be goodbye.

Duke motioned to a bench off to the side.

They sat down next to each other and Duke could see the emotion building on her face. She swallowed hard, pushing back the tears that were already turning her eyes red. Duke took one of her hands and held it both of his own. Goodbyes were never easy but this one seemed more...final than ever before.

"I'm sorry he let you go," he said quietly.

Lenny looked away. "I can't do this here, Duke," she whispered.

"He's a fool, Lenny," Duke continued anyway. He didn't know when he'd see her again and she needed to know these things. "You're going to find someone who makes you as happy as you deserve someday."

"Huh," Lenny laughed sardonically. "You were my backup plan. I thought I'd come home and make a go of it with you but you had to go off and get a girlfriend."

Duke shook his head at her flippancy. He knew she was half-serious. She was heartbroken enough that she would have sought solace in his arms and he wouldn't have been able to say no. But it wouldn't have been real and it would have ruined both of them. Having Natalie cleared up a lot of his confusion in regards to his feelings for Lenny.

"It would have never lasted," he said with a tender smile.

"That's not true." Lenny put on a brave face even as large tears fell on both cheeks. "I could've been happy with you. I could have cooked and cleaned for you and had your babies." Her voice broke and shuddered as she tried to continue, "When I look at you...I see so much of what I want..."

Duke smiled and held her cheek with his palm. "You would never have done that." He touched her tears with his thumb. "You're too good of a person to live a lie."

Her body crumpled against him and she sobbed into his coat, "I know, I would never be able to love you like you deserve."

Duke's heart broke for her. How could he comfort her properly? What could he say to let her know that she was strong enough? That she would heal in time and she didn't need him in order find that out?

"It's time to be grownups, remember?" Duke gently reminded her. "We can't keep playing house our whole lives."

"You're my best friend." Lenny said through her tears.

"And you're mine," Duke's chest burned with restrained emotion.

"But everything's gonna be different now," she whispered.

"Yeah," Duke nodded. "It's gonna be better."

He had spent a great deal of his life loving her, knowing the whole while that he wasn't going to be the one to experience her love returned. She was capable of passion like an avalanche, God save the man who would be on the receiving end of it.

250

***

When Lenny got on the plane, she knew in her heart that Duke was going to be okay...and she would be too, eventually. She was pretty sure that they both knew, without saying, that it was unlikely Lenny would be returning in two weeks. Alaska had a wildness about her that matched a lot of Lenny's insides. She would stay among the danger and adventure as long as it took to heal her. Neither of them knew how long that would be.

Lenny pulled out her notebook. She hadn't written in it since she first started falling for Luke. But it was time to start chronicling her heart's journey again. She knew more about herself than before. Now, she knew she was capable of love. And she knew it was real. And she knew that if she wasn't careful, it could wreck her completely.

She had thought about getting a new one. Her old one had notes and marks in it from Luke and she thought it might be too hard to have to look at that. But, in the end, she decided to keep it. Luke was a part of who she was becoming and she didn't want to ignore that. After all, he was the first man she had ever loved. She wanted to remember that experience as honestly as possible. And honestly, it had been the best thing that had ever happened to her.

***

Luke got home and immediately called a realtor. He decided he hated his house and wanted to sell it. He unpacked his luggage next to the trashcan in the garage. He threw out most of his clothes instead of laundering them. He kept a few irreplaceable things but for the for the most part, it went to the trash. He didn't want anything around that reminded him of her.

Luke was going through the last suitcase of clothes when Mike walked into the garage. Luke had been so focused on his task he hadn't noticed Mike's SUV pull up and park outside.

"Hey," Mike greeted casually. He leaned his long body against the bed of Luke's pickup and stuck his sunglasses in the collar of his shirt.

"What are you doing here?" Luke knew he wasn't being friendly but he really wasn't in the mood for more bullshit.

"Hadn't talked to you in a few days..." Mike watched Luke throw more clothes in the trash. "I came by the other day, you weren't here."

"Yeah, I was stuck in Ohio. But I'm back now," Luke barked.

"You change your mind?" Mike asked, unfazed by Luke's demeanor.

251

"No, Mike. *She* did." Luke looked up at Mike, his face hot with anger. "*I'm* not the one who left. Remember?"

"So that's it then?" Mike's tone was flat.

"What do you want me to do?" Luke growled. "What, Mike! Tell me!"

"Have you tried calling her?" Mike asked pointedly.

Luke sighed heavily. "She's the one who left. If she wants to talk to me, she can call me."

"Wow, that's not childish at all," Mike said sarcastically.

"Maybe you should keep your opinions to yourself," Luke warned darkly.

"Maybe you should nut up!" Mike snapped.

"You know what?" Luke felt his pulse pound in his neck. "I'm tired of constantly having to rescue people around me! I'm tired of trying to convince you lot to stick around! It's bullshit!"

"Maybe if you didn't have such a hero complex, you'd see that *you're* the one who needs to be rescued! From your own arrogant, asinine behavior!"

Luke narrowed his eyes at his friend. He'd never wanted to punch someone so bad in his life.

"Stop being a dick! Stop making yourself a victim and look at reality! What did you expect when you got home? She would hang around, like some sort of friggin' *groupie*? She's so much better than that and she *deserves* better than that!" Mike shook his head in disgust. "Nah, man. You're gonna have to put forth a little effort to get her back. If you want her, go and get her."

Luke grit his teeth together. He didn't respond to Mike. Instead, he threw more clothes in the trash. He finally reached the bottom of the suitcase and paused.

It was one of Lenny's shirts. It must've gotten mixed up in the rush to pack when they were leaving Europe. Luke touched it hesitantly.

"I can't make her come back," he said quietly.

***

"Here's a random question." Mike was annoyed at how stubborn Luke was being. "Did you even tell her you loved her?"

Luke looked up at Mike, brow furrowed.

Mike barked out a laugh of frustration and paced a short distance across the garage and turned back to Luke.

"Wow, you're really thick, you know that?" Mike let his hands slap against his sides in exasperation. "And you can't figure out why she left?

Hello?! You never gave her a reason! You didn't even tell her you loved her, dumbass!"

Luke swallowed hard, "I didn't have to say it. She knew."

"What happened to not giving up on people we care about, huh?" Mike shouted. "What happened to doing everything we could to keep the family together? She's a part of our family now! Why isn't she here, Luke?" Mike waved an arm around the garage, amplifying his point.

"You *do* love her, don't you?"

"Yes! I love her! But she *left*, Mike!" Luke's face was crimson and the veins in his neck were starting to pulse.

"So did I once, but you never gave up on me!" Mike reminded him. "And I did a hell of a lot more shitty things to you than Lenny did. What the hell are you thinking?"

Luke's posture was rigid but Mike knew him better than that. He was the most broken and defeated he'd ever been. Why was he being so stiff-necked about this?

"I know how you feel." Mike tried to bring his voice to a reasonable decibel, despite his frustration. "She's the first woman who ever looked at you and saw past the rock star persona and straight to your soul. You revealed things to her you never would to anyone else. She sees more than the black and white description on Wikipedia and knows every color, shape and flaw that makes up your entire matter. She's still the only think you think about, dream about and want."

Mike's voice choked off and he swallowed hard. Luke stared at him, confused and shocked. His face began to pinch as he tried to push down the rising ache that permeated his whole existence. Mike could see it, because he'd been there. Because he was still there.

"You feel betrayed because when she left, you got sucker punched. Any other girl and I'd tell you to get over it. But she's not any other girl, is she? She's the only one who makes you feel alive. She's the one who stands next to you and makes you feel like this world might not be so bad after all. She's your song, she's your *home!*"

Mike was about to say more when Luke cut him off.

"No, we're done here. You can let yourself out." He grabbed the empty suitcase and went into the house, locking the door behind him.

Mike rolled his eyes and went back out to his truck. Whatever then. He had tried. If Luke wanted to play the blame game and not fight for the girl of his dreams that was his prerogative.

Mike and the guys were still gonna be friends with Lenny and if that made Luke uncomfortable then so be it. Conceited, narcissistic jackass.

***

253

Luke threw the suitcase across the kitchen floor and stalked into his bedroom. He sat down on the bed and looked at the shirt still in his hands. He picked it up and slowly pressed it to his face. He inhaled her scent deeply. It was the scent that had been haunting his dreams since she had left. He felt a lump rising in his chest and he pushed it down. His eyes began to burn and he closed them.

For a moment, she was there with him. Her hair falling on her shoulders and her laugh lighting up his day. Her eyes, so blue they could have been taken straight from the ocean's depths, looking at him with love and adoration. Her hands tangled in his, her lips the perfect distance away for a kiss...

He sighed and dropped his head with regret.

"I don't know how to make you come back," Luke whispered to no one.

Mike's words rang through his head. But what if she still said no? Luke didn't know if he could handle that kind of kick in the teeth. No, it would take some time apart. He would get over her in a while. She wasn't any different than any other girl he'd been with. He held on to that lie, hoping that it would eventually be true.

***

Lenny was in Seattle for her two hour layover before the three hour flight to Anchorage. She had already perused all the little booths and shops in the airport near her gate. She was considering getting a coffee, but wanted to avoid having to use the lavatory on the plane. The airport was packed with travelers and Lenny welcomed the distraction from her thoughts.

"Lenny? Lenny Evans?" A male voice came from behind her.

Lenny turned in her chair and stood when she recognized Ben Calloway, a guy she used to snowboard with back in the day.

"Ben!" Lenny greeted happily.

Lenny hadn't seen Ben in years. They were the same age and competed in a lot of the same events growing up. His parents moved to San Diego during high school and they didn't see much of each other after that. Ben was immensely talented and Lenny had kept up on his achievements over the years.

The last time she saw him, he was a gangly, disproportionate eighteen year old with some serious height in the half-pipe. He had most definitely filled out, Lenny observed. He was at least a whole head taller, wide shoulders and muscles that were apparent through his coat. He had the west coast, surfer boy look going, full tan and shaggy hair.

"What are you doing here?" He asked her eagerly.

"Headed to Valdez for a couple weeks with Federa and them."

"No shit! Me too!"

"Really? I thought I was gonna be the last to arrive. Nick didn't mention you were coming." Lenny was excited, she hadn't ridden with Calloway in a long time.

"Yeah, I had to wrap up some stuff at home before I could leave. It's so rad that you're coming."

"Do you know who else is gonna be there?" Lenny questioned.

"Yeah. Besides Federa and Serge, me, you, Smitty, Shelby Lynn, Travis Jenkins, Shane Brookings and Jimmy Trucker."

Lenny made a face at Shane's name.

"Yeah, I saw all that over the X Games." Ben laughed. "I loved how you stuck it to him. That douche bag had it coming for a while."

"Eh...I'll have to avoid him, I suppose." Lenny said wryly. She wished Nick had told her that Shane was going to be there...oh well.

"Maybe we'll have an appropriately timed avalanche during his run." Ben waggled his eyebrows.

"That's not funny, Ben." But Lenny was laughing anyway.

"Man, it's so good to see you." His sincerity was obvious. "It's been years. You look...really good." He nodded his head in approval.

"You too." Lenny smiled in return. "Who is Shelby Lynn? The names familiar but I'm having a hard time placing her."

"She's this little daredevil from Vermont. She's only seventeen or something but she's blowing up the circuit right now." Ben took a seat across from her and stretched out his long legs in front of him.

"Oh yeah, I remember seeing something about her. She's just a kid, I can't believe Nick is taking her along."

"C'mon, Lenny," Ben chided, "We weren't much older when Nick took us up to Valdez the first time."

"That's true." Lenny rolled her eyes, "Man, time flies."

"True story." Ben agreed shaking his messy hair out of his face. "Hey, you still with the rock star?"

Lenny groaned. "Not exactly."

"It was all anyone talked about after Aspen." He raised an eyebrow at her.

"Yeah, I noticed." Lenny said dryly remembering the tabloid pictures.

"What happened?" Ben was just making conversation, he didn't know that it was weird for Lenny to talk about.

She wrinkled her nose. "It just didn't work out."

255

"Was he bad in bed?" Ben asked suggestively, making Lenny laugh.

"It just wasn't meant to be, that's all." Lenny hedged wishing she could find a way to get him to drop it without being rude.

"Was he a jerk?" Ben frowned.

"No, Luke was really great." Lenny pursed her lips. "It's still kinda raw for me so if we could not..."

Ben nodded, understanding. "Gotcha. Well, when you get to the phase where you want to trash him unmercifully, I have lots of good ones in my repertoire."

Lenny smiled, grateful for his consideration. This trip was going to be fun. Exactly what she needed to help her work through all the turmoil inside. She didn't even mind that much that Shane was going to be there. She felt like she had already kicked that ass and hopefully they could move on like adults.

Her mind drifted briefly to Luke. She wondered what he was doing. Who he was doing it with. She blinked hard, forcing the thoughts away and concentrating on the conversation with Ben. No reason to go there.

"I haven't seen Trucker in years, I had no idea he could still ride." Lenny remarked.

"He's in the geriatrics league." Ben joked, making Lenny laugh again. Yes, this was going to be an excellent vacation.

***

Luke stared out the window of his bedroom from his back. Sleep wouldn't come. The sky was black, the stars floating in the darkness. He could almost feel her forgetting him. Didn't they have something special? Weren't they different from the rest? He knew the longer he waited, the harder it would be to get her back.

He felt gutted. Like a car that had been burned up from the inside out. Empty and charred, waiting to be shuffled off the pavement and taken to the junk heap. The fire leaving nothing useful behind.

He had sold his house. He had a week to get his things out. He didn't even have anywhere to live. He figured he'd place his stuff in storage for now. It didn't matter. Nothing felt like home without her there.

Chapter 19

Deep Inside Of You

Luke suspected that if Lenny knew his suffering, she would feel justified somehow. This is what she wanted, isn't it? For him to be miserable and sleepless and hard to get along with? Well, that's what had happened.

He'd been living with Sway for two days now and hated every second of it. As relaxed and unkempt as Sway appeared to the outside world, he was surprisingly strict about his home. To the point of obnoxious perfectionism. A place for everything and everything had a place. And sometimes he would want it put away before Luke was done using it. Forty-eight hours into their living arrangement and Luke wanted to kill him.

"Listen Luke, you're welcome to stay with me until you find your own place." Sway was making his diplomatic speech for the umpteenth time. "But you have to pick up after yourself. You didn't hang your towel straight after your shower and I had to fix it. We don't want musty towels, do we?"

Luke rolled his eyes. "You don't give a shit about cleanliness on the road. What gives? Are you just giving me a hard time?"

"That's 'Road Sway' this is 'Home Sway.'" Sway responded like it should've made perfect sense to Luke. He walked into the living room and got his coat out of the closet.

"Where you going?" Luke asked. One of the reasons he had asked to stay with Sway was for the distraction. He thought it would be easier to not think about Lenny if he could hang out with some new girls. And Sway was constantly drowning in women.

"I have some people I'm meeting up with." Sway answered casually.

"You need a wing man?" Luke asked.

Sway grimaced as his words. "Wing man? Dude, we're not in college anymore. Besides, I'm insulted that you think *I* would need a wing man." He checked his face in the mirror by the door. He adjusted his long, shiny hair around his shoulders.

"Sorry, I just thought I could come with you. Maybe hookup with someone." The words sounded strange and forced, even to Luke.

Sway turned and frowned at him. "You're looking for a *hookup*?"

He shook his head with disappointment. "Man, you're not like that."

"I used to be." Luke protested, feeling his ego getting testy.

"You're not that guy anymore. You changed with Lenny-"

At the mention of her name, Luke looked down and swore under his breath. No one had said anything to him about her since the day Mike had visited him in the garage. It was a touchy subject for all of them. The guys disagreed passionately about Luke's complacency. And Luke was determined to prove them wrong. He was just doing the worst job at it.

"I know you don't want to talk about her and shit but let's be real for a second." Sway was trying to sound laid back so Luke wouldn't feel threatened but he saw through it. "You guys had something real. I've never had that with anyone…But seeing you guys together gave me hope that I could have it someday too."

"What? Are you saying you're done being a dog and you're gonna turn into a respectable human being?" Luke knew his words were too harsh but he didn't care.

***

Sway wasn't fazed. He was fine being the one Luke took his hurt feelings out on. "Yeah, I'm working on it." He paused as he rested his hand on the doorknob. "You can't come with me tonight, I have a date. A real one." Actually, Sway was on his *third* date with the same girl this week. It was totally new for him. He saw the confusion and disbelief in Luke's eyes and took compassion on him, "We can hang when I get home, I won't be out too late." He promised.

He opened the door and looked at his friend one more time. One of these days Luke was going to have to come to terms with his own hardheadedness. He needed that girl more than he knew. They all did.

***

Luke tried watching TV for a while but there was nothing on. He wondered what Mike was up to. They used to hang out all the time when they were off tour. But Luke didn't want to call him and get another stupid lecture. Mike had no right to tell him how to handle this, he wasn't the one in love with Lenny. *Shit.*

Luke stood up angrily. He was getting so sick of his head leading him back to the same damn train of thought. He didn't want to think about her anymore. It was needless heartache. She was gone and she wasn't coming back. He found himself staring at his phone. Not just his phone, he had already cued up Lenny's number and his thumb was hovering over 'send.' He stood still for a long time, debating in his head if he should call her or not.

He shoved his phone back in his pocket and got his jacket from the closet. He didn't want to talk to her. What else could she say that she hadn't already said. He didn't need to hurt himself on purpose. He left the apartment and went out into the Boston night.

***

Lenny thought she heard her cellphone ring and took it out to look at it. Nope. She didn't even have a signal. *That was weird.* She frowned at the display, she was so sure she had heard it ring...

"Something going on on your phone?" Ben asked from beside her.

She shook her head and put her phone back. "I thought I heard it ring but it didn't." She couldn't shake the feeling that someone was trying to call her.

"You probably won't get too many calls in Thompson Pass," Nick said from the front seat. "You'll have a better signal in Valdez."

Lenny just nodded without voicing her thoughts. She looked out the window of the SUV at the frozen landscape.

It had been years since she had first laid eyes on the beauty of the Alaskan terrain. Valdez boasted an annual snowfall average of 300 inches with some 600-900 more in the surrounding areas. Which is exactly where they were headed. The stark contrast of the crisp white snow against the brilliant blue of the sky made Lenny's heart quicken just a tad. Alaska had always felt like a second home to her.

"It's great that you could join us this year, Len." Nick was saying from the driver's seat. They were barreling down the highway, trying to beat the oncoming snowfall. It was an easy six hour drive inland from Anchorage as long as weather permitted.

"Yeah," Lenny agreed, not really listening. All she could think about was how much more amazing this would all be if Luke and the guys were here.

***

Ben frowned thoughtfully at Lenny. She kept drifting in an out of being totally fine to being completely somewhere else. They had been able to talk quite a bit on the plane ride up, getting reacquainted and rebuilding their neglected friendship. Nick couldn't pick them up until morning and they had both opted to just stay the night in the airport rather than get a hotel.

259

It was fun, they spread their coats out on the floor by the heaters and laid head to head. They continued talking and joking until they got too tired and both fell asleep. Ben had been awakened when Lenny had reached above her head and smacked his face for snoring.

He never felt like he had ever really gotten to know Lenny completely. She had always been this whirlwind of ambiguity. She wasn't shy but she didn't flirt either. Ben was naturally attracted to her and he was usually very good with women but Lenny treated him more like a kid brother than anything else. He didn't mind, they had the whole trip to get to know each other better. And Ben was looking forward to showing Lenny how much of a kid he wasn't.

***

"I thought maybe you and Shelby Lynn could share a cabin." Nick was still talking to Lenny. "You know, since you're the only girls."

"Yeah, that sounds good." Lenny turned her attention back inside the vehicle, her thoughts momentarily put on hold.

"Unless you want one to yourself, I can try to arrange that , too." Nick put in.

"No, I'll share. I hate staying alone."

"You probably wouldn't have to stay alone for long." Ben said under his breath. Lenny frowned at him but he just shook his head like he hadn't said anything at all. She knew what he was implying, but nothing was going to happen there. Ever.

"She doesn't snore, does she?" Lenny raised an eyebrow at Ben. "'Cause I'll probably have to smack her."

***

"I don't know about the snoring, you'll have to let me know." Nick chuckled from the front seat. He glanced in the rear view mirror and saw the brief exchange between Ben and Lenny. He grimaced inwardly.

The wonderful thing about having Lenny along was that she was probably the best rider in the group and would be able to teach the others a thing or two. The hard part was that she was too damn pretty and too damn nice. Nick had promised to take over for Duke in looking out for her among all these dudes. But it was going to be difficult. Hopefully they would get enough snowfall that there wouldn't be much downtime for them to get bored and start looking for other forms of entertainment. Especially since Nick knew that Lenny could take care of herself. He didn't want to be taking guys into town for broken bones and what not.

260

Nick Federa was forty years old this year. He had been doing big mountain riding nearly his whole life. Duke had been his best friend and riding partner for most of it. Nick enjoyed nothing more than to get a bunch of pros all together for a couple of weeks a year in what he considered his backyard. He always tried to invite a variety of riders, guys and girls. But usually the girls opted out. The ones that did make it were pretty fearless and would, on occasion, scare the shit out of him completely.

This year was no different. The group that had come together consisted of legends and rookies but all freaks in their own right. No one looked forward to snowfall more than this group of crazies.

"How's the weather looking for the week?" Ben asked Nick.

"So far so good. But you know as much as I do. That can change." He chuckled to himself. He loved the unpredictability of living in the mountains.

"How soon till we can get on the heli?" Lenny piped in.

"Damn, you're ready to get to it, aren't you?" Ben said with appreciation.

"Oh, probably tomorrow morning, I'll have to check with Jack." Nick answered.

"Kay." Lenny gave a half-smile and looked back out the window.

***

They pulled into the little area where they would 'camp.' Tiny cabins with no plumbing and a couple of nearby outhouses. It was not the most glamorous of setups but no one was there for the amenities. A main Lodge was the focal point of the cul-de-sac. It had plumbing and a staffed kitchen and full service bar. That's where the riders would spend most of their down time. It was nice and rustic with an old pool table and a couple of big screens thrown in for entertainment during blizzards.

Lenny helped unload her gear and Nick directed her to her cabin. She opened the door to the tiny room and smiled. It had been a long time since she was here. The cabin only held what it needed to. It was one room with one set of bunks and one small window. A short table under the window held a few items that belonged to Shelby Lynn and the heater in the corner was roaring. The bunks were piled with blankets and sleeping bags and a single light bulb hung from the ceiling with a pull string.

Lenny set her stuff down and gratefully accepted the top bunk. Shelby Lynn's things were obviously claiming the bottom even though Shelby wasn't there herself. *Probably in the Lodge.* Lenny thought to herself. *Smart girl, don't wanna isolate yourself in this world of testosterone.*

261

Lenny left her things and trudged through the snow over to the Lodge. She might as well join everyone right away. She had been away from the entire snowboarding culture for so long, she wasn't sure what to expect. Would she have to prove herself all over again? Would they welcome her with open arms the way Ben had? Would she be shunned and rejected?

She opened the door to the Lodge and it took a second for her eyes to adjust from the brilliant snow outside to the darker interior. She tried to gauge where she should be as she looked around the open space. It was pretty full since it was a destination restaurant for a lot of folks in Valdez, not just for those staying in the cabins. She took off her coat in the warm interior and hung it on a nearby hook with others. She startled a little when someone came up beside her and put an arm around her shoulders.

"We're all in the back at the bar." Ben said as he guided her that direction.

Lenny was relieved that she wasn't left to fend for herself but she was growing a tad uncomfortable with Ben's familiarity with her. She shrugged her shoulders subtly to push his arm away. He didn't resist, instead he walked ahead of her to the group.

"Hey everyone, look who's here!" He announced Lenny to the group of snowboarders who were having a casual drink at the bar. Lenny gave a small wave and swallowed. *Here we go,* she thought.

Serge immediately patted the stool to his left and motioned with his head for her to join him. She smiled gratefully and took a seat.

Serge was a legend among legends. He was arguably the greatest rider in the world. His talent and technique were unrivaled. Quiet and soft spoken but he always meant whatever he said. His immediate acceptance of her relieved Lenny. That meant that no one else would have a problem with her either.

Serge didn't say much but he bought her a beer and listened to the others talk about their run earlier that day. Lenny relaxed into the conversation. It was fun getting to talk to others who loved what she loved and did what she did. The Lodge was full of activity and soft country music played from a nearby jukebox. It made her heartache seem more bearable.

Nick, Smitty, Ben and Shane were playing a game of pool nearby. The rest of the crew was lined up at the bar facing outward. Next to Serge was Jimmy Trucker, a long haired hippy from Wisconsin who hadn't competed in more than ten years. Next to Jimmy was Shelby Lynn, blonde, unruly hair and sweet innocence wrapped in a stick of dynamite. Next to Shelby Lynn was Travis Jenkins, eight-teen year old superstar from Washington who thought he was a lot cooler than he actually was.

Shelby Lynn and Travis gravitated towards each other naturally

262

because of the age similarity. They had more in common with each other than with the older riders.

Smitty was around the same age as Nick. They had been friends for years, competing in the same circuits and then eventually leaving the competitive side for the same reasons. Smitty used to keep his red hair long but had cut it when he turned forty so he would look more 'respectable.' Smitty and Trucker had been along for Lenny's first trip to AK six years ago and it was comforting to see familiar faces.

And then there was Shane. He kept his eyes focused on the game of pool but they would occasionally flick up to look at Lenny. She wasn't sure how to act with him, they didn't leave things very good in Aspen but maybe they could move past it. He seemed more subdued than his usual, flashy self.

"You looking forward to getting some heli time tomorrow?" Serge asked from beside her.

Serge was from Norway but his English was perfect. Lenny could only detect a slight accent if she listened really hard.

"Yes." Lenny nodded emphatically. "How was it today?"

"Good." He gestured to the pool game, "Smitty took a bad fall but he says he is okay." He nodded over his shoulder at the rookies. "They are a little skittish on the big hills still," he said quietly, his eyes locked with Lenny's. "I was hoping you would be looking for some good vertical tomorrow."

Lenny felt her mouth pull into a half-smile. "Absolutely." Serge had a reputation for pushing the limits of what was physically possible and Lenny felt privileged that he would include her.

"Saw the footage of you in Aspen. That was impressive for not having ridden in two years." He was fishing, trying to see if her hiatus had been real or if she had made up the whole thing for a more dramatic comeback.

"When you want it, you want it." Was all Lenny would reveal. Serge smiled at her response and saluted her with his beer.

She felt her phone buzz in her pocket and pulled it out. Her heart almost stopped when she saw Luke's number on the screen. She excused herself and stepped over to a corner that was more quiet.

"Hello?" She asked, her hands and voice shaking.

Lenny heard lots of voices at once, like from a club or restaurant. She thought maybe he had accidentally pocket dialed her and then he spoke.

"Hello?" He was speaking loudly and didn't sound like himself.

"Luke?" Lenny asked, confused.

"Lenny?" Luke asked in return. Lenny could hear giggling in the back ground.

"Are you drunk?" Lenny was trying to stay calm but she could feel her neck heating up. Did he really call her while he was with another girl?

"I might be drunk." Luke laughed loudly.

"Why are you calling me?" Lenny asked forcefully.

"I'm calling cuz…hold on." She heard him moving around and it got quieter in the background. He must've moved to a different room.

"Lenny?" Luke asked.

"I'm still here," she answered.

It was quiet for a few seconds and Lenny swallowed the lump that had formed in her throat.

"I miss you," Luke finally said.

"I miss you too," she replied. And she did. Oh, how she missed him.

"I need you to come back." His words were slurred and Lenny knew for sure that he was drunk. "Just come home to me and we can fix this whole mess."

"I'm in Alaska, Luke-" she started but he interrupted.

"Why? Are you with Duke? I know he's in love with you! Is that why you left me? For him?" His tone was suddenly combative. Definitely drunk.

"No. Duke is back home. I didn't leave you for anyone." Lenny knew that trying to explain anything to him in this state would be useless. Her arms ached to hold him.

"You said you loved me…" Luke's voice broke and Lenny could feel tears starting to form in her eyes.

"I do love you, Luke," she whispered.

"Then you why did you leave?" His voice kept swinging from heartbroken to angry.

"Luke, we can't have this conversation when you're drunk," she pleaded with him. "Call me tomorrow, we'll talk then,"

Luke seemed to consider her request. He sighed heavily, "Okay. I'll call tomorrow…Lenny?"

"Yeah?"

"I love you, you know."

"I know."

She hung up the phone, her heart heavier than when she started out that day. Words of love could only mean so much spilling from the lips of a drunk. She hoped he would call her tomorrow but knew the chances that he would even remember their conversation was unlikely.

She put her phone back in her pocket and rejoined her group. Ben had noticed her tense phone conversation and came to sit beside her on the vacant stool.

"You wanna talk about it?" he asked.

"No," Lenny smiled at him apologetically. "Sorry, I just wouldn't know what to say I guess." She pushed her beer away, suddenly disgusted by the taste.

"Let me know if I can help in any way." Ben said sincerely.

"I will." Lenny smiled and flagged the bartender down. She ordered some club soda and eased her way back into the conversation around the bar. She tried to not be distracted by her recent phone call. She had wanted him to call so badly. But she hadn't wanted him to call while he was drunk. She tried to push the memory of the girlish giggles in the background far from her thoughts. They weren't together, he was allowed to do whatever he wanted.

***

Luke got home late that night. He didn't really know how he'd gotten home, he just knew he was there now. Trying to get his key to go into the lock. He staggered and fell down in the hallway. He looked up at the door knob and frowned. His eyes couldn't quite focus and he blinked hard to clear the fog. He pushed himself back into a standing position and tried again.

Suddenly the door opened and Sway hauled him inside.

"What the hell?" Sway was angry, Luke could tell and it cracked him up. He laughed loudly at Sway's cranky expression.

"Where have you been?" Sway demanded as Luke stumbled and then fell in the living room.

"I went out," Luke slurred and tried to stand up again.

***

Sway stared at him, in complete shock. Luke hadn't gotten drunk in years. This was so unlike him. This was the old Luke. The Luke none of them could stand.

"You smell like the perfume counter at Macy's," Sway accused.

"Yeah," Luke laughed as he found a seat on the couch, "Girls like me."

"You're joking, right?" Sway was beyond disappointed. Luke looked like hell. His clothes were all a mess and his shirt was barely buttoned. Sway had had enough.

"You're an asshole!" He shouted at Luke. Luke winced but didn't say anything. "You're in love with Lenny! What have you done?!"

Luke stood up angrily. "She left me, Sway! *She left me!*" Luke

265

shouted back.

"So that makes it okay to screw some nobody!" Sway was shaking with fury.

"No!" Luke was shaking his head in protest, confused by his own foggy memories and his overwhelming grief. "I just bought some drinks. I didn't…" His voice faltered, too drunk to think clearly. "I didn't want to be alone…" He collapsed back onto the sofa and hung his head.

"It's just as well she left," Sway said sharply, "You never deserved her." He slammed the door to his bedroom, leaving Luke alone in the dark.

Chapter 20

Learn To Fly

Blake had gone down to the corner store to get a few things. Nothing crucial; fresh produce and some milk. He carried his basket to the counter and waited patiently in line. His eyes casually browsed the tabloid covers, just like anyone else would. He paused on one in particular. He blinked his eyes hard and squinted, thinking he was seeing things. He grabbed the magazine off the rack and stuck it in his basket. He kept his face stoic as he paid for his items and left.

In the elevator ride up to his loft, Blake pulled the magazine out and studied the cover again. He hadn't been seeing things. It was a picture of Luke making out with some chick. The headline read: LUKE CASEY CAUGHT CHEATING! LENNA HUMILIATED AND IN HIDING!

Blake stepped out of the elevator and quickly opened the door to his loft. He set his purchases down on the counter and opened the cheaply printed multicolored pages. Normally, he would never even look at these types of stories. They were always false and misleading, designed to cause trouble. But the sickening feeling in Blake's stomach forced him to look at the rest of the photos.

The magazine had a full spread on Luke's indiscretions. He was pictured sitting in a bar with an unknown girl on his lap. His shirt was unbuttoned and her hands were all over his chest. The article quoted eye witnesses as describing Luke to be "very drunk" and "making out and dancing with several women all night long."

Blake ground his teeth together. This was a local, overnight publication, meaning that the events had happened within the past twenty-four hours and usually within the city limits. But it would go national in a few days. Lenny would see it eventually. That was it. Blake knew, Luke had lost her forever.

***

Luke climbed out of unconsciousness in the spare room of Sway's apartment, his head throbbing. He sat up slowly and winced at the added pain from the minimal effort. He rested his head in his hands as he swung his legs to the floor, trying to clear the fog that had built up in his mind. He couldn't remember anything from last night but he knew he felt terrible.

His stomach felt like he had swallowed pure acid and he wasn't sure if he was going to throw up or not. He hadn't been this hungover in a very long time. He looked down at the clothes he was still wearing from the night before and flashes of memory fired through his brain but he couldn't tell what was real and what had been a dream.

He stood up and made his way to the bathroom for a hot shower. As the steam swirled around him, he tried to focus his thoughts, deciphering reality from nightmare. He had gone to a bar. He kind of remembered Sway being pissed at him when he came home.

He got out of the shower and dried himself off, no better than when he had woken up. He was getting dressed when Sway started yelling at him to come out into the living room.

"What's up man?" Luke wasn't sure if this was just a continuation of their fight from last night or if this was something new. He really wished he could remember more.

Sway threw a cheap magazine on the table and Luke was even more confused than he had been a moment ago.

"You can't stay here." Sway said calmly, his jaw working under his skin. "Not if you're gonna live like this."

Luke frowned and walked over to the tabloid, squinting at the cover. His eyes widened and he flipped to the inside. His stomach lurched and bile rose in his esophagus as he was confronted with the decisions he'd made the night before. The memories came back in a blurry rush and he staggered to the sofa to sit down, unable to speak.

"Does this mean you don't want Lenny anymore?" Sway asked, his face flat and emotionless.

Luke looked around, trying to get his bearings. That's not what he had wanted at all. He just wanted to feel differently than how he'd been feeling. He looked back at the photos with sudden realization, he didn't want her to see these.

He quickly pulled out his phone and checked his call history. He had called her last night. He closed his eyes and tried to concentrate but he couldn't remember what they had talked about. He looked up at Sway with desperation.

"No," his voice cracked, "She's the only one I want."

Sway shook his head and rubbed the back of his neck with one hand.

"Did you sleep with any of those girls?" Sway asked, his face cold and dispassionate.

The memories were muddy but he could almost put them in order now.

"No. I came straight home from the bar, alone." Luke was positive

268

of that. It didn't matter how drunk he had gotten, his goal hadn't been to get laid.

Sway sighed and paced across the living room a few times. "I don't know how you're gonna fix it. You know she's gonna see this eventually."

Luke thought he had reached the lowest point in his emotional fortitude the day before. But this was a whole new level of loss. How was he ever going to get her back now? She was so much better than his behavior dictated. She deserved better than him, no wonder she had left.

Why had he been so determined to prove that he didn't need her? At this point, when he realized what a life without her actually looked like, he knew what kind of a moron he really was. The worst kind.

He'd regressed to old habits to ease his pain and in doing so, may have destroyed any opportunity to get back the one woman that mattered to him.

"Maybe…" Sway began and Luke looked up at him, hope making a tentative step back into his heart. "I might have an idea…" Sway grimaced at him. "But let's be clear about something, I am *not* pleased with your actions. You've really messed up this time." Luke nodded in agreement. "But you've bailed all of us out at one time or another, the least we can do is help you pull your head out of your ass." He sighed with disappointment and ran his hand through his hair, "We have to have a family meeting."

***

Lenny awoke with a smile. The skies were clear and powder was waiting. She dressed quickly and quietly in the early morning, careful not to wake Shelby Lynn who had gone to bed far too late. *All that flirting with Travis Jenkins*, Lenny snickered to herself.

She practically ran to the Lodge for breakfast. She yanked open the door and was greeted with the smell of pancakes and bacon, her stomach growled in happy anticipation.

Ben and Serge waved to her from a table near the back and she joined them. Taking off her coat and hanging it on the back of her chair, she sat down across from Serge and next to Ben.

"Good morning!" She greeted as she poured herself a steaming cup of coffee from the pot on the table.

"You're in a good mood this morning," Ben noticed out loud.

"Uh, duh. I'm in freaking Alaska," Lenny deadpanned. Serge chuckled softly at her.

"Here, fill up." Ben passed her a platter of food and she gladly dug in.

"Nick is gonna take us out for a test run first," Serge said. "Then we'll meet up with the others at their chosen location."

Lenny circled the table with her finger, "Just us?"

Serge nodded but didn't pause in eating.

"You think you can hang with the big dogs?" Ben teased from next to her.

"Do you?" Lenny countered with one eyebrow up, taking another bite of pancakes. She really enjoyed how being at a higher altitude meant you could eat more calories.

"Smitty is teaching the kids how to build a jump out of nothing," Ben added.

"Nice. I hope they give me a crack at it. I haven't gotten a chance to run one of Smitty's kickers in a long time," Lenny said thoughtfully.

"Remember when Duke wrecked last time you were here?" Serge mentioned with a smirk.

"Gosh, yes! I thought he was gonna kill himself that trip." Lenny shook her head at the memory.

"I woulda done it too had I known that you were playing nurse that weekend." Ben laughed and winked at Lenny.

"What?" Lenny smiled, confused.

"Well, it was obvious that Duke was being more reckless to get your attention. We assumed it was because he got to spend more one on one time with you."

"Oh, stop," Lenny made a face. She knew Duke had feelings for her but it was a shock to find out that everyone else knew before she did. What else didn't she know?

"Yeah, he threatened all of us to back off." Ben laughed at Lenny's face.

"Don't worry, Lenny," Serge said seriously, "If anyone wrecks this week, I'll play nurse."

Lenny laughed at Serge's dry humor. She knew he sensed her awkwardness at this particular topic and she was thankful for his appropriately timed joke.

"Can I join you guys?"

Lenny looked up to see Shane standing at the vacant chair. He was addressing Lenny specifically. His unflinching eye contact made her heart skip momentarily.

"I don't mind." Lenny responded with a casual smile and then looked back to her food. That was weird. She was not going to let him get under her skin.

Shane took a seat and began filling his plate. The table was quiet for a few minutes and Lenny couldn't help but feel responsible for that. She was the one who had aired Shane's horrible transgressions to the entire world. And these had been his comrades, his teammates. They shouldn't have had to choose sides in a personal problem that was between Lenny, Shane and Cody.

"Are you coming with us in the heli, Shane?" Lenny asked awkwardly. She'd just a soon put the past behind them. If that meant she had to be the bigger person, than so be it.

"Yeah, Nick asked me if I'd go so he could help Smitty with the jump." Shane kept his face flat and didn't look up from his food. "If that's okay with you, that is," he added at the end.

Lenny swallowed as Ben and Serge looked at her for a response.

"Of course. We're all here for the same reasons, right?" She smiled nervously. "To get some good vertical rides in?"

Serge nodded his approval and went back to eating. Ben studied Lenny's face longer than she was comfortable with and she started to chew on the inside of her cheek.

Shane didn't respond at all. He poured himself a cup of coffee and continued eating. Lenny suddenly felt bad about what she had done to him a few weeks back. This man at the table was not the same flashy, egocentric playboy she had spent so much time hating. This was all new territory.

Before long, they were waiting outside for the helicopter pilot, Jack. They had their gear ready and Lenny could feel her pulse quicken. Being taken to a high peak and dropped off by a helicopter was one of her favorite experiences. Nothing compared. *Well, maybe kissing Luke.* Lenny tried to shake that thought off as quickly as it had crept up on her.

The heli started to get warmed up and they loaded their gear inside. Soon they were cleared to board and take off. The scenery of the Alaskan mountains was breathtaking. Serge spoke with the pilot and they scouted out a stately peak. All the passengers disembarked onto the snowy top and watched the heli fly away.

Lenny pulled her hat a little lower on her ears as the wind whipped past her face. She was terrified and excited at the same time. Duke would have never allowed her to get to a height of this kind. He had always restricted how much alone time she spent with Serge. He was afraid Serge was a bad influence on Lenny's fearlessness and would encourage her to be more risky than was necessary. Lenny felt like a rebellious teenager hanging out with the 'bad boy' in home room. She looked at Serge, he was all business. This kind of extreme was why he had made the trip to begin with.

"Who wants to go first?" Serge asked the group of them after the helicopter had gotten far enough away to hear each other.

Ben looked more nervous than Lenny had ever seen him. Shane was too. Serge seemed to be the only one ready for a ride of this magnitude.

"I'll go first." Lenny found herself volunteering. Her heart was stuck in her throat. She liked to be first to descend for a lot of reasons. The main one being to pick your own line without anyone's influence. But the added bonus of looking like a badass in front the boys was cool too.

She couldn't see Serge's expression behind his goggles and face mask but his approval was apparent in his posture.

"That's insane!" Ben protested. "You haven't dropped a line in too long to be the first at this height." He took a step to get in front of Lenny to stop her.

Shane put in arm up, pushing Ben back slightly. Ben frowned at him, perplexed.

"Dude. She's got this." Shane said confidently.

Lenny looked up , surprised at Shane's sudden support. He was looking at her with different eyes. She had noticed something strange the first night at camp but couldn't quite place it. He was avoiding direct eye contact most of the time anyway. But not now. Now, he was looking at Lenny with eyes of a man who had too many regrets and had decided to do something about it.

"You're kidding, right?" Ben was incredulous.

Shane kept his eyes on Lenny as he answered calmly. "She's gonna be just fine, Calloway. She's the best." He said it without a hint of sarcasm and Lenny tried to downplay the shock that rippled through her.

Ben shook his head like he thought Shane had lost his mind, Lenny knew how he felt. But she wasn't going to let anyone else know that.

"Why'd you come up here if you didn't want to play?" Lenny teased. The adrenaline was starting to kick into high gear.

"I just don't think you should go first." Ben grumbled when it was obvious he had lost the argument.

Serge stood back, completely relaxed, waiting for the squabble to clear. Lenny envied his cool focus.

She dug out her chute and fastened her binders. She grinned at the guys and lowered her goggles, giving a final dramatic salute for beginning her descent.

She started out slowly on her vertical. The angle was steep, probably fifty degrees or more. She was careful, feeling her way as she went. She didn't want to jump past the hard parts and fly to the end. She wanted to enjoy this, every death defying, exhilarating moment.

Interestingly enough, a drum beat started to resonate in her head. It was the opening song for Double Blind Study on the tour. She didn't feel sad or weird, it felt good. And motivating. As her board started it's expert curve down the extreme slope she heard the guitar riff join in and her heartbeat quickened.

The sky was an overwhelming blue. Deep and clear at the same time. The white landscape was bare and open, waiting for her to carve a line right through it. She bent and twisted, feeling the fresh powder cave and respond, propelling her forward. She would speed up and then slow down, controlling her movements, controlling her momentum.

Lenny was flying. She hadn't felt freedom like this in a long time. Far longer than she cared to think about. The air was as clean and pristine as the snow she was slashing in. Her line curved and arced, throwing clouds of powder around her. Creating a beautiful effect for her brilliant blue riding suit to burst through.

***

Shane felt a grin spread across his face behind his mask. He knew she would be fine. He watched in appreciation. He knew Lenny was good. He had just never realized how good. It was like the mountain belonged to her and changed to make her path possible.

"Alright, Calloway," Serge said from behind him and clapped his hand on the kid's shoulder, "You're up."

Ben nodded but he was still pretty nervous.

"You got this, kid." Shane said with a pat on the shoulder. "You can follow Lenny's line all the way down, she's not as crazy as Duke."

Shane waited till Ben got started and then he turned to Serge.

"I assume you'll be last." He nodded at the composed Norwegian. Serge stepped aside in answer, giving Shane room to pick a chute.

In the past, Shane would have never taken this trip. He had always preferred to ride maintained parks and pipes. Back country riding scared him beyond belief. But after losing Lenny permanently and than having his idiocy thrown around the media, he realized that even playing it safe, you can make a mess.

He started small, little trips to the unpopulated runs, trying out fresh powder and learning the feel of riding untamed terrain. It didn't take long for him to get hooked. And when Federa invited him to come to Alaska, he jumped at the chance. This was his largest descent as well but he wasn't scared of the ride. The thing that scared Shane was dressed in blue and coming to a stop at the bottom of the mountain.

***

Lenny came to a halt and pushed up her goggles. She was breathless and heated up from her ride so she removed her face mask and hat as well. She turned to watch Ben cut a smooth line very near hers. It made her feel good, she had blazed a trail to be proud of.

She watched in curiosity as Shane started his own run. He was a little further away from where she had started. She had never seen him ride big mountains before. All the time they were together, he had made it abundantly clear that he was *not* into that sort of thing. He was good in the pipe and that had always been his focus. She was curious as to what had changed his mind.

Ben slid up next to her, and pushed his coverings off his face. He had a goofy grin plastered on and he gave Lenny a high-five.

Shane made his descent with precision and Lenny was impressed. When he reached them at the bottom she impulsively patted his shoulder in congratulations. Shane took off his goggles and gave Lenny a warm look.

"Bet you didn't think I could pull it off." He said with a sideways smile.

"I'm not gonna lie, I was a little surprised." Lenny tried to read his expression but he looked away from her inquisitive stare. Whatever had happened to Shane was a very big deal. He was like a brand new person.

"Damn, check out Serge..." Ben said with awe.

They all turned to observe the living legend take his turn raging down the face. It was a thing of beauty. Serge moved with the fluidity of a spider in an intricate web; in and out, back and forth. The snow bursting from beneath his board as if announcing his arrival to the rest of the world.

"Do you think he knows how good he is?" Lenny wondered out loud.

"He's definitely fearless," Shane remarked. "I'm not that brave." He glanced at Lenny with adoration. "Lenny is, though."

Lenny smiled wistfully, still staring at Serge's perfect form and style.

"Sometimes," she agreed noncommittally.

When Serge finished his run and humbly accepted the group's praise, he radioed the heli and Jack swung around to pick them up again. They flew a short distance away to a smaller slope where Nick and Smitty had helped the 'youngins' build a jump.

"You're gonna fly a hundred feet off that thing!" Nick was hollering at Smitty. They were having an argument about the safety of the jump they'd just finished.

"That was the plan, dummy." Smitty wiped the sweat off his brow and squinted up the hill. "It ain't fun unless you can get hurt."

"Maybe for you and me, that's true. But they're just kids." Nick protested.

"Would you calm down?" Smitty was losing his patience. "They don't have to try it if they don't want to. No one is forcing them."

Nick's mouth twitched in agitation. Smitty was right, but he didn't have to like it.

At the top of the run, the other riders were nervously preparing. No one was talking about their anxiety, they were all pretending like they had none. Lenny laughed to herself. She remembered feeling that way at that age too. Like, if you act like you're invincible than maybe you will be.

"So, who wants to try it first?" Lenny asked with a grin.

"It's Smitty's kicker, maybe he should go first." Trucker suggested.

"I'll go first." Travis Jenkins suddenly spoke up. He wanted to prove his manhood, no doubt. The competitiveness surrounding the entire outing was thick enough to choke on.

Lenny sidled up to Travis as he tightened his bindings.

"Hey." She took a knee next to him and gazed out over the stark white landscape. "We can do this run all day. Save your big stuff for after you get to know the run a few times." Jenkins had a rep for being flashy and bold in the pipe and on the freestyle course. Lenny didn't want his day to be cut short just because he didn't find the right balance.

Travis frowned at her, trying to not to hear her words as a challenge.

"All I'm saying is," Lenny continued, reading his hesitation, "This isn't a park. It's okay to be scared. If you're not a little bit frightened, the mountain will eat you alive." She patted his shoulder as he nodded at her words and got into a standing position.

As Travis traveled down the packed, slick run towards the ramp, Lenny watched in satisfaction. He was controlling his speed and making the slight adjustments that an experienced rider would make. He took the jump at a pretty strong velocity and spun into the air. She could see him tracking the landing already. He set down with a wobble but didn't lose his balance. She was happy he had taken her advice.

Then it was Trucker's turn. Jimmy Trucker was always reckless and never smart. He was addicted to the thrill and possibly the crash. He let out a loud whoop and took off going at a ridiculous speed. The moment he flew into the air, Lenny knew he'd lost control. He didn't just crash, he rolled and bounced and crashed repeatedly. His board disengaged and his body continued on, getting buried slightly in the snow he had disturbed on his way down.

Everyone waited for movement before rushing to him. He flopped over on his back and let out a loud moan.

"I'll check him." Lenny said, tightening her binders. She was cautious on the slick run but had achieved a good speed when she reached the jump. As she flew into the air she got the distinct impression that she was indeed flying this time. She did a quick method to please the onlookers and tracked her landing. The snow was rough and uneven from where

275

Trucker had epically wiped out. She tried to place her board in as smooth a location as she could find at her altitude. Little wobble, nothing she couldn't handle. She turned her board sideways and skidded to a halt near Trucker's crumpled form.

Unhooking her bindings, she jogged over to him and peered down into his face mask.

"Some things never change, Truck," she said with mock disappointment.

He groaned in response. "That's not true. I'm a heck of a lot older this year."

Lenny laughed and began to check his body for broken bones before trying to move him. Satisfied that it was just a couple of bumps, she helped him into a sitting position.

"Thanks, Len," Trucker grimaced at the pain in his ribs as she helped pull him to a standing position.

"You're done for the day," Lenny said apologetically.

"Yeah, I hope I can move in the morning." Trucker attempted a laugh and then held his side.

"Let me take a look at those ribs." Lenny peeled off his coat and pulled his shirt up to expose his left side. It was red and already swollen; tender to the touch. "You might have a few cracked ribs, Truck," she said with concern.

"You know what they say, big mountain thrills equal hospital bills." Trucker tried to laugh again.

"Maybe you should go back to camp," Lenny suggested tentatively.

"Nah, I'll be fine." Trucker dismissed her with a wave as he pulled his coat back on. "I wanna see how everyone else fairs."

"Okay," Lenny relented and trudged over to collect her board. "But stay down here, I meant what I said, you're done riding for the day," she instructed seriously.

"Whatever you say, mama." Trucker smiled and walked over to join Travis who had been watching from a distance.

Lenny whirled, expecting to see Blake but no, it was still Trucker. No one had called her that in a few weeks and it ignited her repressed heartache. She shook it off as she climbed back up to the start where the others awaited.

"Is he okay?" Shelby Lynn looked scared.

"Yeah, he's fine." Lenny waved it off. "He's just gonna be sore tomorrow."

She took this as a teaching opportunity and addressed the remaining riders.

"Smitty builds some pretty gnarly jumps, guys. Take your first run easy. Learn it first before you trick it." She pointed at Jimmy Trucker. "Or you'll spend the rest of the trip watching. And that's not why you're here."

They nodded like obedient children and Lenny suppressed a laugh. A few years ago, no one would have taken her seriously. And now she was one of the 'adults.' Bossing around rock stars all summer had it's benefits.

Ben went next and then Shelby Lynn. Eventually, everyone took a turn. All of them followed Lenny's advice and kept it cautious for the first few runs. They started to get brave and added in little grabs, flips and rotations as they got more comfortable.

"Did I impart wisdom?" Lenny asked Serge as they looked on.

He only gave his quiet, knowing smile. Lenny enjoyed being near Serge. His energy was both calming and ferocious. He reminded her of a cat. He could be completely relaxed one minute, eyes half lidded, nearly asleep and then on the move, twisting and hurtling down the mountainside the next.

"C'mon, Lenny!" Nick called from the top of the slope, "Show us something special."

Lenny smiled and removed her jacket. Even though they were surround by snow, the sun and extra activity was making them all warm. Travis had long since removed his shirt, much to the joy of Shelby Lynn, and Lenny decided to be more comfortable as well. She took off her hat and outer shirt, stripping to her black snow pants and orange tank top. She lowered her goggles and her blonde hair hung in sweaty strands down her back. Serge offered her a fist bump as she strapped in.

The slope was even more slick than before because of all the activity but Lenny liked the extra speed it provided. She would need it for what she was about to attempt.

***

"You have to cool it, Calloway." Serge said from next to Ben. Ben turned, eyes wide with surprise and confusion.

"What?"

"You are not the one." Serge said calmly, as they watched Lenny take off and head towards the jump.

"What do you mean?" Ben asked as he stared at Lenny flying into the air. She did a corked 180 backside, her body a swirl of color and skin, and landed gracefully. The trick was flawless and the other riders applauded.

"I am talking about Lenny." Serge turned his pale, serious eyes on Ben. "You are not the one, do not waste your time."

Ben forced a laugh, embarrassed by the reprimand.

"Who's "The One", Serge? You?" Ben asked, holding his mittened hands up to symbolize the air quotes.

"No," Serge answered and bent down to tighten his bindings for his own run. "Not me. Not you."

Ben watched Serge follow Lenny with an equally impressive run. He was befuddled by Serge's comments. Did Lenny say something to Serge? As far as Ben knew, she was fair game. She wasn't seeing anyone and neither was he. Flirting couldn't hurt, right? Ben's gaze drifted to Shane Brookings who was also watching Lenny. They'd been friendly with each other all day. That didn't mean there was something going on there, did it? *Surely I'm better than that guy!* Ben thought defensively. Shane was a moron. Lenny had to have better taste than that. She wouldn't want to be with someone who was a known womanizer, would she?

Chapter 21

No Way Back

Sway's solution involved a lot of ass chewing, Luke found out very quickly. He had called the guys and with quite a bit of coercing and slight extortion, Sway got them to agree to meet at Blake's loft.

It was like an intervention, Luke noted. His closest friends were there, along with Carl and Harrison's sister, Miranda. It was similar to when they had all confronted Mike on his drug use.

They sat Luke down on the couch and proceeded to tell him all the things he had done wrong and how it had affected their lives. It would have been comical if wasn't so tragic. Luke had been so wrapped up in his feelings for Lenny he never stopped to realize that she was very much a part of the rest of the band. She had been woven into their hearts and music.

How one girl could have such a lasting impact on one band was beyond Luke's reasoning. He knew how she had affected him, but he was in love with her. He was finding out the others loved her as well, but in different ways. She had become equally important and vital to them. They missed her and they wanted her back. And now this thing with the tabloids…

"You're an idiot," Blake said disdainfully.

"Remember, Blake," Miranda quietly reminded, "Use feeling words. I feel…"

"I feel that you are an idiot," Blake restated in exasperation.

Miranda closed her eyes and sighed.

"It's okay, Ran," Luke said, "Blake's right, I am an idiot."

"So what are you gonna do about it?" Blake asked pointedly.

"Well, I was hoping you'd help me." Luke looked around the room at his friends, settling on Sway. Sway nodded and took over.

"We *are* going to help him." He started, giving stern looks to the eye rolls. "Luke has helped us *all* out of terrible things. This is simply an opportunity for us to return the favor."

"What do you have in mind?" Mike hadn't stopped glaring at Luke since he'd arrived and Luke didn't blame him. Mike had tried to help him and Luke had slammed the door in his face. *I'm an asshole.*

"You know that song you wrote for Lenny?" Sway focused on

Luke again and he nodded.

"We're gonna record it and release it. Right away."

The room was silent.

"How does that help?" Luke finally asked, feeling unsure. But *not* listening to his friends hadn't gotten him very far.

"She'll hear it and it'll soften her heart." Sway rolled his eyes at Luke's absurdity and kept going. "And then you gotta go to Jackson Hole and beg her to forgive you for being a complete douche bag. You bring the biggest diamond you can find and you get down on one knee-"

"One knee? People still do that?" Miranda interrupted.

"Get down on one knee," Sway continued, throwing a scowl in Miranda's direction. "And you ask her to marry you."

"You really think he can sing her a little song and she's just gonna forget Skank-Gate and promise to love him forever?" Harrison had been relatively quiet during the whole event. Until now. He stood and grabbed his hair in both hands.

"You have pictures of you playing Who Can Be The Whoriest with a random floozy circulating through the general populous! Am I the only one who has noticed this?" Harrison's voice continued to raise. "Lenny was supposed to be your soul mate! What the hell were you doing with other girls at all?!"

Luke swallowed and hung his head. He didn't have any words with which to defend himself anymore. He knew Harrison was right. And he didn't deserve Lenny's forgiveness let alone a second chance.

"I agree with Harrison." Carl's gruff voice joined in. "Lenny is smart, and she's too good for you." He shrugged and leaned back in his seat, his peace having been said.

The room fell quiet again as everyone stared at Luke. They all knew he had seriously screwed up big this time. Lenny *was* smart, she wasn't going to let some guy treat her like a cheap novelty item and be okay with it.

Luke felt the hopelessness of the situation pulling his insides apart. It couldn't end like this! He had loved her with truth and passion and fury, how could it end with a kiss goodbye at the airport? No fight? No conviction? No effort?

Luke's anger rose to the surface and he bolted to a standing position, making everyone around him jump.

"No," he said forcefully, "It doesn't end like this. Not yet. She might not want me but I still want her. And she needs to know that." He turned to Sway, "Get the studio, tonight if you can." Sway nodded and pulled out his phone. Luke pointed at Harrison. "Don't stop pointing out what a dick I've been." He pointed at Blake and Mike next. "You guys can

280

both punch me if you want."

Mike gave him a small smile and uncrossed his arms, "I'm just glad you're gonna fight for her."

"Me too," Blake concurred.

Luke finally had the conviction he needed to fight for her and it might be too late. This plan might not work but he was willing to try anything at this point. He needed her more than he needed to feel sorry for himself.

***

The song turned out as good as it could for the rush they put on it. The label agreed to release it immediately with no questions asked. Luke was hoping the song would reach Lenny before the photos. She was never one for reading tabloids but that didn't matter. It would be all over TV soon enough. Luke called his manager and told him to set up a few interviews for the next couple of days. He'd try to get out in front of it as soon as possible.

The interviews went as expected. They showed the illicit photos and Luke tried to make it sound like it wasn't as bad as they made it out to be. He attempted to avoid using the phrase, 'we were on a break,' but it came out a time or two. Mostly he tried to focus on the single and how much it meant to him and how in love he was with the person he wrote it for. They asked if it was for Lenny and he would neither confirm nor deny. Again, the hope being that Lenny would hear the words and not see the pictures.

Then he flew to Jackson Hole. He wasn't sure what he'd say when he got there. He just knew that he didn't want to say it over the phone.

The flight seemed to take forever. He rented a car and drove to the Lodge, parking in the empty driveway. He tried to still his flipping stomach as he approached the front door. What if she was angry to see him? What if she was with someone else? What if she was with Duke? He took a deep breath and rang the doorbell.

After a few minutes without an answer, he rang it again. Still nothing. No one was home. Luke looked up at the overcast sky. Maybe she was on a ride. She'd probably be back by dark. Luke got back in his rental and decided to wait.

***

Luke woke up, startled. Someone was knocking on his window. He must have dozed off. It was dark outside, he wasn't sure how long he'd been waiting. He opened his car door to find Duke frowning down at him.

"What are you doing here, Casey?" Duke greeted roughly.

Luke climbed out of the car and tried to look evenly into the taller man's eyes. "I came to see Lenny," he answered as confidently as possible.

"She's not here," Duke replied flatly. Luke saw a flicker of something in his eyes he couldn't place. Either Duke was glad to see him or he was going to punch him in the nose.

"When will she be back?" Luke refused to be intimidated.

Duke's jaw worked under his skin before he finally relented and gestured for Luke to come into the house.

When he walked into the warmth of the Lodge, he noticed how empty it felt.

"She left." Duke said as he hung up his coat and proceeded to the kitchen.

"What do you mean, she left?" Luke followed, feeling his world crash around him. He'd waited too long.

"I mean, you didn't call and she went to Alaska." Duke took out some milk and poured two glasses, offering one to Luke. "She's not here. She's gone."

"When is she coming back?" Luke's memory banks fired and he vaguely remembered having a conversation with Lenny that she was in Alaska. But he hadn't been sure if that memory was real or just a dream.

"Don't know." Duke took a drink of milk. "You should've called."

"I know," Luke responded, feeling more defeated than he had all week. She was even further away now.

"Where in Alaska?" Luke suddenly asked. Why not? He had the money and the time. Why couldn't he just go there? It didn't matter where they were when he told he loved her, she just needed to hear it.

"Valdez. With a bunch of other people." Duke's face was unreadable. He was obviously just as pissed at Luke as the rest of them.

Luke thought for a few minutes before speaking again. "I don't know what to do. I'm so backwards and turned around without her. I love that woman with everything I have. I can't stop trying until I'm positive she knows that."

Duke nodded once and tried to hide his smile behind another drink of milk. "This might be salvageable after all, Casey."

***

It had been an amazing week. Getting up early, fresh rides all day long with the best in the sport, Lenny couldn't ask for more. She'd hardly had time to think about Luke, much less be surprised when he didn't call her back. He had been very drunk. He'd probably forgotten the whole conversation. It was just as well, Lenny thought, they should give each other some space to move on. As impossible as that seemed.

The snow had started to come down in thick waves sometime in the middle of the night. Nick met everyone in the Lodge the next morning and explained that the current storm system moving through might last a couple days. His words were met with groans and complaints. But nothing could be done. They had to wait out the weather and then they'd be able to tackle the mountains again.

The first day of the storm, everyone gravitated to the Lodge and played pool or watched TV. It wasn't so bad. The group was growing closer and more tight-knit and the age gaps weren't as apparent anymore. But by day two, people were going a little stir crazy.

Lenny was watching a very dodgy game of darts between Ben and Trucker when Shane took a seat next to her on the couch.

"I was wondering if we could talk?" He asked gently.

Lenny turned sideways to face him. They were relatively alone. The Lodge was buzzing but no one was close enough to overhear a casual conversation.

"Sure," she answered sincerely. She and Shane had gotten along better during this trip than they had the entire time they'd known each other. The awkward tenseness that she had expected was nonexistent. He had been nothing but friendly and encouraging. It was as if their ugly breakup and following confrontation a few weeks ago had never happened.

"I guess, I just wanted you to know how sorry I am." Shane's amber eyes were pulled down at the sides in regret, taking Lenny off guard. "I feel terrible about what I did to you. You were always so amazing to me and I really hurt you."

Lenny had no idea Shane had wanted to have such a serious conversation. It was as good a time as any, Lenny supposed. She had a few things she'd been wanting to clear up herself.

"Why did you stick around for so long after the accident? You could've just moved on." She searched his eyes as he looked back, unblinking.

"Because I was really hoping maybe you *did* forget what Cody and I had done and we could pick where we left off."

"But there were other girls, Shane…not just Cody." Lenny reminded. Her previous anger had evaporated weeks, ago. It had been replaced with acceptance and curiosity.

"Yeah, I was a horrible boyfriend." Shane acknowledged. He looked at her earnestly. "But, I think I did love you, as much I was capable of at the time."

"What does that mean?" Lenny asked, her eyebrows pulling

283

together.

"I didn't love you like you deserved." Shane's eyes were serious and sad. "But I learned a lot from losing you. And I hope, someday, I can be your friend again."

Lenny studied his face, he had gotten older when she wasn't looking. She had known Shane for a long time. They had a history, not a great one, but it was there nonetheless. She had never seen him more genuine and her heart changed in that moment. She decided to let go of the past.

"I forgive you, Shane." She reached over and laid her hand on his forearm. He looked up at her, relief creeping into his gaze.

"I didn't ask you to," he responded softly, his voice full of hope and wonder.

"No, but we both needed me to." Lenny gave him a crooked smile and moved to sit closer to him on the couch. He hesitantly put an around around her shoulders as she hugged up next to him.

"Thank you, Lenny." He rested his chin on the top of her head and she smiled. They couldn't go back and fix everything, and they would never be more than friends. But at least they *could* be friends and that meant more to Lenny than she had realized.

She glanced over as Nick sat down nearby and started a conversation with those at the bar.

"The storm is actually getting worse." Lenny overheard Nick telling Smitty and Serge. "We may have to move the kids into town till it passes."

And that's exactly what happened. Nick announced a few hours later to pack up what they needed and they piled into a caravan of cars and trucks and headed to a hotel in Valdez.

***

The hotel was nearly empty from other travelers and the group all got their own rooms on the same floor. It was almost like a college dorm, Lenny thought ruefully. Hopefully they would all behave themselves. Snowboarders forced to stay indoors due to inclement weather? Probably not.

She decided to explore downtown Valdez and took Ben, Shane, Shelby Lynn and Travis in tow. They went in and out of little shops and stores, sometimes buying trinkets for family back home. They ate at a small restaurant that served fresh fish and lobster caught in the Sound.

They were walking back to the hotel when Travis pulled the groups attention to a small music store. They entered and casually browsed the

284

various merchandise. CDs, vinyl's, t-shirts, posters; every band imaginable. Lenny was flipping through a stack of old records when a familiar song started to play on the speakers overhead.

She froze, listening to the first few notes on the guitar carefully, *it couldn't be...could it?* Then a low, gravelly voice started in with the lyrics she knew by heart. It was her song. The song Luke had written for her. It sounded a little different, the whole band was playing, it was no longer acoustic. Lenny swallowed hard and looked around for the store's clerk. Spotting him near the register she slowly made her way that direction, trying to not draw any attention to herself.

"Excuse me," she flashed her most persuasive smile. The pudgy, curly haired clerk straightened up as she spoke. "I was wondering what the name of the track is that you're playing right now."

"Oh...uh," he held up a case, "It's Double Blind Study's new single, *Need.* Just got it today." He handed the case over to Lenny for her to examine.

She carefully took the plastic case and turned it over, her hands shaking. It was a stock photo of the band, nothing she hadn't seen a million times.

"It's weird, right?" The clerk said with a laugh.

"What do you mean?" Lenny looked up at him with a soft frown.

"Well, just that guy," he pointed to Luke on the cover. "He writes this song for his girl and then goes off and cheats on her."

"What are you talking about?" Lenny felt a hollowness in the pit of her stomach.

The clerk pulled a tabloid out from under the counter and opened it to the pictures of Luke making out with a random girl. Lenny couldn't help but stare. She felt someone come up behind her but she didn't acknowledge them.

"I wonder if it's a ploy to get more publicity," the clerk continued. "He's been all over TV and radio this week pushing their single and downplaying these tabloid pictures."

Lenny was skimming the article for any mention of her. She knew she shouldn't. She felt dirty for even looking at this piece of trash like it was a legitimate news report but she couldn't stop herself. Yes, she was mentioned: *Lenna Evans, former Olympian, humiliated by Casey's addiction to sex and booze, has been in hiding for weeks.* Well, that wasn't true. Alaska was far away but she wasn't hiding.

"In every interview he's all: This song is for the love of my life. I mean every word, blah, blah, blah." The clerk was enjoying his own Luke impersonation.

"C'mon, Lenny," a strong voice said from next to her. An equally

285

strong arm hooked around her waist and pulled her towards the door. "We have to get back." Shane addressed the clerk, "Thanks, man. You got cool stuff here."

Lenny felt numb as she walked back to the hotel next to Shane. Her head was swirling with the pictures from the tabloid of the girl on Luke's lap with her tongue down his throat. Her hands had been twisted in his hair...the same way Lenny used to twist her fingers in it.

She felt knifed, gutted, a sinkhole where here faith had been. It was so much more than what she had felt the night she had walked in on Cody and Shane. She had been forgotten.

She wasn't sure how she made it all the way to her room and got her key out of her back pocket.

***

Shane took the key from her and opened the door, helping Lenny inside. He gave a reassuring look to the rest of the group who had been watching with worried faces.

"We'll see you guys downstairs for dinner." And he went inside Lenny's room with her.

She was rummaging through her luggage for some clean clothes. Having gone from lifeless to angry in the millisecond he wasn't looking.

"You okay?" He asked apprehensively.

"Sure! Why wouldn't I be okay?" Lenny snapped, throwing her clothes on the floor and rifling through them again.

"I'm not sure what to say, except I'm sorry." Shane tried to offer comfort.

"That's rich, coming from you!" She scoffed openly. "I have great taste in men, don't I? I guess it's true, you all want the same thing. I didn't put out so he replaced me."

Shane frowned, about to protest. He wasn't sure exactly what to say. She had a right to be angry, especially with him. Lenny suddenly took off her shirt and flung it to the floor. She kicked out of her jeans and slid on a pair of shorts. Shane stared for a second before he averted his eyes. She grabbed her running shoes and quickly laced them up.

In only her sports bra and running shorts, Lenny headed to the fitness center downstairs. Shane followed, unsure of what else to do. Lenny let herself into the weight room and immediately started her old routine; heavy weights, heavy squats, heavy presses. Shane recognized it right away. It was part of her physical rehab after her accident. But she was lifting way heavier than she had before. She was clearly going for complete muscle fatigue.

286

"It's a good song," Shane wasn't sure why he felt the need to defend Luke. Probably because the guy wasn't there to defend himself.

"It's a great song," Lenny grunted, "Stupid me for thinking it was about me."

"How do you know it's *not* about you?" Shane countered, knowing he was walking a line that might end up with him getting smacked.

"Oh please. It's just another way to make money. If it was special, it would have stayed special and not been *sold*." She dropped her dumbbells with a thud. "It's fine. We're not together. He can screw whatever tramp he wants."

Shane watched her sweat for a few minutes and then decided it was best to leave Lenny alone. He didn't go far. He sat out in the lobby with one eye on the door and the other on the TV. Maybe Luke Casey would make an appearance on ET or something and fill in some of the blanks.

Shane had been sitting in the same chair for almost two hours when Nick joined him.

"She still in there?" Nick asked, having been filled in on the basics by a very concerned Shelby Lynn.

"Yep." Shane sighed and tossed down the magazine he'd been reading. "She lifted for nearly an hour and now she's running on the treadmill."

"You try talking to her?" Nick asked.

"Sort of. Didn't go well. I'm a little afraid, not gonna lie." Shane pursed his lips.

Nick sighed heavily and rubbed the bridge of his nose with his thumb and forefinger.

"I called Duke…this is gonna get worse before it gets better." Nick spoke slowly, like he was afraid of the next few words he had to say.

Shane narrowed his eyes at him. "What do you mean?"

"Luke's on his way here. His plane landed hours ago and I already checked…he's booked at this hotel."

287

Chapter 22

Victorian Machinery

Lenny's skin was dripping with sweat. Her face was contorted and pinched as she pushed the maximum speed and incline on the treadmill. Her hair had almost completely broken free of the restraint and stuck in thick, sweaty tendrils to her bare shoulders and back. Salty streams ran into her face, blurring her vision and stinging her eyes. She didn't even bother wiping it away. Her lungs burned and her legs were on fire but she pushed on. She had to keep going. At least until she was numb and couldn't feel the hurt that was buried deep inside her.

It wasn't fair. Every muscle fiber in her was screaming, trying to break free from the feelings that threatened to overtake her. She had done the right thing. She had to call it quits with Luke. One of them had to make the sacrifice. One of them had to be the grownup and see their situation for what it really was. Her breathing intensified with her thoughts. If she would have stayed, it could have only ended badly. He would have resented her for changing his life around and she couldn't bear the thought of him looking at her with regret in his eyes.

She felt the sweat running in rivers between her shoulder blades. She breathed heavy out of her mouth, sending sweat spewing onto the display of the treadmill. She should've known better. She should have protected herself and never gotten involved with him. This was her fault. He hadn't done anything wrong. It was his job to write songs that squeezed the soul of the listener. She shouldn't have let herself think she was special. She was a temporary muse. A convenient inspiration. And now that she was out of the picture he was free to do whatever with whomever he chose. Isn't that exactly what Ashton had told her? She was replaceable.

The hollow pit in Lenny's stomach tightened as the pictures flashed in her mind again. This would be a lot easier for her to handle if she didn't have to remember every single thing in perfect detail. Her photographic memory was hell at times. This being one of them. Those images would never leave her mind. Just like she would never forget the things Shane and Cody had said to her. The same way she remembered the accident in vibrant color with all the special effects. It wasn't fair. No one should have to carry a burden so heavy; to see the one man she had ever loved in the arms of a random woman.

Shane reentered the fitness room and took a seat on the weight bench. He clasped a towel in his hands on his lap and patiently waited. Lenny glanced at him and saw that he wasn't going to leave until he talked to her. She jumped to the sides of the treadmill and shut it off. Shane tossed her the towel and she wiped the sweat off her face.

"Feel better?" Shane asked, his face and voice tense.

"No," Lenny shot back. She walked over and stood in front of him. She'd pretty much had enough of everyone's bullshit.

"What do you want, Shane?" She confronted contentiously.

"Nothing." Shane remained tactful, "Just want to make sure you're okay."

"I'm awesome." Lenny said sarcastically and strode to the door. Shane hurriedly got up to follow her.

"I don't need a babysitter, Shane." Lenny snapped. What she needed was this stupid storm to clear and a high vertical.

She felt Shane's large body pressing too close and turned around to tell him to back off when she stopped in her tracks. Her eyes narrowed as a familiar shape came through the front doors and approached the desk. She'd recognize that saunter anywhere.

Without thinking, she marched in that direction; Shane hot on her heels. He was saying something to her but she wasn't listening. All her thoughts and the adrenaline from her intense workout drowned him out. *Hell hath no fury, right?*

"What the hell are you doing here?" Lenny confronted Luke. She crossed her arms over her chest and glared deeply at him. She had controlled her voice to keep from shouting but there was no mistaking the edge in her words.

***

Luke was shocked to see Lenny at the hotel. He thought he'd have to drive inland when the storm cleared. It had been difficult enough just getting from the airport to Valdez in the blizzard. He was tired and discouraged and he wasn't prepared to see Lenny. Especially with the fury with which she was greeting him.

Her face was flushed and her hair was soaked, she was only wearing a sports bra and tiny running shorts. Her perfect skin ran with rivers of sweat, twisting and bending over her lean muscles. She would have looked completely gorgeous if she wasn't staring daggers at him. Luke tried to overlook Shane taking a protective stance behind Lenny. *What the hell is he doing here?*

"I'm here to see you." Was all Luke could think of to say.

Somehow professing his idiocy and undying love seemed inappropriate in the midst of her obvious ire.

Lenny's eyes flicked over to the receptionist and then back to Luke. She was trying to decide if this was, in fact, where she wanted to have the fight that was coming. She decided against it, turned abruptly on her heel and stormed to the elevators.

Luke grabbed his room key off the desk and picked up his bag, hurrying after her.

"Can we talk?" he asked her when they got to the lift. He ignored Shane's warning looks.

Lenny's eyes were severe when she looked at him. She didn't answer as she stepped inside the lift, Luke and Shane following.

The ride to her floor was silent and Luke wasn't sure what to do next. When the doors opened and she charged to her room, he had no choice but to pursue her.

She unlocked her door and let herself in, slamming it in Luke's face. He sighed and knocked.

"Lenny...please, can we talk?" He asked through the thick wood.

After a few moments without an answer, Shane touched Luke's shoulder.

"Maybe give her a few minutes. She's pretty pissed at you right now."

Luke frowned at him. *When did I switch places with Shane? Doesn't Lenny hate this guy?* Luke swallowed the words that wanted to lash out at Shane and took his key card from his pocket. He walked down the hall a few paces to his room that happened to be right next to Lenny's, he noticed wryly. He dumped his bags and his coat and went back to Lenny's door.

Shane was still standing outside of it like some sort of bodyguard and Luke felt his anger at the situation growing. This was not part of the plan. He needed to talk to Lenny, and having this gargoyle watching his every move wasn't helping.

He knocked on the door again.

"Lenny, please." Luke tried to reduce the frustration in his voice. "Can we talk?"

Some doors down the hall opened and the rest of Lenny and Shane's group peaked their heads out in curiosity. Luke was positive they had all heard the rumors about their wild love affair during his last tour. Most of them had probably been filled in on the tabloid pictures and the recent song release. And they had all, more than likely, formed their own conclusions. Luke wasn't the good guy in any of them. They knew Lenny, of course they would be on her side. But that didn't mean they couldn't gawk at the rock star.

Luke looked uncomfortably at the small audience that was gathering twenty or so paces down the hall. He knocked on the door again.

"C'mon, Lenny." He tried to plead again. "Can we please talk?"

The door suddenly flew open. Lenny backed Luke up into the hallway. Her jaw clenched and her mouth formed in a hard line.

"Sure. Let's talk." Lenny crossed her arms over her chest. "Who is she?"

"What?" Luke's eyebrows pulled together.

"The tart checking the depth of your throat with her tongue!" Lenny took a step towards him and he backed up again.

"She's not...I...uh..." Luke had never been on the receiving end of Lenny's fury. He was at a loss for what to do.

"Wow." Realization hit Lenny. "You don't even know her name, do you?" The onlookers let out a collective gasp.

"Did you hear your song?" Luke was flailing and he grabbed at his only defense.

"Oh, the song you *said* you wrote for me but then *sold?*" Lenny stretched her hands out to the sides and let them fall, slapping against her thighs. "You run out of ideas? Is that why you're here? You need me to help you find that next hit?" She took on an aggressive stance and put her hands on her hips. "What, hard up for cash after the tour? Being a philanderer must get expensive fast!" Her voice dripped with sarcasm.

"Hey!" Luke had about had enough. He pointed to his chest with both hands. "How do you think I felt when you left?! I was lonely and I missed you and I'm sorry about the girl, it just happened!"

"Really? You were minding your own business and she tripped and fell and you caught her with your tongue?" Lenny yelled.

"You LEFT!" Luke shouted, taking a step forward and leveling a finger at her face. He knew he wasn't helping the situation but he couldn't stop himself. He was still angry with her for walking away. "Besides, how do you think I feel when I get here and you're with *him*?" Luke pointed at Shane. "Is he helping keep your bed warm in Alaska?"

Luke knew he had crossed a line. He regretted it the moment he said it. The hurt and anger in Lenny's eyes tore through him. Before Luke could take it back, Lenny's hand flew to his face making a loud 'smack' that was followed by silence.

He stared at her in shock. Luke had never been slapped before. His cheek stung with the heat from her hand. Lenny's eyes glossed over with tears and Luke instinctively reached for her but Shane, misreading Luke's intentions, stepped in between them. Lenny spun and retreated, slamming the door to her room.

Shane's eyes bored holes into Luke's. Luke tried to step past him but Shane stood firm, his powerful body rigid.

***

"Alright, everyone." Serge's calming voice cut through the tension. "The show is over, it is time to get downstairs for dinner." He herded the wide-eyed onlookers towards the elevators. Luke and Shane stood toe to toe, neither one of them moving.

Serge and Nick sent the elevator on its way and approached the testosterone fueled standoff.

"This is needless," Serge reproved them. "Shane, you should come downstairs with me."

"I'm not leaving him alone with her," Shane seethed.

"I would never hurt her," Luke responded in kind.

"You already have," Shane took a step forward.

"So have you," Luke reminded, closing the gap between them.

"This isn't a pissing contest!" Nick snapped, pushing the two men apart. He narrowed his eyes at Luke. "You need to give her some time. Why don't you cool off and get something to eat with us?"

"No, thank you," Luke growled. He backed up and sat down with his back against the wall, facing Lenny's door.

Nick sighed and grabbed Shane by the arm.

"Let's go." He pulled Shane toward the elevator but not before Shane gave Luke one final, threatening scowl.

***

A heavy silence descended over Luke as he waited in the hallway. He rested his arms on his bent knees and leaned his head against the wall. This was the last thing he had expected. He had thought that she might be a little mad, maybe hurt. Mostly he was hoping she would be happy to see him. He'd come so far just to have the door slammed in his face. Twice. And why was Shane being all possessive? Were they back together?

Luke rubbed the hot skin on his face where she had slapped him. He knew better than that. Lenny wasn't sleeping with Shane. It wasn't in her character. Of course, she probably had believed the same thing about him and look how he had treated that belief.

The only thing that had been on his mind on his entire journey here was telling her he loved her. Instead, he had yelled at her and pushed her even further away.

293

After Lenny had slammed the door she retreated to the bathroom. Her hand stung from where she had struck Luke's face. She looked at herself in the mirror and noticed the tears that were spilling down her cheeks. She wiped them away angrily and turned the shower on.

The hot water poured down her back and Lenny gave way to heaving sobs. She leaned against the wall of the shower and cried. How could he be here? Why? What purpose did it serve for him to torture her up close? Couldn't he let her suffer from a distance? Everything about this was wrong. Completely and totally wrong. On one hand, she wanted to push him down a flight of stairs, along with the tramp from the photos. And on the other...all she wanted was to have him fold his perfect arms around her and believe that they could start over and none of that other stuff mattered.

Lenny slammed her fists against the shower wall in frustration. She was still going to have to deal with this. Slapping his face and slamming the door were only minor interruptions in the fight they were in the middle of. It would take a lot more than that for this to get solved. But Lenny didn't want to. She wanted to go back to a few days ago, when the powder was perfect and Shelby Lynn had called her Snow Goddess. When she was so busy with living her life that her heart had, albeit briefly, stopped aching for a minute. How could the presence of one person completely turn her world upside down?

She somehow managed to wash her hair and scrub herself clean. The tears abated for the moment and Lenny wrapped a towel around herself. She stealthily crept to the door and looked out the peep hole.

Predictably, Luke was sitting just outside, facing her door. Lenny dug through the pile of clothes she had dumped out on the floor earlier for some sweats and a shirt. Nothing was particularly clean or attractive and she decided on a pair of gray, lumpy sweats and an old college sweatshirt that she had 'borrowed' from Scott years ago.

She slowly combed out her long, wet hair and thought about what to do next. She could let Luke in and the fight would probably start again. Maybe even causing them to get kicked out. Or she could go to bed and hope that he'd get the hint and fly back to wherever he had come from. The last thought scared her more than the first. She didn't want him there but the idea of him leaving the way things were made her want to panic.

She should go out there and talk to him. She knew it inside but it was difficult to figure out what to say. She had said everything she needed to when she had left the airport. Why did it feel like they were still connected? Shouldn't it be over? But no, she could feel him from the other side of the door, waiting for her.

The rigorous workout that Lenny had subjected her body to hours before was catching up with her. So was the emotional stress of Luke's presence. Lenny curled into a ball on her bed and tried to focus on her breathing. The fatigue took over and she fell into a dreamless sleep.

***

The others came back from dinner and a hush fell over the group as they stepped over Luke's rumpled form in the hallway. He didn't even look up at them. Nick ushered them to their rooms and told them to turn in early. They didn't need convincing.

Shane waited in his room long enough for the others to think he'd gone to bed and then he stepped into the hallway. He paused, waiting to see if Luke would notice his presence. If he did, it wasn't obvious. Luke was more exhausted then Shane had first noticed. His clothes were wrinkled and unwashed. His eyes were sunk in and dark from days, possibly weeks, without sleep. He hadn't shaved either. Shane wondered when he had eaten last.

He made his way slowly towards the singer and took a seat next to him on the floor.

"I don't want to fight with you, Brookings." Luke said roughly. His eyes heavy with fatigue and discouragement.

"That's not why I'm here." Shane answered flatly. He clenched his jaw. Being a dick was so much easier, but Shane wanted to be a better person. How he hated himself right now.

They sat in silence for a while, the ice maker down the hall and a movie with explosions in the room behind them, the only noise.

"She hasn't slept with me." Shane said, his voice echoing in the silence. He felt an indescribable need to defend Lenny's honor. Maybe because he had been the one to ruin her in the past, it would be a way of making amends. Shane wasn't sure. He didn't particularly *like* Luke Casey but he knew Lenny cared for him. And that was important to Shane.

"I know," Luke sighed in frustration.

"Then, why did you...?" Shane's voice trailed off.

"I was mad. And I still don't know why you're here." Luke threw a small glare in Shane's direction.

Shane shrugged. Luke had a point. It did look suspicious at first glance.

"I'm not after your girl," Shane declared.

Luke 'hmphed' and leaned his head back, looking up at the ceiling. "What makes you think she's still my girl?" He asked the ceiling more than

295

Shane.

Shane considered his words carefully before saying them. "I've known Lenny a long time," he began slowly, "And she's never slapped anyone. Kicked the crap out a couple of guys and has definitely thrown some punches but never slapped."

"And that helps me how?" Luke let out a disgruntled chuckle.

"I think...you have to care really deeply for someone to let them get to you that much." Shane shook his head and looked into his lap. "She never even fought with me."

Luke frowned and looked over at Shane. "Never?"

"Nope. She'd just shut herself off or leave town for a while. I guess I always knew I wasn't worth her time."

"So, you're saying the slap is a good thing?" Luke asked skeptically.

"Yeah, that's what I'm saying." Shane's serious face cracked a smile. "But that's Lenny for ya, when she loves, she goes all in."

***

Luke swallowed hard. He missed her. He wanted to start pounding on her door and demand to work this out. But he thought she might be sleeping and he didn't want to disturb her. She had looked so tired.

"Did you really get a tattoo of her name on your arm?" Luke suddenly asked.

"Ha, yeah. You wanna see it?" Shane pulled up his sleeve to reveal his perfectly sculpted bicep and a simple script:

Free Bird

"Why did you do that?" Luke asked.

"What can I say, I'm a lifelong fan." Shane shrugged and smiled, lowering his sleeve.

"Get some sleep, man." Shane started to stand up. "If this storm breaks tomorrow, she's gonna head for the highest peak." He raised an eyebrow, "You ready to chase her?"

Luke gave a crooked grin through his weariness as an answer. "I'll think I'll sleep out here...just in case."

Shane nodded and headed back to his room. He grabbed a couple of the extra pillows and a blanket and brought it to Luke in the hallway.

Luke nodded his thanks and Shane left it at that. He hoped that Luke could put things right. He wasn't a bad guy, he'd just made some piss poor choices. Shane had been there. But Lenny had forgiven Shane, so she would probably forgive Luke as well. Hopefully, sooner rather than later. Those two belonged together.

Chapter 23

Get Around This

Lenny's growling stomach is what woke her up. She was starving. Her first thought was for pancakes. Her second thought was Luke.

She crept to the door to look out the peep hole and held her breath. What if he wasn't there? What if he had left while things were still ugly between them? Lenny let the air out of her lungs as she observed Luke's slumped over figure in the hallway.

He looked pitiful. He'd tried to stay propped up but had nodded off sometime in the night and was slouched, painfully crooked. Lenny's heart squeezed inside of her chest. What kind of a man would sleep outside of the door of the girl who had publicly chastised him and then slapped him?

Luke Casey was that kind of man.

Lenny went to the bathroom and rushed through her routine. She shook her head to herself as she contemplated what her next move should be. She couldn't see a way out of talking to him. He obviously wasn't going to leave until she did. She brushed her teeth and pulled her silky hair into a loose ponytail at the nape of her neck. She looked down at her pajamas and decided she didn't want look like a total mess.

She tried to find something clean to wear amongst her pile of dirty clothing. Settling on some well-worn jeans and her black, lace-back riding tank, Lenny quickly changed. She slipped on some thick socks and laced up her boots. She grabbed a black and white flannel from off the floor and shoved her arms through the sleeves, not bothering to button it up.

She closed her eyes to steady her breathing before opening the door. She pulled it open quietly and slowly stepped into the hall. Luke didn't stir. She looked up and down the hall but didn't hear any other activity aside from the small click of her door closing behind her. It was still early, the rest of the group would probably be asleep for at least another hour.

Lenny looked down at Luke and noticed his appearance for the first time. She had been so upset with him the night before that she didn't see the circles and puffiness under his eyes. But he was still as handsome as she remembered, his long hair nearly to his shoulders and partially covering his face.. She knelt down next to him and readjusted his pillow.

Luke's eyes opened slightly and then closed again. Lenny gently touched his face, brushing his hair away. His eyes opened again and fixed on her. Lenny smiled slightly as his brain caught up with his vision.

"Lenny?" His voice croaked.

"What are you doing sleeping in the hallway?" She asked softly.

Luke pushed himself into a sitting position and tried to reorient himself. He rubbed the sleep from his eyes and looked at his surroundings. His vision came to rest on Lenny and he looked her up and down, finally settling on her face.

She tried to work the moisture back into her mouth, suddenly at a loss for words under the scrutiny of his crystal blue eyes. Her anger from the previous evening momentarily forgotten in his larger than life presence.

"You wanna get some breakfast?" She couldn't think of anything else to say. She knew they needed to talk but she didn't know where to start and she didn't want to be in the hallway when the others started to rise from their comas.

Luke nodded once and got into a standing position. He gathered his pillows and blanket and silently deposited them in his room. He disappeared for a few minutes, leaving Lenny in the hallway. Just when she was afraid he wasn't coming back, he reemerged, his face washed and breath fresh. His eyes brightened when he looked at her, or did she imagine that?

They didn't speak as they got on the elevator and walked to the small café that was part of the hotel. The hostess seated them and they sat silently, staring at their menus. Lenny couldn't help but feel incredibly awkward. Maybe this was a bad idea. She looked sideways out the windows and silently cursed the continuing blizzard. She wanted nothing more than to run out into the swirling snow and disappear from the uncomfortable conversation they had yet to begin.

The waitress came and got their order and then left them to sit in their silence again. Luke shifted in his seat and finally leaned against the table, putting his elbows on the top and resting his chin in his hands.

"I'm sorry about the thing with the girl in the bar. It was stupid and I have no excuse." His normally smiling eyes were tired and forlorn.

"Luke-" Lenny started, closing her eyes. Not anticipating the pain that would accompany the strangeness of his apology.

"I don't have a right to ask for anymore chances or even for forgiveness." He slid his hand across the table and tentatively touched the top of her fingertips.

Lenny sighed heavily. He didn't understand, how could he?

"I'm also sorry about releasing your song. You were right. It was special, I should have kept it special." Luke's mouth turned up on one side slightly. "That's what I get for listening to Sway."

"You took relationship advice from Sway?" Lenny asked, aghast.

298

"He has a girlfriend now," Luke defended.

"No way." Lenny smiled suddenly and Luke grinned in response. "I miss those guys," she added quietly.

"Then come back," Luke pleaded frankly.

"Luke, you know that wouldn't be a good idea." Lenny swallowed the lump that rose in her throat. He wasn't going to make this easy on her, was he?

"Why?" Luke asked, covering her hand with his. "We're great together. Why is this such a bad idea?"

Lenny's skin awakened when his hand grabbed hers and she got mad at herself inwardly for having such a reaction. If she was going to explain this to him than she need to keep her wits about her.

"Did you not notice the epic fight we had last night?" Lenny looked at him earnestly. "Being on tour put us in a kind of bubble. It protected us from reality. When I first left, I thought that maybe I was making a mistake because I missed you so bad but..." she looked out the window and shook her head. "Seeing you in those pictures hurt more than I thought possible. Our relationship doesn't translate into our regular lives." She pulled her hand away from his and took a sip of water. "If you think about it, I think you'll see it too."

Luke looked down at the table. His shoulders slowly sagged into a defeated posture and Lenny thought that maybe she had reached him after all. Maybe he could see what she could see.

Their food came and they ate silently. Luke wouldn't look at her and Lenny felt like she was leaving him all over again. Why had he come to Alaska? What purpose did this serve? He was obviously moving on back in Boston. The pictures flashed into Lenny's mind again and she visibly shuttered, getting Luke's attention.

"Something wrong with your food?" He asked, concerned.

"No," Lenny took a drink of water, "Just an unpleasant memory."

Luke nodded and went back to his meal.

"Hey, guys." Nick approached their table cautiously.

"Nick," Lenny greeted and nodded at Luke, "This is Luke Casey, Luke this is Nick Federa. He runs the place up in Thompson Pass."

"Yeah, we met briefly last night." Nick offered his hand and Luke shook it. "The storm should clear out by today," Nick was addressing Lenny again, "We should be able to go back to the cabins by tomorrow."

Nick must have noticed the tension at the table but he decided to add an invitation to Luke, "You're more than welcome to join us, if you want."

"Luke probably won't be staying." Lenny interjected before Luke could answer.

Nick shrugged and then moved to his own table where Smitty and Trucker were seated.

"Are you asking me to leave?" Luke asked, his voice rough.

Lenny looked up, seeing the rejection on his face and her heart sank. "I just thought, it might be weird for you to stay since...you know."

"No, I don't know." Luke's eyebrows pulled in tight.

Lenny mirrored his frown. He was more stubborn that she had anticipated. How could he not see the eminent devastation that was their relationship?

"I just meant, you might want to get back home, that's all."

Luke lowered his glower to his plate of food and shoveled in the last few bites of omelet. He swirled the coffee in his cup, took a drink, and looked up at Lenny again. His face was resolved.

"I'm staying," he said simply. Lenny's mouth fell open but before she could protest, Luke stood up and pulled his wallet out of his back pocket. He tossed a couple of twenties onto the table, more than enough for both of their breakfasts.

He pushed his face into her personal space, demanding eye contact. "This," he pointed between himself and Lenny, his voice a dark whisper, "isn't over." He held her eyes for a heartbeat longer than Lenny was comfortable with before he turned to leave.

Lenny watched his back in silent frustration. Her face was warm from the intensity of Luke's final stare. Why was he making this harder than it had to be? What could be solved by his staying here? What was he possibly thinking?

***

Luke had a plan. It wasn't the best plan that he'd ever made but he finally had one. Lenny thought their relationship couldn't last in the real world. She thought he didn't care for as much as he did. His plan was to prove her wrong. And the best way to do that would be to join her in her world.

Luke had been snowboarding recreationally since he was a kid. He wasn't the best but he was better than most. Duke had set him up with a bunch of gear before leaving Jackson Hole. He had all the equipment he would need to join the other seasoned riders for the remaining week. He just hoped it wouldn't take long for Lenny to figure out what he already had. They were meant to be together.

He showered and dressed quickly, knowing he was going to have to permeate Lenny's life in a way he never had before. He had to learn about her friends and colleagues. He had to dedicate himself to being her friend

300

again. And when she was ready, she would let her guard down and Luke would swoop in and steal her heart.

He was pulling his shirt over his head when he heard her come back from breakfast. He grabbed his coat and went to her door and knocked. He noticed her dumbfounded face when she opened the door. She stood there awkwardly for a few minutes until he spoke.

"Can I come in?" He asked, trying to sound as platonic as possible.

"I was just leaving, actually." Lenny replied, eying him suspiciously. "I have to get some of these clothes washed before tomorrow."

"I'll help you." Luke stepped into her room, ignoring her annoyed look and grabbed the couple of laundry bags she had filled. He turned to find her staring at him.

"Let's go," he prompted.

Lenny hesitated before reluctantly opening the door to the hallway. She grabbed her coat and slipped it on. Luke did likewise and they traveled in complete silence from the hallway to the elevator and down the street to the laundry mat.

***

Lenny self-consciously sorted her clothes while Luke got change. She hadn't brought anything too embarrassing with her. Just the basics; jeans, t-shirts, underwear, socks, a couple sweaters and some flannels.

Luke came back and handed her a stack of quarters and she hurriedly started two loads at once. The sooner this was over with the better.

As the washers began their cycles, Lenny took a seat and Luke joined her. She was decidedly uneasy. Luke's presence still had an overwhelming effect on her. She felt calm, relaxed, giddy even but that was coupled with the fear, dread and paranoia that everything was about to go terribly wrong.

***

Luke could sense her tension and he got up and bought a couple of waters from the machine. He handed one to her and took his seat again.

"So, you get any good runs in since you been here?" He tried to sound as casual as possible but his heart was racing. Being in such close proximity to Lenny was like being trapped in an open space with a tornado bearing down on him.

"Yeah, it's been nonstop until this blasted storm." Lenny gestured to the snow that was starting to taper off but still heavy.

301

"Tell me about your favorite day." Luke saw her eyes light up and he was happy that she was feeling a bit more lenient to opening up to him.

Luke paid attention to every detail. He asked for specifics and tried to memorize all the people that Lenny was close to. If he was going to gain her trust again, he was going to need to give it everything he had.

He loved listening to her voice and how, when she was really excited about something, her smile was permanently crooked, making her talk out of the side of her mouth. Sometimes he'd get distracted by the perfect shape of her lips and he'd remember what it had been like to taste them. He'd have to pull himself back into reality. If he was ever going to get an opportunity like that again, he was going to have to earn it.

***

Luke helped Lenny switch her loads to the dryer. She continued to tell him all about her week in Alaska. She recounted everything in vivid detail, using her photographic memory to the best of its ability. Sharing with Luke the adventure she'd been on made it feel like he had been there with her. And for a moment, fleeting though it was, Lenny forgot about the tabloid gossip and pictures. She was simply sharing her life, turn by turn, with the one person she had wanted to be there all along.

***

Luke hung on her words. Thankful for the time he could spend with her. At first, he had been jealous of the others who had gotten to share in the actual events of the week but her memory was so perfect and clear, he knew she wasn't leaving anything out. He had noticed this about her memory before and he had a hunch. Taking advantage of the relaxed and warm atmosphere of the laundry mat, Luke decided to ask her about it.

"Do you have a photographic memory?" He didn't miss the subtle intake of breathe at his words. "I've just noticed that you never miss a detail." Luke was trying to sound complimentary.

"That obvious, huh?" Lenny's eyes turned down like she was embarrassed.

"Only to those who are paying attention." Luke touched her fingertips and she looked up at him.

"Yeah, I do," Lenny confessed with a sigh. "It's my best kept secret. Duke is the only one who knows…and now you."

"Why do you keep it a secret?" Luke asked gently.

"I'm afraid they won't let me compete or people would be too afraid to get to know me." Lenny let her gaze drift to the outside world and

302

her eyes unfocused. "I guess, that's why I love the back country so much. It's unpredictable and it always surprises me."

"You like to be surprised?" Luke's question held a subtle double meaning and Lenny didn't miss it. But instead of turning away from him she held his gaze.

"Some surprises are no fun at all," she answered simply. He knew she was referring to the pictures with the other woman. Luke cringed internally. Knowing her perfect memory now, he could see why that would be so hard to move past. It's not that she was choosing to remember it, she literally could not forget. He hated himself even more.

"I don't know if I can do this, Luke." Lenny blurted out. She ran a hand through her long hair nervously.

"Do what?" He frowned, his heart flooding with panic.

"It's too weird. You showing up here after not calling me, making out with random girls and then our meltdown in front of my friends last night." She looked weary and sad. "And you want to act like nothing has changed, act like we're friends and you can put the pieces back in places where you think they fit. But they just don't."

Her brows pulled together as she tried to explain to him what he refused to accept as fact. "I can't pretend like I'm okay. I'm not. I know I left, because I thought it was the right thing to do. But you let me go. You made it kind of obvious that you were fine with me being gone."

"I was the opposite of fine, Lenny. I was a mess." Luke calmly confessed. "I realize that it might take some time to get back to where we were...but I'm not going anywhere. I think we can fix this...together."

Before Lenny could answer, the dryers buzzed simultaneously causing her to jump up and begin putting her dry clothes on the folding table. Luke stood up slowly and joined her. Again in silence, they sorted and folded her clean laundry. Lenny was careful to make sure she folded all of her own bras and panties, not letting Luke even touch them.

He found it amusing that she was so protective of her undergarments. He didn't get to see Lenny behave like a typical girl very often and he liked it.

He finished folding a shirt and reached for another. He pulled a large blue t-shirt from the pile and frowned. It looked familiar, and it was obviously a man's shirt. It clicked in an instant. It was his shirt. The one he had given her back when they were on tour. He glanced over at Lenny who hadn't yet noticed what he was holding and he couldn't help but smile. She had brought it with her. And it had ended up in the laundry which meant she had been wearing it.

And that meant she still had feelings for him.

He felt a sly smile tug at the corners of his mouth. She was totally in love with him. And he knew it. He was definitely not giving up now.

***

Lenny saw Luke looking at her out of the corner of her eye and she glanced quickly in his direction. Seeing the shirt he was folding, her eyes went wide. She turned back to her task, maybe he didn't recognize it.

"So, you're still wearing my shirt?" Luke sounded amused.

Lenny grit her teeth and grabbed the shirt from him. She threw all her clothes back in the bags, not bothering to fold the rest.

"C'mon, Lenny," Luke's voice softened, "I was just teasing."

"I know." Lenny answered flatly. "Maybe I don't feel like being teased right now. *Especially* about that." She put on her coat and charged out the door.

She heard him follow a few seconds later. When he caught up with her, he took the heavy bags from her hands and continued forward.

She glared at the back of his head but she followed him anyway. In the elevator, Luke's eyes twinkled with mischief. Lenny kept her face straight, she refused to smile at him.

"Do you sleep in it?" He asked suggestively.

Lenny rolled her eyes, silently staring at the door of the lift. Luke laughed at her avoidance of the question. Outside of her door she fumbled with her key, clearly having been made uncomfortable by Luke's line of questions.

Luke leaned against the door frame, watching her.

"You're gorgeous, you know that?" He said, oozing as much sensuality as his longtime experience as a rock star would allow.

Lenny dropped her key on the floor and when she bent down to retrieve it, Luke put his hand on hers. She looked up into his penetrating gaze, their faces inches apart. He leaned in fractionally and Lenny bolted upright. She slid her key in the lock and quickly opened the door. Luke stood up and Lenny grabbed the bags from his hands, throwing them into her room.

"Thank you for your help with my laundry," Lenny said politely and then closed the door. She heard Luke chuckle softly from the other side and it irritated her. He knew what kind of power he held over her and it wasn't fair for him to use it against her like that.

Luke knocked softly on the door. "I'll just wait out here until you're hungry again." He joked playfully from the other side.

Lenny paced in frustration. He had her there. She ate around the clock and there was no food in her room. Besides, she couldn't keep avoiding him. Especially if he was planning on coming with them tomorrow.

The worst part was that she didn't want to avoid him. She had thoroughly enjoyed the entire day with him. He had been sweet and attentive and adorable. But, again, this was a bubble. As soon as real life got involved, it would go straight to hell.

"I was thinking pizza for lunch." Luke continued through the door. "I saw a little place up the road that I wanted to try."

Lenny couldn't help but smile. He was persistent, she would give him that. She had missed him so much. She found herself opening the door, against her better judgment.

Luke was leaning against the frame and he gave her his most charming smile.

"Hungry?" He asked coyly.

She tried to hide her smile but she couldn't. She sighed and entered the hallway again, he fell in step beside her on the way back downstairs.

"I'm assuming that you're paying?" Lenny asked in the elevator.

"No way. The rule is, if I pay it's officially a date," he winked at her, "Unless this is date?"

Lenny's heart skipped at his wink but she maintained composure.

"Nope, just friends. I'll pay for myself." She looked straight ahead, refusing to get sucked into his playful gaze.

***

When they were seated in the booth at the small pizzeria, Lenny tried to relax again. Luke's presence was always unnerving but even more so now that he was completely hell bent on flirting with her. She couldn't deny that it felt good to have him there. Her body no longer felt like it was missing a vital organ. She glanced around and saw some of the people from her group at a different table.

She shifted, as they openly gawked. The shouting match that had taken place in the hallway last night flashed in her mind. They looked confused and curious and she couldn't blame them. What was she thinking? Luke was going to be entering a hornet's nest with this group. They would undoubtedly see him as the villain and ostracize him.

"This was a bad idea," Lenny said as she swirled the ice in her drink.

"It's okay, Lenny," Luke tried to get her eyes to meet his. "I can take my lumps. I'll do whatever it takes to prove that to you and anyone else who cares."

Lenny pursed her lips together. They both had separate agendas. She was trying to prove that they couldn't possibly work and he was trying to prove otherwise. What a fine pair they made.

***

Luke saw a thousand emotions roll across Lenny's face in an instant. She seemed to settle on casual indifference and Luke felt a new wave of regret course through his veins. He wondered if he hadn't have gone out that night...would she have been this reserved now? How much distance did he put between them with his selfish choice?

He missed the familiarity they used to have. Now, she was on guard, distrusting, reserved. He missed the way she would look at him and he knew she felt safe.

Lenny cleared her throat and looked at him expectantly. Luke realized that she had asked him a question but he hadn't heard it.

"I'm sorry, what?" He asked apologetically.

"I said, when is your return flight?" Lenny frowned at his faraway look.

"Uh, I don't have one." Luke answered uncomfortably. He saw the question on her face so he added. "I bought a one way."

***

The group of other riders finished their meal and gave curious glances as they departed. Shelby Lynn waved at Lenny shyly and then went outside.

"What was that all about?" Luke asked.

"Oh, you haven't heard? I'm awesome." Lenny said saucily and laughed at her own bravado.

"I have, actually, heard that. And humble, too." Luke smiled at her.

They were interrupted when Ben stepped over to their table.

"We're going bowling tonight." He openly glared at Luke, "Nick said you're coming back up to the cabins with us tomorrow." Luke gave a curt nod and Ben continued, "So you can join us tonight if you want."

"You make me feel so welcome," Luke said, impatience in his voice.

"They'll be other girls there, you sure you can control yourself?" Ben asked darkly.

"Ben!" Lenny snapped, mortified by his behavior.

"It's okay, Lenny." Luke calmly stopped her and addressed Ben squarely. "Look man, I made some bad choices. I'm not making excuses for that. But I love this girl and I'm not gonna give up just cause you spent

306

half an hour coming up with an insult." He took a drink of his soda. "We'd be happy to join you for bowling tonight."

Lenny could see Ben was trying to think of something witty to reply with but came up empty. He grunted and left.

Lenny's head was swirling with a million thoughts. And they all centered around one thing. Luke had said that he was still in love with her.

***

Luke went back to eating, completely unfazed. He looked up to see Lenny watching him with curious eyes.

"What? Do I got pizza on my face?" He asked, making her smile.

"Nothing," Lenny replied but something had changed, infinitesimally in her eyes when she looked at him. He had no idea what he'd said in the past few seconds to propel any kind of change, but he was happy for it.

***

The afternoon passed quickly. Lenny found herself getting excited for Luke to join them on the mountain tomorrow. She had wanted him to be a part of her life before, but the timing had been all off. She couldn't believe that he had bought a one way ticket to Alaska.

She still felt a need to show him that a romantic relationship was impossible for them and probably a terrible idea. But he was making it hard. He flirted with her openly all day long. She did her best to ignore his comments and gestures, not wanting to encourage him. If he stood too close, she moved away. If he reached for her hand, she'd put them in her pockets. Part of her was scared that her plan would work and he'd give up, but he only tried harder. Finding new and clever ways to flirt and catch her off guard.

At the bowling alley, the others tried their best to give Luke the cold shoulder but Luke's gregarious personality and authentic charm won them over pretty quickly. Even Ben, who held out the longest, was eventually high-fiving Luke and buying him nachos.

"Damn, Lenny," Trucker complained. "You're kicking our asses! Is there anything you're not good at?"

"Yes," Shane answered from behind her, "She's a terrible dancer."

"What!" Lenny whirled to give him a glare but he just laughed.

"You are a horrible dancer, don't deny it." Shane handed her a soda.

Luke was getting along with everyone so well that Lenny found

307

herself unusually miffed. He was attentive and alert. He answered their questions but downplayed his rock star status. He joked around and looked genuinely at ease. He was freaking perfect.

"Don't be grumpy," Shane rebuked as he sat down beside her.

"I'm not being grumpy," Lenny protested even though she knew he was right.

"You have a very effective frown but this is neither the time nor place." Shane reprimanded with a smile.

"Is it weird that he's getting along with everyone so well?" Lenny shared her thoughts with Shane.

"No, what's weird is that you're avoiding him so obviously."

"Hey, you were on my side not twenty-four hours ago." Lenny reminded him.

"Yep," Shane admitted. "But then we had a bro talk."

"You what?" Lenny's slack-jawed face caused Shane to burst out laughing.

"Yeah, Luke and I are bros now." Shane grinned at her.

Lenny put her hand to her forehead in shame. "My life is so weird," she muttered, making Shane laugh again.

"I think you should give him another chance, honestly." Shane added.

"There's no 'another chance' to give! Am I the only one who can see this as an impending disaster?" Lenny's tone was desperate but Shane laughed her off again.

"You forgave me, don't forget." Shane reminded.

"What's your point?" Lenny shot at him, irritated with his blasé attitude.

"Well, I would think it would be easier to forgive Luke," Shane answered seriously, "You're in love with him."

Lenny pursed her lips indignantly, "I hate your face." Shane guffawed as Luke sat down on the other side of her.

"What's going on over here?" He asked, grabbing Lenny's soda and taking a big drink.

"Nothing," Lenny answered quickly, giving Shane a warning glare.

"We were talking about how she needs to give you a one on one lesson on the slopes tomorrow." Shane winked at Lenny.

"That's sounds sexy," Luke arched an eyebrow at Lenny.

"Yeah, it should be real hot with all the layers of clothing involved." Lenny answered dryly. She was not amused. How had both of her exes become best friends?

"You bunking with me tomorrow?" Shane asked Luke.

"That's what Nick said." Luke nodded, draining the last of Lenny's

308

soda.

"Sweet," Shane fist bumped Luke and then headed to take his turn. Lenny gave Luke a look that made him laugh.

"What the hell is that all about?" Lenny asked him.

"Shane's a good guy." Luke didn't give more of an explanation.

"When did this happen?" Lenny was confused and annoyed at the same time.

"Last night. He brought me a pillow after you slapped me silly." Luke answered with a sly smile.

"I did not slap you silly." Lenny objected. "And I'm sorry about that, by the way." She added softly.

"You don't have to apologize, I deserved it." Luke nodded towards Shane, "We have a lot in common."

"Oh yeah, like what?" Lenny asked in disbelief.

"Well, we both have excellent taste in women." Luke smiled at her glare and got up to refill her soda.

As the night continued on, Lenny found herself in conflict. Why *was* she pushing Luke away? To prove a point? Shane was right, she was in love with him and she didn't want him leave. She wanted him to stay. Nothing made sense anymore. Her previous resolve seemed so foolish and foreign with Luke's overwhelming presence all around her.

When they made their way back to their rooms and turned in, anticipating the early departure tomorrow and the promise of fresh powder, Luke stalled outside Lenny's door.

Lenny unlocked her door but didn't go in right away. She paused, holding the door open with an arm, and looked up into Luke's hopeful expression.

"I had fun today," she said sincerely.

***

"Me too." Luke reached up and brushed a stray hair off her face. She didn't pull away this time.

Luke wanted to kiss her. His eyes drifted to her lips and he stared at their perfect bow shape. But it was too soon. He still had work to do and kissing her right now wouldn't help. Instead, he touched her cheek with his palm and pressed his lips to the top of her forehead.

"Get some sleep, beautiful." He smiled down at her. "You have to teach me how to fly tomorrow."

***

Lenny smiled in return and went into her room, slowly closing the door behind her. She sat down on the edge of the bed in a daze.

Oh no, she thought with dread, *I'm in way over my head.*

Chapter 24

All In

The four day storm had covered Thompson Pass and the Chugach Mountains with a perfect, unblemished blanket of snow. It was pristine and lush; Lenny literally salivated when she beheld it. The drive up had been very different than the week before. This time, Lenny rode in the back of Nick's SUV with Luke and Serge. The atmosphere was cheerful and mild, probably due to the presence of the unshakable Norwegian. But it may have also been Luke's solid resolve from beside her.

Lenny's discontent had taken a backseat. She had awoken that morning feeling refreshed and alive. Knowing Luke was going to be there gave her soul a little boost. She didn't entirely know what that meant. She wasn't ready to just declare all forgiven and agree to move to Boston. But she would be lying if she said she hadn't thought about it more than once. Luke brought a peace out in her that no one else ever had. And it really wasn't anything he did. It was who she naturally became when then were together.

***

Luke had finally gotten a good nights sleep. He hadn't rested since Lenny had left Boston. The first night in Alaska when he slept outside her door had been his first real sleep in weeks. Just knowing she was close by had been enough to allow him to doze off for a few hours. But after he had walked her to her door last night, he fell asleep before his head hit the pillow. He'd been so upside down without her, and having her around had finally righted him. Even if this was as close as they ever got, Luke knew without a doubt that they needed to be a part of each others lives. She was his best friend. And he was never taking that relationship for granted again.

They quickly unloaded their gear into their cabins and then gathered by Nick for another rundown of basic avalanche survival training. Everyone except for Luke had already taken the training when they had first arrived but with the new snowfall, Nick wanted everyone to be refreshed before going out there.

They all passed the basic tests without any problems. Nick

reminded them that the mountains are unpredictable. Especially with the new powder, no one would be able to tell what's sturdy and what's soft until they're in the middle of it.

***

"No pressure, guys," Nick spoke through his headset in the helicopter. "We're just gonna go out and make a few turns."

Lenny nodded when Nick glanced behind to make sure they had heard. She looked at Luke who was his usual, the most relaxed and confident person in the room. She had no idea how he could be so collected even when he was obviously out of his element.

After the chopper had set them down and then took off again, Lenny pulled Luke off to the side.

"You don't have to do this, you know." She saw his eyes shift to the mountainside and then back to her.

"Yes, I do," Luke said calmly with a smile. "Besides, if I get hurt, you can give me mouth to mouth." He laughed as she rolled her eyes. She feigned annoyance but the idea of her lips on his again made her heart stutter. And that annoyed her a little bit more. Why wasn't he taking this more seriously?

"You need to be a little scared, you know." Lenny's concern was growing.

"I know. And I am. Totally terrified." Luke grinned at her again as Shane joined them.

"Ready to have your life change?" Shane asked.

"Do your worst." Luke accepted the challenge.

Lenny realized that *she* was the one who the most nervous about Luke riding. If anything happened to him…Her stomach was full of butterflies as Shane gave Luke some pointers. This was a bad idea. Lenny shook her head and finally had to say something.

"No. Don't do that." Lenny stepped in between Shane and Luke. "No offense, Shane." She said over her shoulder then back to Luke. "Just take it slow. We can ride this hill all day. Don't worry about speed." She looked down at Luke's board and bindings and realized why they had looked so familiar. "Do you have Duke's stuff?"

"Yeah, he said I would need it." Luke looked at her sheepishly. So he had been to see Duke first. Was she really the only one who saw the ridiculousness of the situation?

"Well, he's not wrong. Duke always had the best stuff," Lenny conceded. She would have to address that Duke issue later.

"Just go slow for your first few turns and see how it feels. Wait till

312

you can feel how the board responds. We're not racing."

Luke put his hands on her shoulders and looked her in the eye. "Hey, I'm gonna be fine. I promise not to do anything stupid," he said reassuringly.

She smiled, seeing the honesty in his face and tried to relax her back-flipping insides.

"C'mon, Casey," Shane waved his arm and started on his run. Luke pulled his goggles down and joined him.

Lenny held her breath as she watched them curve in and out and back and forth. Luke was good. He was actually very good. He kept up with Shane just fine and Lenny could tell he was a strong rider. His technique was a little shaking. *But that can be cleared up with practice back home.* Lenny muttered a curse under her breath for that thought. Luke was not coming home with her.

She wasn't even surprised that Luke had been to see Duke. She figured he had either talked to Duke or Harrison because they were the only ones who knew she was in Alaska. She wished she'd gotten a little more of a heads up though. She'd have to give Duke a hard time for that one.

She was a little shocked that Duke had loaned his stuff to Luke. That was the equivalent of letting someone take your firstborn across the country. Duke never let anyone touch his stuff. Either Duke was getting soft in his old age or this was his version of giving Luke his blessing. Lenny suspected the latter. And that thought only added to her frustration.

Her heart stumbled in conjunction with Luke's wipe-out. He had been doing fine when he lost control and tumbled end over end. Shane had led him over a small lip and he caught air. He was clearly unprepared for it and he lost control before he'd even landed.

Lenny didn't even wait for him to come to a complete stop. She was already flying that direction, her heart in her throat.

She edged her board to a stop so fast, she could have had her own fall if she wouldn't have already disengaged her binders and was in near sprint across the snowy terrain. She threw off her goggles and hat and sank to her knees in the snow next to Luke's upturned figure.

He was flat on his back, his arms outspread. She cleared the snow that had packed in around his face, her breath coming laboriously.

"Luke?" She pushed his goggles up and stopped. His perfect blue eyes were looking at her with a bemused, almost whimsical expression.

"Were you worried?" He asked, his mouth making a crooked grin.

Lenny wanted to hug him and kick him at the same time. She bit her bottom lip and shook her head.

Luke pushed himself into a sitting position and grinned at her. "You came rushing to my side at the first sign of trouble. I've taken worse

313

falls off the stage." He raised his eyebrows as if to make some point.

"I'm glad you're okay." Lenny finally said as she returned to her feet. She was blushing at her reaction to his mini-wreck and she was glad he couldn't tell due to the cold air on her face.

"What if I would have gotten hurt?" Luke asked as he disengaged his board and stood as well. He put his hands on his hips and looked at her with a cocky self-assurance. "Would you be sad?"

Lenny rolled her eyes and walked back to where she'd left her board near-buried a short distance away.

"You woulda cried, I bet." Luke followed behind her. She smiled to herself, glad he couldn't see her reaction.

The rest of the day went by smoothly. No injuries, no avalanches. Shane and Luke brought an energy to the group that hadn't been there the week before. They had bonded quickly and Luke was a complete natural on the mountain. Just like the night before when they were all bowling together, Luke was everyone's best friend. He fit so perfectly in the group that Lenny was actually shaken up by it. Not in a scared way…well, maybe in a scared way. Had she been wrong this whole time? Was her fear of the oncoming heartache all in her head? Was she really the only one who could ruin this?

They returned to base camp that night and Trucker and Smitty built a bonfire. The crew was still amped from an easy day on the slopes and they needed to expel a little of that extra energy.

The fire burned tall and bright against the blackness of the Alaskan sky. Some people were roasting marshmallows, a few were drinking beers. Light conversation and laughter floated through the air.

Lenny sat on a log near the fire, a little removed from the group. She stared into the orange glow and let her tense muscles relax with the buzzing of her friends voices nearby.

So much had happened in the span of a few days. The emotional ups and downs had been hard to keep up with. And now, she had to get her head together and figure out what the next step was. She thought she had this all figured out when she had left Europe but it had hurt more than she had anticipated. She wasn't sure, that when push came to shove, she could willingly walk away from Luke again. Even if it was better for them both. It hurt too much.

Luke sat down next to her on the log, pushing close against her side till she moved over so he had room.

"Did you have fun today?" He asked her, pulling a charred marshmallow off of a stick.

"Yeah, did you?" She asked giving him a small smile. She was desperately trying to keep an emotional barrier between them. Luke always made her question every single one of her rational thoughts.

Luke popped the mallow into his mouth and grinned at her. She couldn't help but grin back, his happy smile was infectious.

"I always have the best day when it's been a day with you." Luke said after he swallowed his mouthful a little more serious as he spoke. Her heart strangled in her chest. That's exactly how she felt too.

Lenny had always been extremely independent. Which is probably why she'd chosen snowboarding as the first love of her life. It was free and wild, just like her. She loved her family and they had always supported her. But even they couldn't explain the side of Lenny that came out when she was shredding a gorgeous line. Traveling and boarding all over the world, she had gotten to meet some exceptional people. She never had a problem making friends but she hadn't truly made any deep connections. Not until she ran away with rock stars.

Even now, without Mike, Blake, Harrison and Sway here, she felt...homesick. Luke's close proximity only made that feeling stronger. She had tried, really tried, to keep her barrier intact. But those rowdy group of men had won over her heart. And one of them in particular held more of heart than she had consciously agreed to.

She gave a sideways glance to Luke and tried not to stare at how the fire reflected in his pale blue eyes, making them glow even more intensely. The entire tour he hadn't so much as looked at another woman. Not that there weren't any around. Women were constantly throwing themselves at the band. They would do horrible things to get attention. Shameful, self-depreciating things. But the guys were professionals, and the tour had been clean and relatively easy. That's what had been so shocking about the paparazzi photos of Luke with whoever that had been. It was so uncharacteristic of the Luke that she knew. But there it had been, in full, high definition color, the truth of what a life of fame often entailed. Lenny wasn't sure if she could live that life.

"Do you want a mallow?" Luke asked her, reloading his stick.

"Um, sure." Lenny tried to pull her thoughts back to the present.

Luke lit the marshmallow on fire and slowly turned the stick so it burned evenly all the way around. He presented the perfectly roasted mallow to Lenny and she gingerly removed it from the stick. She couldn't help but smile at his proud grin.

Luke leaned against her as she stuck the gooey treat in her mouth. He rested his chin on her shoulder, looking directly at her face.

"Is it good?" He asked, eyebrows going up.

Lenny laughed out loud at his behavior and playfully shoved him off of her.

Luke chuckled, that low, hearty chuckle that sent shivers through her. She knew she was blushing but was hoping that the glow from the fire was covering it up.

Luke casually let his arm drape across her back and she instinctively leaned closer to him. After a few moments Lenny rested her head on his shoulder. They sat in silence, staring into the fire. Luke pressed his cheek against the top of her head and let out a contented sigh. Lenny knew what it meant because she was feeling the same way. It was like finally coming home.

No one bothered them. They left them in their own little world. Lenny had started to pick up on the collective thought of the group that she needed to stop resisting Luke's attempts at reconciliation. She had feared they would hate him, nearly the opposite had occurred. It seemed Lenny was the only one who was still unsure. No, that wasn't it. It's not that she was *unsure*, it was that she was the only one who hadn't gotten caught up in the romanticized scenario that had been playing out for all of them to see. She was the only one who could see the truth. And the truth was that Luke's life came with certain...complications.

If she went back with him, it might be great for a while. But eventually, they wouldn't be able to see each other every day. And Lenny didn't know if that would count as being 'on a break' for Luke again. Would he seek solace with someone else? Or maybe he'd get tired of her all together and trade her in for someone far prettier and more...experienced. She swallowed at that last thought. She didn't really have much to offer.

***

Lenny sighed and Luke glanced down at her face, lit by the roaring fire. He was beyond happy to be this near to her again but he was still intimidated by her presence. She was strong and brave and tender. Her eyes missed nothing, her heart felt everything. She was completely different than any woman he'd ever met. She spoke her mind but with kindness. She'd risk everything to protect those she loved. She was always trying to do the right thing, not just what felt good in the moment. Luke had no idea how he had ever gotten her to look at him in the first place. She could honestly have her pick of anyone out there.

But Luke knew he was the only one who was willing to fight this hard to keep her.

***

After a long while, the fire started to burn down and the other riders started to go to bed. Lenny knew they should probably turn in as well but

316

she didn't want to move. If they got up and went to their separate cabins then she would have to face reality again. And she still hadn't made any definite decisions.

"It's getting late." Luke murmured against her hair.

"Mmhm." Lenny confirmed, still not moving away.

"C'mon," Luke stood up, pulling Lenny with him. "I'll walk you to your cabin." His fingers found and intertwined into hers and they slowly walked across the snow packed ground.

The light inside was on which meant that Shelby Lynn was in there and awake. Lenny slowed as they got closer to the door. Not wanting the peaceful moment to end.

Luke stopped walking and turned to face her, pulling her into his strong embrace. He hugged her tight against him and she wished there was more time.

"How about if you meet me for breakfast tomorrow?" Luke asked.

Lenny nodded, swallowing away the emotion that came out of nowhere. Why was it so hard to say goodnight? She would be seeing him again in the morning. *Because every goodnight is closer to goodbye. Again.*

Luke leaned down and kissed her cheek softly. His lips were warm on her cold skin and Lenny felt a tingle run through her. She gave him a shy, sad smile before going inside.

Shelby Lynn was propped up on one elbow when Lenny came through the door. She watched quietly as Lenny changed and crawled up the ladder into the top bunk.

"Are you gonna take him back?" Shelby asked as Lenny reached for the string to turn the light off.

Lenny paused at the question. She wasn't sure how to answer. Was Luke really hers to take back?

"Why do you ask?" Lenny asked instead, pulling the switch and enclosing the room in darkness.

"Because we all think you should."

Lenny smiled in the dark room. "All of you think that, huh?"

"Well, it's just been the most exciting thing that's happened all week. We obviously talked about it." Shelby adjusted her covers making the wooden structure rock slightly.

"It's not a reality show, S.L." Lenny pointed out. "The audience doesn't get a vote."

"I know." Shelby was quiet for a few minutes and then she sleepily sighed, "You guys are so great together."

Lenny pursed her lips up at the ceiling. The cabin grew quiet, Lenny heard Shelby's breathing even out and knew she had fallen asleep. Lenny wasn't so lucky. She lay awake for a long while after that, trying to figure

317

out why Shelby's logic seemed so sound.

***

The next day brought more adventure and even more confusing thoughts for Lenny. The group stayed together again and took some turns. Travis and Trucker started a slight competition with a small jump and pretty soon everyone was being a little more risky with their lines.

Luke was his amazing, charming, smooth self. Lenny loved how he fit in perfectly with her group of friends but that didn't mean what she knew he was hoping it would mean. She still couldn't shake the thoughts from the night before. He was a rock star. He would always be a rock star. And it would take a special kind of woman to be able to deal with all the things that came along with that. Lenny wasn't sure if she would ever fit into that category.

***

Luke was having a blast. Snowboarding was his new favorite thing. Lenny's friends were awesome and being around Lenny was...intoxicating, as usual. She was unbelievable on the snow. Everything she did seemed effortless.

She had raced Serge to the bottom of a very steep mountain, tying Luke's stomach in knots. But he couldn't help but let his heart swell with pride at her confidence and talent.

When the others started doing some risky flips and rotations, she blew them all away. They had gotten heated and Lenny had removed her coat and flannel. She was wearing her black snow pants and a form fitting black tank with the entire back made out of lace. Luke assumed that every guy was checking her out but there was nothing he could do about it. She was captivating. Her perfect body twisted and soared in the air, her blonde hair glowing like a halo in the bright sunlight. She had no idea how beautiful she was.

When they got ready to head back to base, Lenny put her coat back on and Luke knew he heard some sad groans from the guys around them. She didn't even notice. Of course she didn't. She wasn't one of those girls. She had no clue that very often she was the most gorgeous woman in the room. Luke had a devilish thought then. If Lenny knew how hot she was, with her confidence, the world would be doomed.

He chuckled at himself as he followed her into the helicopter. She gave him a frown that was more of a question and he just shook his head.

Everyone gravitated to the Lodge for the evenings activities. Luke

318

sat up at the bar and watched Lenny try to teach Shelby Lynn how to play pool. It was comical and sweet at the same time. Lenny was good, like everything else in her life, but Shelby Lynn was very uncoordinated. She kept getting frustrated and would want to give up but Lenny's patient words would bring her back to try again.

Shane took a seat next to Luke and nodded at the bartender for a beer. When he got it and took a sip, he chuckled at Luke.

"You're so obvious." Shane laughed again and Luke smirked, knowing he'd been caught watching Lenny.

"I can't help it." Luke replied honestly. Lenny looked up and caught his stare. He didn't even try to hide it, instead he winked at her. He thought he saw her blush slightly before shaking her head and going back to Shelby Lynn.

"Have you guys talked anymore?" Shane asked curiously.

Luke sighed heavily. "No, not really." He frowned slightly. "She's being pretty stubborn."

"Yeah, that sounds like Lenny." Shane smiled around the lip of his glass.

Luke scanned the room, trying to come up with some kind of profound plan. He had thought that just spending time in Lenny's world would prove that their relationship could work. But he was starting to get the feeling there was more to her rigidness than that. She wasn't being completely forthright with him and he needed to get her to open up to him. Once and for all.

That's when Luke spotted the unused dance floor tucked back in a corner. It was just beyond the jukebox. The lights around it weren't on so that's why he didn't see it. It wasn't in complete darkness but it would provide a nice little private space for them to talk without her feeling completely trapped. All he had to do was convince her to dance with him.

Luke grinned at Shane, "I have an idea."

He hopped off his stool and made his way to the jukebox. He glanced over the song lists and starting pumping quarters in the machine. He thought he'd need about six songs for a decent conversation. He chose all slow, cheesy ballads, knowing she'd at least find humor in it if nothing else.

As Neil Diamond's husky voice started to sing 'Hello Again,' Luke approached Lenny from behind. He saw Shelby Lynn's eyes get wide but Lenny didn't turn around. Luke smiled and gently clasped her wrist, slowly twisting her to face him. She was curious and her eyes sparkled. Luke didn't say anything as he gently tugged her towards the dance floor.

He put his hands on her waist and she automatically rested her hands on his shoulders. She looked uncomfortable and Luke noticed right away that she was not a very good dancer at all. He kept the pace slow and she focused on the center of his chest, concentrating on the movements of her feet.

"I think we should talk," Luke began in a hushed voice. He saw Lenny swallow and she subtly nodded.

"I want you," Luke said plainly. Lenny's eyes flashed up to his and her face flushed with his choice of words. He chuckled as he realized how that sounded. "I mean, I want you with me." His face growing more serious. "I want you back in my life."

Another verse went by as he waited for her response. When she spoke, her words came out stiffly, like it was hard for her to say them.

"Luke…" She began slowly, "You're a rock star…and with that comes certain…complications."

Luke frowned down at her face but he didn't interrupt.

"I don't know how I can be…okay, knowing that the moment we're not together for a few days, you'll have women standing in line to fill that void for you."

"It's not like that." Luke protested. "I made a really bad choice-"

"Luke, we had only been apart for a little while and you…" Lenny swallowed again. "You-"

"I know." Luke began to plead. "I really screwed up, but it won't ever happen again."

Lenny's eyebrows pushed together with confusion. "But, Luke, when you love someone, it doesn't matter if you're on a break. That person should still be the only one…"

Luke's heart froze in his chest as he realized what she was telling him. He couldn't undo what he had done. She was right. He had been in love with her and had allowed himself to look into…other options. If she had been out kissing other guys he would have felt completely betrayed. He had never put himself in her position. The idea of Lenny with someone else…kissing him, holding him…loving him. His pulse began to quicken with the rising panic of losing Lenny forever.

"It's hard to…start over." Her words were tiny slices in his heart, stripping away the hope he had left. "I can't forget-"

"I know, you can't forget. But maybe you could forgive." Luke's grip around her tightened, like he was afraid she would walk away from him any minute. "I'm so madly in love with you I can't think straight. You're all I want. I can give up the band, the music, Boston. All of it. Anything. Just not you." Luke's words were pouring out, he couldn't stop them if he wanted to. "I know I messed up. I hate what I did. I never wanted to hurt you. Ever. I should have fought for you from the beginning. I should've never let you walk away…I need you in my life. You're…" Luke's voice cracked. "…you're my best friend, Lenny."

***

"Try to think about the future, Luke." Lenny's voice sounded small, even to her but she needed to get it out. "What happens when we're separated? When I'm competing, maybe, and you're around the world? And you get lonely? You're the sexy lead singer of a major band, in case you've forgotten…you wouldn't be lonely for long…and I don't think, no, I *know* I can't compete with that. I'm just…" Lenny searched for the right explanation. "…a regular person." Her eyes settled on his chin as she said the words.

"You are *not* a regular person." Luke's firm voice brought her eyes back up to his. His jaw clenched in seriousness. "You are a hell of a woman." His eyes shone with emotion. "You're it." He brought one hand up to rest on her cheek. "There is no competition. You have my heart."

Lenny had no words left. She couldn't deny that her heart still ached to be near Luke. That the only time she'd felt any kind of peace in the past couple of weeks was when he had shown up in Valdez. She couldn't refute that even the simple act of him holding her in his arms on the deserted dance floor made her whole body tremble with excitement.

"I have never known anyone like you, Lenny. You are brave and strong and beautiful. You make me think I can be a better person. More importantly, you make me *want* to be a better person." He took a careful breath. "I know we don't have it all figured out. I know I'm probably gonna screw up a few more times and make you mad at me. But I also know that you're the one I want to be with to figure these things out. I don't want to do this life without you, my best friend. I'm crazy in love with you."

Luke pulled her closer, holding her tight. He touched his forehead to hers so he could look her directly in the eye.

"Please, Lenny. Please," Luke whispered, his deep voice raspy. "Forgive me…I should have told you every day that I loved you. You're the most amazing woman…I…you're…everything to me…you deserve better than me but, dammit! I'm not gonna ever stop trying to show you how incredible you are and how incredible *we* are when we're together."

In that moment Lenny knew her heart had been misleading her the whole time. She had been so afraid of following it blindly that she had made all of her decisions based on fear. And they had been the wrong ones. Luke in her life was the only thing that made sense.

She closed her eyes, and licked her lips slowly. "Okay." She whispered.

Before she could open her eyes to see his reaction his lips crashed

321

into hers. His hands pressed into her back drawing her body flush against his. She tangled her fingers in his hair and pulled his head in, deepening their kiss. Her body reacted forcefully, feeling like it would never be close enough to him.

Lenny surrendered her heart fully to him. No more second guessing or hesitation in her thoughts. This was it. No matter what happened in the future, she knew that Luke's arms would forever be her home. She could never go back to a life without them.

The room broke out into applause and Lenny disrupted her kiss with Luke, laughing. She had forgotten that they were surrounded by a bunch of people. Luke still didn't seem to notice or maybe he just didn't care. He continued kissing her face and neck. He finally stepped back and addressed the onlookers.

"Thank you, thank you." Luke bowed and Lenny shook her head at him, a smile still on her lips. Always the entertainer. He grabbed her hand and kissed it affectionately and tugged her in the direction of the bar.

"You finally get all that figured out?" Shane asked with a grin.

"Not all of it…" Lenny looked over at Luke who was beaming at her and he slipped an arm around her waist, pulling her to his side. "But the rest is just details." She finished with a content smile.

"Good." Shane handed them each a beer and then toasted them.

Lenny wasn't sure what was going to happen next but as she looked up at Luke and he pulled her tighter against him, she knew…they would get through it together.

***

Luke couldn't believe the peace that had descended over him. He looked down at Lenny's laughing face and he knew…everything was going to okay now. He wasn't going to screw this up again.

She caught him looking at her and her face took on a puzzled expression.

"What?" He nuzzled her neck. Staying away from her was going to be even more difficult now.

"Why me, Luke?"

He pulled away, unable to hide the shock on his face. "Why you? Are you serious?"

Lenny smiled shyly and bit her bottom lip. "Yeah, why me?"

"Because you're smart and funny and a good kisser." He grinned when she smiled. "Because, you make me feel like I'm worth a damn. Because when the rest of the world doesn't make sense, you do. Because when we're together, we're unstoppable." He rested his forehead against

322

hers and looked her in the eyes. "Because you're my very best friend in the whole world and I'm never gonna let you go."

Epilogue

Sweetness

Mike adjusted his tie in the mirror and took a deep breath. Today was a big day. It had been building for a while, nearly a year. But today it would be official. Today, they would all take the next very important step of being responsible adults. With Luke, their fearless leader, right out front.

"You still have the rings?" Sway plopped down on a plush sofa in the hotel suite where they were getting ready. His blond hair pulled back into a sleek ponytail made him look almost respectable. But the flash of his purple socks showing at the ends of his pant legs said something else.

"Yep" Mike patted his coat pocket. He had already checked fourteen times this hour to make sure.

"Is this fast? It seems fast," Harrison questioned from his area of the room. He'd been occupying the balcony for a large part of the day and would sometimes step inside to ask a question or state some random fact. This was one of the question moments.

"Harry, we live fast. It's sorta the rock star life motto," Blake—whose tux was still not on—remarked from his reclined position on the bed. He'd been watching a boxing match and claimed he'd get dressed as soon as he absolutely had to. For now, he was in his tuxedo pants and white undershirt.

"It's just... so... fast," Harrison muttered under his breath and went back out onto the balcony.

The door to the suite swung open and Luke strode through it. Elegant black tuxedo, blond hair cut short, but still messy the way he liked to wear it. Grin as cocky as ever.

"Beautiful day!" If his smile had a wattage, he would have exceeded his recommended limit hours ago.

"And where have you been?" Mike asked, raising an eyebrow. "Not bothering the bride I hope. You know there are rules for those sorts of things."

"I've never been very superstitious." Luke winked and sauntered to the balcony where he clapped Harrison on the shoulder. "This view is amazing."

"And to think, he hasn't even had sex yet," Sway remarked soberly, sitting up straighter on the sofa. Mike glanced down at the bass player's pensive face. They were all handling this event so differently from each other.

"It suits them, Sway," Mike reminded casually.

Sway looked up at Mike and nodded, "Yeah. I know. I was just... noticing, I guess." He took a breath and faced Mike more directly, leaning forward on his knees with his elbows, back towards the open balcony door. "He really loves her." There was no question in his words, but maybe a little bit of awe.

"Yeah, man," Mike confirmed. "He really does."

Sway sat back against the sofa. "That's wild."

***

Lenny didn't get nervous. It wasn't in her nature. So what was this feeling that had settled in the pit of her stomach?

She smoothed out the front of her dress and watched her hands move in slow motion in the mirror.

It was a gorgeous gown. Simple and elegant. A pure white, satin sheath that reached to the floor and only an afterthought of a train that spilled out from behind her. The straps were skinny, barely a thread, and the v-neck swooped gracefully along her neckline. She'd picked it out herself, knowing instantly that this was the dress she wanted to wear when she pledged her forever to Luke.

Her gaze traveled up to her face. Her hair had been arranged in a romantic knot at the back of her head, leaving enough room for her veil to be added soon. Simone had done her makeup, keeping it simple as well. Charcoal around her eyes, bubble gum pink on her cheeks with a dab of gloss on her lips. She looked like herself, just a much more put together and beautiful version of herself.

"You feeling okay?" Natalie asked, coming up behind her.

One of the more stressful parts of planning this wedding was figuring out who to ask to be bridesmaids. Luke wanted all of his band mates to be groomsmen, leaving Lenny to come up with four bridesmaids. Not the easiest task for a girl who wasn't very good at making female friends and who had severed ties to her best friend a few months prior.

She asked Felicity, her brother David's wife, to be her Matron of Honor. Scott was in an on-again spell with Simone, so she asked her. And then Duke, surprising the entire world, up and married Natalie while Lenny had been in Alaska figuring things out with Luke. So that seemed like an obvious choice. Leaving one more spot to fill. Lenny had texted E, the personal trainer she had an almost friendship with after meeting her on tour.

Low and behold, E and Sway were friends. Sway, having stolen Lenny's phone and gotten E's number, had been texting her daily for the remainder of the tour. When Sway had returned to Boston he'd met up with E a few times and they even tried dating for awhile, but decided that they were better at being friends. Of course, all of this was news to Lenny. But that made it much less awkward to ask her to be a bridesmaid.

"I think," Lenny started to answer Natalie's question, "I'm just really excited." She felt her neck begin to heat up and Natalie snickered at Lenny's sudden smile.

"Good, you should be excited," Natalie agreed.

"I don't know if anyone is looking forward to this more than your groom," Simone remarked. Her gorgeous red hair was pulled into a fancy twist with little sparkles tucked into the sides and she kept reapplying hairspray every chance she got. "I had to chase that boy away from the door again. He wants to get a look at you so bad."

Lenny smiled and looked down at the empty place on her finger where his ring would be before the day was over.

"Oh, you loooove him," Felicity teased, seeing her face reflected in the mirror.

"More than I thought possible," Lenny whispered.

***

Sway: *is she getting nervous?*
E: *yeah but in a good way. How are you guys doin over there?*
Sway: *I'm wearing purple socks*
E: *this is why we can't be together*
Sway: *they're actually kinda lavender*
E: *I'm turning my phone off now*

***

Having the Grand Tetons as the backdrop to their wedding day was Luke's favorite detail. After only spending ten minutes with Kelli Evans, he was sure that a lot of planning and attention had been given to the dresses, flowers, food, and candles. But marrying Lenny in the shadow of the mountains that had helped mold her into the woman he loved was fantastic.

The guys hadn't understood at first why he pushed to have the wedding in Lenny's hometown. But they didn't try to talk him out of it. Mostly, they were shocked it was happening so quickly. He agreed, from their perspective it did seem rather fast. But in Luke's mind, he would have married her months ago.

Today couldn't have gotten here fast enough.

He'd proposed to her on the flight home from Alaska with a ring he'd

327

purchased from a jeweler in Valdez. She'd cried. He had immediately started trying to set a date. By the time they had landed, they had agreed to two months from that day, in Jackson Hole.

They picked the large resort hotel set in the mountains for two reasons: it would be easy to control the guest list, and it afforded them more privacy than a church or outdoor wedding would. And Luke really didn't want to share this day with the press.

He was marrying Lenny in less than a year since he had met her. On paper, it looked rushed. In his heart, he'd been ready since that first meeting, he just didn't know it at the time.

Luke took a deep breath as the string quartet played the gentle procession and the last of the bridesmaids and groomsmen filed down the aisle toward him. This was it, Lenny was next.

"This is it," Mike muttered his exact thoughts over Luke's shoulder. "You ready?"

Luke's eyes were focused on the doors at the end of the aisle. "Absolutely."

The doors opened while the quartet began their own rendition of The Wedding March. Luke thought he was ready, he really did. But then Lenny stepped into view on her father's arm and he couldn't breath.

She was a vision in white. Never had Luke beheld such and angel. Her shy smile lit her face and her sapphire eyes were instantly locked to his. She was exquisite.

The rest of the wedding party ceased to exist in his peripherals, the friends and family in the chairs facing him became an ambiguous swirl of color. All he saw was Lenny. She was all he wanted to see for the rest of his days.

The way she was looking at him, like he was the only man in the world, forced him to take a breath, which started his heart pounding. Everyone had kept saying what a lucky man he was and with every step she took towards him, he felt that truth deep in his core. But it was more than luck. God, in all His divine grace and glory, had seen fit to bless him with the love of this woman. And Luke promised right then, he would hold on tight to this blessing. Nothing on this earth would ever convince him to let go. Not even for a second.

***

Vows.

Promising forever with one person in front of God and everyone.

Promising God that you'll fulfill those promises that you made in front of everyone.

Blake didn't get it.

He used to think that maybe he was the marryin' type, but over the years he'd decided that just wasn't for him.

He wasn't against it by any means. Some people were clearly happy going from an "I" to a "we," sharing their good and bad, triumphs and struggles, and total hearts with another person. Luke and Lenny were those type of people. They belonged to each other, anyone could see it just by looking at them. And it had nothing to do with that goofy grin that Luke had on his face every time Lenny walked into the room.

Blake swallowed away the bitterness that had crept into his mouth with his thoughts. He was happy for his brother, truly. He didn't want his own issues to sour the beauty of the day. His faults were his own. They had nothing to do with what was happening here today.

Lenny whispered, "I do," and a glimmer of a tear dropped onto her cheek. Blake swallowed again and wondered if all brides loved their grooms as much as Lenny loved Luke. Did they all look at the man across from them with such devotion and conviction? Did the world cease to exist for them? Was the man on the receiving end of her promise worthy of such a woman the way Luke was?

Blake was deluding himself if he thought he didn't want that. What he wouldn't give to have the woman of his dreams promise to stand by his side no matter what was to come. But she had already promised that to someone else, hadn't she?

He pushed those feelings of betrayal that cut his insides wide open into the box in his head marked "REASONS TO HATE MYSELF." He could think of that later. Today was not about that.

Today was a celebration.

***

"Look who's the most popular girl at the dance!" Sway nudged Harrison with an elbow.

Harrison smiled sheepishly and shook his head. It was true, he'd hardly gotten a break to get a drink of water. The single ladies at the reception had been keeping him busy on the dance floor most of the night. "You're more than welcome to take them off my hands."

"Nah, I'm taking it easy this weekend. I promised Lenny I'd be on my best behavior." Sway grinned and Harrison knew he was enjoying the switch in roles.

Sway was always the ladies man. It came naturally to to him. Women flocked to his pretty face and charming disposition. Not tonight for some reason. Harrison looked around the group of revelers as he took a long drink

329

of ice water and something occurred to him.

He narrowed his eyes at Sway as he lowered his glass. "Did you do something?"

Sway barked out a laugh and shoved his hands in his pockets. While Harrison had taken off his tuxedo jacket and tie long ago because he'd been getting so heated from dancing, Sway was still in full dress.

"What makes you ask that?" Sway inquired jovially.

"I notice you haven't really answered my question." Harrison frowned hard at him.

Sway chuckled and looked around the room, catching Blake's eye. They nodded their chins at each other and Harrison was now certain they had arranged for this to happen.

"You were so uptight today," Sway began to explain, a satisfied grin on his face. "We thought we'd try to help take your mind off your worries. And what better way to do that than get you to dance with every pretty girl here?"

"Did you bribe them or something?" Harrison accused, reaching for the pitcher of water on the table and refilling his glass.

"Didn't have to." Sway grinned. "We just told them that you were single and loved to dance. The rest was up to them."

Harrison raised a slightly surprised eyebrow. Well, it had definitely turned into a fun evening, so he really couldn't complain. And he didn't have a reason for why he had been acting nervous all day. He supposed he'd been afraid that maybe something would happen and the wedding wouldn't proceed as planned. He loved Lenny, and adding her to their little family was the exact right thing to do. He had been a little apprehensive that Luke would screw it up at the last second. The moment after they were announced as husband and wife, Harrison took his first easy breath of the day. It was done. Complete. They couldn't back out now and he finally allowed himself to participate in the celebration.

"I love weddings," Sway declared, loosening his tie and taking a seat. "So much joy and love. Plus the cake is always excellent. Have you ever noticed that? Wedding cake is the best cake."

"Think you'll ever find yourself as the groom in one of these?" Harrison asked, reaching to the empty seat next to him and taking the piece of cake sitting there because Sway was right—wedding cake was the best.

"Maybe." Sway shrugged. "If I find the right girl."

"Haven't found her yet?" Harrison knew Sway, having been inspired by Luke and Lenny, had been trying the whole relationship thing for the past few months. They had all fizzled out but, Sway remained upbeat about the entire thing.

"No, not yet."

330

"You sure? The girls you've been choosing have been great. And they all have seemed to really like you."

Sway pursed his lips and his face went introspective. "I know. That's why I end it as soon as possible. I just know, that when I meet her, I'll *know*. You know?"

"I don't know," Harrison responded dryly and Sway chuckled.

"I'm not gonna lead a girl on if I already know she's not the one. It wouldn't be fair to her and sure as hell wouldn't be fair to the girl who's out there waiting for me." Sway's small smile took Harrison by surprise and his mouth fell open. Sway saw him gaping and laughed out loud. "Don't look at me like. How many times have I told you that I have layers?"

Harrison tried to wipe the shocked look off his face. "Yeah, but I haven't actually *seen* any of them before. This is kinda cool, Sway."

"Don't go spreading it around, bud." Sway grinned. "When I meet her, I want to be able to knock her off her feet."

"I have no doubt that you will."

* * *

Luke's fingertips dug into Lenny's waist as he pulled her closer on the dance floor. Her eyes darkened to a deep midnight blue as her lips slightly parted. He could hardly believe that she was his wife now. His *wife*. Forever.

"My God, you're beautiful," he breathed. She smiled and looked down shyly at the center of his chest. He dipped his head, his lips brushing the shell of her ear. "You wanna get out of here?"

Her breath hitched and he pulled back to look her in the eyes again. She licked her bottom lip slowly. "But we've invited all of these people."

"So? They can stay and dance all night, eat all the cake. But I," he paused for effect, "don't want to share you anymore. And probably not for the rest of the night."

Her cheeks blushed to hot pink and he smiled, loving that she was getting flustered. She glanced around at the revelers and chewed on the inside of her cheek. He knew Lenny pretty well now, and the cheek chewing thing was what she did when she was thinking. She had no idea she was doing it usually and he thought it looked pretty adorable.

"If we try to leave, people will want to stop us," she pointed out, voice hushed like she was afraid someone might overhear them.

"Just make a bathroom break, then get in the elevator and go to the top floor. I'll wait two minutes and then join you." He'd had a plan for this since this morning when he timed how long it would take to get from the reception hall to their bridal suite. Yeah, he was more than a little excited.

331

She swallowed and took a deep breath. "Okay, you talked me into it."

"I want to point out that it wasn't that hard." He raised an eyebrow and her smile widened. He dipped his head again, pressing his lips to her cheek. "Two minutes," he reminded and then released her.

She backed away from him, not breaking eye contact for a few steps. Then turned and headed straight for the door. People immediately started to converge on her, but she waved them away gracefully as she pointed to where she was going.

"You guys are sneaking out, aren't you?" Someone asked at his shoulder. Luke turned to look into Duke's playful gray eyes.

"That obvious?" Luke grinned, the two minutes ticking by in his head.

"Don't worry, I'll cover for you." Duke lifted his chin and winked. Then he slapped him on the back of the shoulder. "Take the stairs, your band mates have commandeered most of the elevators for a race."

Luke chuckled, not even surprised. "Thanks, man," he nodded his appreciation.

"Don't mention it." Duke gave him a nudge with his fist and Luke headed for the exit.

He didn't have to worry about anyone stopping him , he wasn't as pretty as the bride and attracted a lot less attention. Entering the hall, he spied the door to the stairs quickly and pushed through it. Taking them two at a time at a full sprint, he was breathing heavier once he got to the top. But he was far from being tired out.

***

Lenny waited by the elevators, her heart pounding. She had no idea which room was even theirs, so all she could do was wait for Luke to join her.

She twisted her fingers together in front of her, feeling anxious. It had been a beautiful day followed by an amazing night and it wasn't over yet. The part she didn't know anything about was coming up.

Okay, it's not that she didn't know *anything*, but she was definitely a novice to the sex part. She really hoped she didn't disappoint.

A warm hand slid over the top of her shoulder and she spun to find Luke grinning that cocky grin that she loved.

"Where did you—?" she started but he jerked his thumb over his shoulder.

"Stairs."

"Oh."

They stared at each other, the moment full of heartbeats, then Luke took her hand, lacing their fingers together and led her down the hallway.

She tried to keep her breathing steady, but her anticipation for this night was heady. He paused at the door to their room, slid the key card in, and turned the knob. He pushed the door open and ushered her through.

Her heart felt like it swelled to twice it's size as she took in the lit candles, the roses and the dim lighting. How had she not seen this coming? Of course Luke would have thought of everything.

"Thank you." His deep voice caused her to turn back to face him. With hands in pockets, ice blue eyes watching her intently, chiseled jaw that was more pronounced in the candlelight, he was the most handsome he'd ever been.

"For what?" she questioned with a slight smile, feeling her pulse speed up as she took in all that he was. With no one else around to serve as a distraction, she could finally drink him in. Absorb his gorgeous face, his strong frame, the way he moved as he took smooth steps towards her. She felt his hands cup her face but the tingle reached to her bellybutton. He angled her face to his and took his time looking it over. As if he wanted to memorize every detail. She felt adored. Beautiful.

He swept a thumb across the apple of her cheek. "For changing my life."

Then his lips brushed hers lightly and she closed her eyes, surrendering to the kiss. It grew in fervor even as Luke took his time with it, letting his hands travel to her hips and then her back, pressing her closer to him. Her arms slid up his chest and her fingers pushed into his hair.

He kissed her slowly.

Intentionally.

Not rushing.

She realized they never had to rush again. They had all the time in the world to make it perfect.

Any trace amounts of anxiety or apprehension about tonight vanished in that kiss.

Lenny just knew, it was going to be amazing.

Because everything they did together was amazing.

***

One month later

"All I'm saying is, I think four weeks is more than enough time for a Honeymoon."

Sway was bitching again. Harrison rolled his eyes and continued to pretend he was reading…*What magazine is this again?*

"We have to be in L.A. in two weeks and we don't have anything good to work with yet and he's 'unreachable.'" He put his fingers in the air to symbolize the air quotes while making a snotty expression.

"Dude, shut up," Mike looked at Sway with his eyebrows raised. "Blake and I have written some kick ass stuff so stop insulting us." He got up from the couch and moved to the fridge. "Besides, Luke gave us everything he had before he left."

Sway made a disgruntled noise in the back of his throat and flopped himself into a chair, looking dejected.

***

"Let the man enjoy his honeymoon, for Pete's sake." Mike said from Blake's kitchen. He pulled out some leftover pizza still in the box from the fridge, opened the lid and gave it a cautious smell. *Nope, no should eat that, they'll die.* He left it on the counter.

"Is Sway still bitching?" Blake asked as he reentered the room. He picked up a slice of the cold pizza off the counter and took a bite. Mike eyed him warily but didn't say anything.

"We should be able to call him." Sway grumbled.

"No man." Mike frowned severely at him. "Let him enjoy his wife."

"What could possibly be so important that they needed to disappear for a whole month?" Sway asked like he had a point.

Mike stared at him incredulous. "Are you really that thick?" He asked honestly.

Sway frowned back, looking like a belligerent teenager.

***

"They're probably having sex!" Harrison finally snapped.

"So, I've had lot's of sex." Sway almost grinned at his own words.

"Yeah, well, they're not you." Harrison tossed the magazine aside and looked at Sway seriously. "Luke and Lenny waited to get married. And Lenny was a virgin." Harrison felt his face heating up. "I really can't believe I have to explain this to you."

Sway stared at him for a few minutes as he processed his words. Suddenly the proper synapses in Sway's brain fired and understanding dawned on him. His eyes grew wide.

"Ooohhh." He drew out the word making Blake chuckle and Mike and Harrison roll their eyes.

"You're such a dumbass." Blake laughed again.

Harrison ran both hands through his thick, dark hair and addressed Mike. "You suppose they'll get their own bus?"

"I hope so." Mike sniffed, "I really don't want to share a bus with

334

newlyweds." He picked up the phone to dial for fresh pizza.

"Where do you think they'll live?" Harrison asked Blake.

Blake chewed thoughtfully and swallowed before answering. "I don't know. Luke is technically still homeless."

"Yeah, he ruined all my towels." Sway spoke up.

"Maybe he'll move to Wyoming." Blake pointed out.

"Yeah, maybe." Harrison grew quiet. He was really happy for his friends but he also hated change. "Do you think they might get a place here?" He asked hopefully.

"Maybe." Blake nodded and started on another piece of cold pizza.

"I bet Lenny is gonna be super hot when they get back." Sway said with a wistful expression. "She'll be all tan from spending a month in Hawaii." He made a clicking noise with his tongue.

"No." Blake corrected him, shaking his head. "You can't check Lenny out anymore."

"Why not?" Sway was getting overly frustrated.

"Cuz they're married now. That would be like checking out your sister." Blake answered matter of fact.

Sway sighed heavily as he thought that one through. "Fine." He slumped his shoulders in resignation.

***

"What happened with that girl you were seeing?" Mike asked now that he was off the phone. Sway was always a little tamer and easier to get along with when he was in a relationship. His attitude indicated he was single again.

"Eh, she left me for a stunt man." Sway mumbled.

"Really? I'm sorry man." Mike meant that, he didn't like to see his friends get hurt.

"It's all right. Apparently he can set himself on fire." Sway tried to lighten his expression. "How can I really compete with that?"

Mike still found it amazing that Sway had been in a monogamous relationship for more than a month. It really showed growth.

Of course, they were all growing, weren't they? Luke getting married was just the first big step. It would only snowball from here. As he looked around Blake's loft at his closest friends, he felt a peaceful energy deep inside. He, for one, was looking forward to what the future would bring. It was time to see what they were capable of in real life.

The End
The Double Blind Study series will continue with Blake Diedrich in In Your Honor.

Acknowledgments

I'm not sure this story would have ever gotten completed if it wasn't for Scott Colby and the fantastic ladies of FFP. Your strength and encouragement helped push me through so many obstacles at once. Thank you for all that you are.

To my lovely group of beta readers. Those of you who read the first and ugliest draft and encouraged me to keep going until it was better: Laura, Emily, Jennifer, Lisa, Tania, Jodi and Julie. And of course everyone who stuck with me through every draft after that, pushing through endless revisions and providing tireless feedback and support: Laura (always Laura, forever Laura), Amy, Des, Marissa, and Steven. And my loyal fp fans, vivkifay and chocoyum94, I love you so much!

To my fabulous editors Hillary and Dan. For putting up with my freakouts and insecurities and being patient and kind to me despite it all.

Thanks to the Foo Fighters who provided the soundtrack in my head as I wrote every word.

To my parents who instilled a passion for great music and great love in my life. I love you both more than I can express and am forever thankful for you.

To my husband, Charles. Because it's not possible for me to hear "Everlong" without thinking of you. Because you've changed my life in amazing and unexpected ways. Because I'm so incredibly thankful for your presence in my life. Because you are my very best friend.

Thank you, God, for giving me this life and these people in it. My cup runneth over.

Discover more titles from Heidi Hutchinson

Double Blind Study series:
Learn to Fly
In Your Honor
Tectonic
Deepest Blues
The Hope That Starts
Brand New Sky

Anthologies:
Naked Came the Trio (poetry)

heidih.net

About the Author

Heidi Hutchinson is an incorrigible idealist with a deep love for art, coffee and fabulous music in general with rock and roll in particular. She writes about all of these subjects as often as life allows.

She lives in the Midwest with her alarmingly handsome husband and their fearless child where they eat more pizza than God intended.

Keep reading for a sneak peek at In Your Honor!

In Your Honor
(Double Blind Study #2)
© 2013 Heidi Hutchinson

Prologue

Cologne, Germany
Three Years Ago

Blake rested his spinning head in his hands, pressing the heels into his eye sockets. He was way too drunk for what was happening. The sterile surroundings of the Catholic hospital made his intoxicated confusion more pronounced, and he felt humiliation take a seat right next to his overwhelming dread.

A soft figure sat down next to him and he slowly rotated his head to see the tiny figure of a nun looking at him with kind eyes. She extended a cup of coffee his direction and he took it. She said something to him that he didn't understand.

"I'm sorry, I don't speak German," he said with a grimace.

She nodded and patted his knee gently. "You must have coffee." Her English was good, but he could tell she was a little unsure.

"Yes, thank you." He raised the cup she had given him. "Danke." He knew a few basic words but not enough for a conversation. Especially right now.

"Your friend," she raised her eyebrows in question, "he is sick?"

"Yes." Blake felt a wave of anguish wash over him. "Very sick."

Mike was more sick than any of them had realized. They should have, though. They did. They just didn't want to have to deal with it. They were all too busy with their own shit. And now, Mike might not make it. It was insane how much had changed in the past couple of hours.

When Carl had finally gotten through to Blake and Luke at the bar, Mike was already unconscious. Luke had been in the hospital room with him since they had arrived. Blake wasn't ready to go in yet. He was too ashamed. And scared. And *so* drunk still. He reached up to rub his

341

forehead with his fingertips.

He wanted to blame someone. Maybe he could blame Ilsa, he'd never trusted her. She was so demanding of Mike's time and energy. Blake had known she was a user too, but he chose to ignore it. He chose to worry about himself despite the promise that all of them had made years ago to run this band like a family instead of a hobby.

"You have someone." The nun interrupted his blurry thoughts again. He frowned, not sure what she meant. She gestured to the phone he clutched in his hand. He looked down at it and remembered that he'd been getting ready to call someone. But he didn't know who. He knew who he *wanted* to call. But he had promised never to call her drunk again.

"She'll be mad at me," he said out loud, not caring if the nun understood at all.

"Maybe," the nun replied noncommittally, which made Blake almost smile.

"I made a promise." He stared at the floor in front of him, his head a complete mess. He had promised to stay away forever. But all he wanted at that moment was to hear her tell him everything would be okay.

"Promises can be remade." The nun patted his knee again and he glanced over at her. She smiled secretively and then stood up, leaving him alone.

His stare returned to his phone. The loneliness in his chest caused him to cue up her number and press Send before he sobered up enough to talk himself out of it. He pressed the device to his ear and hoped she would answer.

She picked up sooner than he expected.

"Hello?" she answered tentatively.

"Hey," Blake croaked, his vision suddenly blurring with unexpected tears.

"What's wrong, Blake?" He could almost see the concern on her face as it radiated through the phone. No anger, or accusation. Only genuine worry. He had never deserved her.

"Mike overdosed." He pushed the words out heavily. He heard her alarmed gasp and he continued, "I know I said I'd stay away. But you're the only one I can call. I'm really scared. He's in a coma. Luke is with him right now, but we have no idea what's going to happen. And I'm really drunk and confused and I feel bad for calling you but I... I just didn't know what else to do."

"It's okay, Blake. I'm glad you called me." She was trying to calm him down. From thousands of miles away he could feel the overwhelming comfort that she was practically made out of. He missed her. He wished she was there with him right now, to hold him and tell him it was going to be

342

okay.

"I miss you," he confessed, and he didn't care how it sounded.

"I miss you, too." She was quiet for a moment. "I'm sure Mike will pull through. All you boys are tough. How is Luke holding up?"

Blake really couldn't believe how amazing she was. They had left things so messy and ugly. And here she was, holding him one more time.

"He's scared too." Blake reached up and wiped the tears off the side of his face. "I wish I had done things differently."

"Blake, don't do this to yourself. Not right now," she pleaded tenderly over the phone.

"How do we fix this? I never saw this coming. I have no idea what to do." Every word had two meanings, and he knew she knew it. He needed her to. He needed her to know that he wasn't proud of anything he had done. "Is it all really over? I mean, maybe I could start doing things differently now. Maybe I could figure this whole thing out."

"Blake..." His name hung off her lips and he desperately wanted a do-over on life.

"Don't." He ran his hand over the back of his head in frustration. "Don't say what I know you're gonna say."

Then she did what she always did. She reached across the miles and gave him exactly what he needed to get through this moment.

"Tell me about Europe. Are the crowds are as crazy as I've heard?"

Blake leaned back and sighed. He told her about the shows and the flights and the cities they'd been to. They discussed the music and the latest album. Sway and Harrison arrived but sat silently nearby. She kept him distracted until he was sober and the sun was coming up outside. It had to be in the middle of the night where she was, and still she continued the conversation.

Blake saw Luke coming down the hallway towards them and knew they were all getting ready to have a difficult conversation.

"I have to go," he said painfully, not knowing when he'd ever hear her voice again. "Thank you. For everything."

"You're gonna be okay, Blake. Y'all will," she said, her soft accent making him smile one last time.

"I'm sorry I broke my promise of not contacting you again," he said quickly as Luke got closer and goodbye was imminent.

"Tonight doesn't count," she tried to reassure him.

"It counts for me." He took a quick breath before he had time to change his mind. "I love you." He hung up the phone without waiting for a reply because he knew those days were over. He couldn't go back and she had asked him not to. But he had to tell her at least once more.

He doubted that he would ever feel like he had told her enough.

Chapter 1

Nothing

"You want another?" The bartender's gruff voice broke through Blake's melancholy study of his empty glass.

He licked his dry lips, chewing on the bottom one briefly before nodding and pushing the glass towards the barkeep. His eyes glazed over as he stared at the warm, brown liquid refilling the glass. He couldn't remember how many he'd had at this point. Probably too many. His thoughts were still too clear for his own comfort. He swirled the cheap whiskey once before downing it.

"Mmm, I see you went for the good stuff, must be a party." Sway's sarcastic quip from Blake's left caused him to roll his eyes.

"Piss off, Sway," Blake slurred as he nodded at the bartender again.

Sway made himself comfortable on the stool, resting his elbow on the bar and his chin in his hand, and looked at Blake.

"You saw the schedule, I take it?" Sway stated the obvious.

"Oh, yeah." Blake threw another shot back and relished the burn as it traveled down his nearly numb throat.

"I bet I could get it switched if you want me to," Sway offered, but they both knew how absurd that sounded.

"Don't bother. It was bound to happen eventually." Blake rubbed his forehead with his right hand, feeling himself break out into a sweat. He slammed his palm back on the bar. "I have to grow up someday, right?" He chuckled cynically as he tried to stand.

"Whoa," Sway cautioned him as he grabbed Blake's arm, keeping him from toppling over. Yep, he'd almost had enough.

"I gotta take a piss," Blake mumbled and he staggered to the bathroom at the back of the dimly lit and mostly empty bar.

He liked this bar. It wasn't his favorite, but it was out of the way enough that most of his friends wouldn't find him here. Also, it wasn't a very successful establishment, so he never had to worry about being recognized. It was the closest thing to a hick bar he had been able to find in

Boston. He didn't need it often, just when he thought about stupid shit.

He leaned against the wall for support as he made his poorly aimed deposit in the urinal.

It really wasn't anyone's fault that he had felt the strong need to get hammered. He had seen the touring schedule and had immediately hailed a cab. He needed a drink. He was going to need a lot more before he hit the road too. He had no idea how he was going to cope with being on another friggin' dry tour.

He washed his hands in the grimy sink and looked at his red, watery eyes in the mirror. His normally stylishly messy black hair wasn't stylish at all, and his shoulders sagged like a man defeated. Maybe he could stay away this time. Maybe he wouldn't have to stop at that godforsaken diner and order a frickin' piece of frickin' apple pie. It's not like she'd be there anyway. She was married by now, or so he'd heard. Living her happily frickin' ever after.

Blake pushed away from his reflection and made his way back to the bar. He ignored Sway's disapproving head shake as he ordered another shot. If she was still creeping into his thoughts, he hadn't had enough.

***

Sway made an obvious show of wiping off the rim of the glass with a napkin before taking a drink of the water he'd ordered while waiting for Blake. He hated this place. It was gross and not up to the standards that Sway felt a reputable musician should frequent. He looked over at Blake, who was back from the bathroom and already downing another shot, and grimaced. It was going to be a long night. Again.

"How about we head home early tonight," he tried to suggest casually, knowing it would fall on deaf ears.

"Go ahead." Blake dismissed him with a sloppy wave of his hand.

No, Sway couldn't leave him. Not like this.

"Maybe we could try a different bar at least." Sway ignored the glare from the bartender.

"I like it here," Blake declared a little too loudly.

"Whatever you say, man," Sway relented. He wished he knew how to better handle one of Blake's 'episodes.' One tiny insinuation about his hometown or state, and he went straight to the nearest bottle of Jim. Sway wasn't even sure of the last time Blake had even *been* home. They usually avoided traveling anywhere near his triggers, Virginia Beach being the exception. He wasn't even clear on why that place had caused Blake to go ape shit last year, it just had.

But the band always knew when he was thinking about home. Thinking about her. He was pretty easy to read in that regard. That's why Sway knew right where to look when he saw the schedule and Blake

346

wouldn't answer his phone. Two dates this year had been booked in Oklahoma.

"I have a great idea," Blake announced, cutting into Sway's thoughts. "Let's work on the tattoo."

Sway was already shaking his head. "No, no, no, we don't do that drunk anymore, remember?" Blake was already pulling his coat on and walking a little sideways towards the door.

"Fine, ya big girl, you stay here." Blake laughed at his own insult and pushed outside.

Sway was close behind him. "C'mon, we talked about this like a hundred times. You made me promise not to let you do this again."

Blake chuckled and put an arm around Sway's shoulders more for support than for a hug. "Yeah, but you always give in."

Sway sighed. That he did. Fighting Blake when he was like this was never the best option. He was going to do what he set out to do, with or without approval. At least Sway would be sure that he got home safe tonight.

The tattoo parlor that Blake had been going to since he'd moved to Boston was only a couple of blocks away. They wouldn't care that he was drunk. It wouldn't be the first time.

The particular tattoo that Blake was referring to had been years in the making. It was mostly dark clouds and lightning that covered the left side of his chest and wrapped around his shoulder and most of his left arm. Two wild horses, their manes made of lightning and water, were screaming out of the center of the storm. A small section of the clouds broke apart high on his chest to reveal a star-filled sky. The colors and shading were exquisite, and Sway knew that Zeke loved the work he had put into it.

They entered the small establishment and the girl sitting at the counter took one look at the two of them before hollering over her shoulder, "Zeke! The rock stars are here."

"Thanks, Tab." Sway nodded to the willowy chick with porcelain skin and traffic cone orange hair that looked more supple than it should for how processed it was. She smiled sweetly as she opened the door next to her, letting Blake stagger through.

"Does Zeke even have an opening?" Sway asked, staring at the gauges in her ears; they were way bigger than the last time he had been in here.

"Yeah, it's been slow today. Besides, he would make time for Blake no matter what." She leaned across the counter and ran a finger over Sway's bottom lip. "I wish you'd let me pierce that pretty face of yours."

Sway gave her a sideways smile. "I love it when you flirt with me, Tabitha."

She flashed a smile and he stepped through the open door to help Blake into his usual chair.

Zeke emerged from the back and chuckled, rubbing his shaved head with an open hand. "I could smell the Jim Beam from the back office. Let me guess, you wanna work on the side piece?" He settled onto his stool as Blake struggled with removing his shirt.

"I wanna add the words today." Blake leaned back and put his arms over his head.

Zeke raised dark, speculative eyes at Sway in question. Sway shrugged. "I know, I tried to talk him out of it."

"All right, buddy." Zeke put on a pair of gloves and started setting up his station.

Sway took a seat nearby and Tabitha swiveled on her stool to face him. His gaze started at her hot pink heels, then moved up her long fishnet legs to her black shorts that were connected to matching hot pink suspenders.

"I always like the view here," he praised, and she raised a pierced eyebrow.

"I wish you guys would come by more often instead of only during the random bender." Tabitha tucked a neon orange strand of hair behind her ear.

"You and me both." Sway rolled his eyes. "So what kind of things do you pierce?"

"We have this conversation every time, Sway," she chided.

"I know, but I forget. Indulge me." He gave her a crooked grin and glanced over as the tattoo gun started to whir against Blake's side. The words were the last little bit to be added. Blake had held off for a long time, saying that he wasn't ready to put that nail in the coffin quite yet. Sway had to wonder if this would actually change anything.

The shop remained relatively quiet as Zeke worked. Tabitha helped a few patrons get scheduled for later in the week, and Sway toyed with the idea of texting Luke to tell him what was happening. They had all previously agreed not to let Blake get this carried away again. Pulling him out of the black hole he had the propensity to throw himself down was exhausting. Not to mention depressing. But Sway wasn't feeling like ratting out his brother. Not tonight.

"You know," Tabitha looked over at Blake as she spoke to Sway, "my friends and I are going out tonight. I have a girl or two that are kinda into the brokenhearted thing. I'm sure they'd make him forget his sorrows. At least for a few hours."

Sway pursed his lips and thought about it. "What do you say, Blake? You want some female companionship tonight?"

348

Blake twisted his head to glare at the both of them. "No."

Sway grimaced apologetically at Tabitha. "Sorry, gorgeous. Not tonight."

She nodded solemnly. "It's too bad. I hope he gets over her eventually."

Tabitha and Zeke knew the story well. The whole shop knew. Whiskey made Blake a talker and they'd all been regaled with his tale of lost love and heartache. Although tonight, he was more somber than usual.

"How's it look?" Blake stood up for Sway to inspect after Zeke had finished applying the ointment.

Sway pushed his blonde hair out of his face and squinted at the black ink scrawled across Blake's left side ribs in delicate lines that seemed somehow appropriate within the turbulent, roiling storm. He pursed his lips as he read the words that stood out on the angry, red skin.

this Honored heart bears Lucky scars

Sway blew the air out of his lungs. "Looks good, Blake." It did look good, but Sway knew Blake would be seriously pissed in the morning. He always did this. Took it too far. Sway would never understand.

"I think I'm ready to go home now." Blake's eyes sagged at the corners and Sway could see the fight in him had waned considerably. Maybe adding the words had finally settled things in his mind after all.

Sway nodded and helped his friend get a cab. The long ride back across town was silent and Blake leaned his head against the window, staring listlessly at the passing buildings. Sway went to exit the vehicle with Blake but was stopped by his friend.

"It's all right man, I've pretty much sobered up now." Blake met his eyes briefly and then looked at his feet, shoving his hands in his pockets.

"You feeling okay?" Sway frowned, trying to decide if he should go with his gut or listen to the guitarist.

"No," Blake answered honestly. "But I'd rather be alone if that's okay."

Sway looked up at the building, knowing that Harrison and Mike would be nearby if something should arise. He would text them and give a heads-up. "Right. Well, call me if you need me."

"Thanks, man." Blake nodded his appreciation, his mouth maintaining a hard line.

Sway stepped out of the cab briefly to give Blake a 'man-hug' before heading to his own apartment. He sent a quick text to his bandmates and tried to let go of the uneasiness that wanted to settle in the pit of his stomach.

***

Blake leaned back heavily against his door as it closed behind him. Nope, he hadn't gotten nearly drunk enough. He would no doubt dream

349

about her tonight, but he wouldn't have the luxury of not being able to remember it.

He tossed his keys on the coffee table as he took slow steps towards his bed. His empty, unmade bed. He stripped off his coat and t-shirt and collapsed on the thick comforter. He pushed the pillows onto the floor and rolled onto his back. Bringing his hand up, he gingerly touched the gauze that covered his latest marking.

"Please be happy." He whispered his wish to the ceiling before passing out.

***

Carl winked at the waitress as she refilled his coffee, and he took pleasure in seeing her blush. He had been waiting in the corner booth for close to forty-five minutes now and Lenny still hadn't showed. Not that she was late. Well, she was kind of late, for Lenny. Ever since she had ceased to be Lenny Evans, assistant extraordinaire, and became Lenny Casey, super hot wife of equally hot rock star, she had different priorities. Mostly, she ran on time now instead of a half hour early.

He saw a flash of golden hair enter the restaurant and he waved her over.

"Hey, Carl," Lenny greeted him with a wide smile as she slid into the booth, her cheeks rosy.

"Hey, kid," Carl grunted in return, suppressing his own smile at seeing her. He would never tell her to her face, but Lenny was one of his favorite people. She was like the daughter he thought he would have had, had he ever had kids. But he wasn't going to start telling people that, he had a reputation to maintain.

"Is the coffee good?" Lenny asked with an eyebrow raised.

"It's decent," he answered as he set his mug down and waved at the waitress for another cup for his companion.

"So," Lenny started, slipping her jacket off and leaning her elbows on the table, her damn blue eyes sparkling, "what's this about? Carl Darrow doesn't call without a reason."

He felt his mouth twitch up on one side; he had missed her. He decided to skip the bullshit and get to the point. Lenny never seemed to mind his methods. "You want your old job? I mean, I know you're coming along anyway. Luke bought a whole damn bus for you. I haven't been able to find a replacement, and we're coming up on crunch time."

"You haven't even looked." Lenny called his bluff and he almost grinned at her. "I don't know, Carl." She thanked the waitress for the coffee before continuing. "It's a lot of work and I kind of wanted to spend some quality time with Luke... if you know what I mean."

Carl rolled his eyes and she laughed at him. "I know all that. But what if I doubled your salary?"

"You know it was never about the money," Lenny chastised gently. No, the job was never about the money. She was a highly successful snowboarder who had run from her responsibilities, joined Team Double Blind Study, and subsequently fallen in love with the lead singer and become part of the family. It had been about a lot of things, but definitely not the money.

"What if I let you hire your own replacement?" Carl proposed. He knew she didn't want her old job back. But he didn't want to have to go through all the trouble of finding a person who would never hit the standards that she had set for him on the previous tour. Lenny was the best.

Her brow furrowed in thought. "That's not a bad idea, actually." Carl mentally high-fived himself. Of course it wasn't a bad idea, it was a great idea.

"Would you be willing to train them and everything?" Carl looked down at his coffee, afraid she'd read his mind if they had eye contact.

"I guess I could... I mean, that would be the easiest option." Lenny tapped her finger against the handle of her mug. "Yeah, okay, I can do that."

"Great." Carl picked up a stack of applications sitting next to him in the booth and slapped them on the table. "Here are your candidates. They need to be on the crew bus on Monday." He ignored Lenny's slack-jawed expression as he stood and slipped on his coat. He clapped his hand on her shoulder as he strode to the door. "Thanks, kid, it's good to have to you back."

***

Lenny shook her head and chuckled lightly at Carl's abrupt departure. She should have seen that coming. Carl didn't do anything without making a plan first. She pulled the stack of applications towards her and thumbed through them, probably close to fifty. *This is going to take awhile.*

Her phone buzzed in her pocket and she pulled it out, grinning automatically when she saw Luke's name on the screen.

"Hey," she greeted her husband.

"Hey, you left before I was ready to go." He sounded wounded but she knew it was only an act.

"I was already running late and you know how Carl hates to wait," she replied, skimming the top application.

"Are you at the corner diner?" She could hear him moving swiftly, he must be on his way.

"Yes, you want me to order you anything?" she asked, flagging the waitress down.

"Yeah, pancakes. Be there in a bit." He hung up and she set her phone on the table just as the server walked over.

"I'm gonna need your biggest order of pancakes and a western omelet. Oh, and more coffee." She smiled her thanks as the girl went to place her order and then refocused on the applications.

A few moments later, Luke kissed her on the neck before sliding into the booth across from her a few moments later.

"What's all this?" He gestured to the papers.

Lenny rolled her eyes. "Carl got me to agree to hire the new assistant for the tour."

"Makes sense." Luke nodded his approval and picked up the top sheet, giving it a thorough scan.

"You always take his side," she chided.

"Of course, he hired you." He winked at her and she felt the blood pulse in her veins. The simplest of expressions coming from Luke could make her forget her name. "Besides, he has those higher-ups breathing down his neck to make sure the tour is as successful as the last one."

"Maybe I should appeal to his boss then." She raised a suggestive eyebrow and Luke narrowed his eyes and made a growl sound in the back of his throat.

"That sounds like a *very* good idea."

"You're terrible." She laughed at his playful expression and he grinned.

It was true, though, it was a whole new regime. The band's contract had expired after the last tour and they had decided to start their own label. No more being pushed around by people who didn't care about anything but the bottom line. They could be musicians again. Real ones.

As such, a lot of vetting and hiring had taken place in the past couple of months. The band had recorded and released their first album on their own label, and a touring schedule had been created. A new bus had been purchased for the newlyweds, and Carl had been given a significant raise. They had been so busy that Lenny was more thankful than ever for the month-long honeymoon they had gotten to take before the craziness began.

"You suppose Carl will flip out if I hire a girl?" Lenny asked as the waitress set down her omelet and Luke's pancakes.

"Probably," Luke muttered as he poured the syrup. "Why? Did you find a good one?" He nodded at the paper Lenny was holding.

"Maybe." She chewed on the inside of her cheek. "She's still in college, a business management major..."

"What?" Luke asked when Lenny didn't speak again for a few seconds.

"I don't know, gut feeling. I think I'll call her, set up an interview." She pulled out her cellphone.

"And then can we have breakfast as husband and wife?" Luke's crystal blue eyes sparkled and she felt a tingle go from her toes to her earlobes.

"Yes, my love." She gave him a crooked smile as she dialed the number on the application. Damn, but she loved him.

Chapter 2

But, Honestly

The slight breeze blew the thick, wild hair across Harrison's forehead as he leaned his back against the tour bus. His large, mirrored aviators covered most of his face as he watched the last of their belongings being loaded. He crossed his arms over his chest and kicked the dirt at his feet.

He was anxious for the tour to begin. A lot of changes had taken place in a short span of time, and Harrison had never been a fan of change. He wanted to get out on the road, feel the shows, meet the fans, and return to the flow that he was comfortable with. Not that he didn't like the changes. He did, they had all been great. He just struggled with adapting.

"Mister O'Neil?" a small female voice said to his left. "I... uh, I'm sorry to bother you..." She sputtered and stopped as Harrison turned his gaze in her direction.

"Kendra, I told you, just call me Harrison," he patiently reminded the new assistant.

"Right, Harrison, sorry." Her tanned skin blushed deeply and she tried again. "I was wondering if you, um, if you had decided which bus you were going to be on."

Harrison had no idea where Lenny had found this girl. She was sweet enough but she was so damn nervous she could hardly get her words out half the time. He didn't know how she would hold up under the pressure of touring. Or the scrutiny of Carl.

She was thin and lithe, a former ballerina who had injured her knee and changed direction with her life. Her light brown hair had professionally applied streaks of red and she had a cute button nose that Harrison had noticed instantly. He liked noses. Her wide hazel eyes were adorably innocent. And always nervous.

"I'll be on the blue bus with Mike," he answered, wishing he could give her confidence like a stick of gum.

"Okie dokie." She blushed again. "Sorry, that was stupid." She gripped her clipboard to her chest as she hurried away, her ponytail bobbing up and down with her stiff steps.

"How long till you think we have to buy her a ticket home?" Mike remarked as he came up next to him.

Harrison shook his head. "I have no idea... a week, maybe."

"Lenny seems to think she's perfect for the job, and she's not usually wrong," Mike reminded him as he shoved his hands in his pockets and settled against the bus with Harrison.

"Yeah, but she's just so... jumpy." Harrison scrunched up his nose.

"I don't know... people can surprise you," Mike said thoughtfully. "Don't write her off just yet."

Harrison studied his shoes for a few minutes, trying to word his next question carefully, but there really were no better words for it. "How do you feel about the schedule?"

Mike's deep intake of air told Harrison what he needed to know. It was going to be an emotionally jarring trip for at least one of them. But it really couldn't be helped. Harrison had been part of the planning process, and he had done everything in his power to protect his friend from having to face his issues. But maybe it was time for him to face them.

"We'll find out when we get there." Mike's voice was low, noncommittal.

"He always has us. He doesn't have to do anything alone." Harrison murmured more to himself than to Mike.

"I know." Mike chuckled. "And I promise I won't let him get any misguided tattoos on my watch."

"I can't believe he did that." Harrison shook his head in wonder. "He wasn't as mad about it as I thought he would be."

"He's still in love with her. I think it's a bigger problem than just the tattoo," Mike said pensively.

"What's gonna happen when we actually get to Oklahoma?" Harrison worried out loud.

"I don't know. But we should probably warn Lenny and Kendra so they don't freak out." Mike sighed and pushed away from the bus.

"Family meeting?" Harrison questioned.

Mike paused before answering. "Not yet. Let me talk to him about it first. No one likes their dirty laundry aired without their permission. I know that better than most."

Harrison watched his back as he went around the corner towards the hotel. Yep, this tour was going to be a whole new rodeo.

***

Kendra Salem pushed her heavy, sweaty hair out of her eyes as she tried, once again, to convince her shoe-laces to stay tied. Double knot, triple knot, nothing was working and she was getting frustrated. It was only her first day on the job and she had never felt more alone in her life.

The band was friendly enough and the crew was trying to be as helpful as possible, but Kendra still felt like the outsider. Because she was. They were a family and she was the new girl. What had she been thinking when she had even applied? She couldn't take care of rock stars, she could barely keep a goldfish alive.

She straightened from her task and trudged to the crew bus. She still had another page of items to check off the list before she could retire to her hotel room where she planned on eating her weight in ice cream before crying herself to sleep.

She still hadn't figured out why Luke Casey's wife had hired her. The interview had been a disaster. She had overslept and dressed in such a rush that her shirt was on inside out and backwards. She froze up during most of the questions and then tripped and fell in Luke Casey's lap before leaving in humiliation.

She came around the back of the red bus and collided with a hard, male body. Her tiny frame flew to the ground and she scrambled to her feet, feeling the color change on her face.

"I'm so sorry," she apologized as she tried to chase the papers that had disengaged from her clipboard and were blowing around her feet.

"New girl, you have got to chill." Blake's voice caused a fresh surge of embarrassment to flood her veins. She couldn't handle humiliating herself in front of the band members. She wanted to quit. She had to talk to Lenny, she couldn't do this. She wasn't cut out for it.

Strong hands gripped her shoulders and she looked up into friendly green eyes.

"I'm sorry, Mister Diedrich..." was all she could say.

"Calm down, darlin'." Blake spoke to her slowly and waited for her to catch her breath. "You're doing a good job, there's no need to be so jumpy."

Kendra felt tears burn her eyes and she swallowed hard. Crying right now would only make things worse.

"Hey, hey, hey," he soothed, and pulled her against his chest in a hug. "Don't cry, I can't handle it when girls cry."

Kendra sniffed back her tears with a small laugh. Blake held her at arms' length again and looked at her seriously.

"We're regular people. Just like anybody else. You don't have to be as worried as you are." He paused, and one corner twitched in a hint of a smile. "And for Pete's sake, please call me Blake."

Kendra nodded, feeling her racing heart begin to calm down. He

357

oozed confidence and she desired nothing more in that moment than to be as sure of things as he seemed to be.

"I don't want to let any of you down," she suddenly confessed.

"You can't. Lenny has total faith in your abilities and she's never wrong. You already possess the skills you need, you just have to tap into them." Blake grinned at her, and Kendra felt her shoulders relax a bit at his encouragement. She took a deep breath and nodded.

He patted her shoulder. "Chin up, chick. Now, I have to go see a man about a dog." He gave her a final smile before disappearing around the side of the bus.

Kendra picked up her clipboard and brushed the dirt off. Maybe Blake was right, maybe she just had to believe in herself. *Please let that be true.*

***

Blake chuckled, remembering the look of absolute horror on the new girl's face when she had run into him. It was hilarious but he was glad he hadn't laughed at her. She was obviously having a hard day. He didn't envy her, trying to fit into a ready-made family would be a challenge for anyone. And he knew they weren't the easiest people to get along with.

He claimed his usual bunk in the red bus by covering it with his stuff. Then he returned to his hotel room to drain the mini bar before they departed the next morning. Had anyone explicitly told him that this was a dry tour? Not really, but it was heavily implied. And he would honor that as much as his frayed nerves would allow. But until the tour officially started at dawn, he was allowed to get as shit-faced as he wanted.

He probably wouldn't be this anxious if he had had more time to prepare for what was coming. Or, at least, that's what he told himself. He had seen the schedule a week ago and they would be in Pryor in four days. Definitely not enough time. They had a show tomorrow night in Des Moines, the night after that in Omaha, the night after that in Kansas City, and then he would wake up in his hometown. And he'd be there for two days before playing at Rocklahoma. Two frickin' days.

Blake chucked the empty bottle of vodka across the room to the trash can. He hated vodka, that stuff was the worst. But maybe, just maybe, it would help him fall asleep tonight. A hearty knock at the door told him otherwise.

He shoved himself to his feet and looked through the peephole. He had thought it would be Mike, but no, it was Luke. He pulled the door open and returned to the minibar without so much as a greeting.

The door closed behind him and he flopped into a chair, twisting off the lid of his next dose of therapy. He smiled at Luke and waved to the fridge.

"Help yourself."

"Thanks, I'm good." Luke looked uncomfortable, and Blake wondered how the conversation had gone between him and Mike about who would try to come and talk to him. Maybe they had just flipped for it. Either way, Blake wasn't planning on putting up a fight. He'd be honest if the right questions were asked.

"You gonna make it through this one?" Luke got right to the point as he settled in the chair across from Blake.

"Hope so. Wish someone would have told me the plan ahead of time," he said pointedly.

"We thought the less time you had to think about it, the less damage you'd do to yourself," Luke admitted. Blake couldn't fault him for that. He had no idea how he would have handled it if he'd known sooner, but it probably would have been something akin to a train wreck.

"Why do we have to spend so much time there?" Blake asked, his voice rougher than he preferred.

"I got a couple tips on some local talent there and I wanted to see their act. We still need an opener for the tour and we have to go after unsigned artists." Luke's face was sympathetic and Blake couldn't be mad at him. He was making the best decisions available for the band as a whole. He always did.

"I get it," Blake sighed. He did get it, but he still didn't like it.

A few minutes of silence passed before Luke spoke again. "You gonna try to see her?"

Blake closed his eyes and resisted the urge to scratch the ink that was still healing on his ribs. "Nah, I need to let her live her life. It wouldn't do either of us any good." It was the clearest and most direct thought he'd had on the matter all week. "I'll probably stop at the diner and reminisce a little, though," he added as an afterthought.

"You don't think she'll be there?" Luke asked quietly.

Blake swallowed hard. "No, I heard she married some rich guy and moved to Tulsa. She was always too good for that town anyway." The words tasted bitter as he said them, and he knew he wasn't convincing Luke that he was as fine with it as he wanted to believe himself.

"Will you do me a favor?" Luke asked, his brow furrowed in concern. "Will you take one of us with you... just in case?"

Blake chewed on his bottom lip as he considered the request. It wasn't that big of a deal. If it made Luke more comfortable then he could do that. He shrugged. "Sure."

***

The drive across Iowa was boring. Like, want to rip your hair out and set it on fire just to freak out the bus driver boring. Blake regretted not sneaking some contraband onto the bus before they had pulled out of town. Chances are Kendra wouldn't have found it, she wasn't as thorough as Lenny had been. But that thought made Blake feel like shit. Hadn't he been the one to tell her that she was going to do a good job?

Come to think of it, Blake had no idea where Kendra even was. Crew bus? Blue bus? Not in the Love Nest, that was for sure. Lenny and Luke's bus was brand-new and gorgeous. No one was allowed on it, Luke's rules. Which left Blake with more room than he'd ever had on tour, since his only company was Sway. After all those times he thought he needed more space, it turned out that being alone with his thoughts was not the greatest feeling in the world. Especially with the destination that loomed on the horizon three days from now.

"New girl didn't miss a single thing, and I had a lot of bullshit on my 'must-have' list." Sway opened the fridge in the kitchenette and lobbed a soda in Blake's direction.

"Kendra," Blake replied, catching the can and cracking it open.

"What?" Sway frowned and sat on the sofa, kicking his shoes off.

"Her name is Kendra." Blake rolled his eyes.

"Right," Sway nodded. "Kendra," he repeated slowly, trying to commit it to memory. "She's not bad looking either."

"You know you can't—" Blake frowned at him.

"I know, I know," Sway waved him off. "I wasn't saying anything like that. I'm just... I don't know, making conversation."

"Awkward," Blake stated flatly.

"What else are we supposed to talk about? You don't want to talk about," Sway paused, pointing at Blake's side, "you know. And Iowa is the most boring drive in the world, and Harrison took all of the good video games 'cause he thought *that* would be funny." Sway looked exasperated and Blake cracked a smile.

"You wanna work on some music?" he suggested.

"Like nothing else." Sway's face lit up in relief and excitement.

They had been working on some things the past few months that they didn't intend to present to the rest of the band. Playing around mostly, experimenting with lyrics and different technique. But they had agreed to set it aside for the tour so they could focus on the band. That lasted all of six hours.

***

Lucy Newton wiped down the end of the counter one final time before throwing her rag in the mesh bag around the corner. She stretched the overworked muscles of her back and shoulders and untied her apron.

"You ready to go home, Lucy?" Mac called from the back room.

"Yeah, you almost finished?" She released her tired hair from its restraint and shook out the wild, chestnut waves that tumbled down her back. She checked the back door again to make sure it was locked and started shutting off the lights.

Another long, busy day for the oldest diner in Pryor, Oklahoma. And Lucy was proud of that accomplishment. She touched the framed photos of her grandparents by the cash register on her way to the front door where Mac was waiting.

"What time do you want me to be back tomorrow?" her cousin asked as he pulled the door open for the two of them. She grabbed her large purse that was more of a small saddle bag than a traditional purse and slipped it over her head.

"After lunch; that should give me enough time to change my clothes before heading to rehearsal."

"You sure you don't want me to work the whole day for you? I really don't mind." He scratched the top of his head, hair the same shade as hers and just as thick as they paused in the parking lot.

"No, you'll be working for me during the show, too, so I don't want to take advantage of you." She smiled and lightly punched him in the arm. "Go home, get some sleep, snuggle that new baby of yours."

"Okay, Lucy, whatever you say." He chuckled as he walked to his car and unlocked the door.

Lucy paused and took a deep breath. Then another one. She squinted towards the horizon but couldn't see anything beyond the black prairie sky.

"What's up?"

She turned to see Mac watching her, perplexed.

"Nothing... I just..." She smiled as she realized her absurdity. "I thought I smelled rain."

Mac chuckled and climbed into his car. He rolled the window down and teased her, "Storms come out of the west, Lucy. Usually not the north."

Lucy frowned and realized she had been looking northeast. That was a weird mistake to make. "Yeah, usually," she murmured to herself.

"Besides, they're predicting clear skies all week. You're tired. Get some rest tonight." Mac gave one final, amused head-shake and drove off.

Lucy stood very still for several minutes as her head tried to explain to her heart that it was crazy and she was, indeed, just tired. She inhaled deeply again.

She hadn't imagined it. It was definitely going to rain.

***

"I thought Des Moines was lovely." Harrison ran his hands through his curly hair and bounded into the bus.

"Yeah, they definitely had some energy," Mike agreed right behind him.

361

"Sway and Blake seem to be getting along just fine," Harrison added, as he took his seat on the floor and hooked up the video game system. "I thought there might be more bitching about me jacking all the games, but they didn't seem to care."

"I'm just glad Blake was sober, he's hard to play with when he's wasted," Mike said as he changed out of his too-sweaty shirt.

"Says the drummer with the longest record of forgotten performances in the history of rock and roll, and that includes Keith Moon," Harrison reminded him.

"True story. I shouldn't talk." Mike caught the controller that Harrison flipped his way and settled onto the floor.

"Do you guys want those sandwiches now... or..." Kendra's voice made Mike suddenly realize she was on the bus with them.

"Are you riding with us tonight?" Mike asked the first question that popped into his head.

So did Harrison. "What sandwiches?"

Mike rolled his eyes at the guitarist.

"Um, yes," Kendra answered Mike and then moved silently to the kitchenette where she retrieved two foot-long subs. She handed them both over and then sat quietly in a chair.

Harrison immediately started eating, but Mike was still confused.

"Why are you on this bus?" He didn't want it to sound like he was upset by her presence, because he wasn't. But he was still very much bewildered.

"Because Carl has me on the blue bus for the first week." Kendra's voice was clear, but he detected the hint of a tremble. She was afraid she was in trouble. That was his fault. He tried to start again.

"I just meant, where did you ride last night?" Mike tried really hard not to frown, but he knew it was happening anyway.

"I was... here..." Kendra's eyes were so round and wide that Mike was a little worried they might fall out of her head.

"Yeah, dick," Harrison said around a mouthful. He smacked Mike in the chest with the back of his hand before swallowing. "She's been with us since we left Chicago."

"What?" Mike felt it was okay to frown at Harrison. He also felt it was okay to smack Harrison upside the head if the need should arise, which could be any minute.

"Um, self-involved much?" Harrison rolled his eyes.

Mike looked back to Kendra, who looked like she might cry. "I'm sorry, Kendra. I guess I'm an idiot." He attempted to make her feel better.

"Yeah, you are." Harrison started laughing, but his mouth was full again and he choked.

Mike narrowed his eyes at Harrison, then turned to Kendra. "Thank you for the sandwiches." He nodded at the timid assistant and turned to face the game again. His mind was spinning. Was she really that quiet and sneaky that she had been on the bus with him the whole time and he hadn't even noticed her? *Oh man, Lenny knew exactly what she was doing.*

An invisible assistant. Well played, Lenny Casey, well played indeed.

***

"What's bothering you?"

Luke looked up to see Lenny watching him from the doorway of their room on the bus. She was dressed for bed, tank top and little shorts, her blonde hair almost reaching her waist. He let out a contented sigh as she crawled across the bed on her knees and curled up next to his side.

"You're gorgeous, you know that?" he asked as he kissed the top of her head.

"That's why you were thinking so hard just a minute ago?" she asked playfully.

"No... I was just thinking about stuff." Luke wrapped his arms around her and held tight.

"Tell me," she whispered gently.

Luke pondered her request. It's not that he didn't want to tell her, he did. He just wasn't sure how to say it. He barely knew how to think about it. He had already told her his concerns about Blake, and she'd been receptive and thoughtful. He didn't want to disrupt their happy family, but he couldn't shake the feeling in the pit of stomach that something big was coming.

"I have the feeling..." He paused, a little afraid he was going to sound stupid, but he pushed past it. "I mean, things have been going really great. And I guess... I'm wondering why it feels like there's a storm coming."

Lenny traced the lines of his tattoos on his bare chest for a few minutes. He enjoyed feeling her warmth by his side. Like she fit in the place next to his heart where he hadn't realized there had been a hole.

"There's always a storm coming," she said at long last. "But we'll get through it like we do everything else. Together."

***

Lucy put her old guitar away, being careful to tuck the aged blanket that her mother had made around it before closing the case. It had been a good practice. They were getting better and better, but she was still apprehensive they wouldn't be ready in time for the show Thursday night. She had been a last minute fill-in for the regular guitarist, Bobby. He had gotten stage fright as it got closer to the date and had bailed.

Taylor Stevens had frequented the diner for several weeks and he had become friendly with Lucy. He knew she played guitar some, and who her

363

father was. It didn't come as a real shock to her when he asked her to fill in. What was shocking was how well they all seemed to work together. This wasn't a garage band made up of friends from high school. No, Taylor Stevens was serious about his music, and he hand-picked the musicians he would play with. Truthfully, Lucy was honored.

"Good job, Newton. Same time tomorrow." Taylor gave her an earnest nod as they left their rehearsal space. His full, manly beard and clean-shaven head, thick shoulders and athletic build made him look more menacing than he really was. The only thing he took seriously was his music, otherwise he was fairly easygoing.

Lucy cranked the motor on her 1970 Pontiac GTO that had really seen better days. The color was supposedly called *Palisade Green,* but it was more of a dirty avocado to Lucy. Not that she minded, it went nicely with her infrequent trips to the car wash.

She loved her car, it was a gift from her father as one of the first things he bought for himself when he started to make money from his music. Someday she would have it restored and possibly repainted. But not while she was still running the diner full-time and singing at Red's on the weekends.

The drive across town was fast, a benefit of living in a place with a small population. She had hated the year she'd spent in Tulsa. Big city life had never been her fit. She supposed it probably would have grown on her in time, but she didn't have to worry about that anymore. She was home. This is where she belonged.

The parking lot at the diner was full, and she was worried for a moment that they would be behind, but as she entered the kitchen through the back she saw that Mac had things under control. As usual. She loved having her family help out so willingly in the business that her grandmother had built with her tiny, bohemian hands.

Having taken over the diner right around her eighteenth birthday, it had been an important part of her rise to adulthood. Even after her year away, she came right back to it, easy as pie.

"How was rehearsal?" Mac asked as she pulled her hair into a tight bun at the nape of her neck.

"Good. I wish you could be there to see us, it's going to be a huge venue." Lucy grabbed a nearby apron and tied it around her waist.

"Are you nervous?" Mac asked with a wink and handed her an order ready to go out.

"Never." Lucy smiled widely and pushed through the doors to the front. "Comin' out!" she called.

The night went by fast, and Lucy was looking forward more and more towards Thursday's show. She was humming and singing to herself as she waited tables, took orders and bussed the front. Completely wrapped up in one of Taylor's songs while she swept behind the counter, she didn't hear the question that Mac asked her until he put a hand on her arm and she jumped.

"Hey, kid, calm down." He laughed at her reaction. "I was just asking how many pies you wanted for tomorrow."

"Oh, probably one apple and one cheesecake," she answered quickly, and then frowned as she thought about it some more. "But make an extra apple tomorrow."

Mac made the note on the whiteboard. "You're the boss. Why an extra apple? You expecting to sell more on Thursday?"

Lucy didn't have an answer; her gut spoke and she listened. It only worked out for her half the time, so she wasn't sure why she still listened to it.

61962096R00220

Made in the USA
Lexington, KY
26 March 2017